Ambrose B. Carlton

The Wonderlands of the Wild West

With sketches of the Mormons

Ambrose B. Carlton

The Wonderlands of the Wild West
With sketches of the Mormons

ISBN/EAN: 9783337297701

Printed in Europe, USA, Canada, Australia, Japan

Cover: Foto ©Andreas Hilbeck / pixelio.de

More available books at **www.hansebooks.com**

CONTENTS.

PART I.

PART II.

PART III.

The Anti-Polygamy Law of 1862.
The Poland Law of 1874.
The Edmunds Law of 1882.
The Edmunds-Tucker Law of 1887.

APPENDIX.

THE WONDERLANDS OF THE WILD WEST.

   *   *   *   *   "of antres vast and deserts idle,
Rough quarries, rocks, and hills whose heads touch heaven,
It was my hint to speak ;   *   *   *   *
And of the cannibals that each other eat,
The Anthropophagi, and men whose heads
Do grow beneath their shoulders."—*Othello*.

A SOJOURN for nearly seven years in Utah, as one of the Board of Commissioners appointed by the President of the United States, under the provisions of the so-called "Edmunds Anti-polygamy Law" of Congress, has afforded the writer of these Sketches ample opportunities to become acquainted with the Mormons or Latter-day Saints, as well as some of the most remarkable and picturesque scenery of the Wild West.

As to the people called Mormons, I shall "speak of them as they are—nothing extenuate, nor set down aught in malice." I shall condemn where censure is just, and give credit where it is due. It is seldom that we find great bodies or classes of people as bad as they are painted by their enemies. Much that is said concerning an unpopular and hated people should be received *cum grano*, for it is easy as well as agreeable for many persons to deal largely in hyperbole and fiction against those whom it is the fashion to despise.

The Mormons have grievous faults, and grievously have they answered for them. The odium that has

2 "

attached to them by the adding of polygamy to their former beliefs, has so prejudiced the public mind against the Mormons that they are seldom credited with the virtues which they really possess.   But the candid and impartial observer who has mingled extensively among the people, will agree with the views promulgated by the Utah Commission, (the Board above referred to) in their annual report to the Secretary of the Interior of 1887:

> The majority of the Mormons are a kindly and hospitable people. They possess many traits of character which are well worthy of emulation by others.   In their local affairs they strive to suppress the vices which are common to settled communities.   In matters of religion they are intensely devotional, rendering a cheerful obedience to their church rules and requirements.   They possess many of the elements which under a wise leadership would make them a useful and prosperous people.

The manuscript for this work was prepared from time to time from the summer of 1882 to 1890 ; and for the most part the sketches were written contemporaneously with the events, some times in haste, with more regard far the matter than the manner, but always with a scrupulous care to state the facts truly, and to give my impressions and opinions, formed at the time, "without fear, favor, or affection."

THE PLAINS AND ROCKY MOUNTAINS.

Many a "cultured" denizen of New England and elsewhere on the Atlantic seaboard associates with his idea of the Wild West, such regions as the highly civilized and enlightened State of Indiana ; and would be surprised to learn that on the banks of White River, or the Wabash, there are no wild buffaloes, no antelopes, painted Indians or grizzly bears.

My subject is not the Old West, but the New West, the wonderland of this continent. I have traveled in the far west with some intelligent tourists who have visited the most famous natural scenery to be found in the Old World, and they do not hesitate to declare that they have seen nothing beyond the Atlantic to compare with the wonderlands of the Rocky Mountains and the Sierra Nevadas.

In order to furnish a thread of continuity on which to string some observations on men, manners and mountains, and the wonderful scenery to be found in that vast region lying between the Missouri River and the Pacific Ocean, I will have you go along with me across the continent, from Kansas City, at the western boundary of the State of Missouri, to the Golden Gate of the Pacific, at San Francisco. I will not dwell long on the way, nor will I weary your patience by relating the ordinary incidents of travel. We will go along rapidly, for we now travel by railroad in a Pullman Sleeper over those trackless plains and deserts, and rugged and inhospitable mountains that were traversed by the Argonauts of '49, in their long and toilsome journey of many months. In the eastern half of Kansas we pass through a rich and well-cultivated country. In the western part we reach the beginning of the arid region, which stretches for a thousand miles toward the west, and includes the regions of the Rocky Mountains, the Great Basin and the Sierra Nevadas.

In Kansas and Colorado, the untraveled tourist will feast his vision on those vast prairies or plains, of which he has heard so much. Day after day, until we reach the foothills of the Rocky Mountains, we pass over these everlasting, boundless, illimitable "plains," until the brain reels and the eye is tired in looking upon the vast expanse; and, if the traveler is of a poetic turn of mind, he will recall the graphic lines of William Cullen Bryant:

> "These are the gardens of the desert, these
> The unshorn fields, boundless and beautiful
> For which the speech of England has no name—
> The prairies.   I behold them for the first ;
> And my heart swells, while the dilated sight
> Takes in the encircling vastness.   Lo ! they stretch
> In airy undulations, far away,
> As if the ocean in his gentlest swell,
> Stood still, with all his rounded billows fixed,
> And motionless forever."

This description refers to the rolling prairies which are found in Missouri and Iowa, and the eastern portions of Kansas and Nebraska; but as we go further west, the prairies or plains for hundreds of miles, appear to be almost as level as a billiard table, with nothing to relieve the landscape, except, now and then, a herd of graceful antelopes, or the grand illumination of a prairie fire.

Where are the wild Indians, the buffaloes, the trappers that beguiled our youthful days in Cooper's novels? They are things of the past, along this line of travel. They have vanished before the advancing steps of civilization.   No buffalo are to be seen from the Missouri River to San Francisco, although, at the time of the construction of the Kansas Pacific Railroad, through Kansas and Colorado, about twenty-one years ago, the trains were sometimes stopped by herds of tens of thousands of buffalo; and at present Indians are rarely seen until you reach Utah or Nevada.

All the way from the Missouri River to the foothills of the Rocky Mountains, we have gradually ascended, until now, at an elevation of five thousand or six thousand feet, still on the plains, we catch the first view of the

AN INDIAN "BUCK."

Rocky Mountains.   Looking to the south-west the snow-capped summit of Pike's Peak towers aloft in awful sublimity, some seventy five miles away.   Soon afterwards we reach Denver.   Thence we go north one hundred and twenty miles till we arrive at Cheyenne, the capital of Wyoming, intersecting the main line of the Union Pacific Railway.   It is midsummer, but to the left of us, we are in constant view of the Rocky Mountain range, covered with eternal snow.

.   Soon after leaving Cheyenne we begin to ascend the Rocky Mountains rapidly until we reach Sherman, the highest point on the railway between the Missouri River and the Pacific Ocean, the altitude being eight thousand two hundred and thirty-five feet above the level of the sea.   In Wyoming and Utah, as far west as Ogden, we pass over a mountainous country, for four or five hundred miles, some parts of which are very picturesque; particularly Echo and Weber canyons.   Further mention of these canyons and other scenery on this road is now pretermitted, because we shall presently visit other mountain scenery far surpassing, in beauty and grandeur, anything to be seen on this line of travel.   Soon after leaving Evanston, we enter the world-renowned Mormon land, the territory of Utah.   In sketching the wonderlands of the west, it would be like a deed without a seal at common law, a most unpardonable *casus omissus* if we fail to notice this strange and peculiar people, the Latter-day Saints.   But before entering on this, we will make a detour to the capital of Zion, and give some account of the physical geography of the country.

We arrive at Ogden, Utah Territory, on the evening of the fourth day's travel from Indiana.   Here we take the Utah Central Railroad* and run south thirty-

* Now [1891] a branch of the Union Pacific Railroad.

seven and a half miles, skirting the Great Salt Lake on our right, and reach Salt Lake City at eight o'clock on the same evening, having traveled one thousand seven hundred and fifty miles from Terre Haute, Indiana.

The area of Utah Territory is about eighty-four thousand square miles, a great portion of which is covered with mountains; many of them of stupendous height. Being situated within the arid region, the cultivation of the soil depends mainly upon the facilities for irrigation; and this leads us to a notice of the mountain ranges and the canyon streams of Utah.

And what is a canyon? It is a Spanish-American word, used to express what can be better understood by a description than a definition.

In that remote geological era, when this western region was so awfully convulsed by the throes of Nature, and these lofty and rocky mountains were upheaved, in ranges, generally running in a north and south direction, there were great seams or gulches made transversely with the ranges. These are called canyons.

The whole three hundred and fifty miles of the length of Utah is traversed north and south by ranges of mountains, the principal of which is the Wasatch range, a part of the Rocky Mountain system.

The western side of this range is bold and precipitous, many of the peaks rising ten, eleven and thirteen thousand feet above the level of the sea. This mountain range is cut transversely on the west side by canyons, at intervals of three to five or eight miles. Issuing from each canyon there is a stream of water flowing down from the melting snow of the mountains, which is often drifted to the depth of fifty or sixty feet. These streams, flowing from their source from ten to thirty-five miles through the canyons, down into the valleys at the base of the mountains, are utilized for the purpose of irrigating the fields. The soil being very rich, and productive when cultivated by irrigation, the Mormons have made many of these valleys to "blossom like the rose."

One of these canyons will now be described; and it will serve as an illustration of hundreds of others in the west.

On a warm July day, we start on an excursion to Little Cottonwood Canyon to the southeast of Salt Lake City. We set out early in the morning, on a train of the celelebrated scenic road, the Denver and Rio Grande Western Railway. Running south eleven miles, through a rich and well-cultivated valley, we reach Bingham Junction, where we intersect a branch railroad, which runs west to the Bingham mines, and east to the mining camp of Alta, at the head of Little Cottonwood canyon. Changing cars at Bingham Junction, we run in an easterly direction about eight miles to a little town called Wasatch, just above the mouth of the canyon. Here we leave the steam cars and continue our journey about eight miles up the canyon on a tramway, the cars being drawn by mules working tandem. At the mouth of this canyon are the granite quarries, where the material is procured for the building of the Mormon Temple at Salt Lake City. On each side of the canyon, for several miles above its mouth, there are great mountains of granite, rising some two or three thousand feet above us; and it has been estimated, or guessed, that there is enough granite here to build a hundred cities as big as New York. Along the narrow valley, or rather defile, there are many granite boulders, from the size of a collossal elephant to a meeting-house, which appear to have been broken off and rolled down from the almost perpendicular sides of the mountains. Thus far the Mormons have quarried only from these enormous loose rocks for the building of their Temple, which has been in course of construction since 1853. This granite is first-rate building material, and the Temple, when finished according to the design, will be one of the most durable and beautiful buildings in this country.

At these quarries our attention was called to some handsome white tents on the other side of the canyon stream, and we were told that there was something over there worth seeing. Crossing on a foot-bridge over the dashing, foaming mountain stream, as white as milk, we found ourselves in a scene of enchantment and rural beauty, rarely to be seen anywhere in the wide world! Hid away among the bushes of maple and cottonwood and wild roses, there were a great many tents of snowy whiteness; within were nice clean beds and pictures, and other light furniture. This umbrageous village of tents is occupied in warm weather by the quarrymen and their families, and picnic parties are sometimes held here by the young people of Salt Lake City. All through the grounds were beautiful walks, fringed with flowers of many kinds; streams of pure mountain water were flowing everywhere. some in little wooden flumes, and some in graveled channels, while many tiny jets were cooling the perfumed air. This gem of the mountains, this quiet scene of rural beauty, was "worthy of the golden prime of the good Haroun Al Raschid."

But let us continue our way up the canyon. The tramway is (or has been) enclosed with a continuous snow-shed, the whole eight miles, constructed at great expense; but in many places this structure has been carried away by snow-slides.

The scenery in this canyon is very grand and beautiful, the narrow defile being enclosed on both sides by rugged mountains a half mile high above the stream, and the stream itself some miles above the mouth of the canyon being seven or eight thousand feet above the level of the sea.

In many places these stupendous mountain walls are almost perpendicular, and often indented with awful gorges, where the immense rocks are fashioned into all sorts of grotesque forms, resembling castles, cathedrals, towers or animals of monstrous size and shape. Far up the mountain sides we see little *bushes* of evergreens —that is, they *seem* to be little bushes; but, in fact, they are large pines and firs, probably one or two feet in diameter and seventy-five feet high—large enough for the masts of a frigate. Now and then we catch a view of a beautiful cascade of silvery whiteness and gauze-like appearance, dashing down the rugged declivity, and sometimes making a clear leap of hundreds of feet.

As we proceed along the stream, we are rapidly ascending, and the temperature is becoming colder; the tops and sides of the mountains are covered with great patches of snow, a curious sight for midsummer! But this canyon stream is "a thing of beauty and a joy forever." It is very rapid, cold and clear, and goes dashing, roaring, and foaming among huge rocks, with many hundreds of rapids and cascades.

At length we arrive at Alta, four hours from Salt Lake City. The air is pure, dry and cold. Several of the party are shivering. One lady in delicate health is almost overcome with the cold, but is soon restored by extra wraps and a roaring coal fire. The little children of the party find an acre of snow close by the hotel, and amuse themselves with snow-balling.

Alta is surrounded on all sides but one with high mountains. Several noted silver mines are here, among others the celebrated Emma Mine, concerning which Minister Schenck had so much trouble several years ago, in England.

To give you an idea of a winter in the Wasatch Mountains, Alta will serve as an example. The snow is often thirty feet deep in the town, and sometimes over the tops of the second story windows, while in some instances nothing can be seen of the houses except the tops of the chimneys. The people get about through tunnels which they excavate under the snow. "Beware of the dreadful avalanche!"—is not mere poetry to the denizens of Alta. It has several times been almost completely destroyed by these snow-slides, and one time and another more than one hundred and fifty lives have been lost. In the spring of 1884 there were twelve lives destroyed there, by an avalanche, and in the spring of 1885 there were twenty more deaths by the same sort of disaster.

So much for the canyon. In subsequent pages I will call your attention to some other of these remarkable chasms in the west, such as the Grand Canyon of the Arkansas, the Royal Gorge, the Black Canyon of the Gunnison, etc.

But the most remarkable and stupendous chasm on this globe is the Grand Canyon of the Colorado, partly in Utah and partly in Arizona. For awful sublimity and grotesqueness, this tremendous gorge has no parallel upon the earth. It is three hundred or four hundred miles long, and in many places half a mile, and in some places more than one mile deep.

At the bottom flows the dashing, foaming, turbulent waters of the Colorado River, compressed within narrow limits by the huge and rugged rocks that rise in many places perpendicularly from three to six thousand feet.

What an awful spectacle, to stand beside the dark
and rushing waters of the stream, fifty feet deep, and
look up at the buttressed and battlemented walls which
seem to reach the sky, walls so high that the perspective
appears to close them at the top so near together, that
only a thin streak of sky can be seen!

How trifling, how infinitesimally small and insignificant is man, with all his boasted works of art,—his Par-
thenons, his Coliseums, his pyramids, his capitols, and
temples,—compared with these stupendous, titanic, awe-
inspiring works of nature! Words are vain and feeble
—wholly inadequate to convey to the mind a full con-
ception of these Cyclopean wonders of the west. They
are ineffable; but the thought of them will remain
through life, and you will always feel proud that you
have seen them.

Before I come to a description of the city of the
Saints, I will take time to make only brief mention of
Marshall's Pass, where the great scenic railway crosses
the backbone of the Rocky Mountains at an elevation of
ten thousand eight hundred feet above the level of the
sea. The elevation is so great that you shiver with cold
in July, and the road is so crooked, in order to make the
gradual ascent, that, looking down the mountain sides,
you think you see six or seven different railroad tracks.
But this is not so crooked as the narrow-guage railroad
between Georgetown and Plume City in Colorado, where
it doubles up and crosses itself in a loop; nor will it
compare with the Southern Pacific Railroad at Tiha-
chapi Pass in Southern California, where (it is not
much exaggeration to say) the road is so crooked
that it ties itself into a double-bow knot. The road
runs through a tunnel, and then describes a complete
circle around the peak of a mountain; then crosses

itself seventy-eight feet above the tunnel, and in a short distance makes another circuit and crosses itself again. This is called the Lover's Knot.

Salt Lake City, the capital of Utah, is one of the most beautiful and attractive cities I have ever seen. On a fine spring day we take a carriage drive to view the place.

A VIEW OF SALT LAKE CITY.

Our driver said he had been a Mormon, but had had nothing to do with the Church for a long time. He had resided in Salt Lake City for twenty years. He was an excellent guide, and knew where everybody lived, and all the places of interest. Going east on South Temple (or Brigham) Street, we passed the Temple Block on which are situated the Tabernacle, the Temple, the Assembly Hall and the Endowment House. East of these are the Tithing Yard and buildings, the *Deseret News* office, the Lion House, the Bee Hive House and the Eagle Gate. Across the street from the Bee Hive House is the Gardo House, commonly called by the Gentiles The Amelia Palace.

The Temple block contains ten acres and is enclosed by high walls. The Tabernacle is the great meeting-house of the Saints, in which they hold religious exercises every Sunday, except in cold weather, when the meetings are held in the Assembly Hall. The Tabernacle will seat 12,000 people, and, with standing room, has upon some occasions held 15,000. In the west end is an immense organ, which at the time it was built, was the largest in the United States. It is the work of resident mechanics and made of the native woods of Utah. The choir when full, consists of one hundred and ten singers.* The Tabernacle when seen from a distance looks like a huge turtle. It is two hundred and fifty feet long by one hundred and fifty feet wide, and eighty feet from the floor to the ceiling. It is elliptical in shape, and without a column inside to support the roof. The foundation for the dome of the building is a succession of red sand-stone pillars, each about six by ten feet and fifteen or twenty feet high. Around the building there are twenty doors.

The Temple, however, is to be the glory and pride of Zion. It was begun in 1853, and with some intermissions, work has been going on ever since. It is thought it will be finished by the year 1893. The material is a first-rate gray granite, found in the mountains about eighteen miles from the city. The walls are nine feet and three inches thick, and have already been carried up above the square. The work on the spires is now going on. When finished according to the Architect's plan, it will be a magnificent and substantial building. The cost of construction up to March 12th, 1883, was $1,687,000, and at this time it must be considerably over $2,500,000.

The Assembly Hall is a new and substantial building, of granite, of excellent architectural design, in which the meetings are held on Sundays when the weather is cold. Its highest steeple is ornamented with an effigy of Gabriel blowing his trump. The inside of the hall is decorated with many pictures illustrative of scenes in Mormon history.

The Endowment House is a plain and unostentatious adobe structure in the northwest corner of the Temple Block. Here various mysteries and ordinances

---

* The Choir now [1891] numbers more than three hundred singers.

of the Mörmon theology are celebrated, among others marriages.   The Endowment House is a *sanctum sanctorum* into which Gentile "misbelievers" are not admitted.*

Proceeding eastward on Brigham Street we pass on our left the Lion House, a large building, plain in style, but well built and well finished.   On top of the portico facing the street is a well-executed stone lion, of life size.   (Brigham Young's poetical sobriquet was The Lion of the Lord,)   In this house a majority of his many wives were domiciled, during his life-time.   A short distance east of the Lion House is the Bee Hive House, the principal residence of the late President.   It takes its name from a bee hive on the top of the house.   The bee hive is the emblem of the Mormons and the coat-of-arms of the State of Deseret— by which name they formerly sought to be admitted into the Union as a State.   On the front door of the Bee Hive House we find the door plate still remaining, inscribed in plain Roman letters, Brigham Young.

Across the street, south of the Bee Hive House, is the Gardo House or Amelia Palace, built by Brigham Young, as is generally said, to please his ninth wife, Amelia Folsom Young, at that time the light of the Harem, and the reigning queen of his capacious affections.   This is a very elegant and costly building, and would appear to good advantage among the most sumptuous residences of our eastern cities.

Passing by the Eagle Gate constructed by Brigham Young, consisting of four high pillars, surmounted by a spread-eagle standing on a bee hive on top of the arch of the gate-way, we see a great many fine resi-

---

* The Endowment House was pulled down in 1889.

dences.   On our left was pointed out to us the "White House where Brigham's first wife resided until her death in 1882;—on the right we saw the former residence of the recalcitrant Ann Eliza Young.   Further on we passed, on our left, the elegant residence of Brigham Young, a son of the late President, and now one of the Twelve Apostles.   On this street also are several fine residences belonging to mining and mercantile nabobs among the Gentile population.

Brigham Street* is the aristocratic thoroughfare of the city.   It is situated on the southern declivity of the "bench" of the mountains.   Streams of pure cold water are brought in artificial channels, from the City Creek Canyon, in the adjacent mountains, on to the beautiful deep green lawns of English lawn grass, and the rich gardens, orchards and vineyards.   Apple, peach and plum trees, as well as strawberries were in full bloom.   On this street, and in other parts of the city we found a great deal of lucern (or alfalfa.)   It is growing luxuriantly, of a bright emerald green, and contributes greatly to the beauty of the landscape.   It is cut for hay, and three or four crops are mowed during the season.

From Brigham Street we drove some distance up on the bench to a place called lookout point, from which we had a magnificent view of the whole city, Great Salt Lake, many towns, villages, and settlements, and the snow-covered mountains twenty and thirty miles away, some of the peaks being twelve or thirteen thousand feet above the level of the sea.   Of a clear day Mount Nebo in the south can be seen, eighty miles away.

The whole scene reminded me of Irving's descrip-

---

* More properly South Temple Street.

tion of the city of Granada, at the time of its conquest by the " harnessed chivalry of Spain"—the same rugged mountain scenery, and the silvery streams irrigating plains and meadows, gardens, flowers and fruits.

Returning to Brigham Street, we proceed to Camp Douglas, a military post about three miles east of Main Street, then commanded by Col. Alexander McCook. This place is six or seven hundred feet higher than Salt Lake City, and commands a fine view of Zion. The officer's quarters are built of fine red sandstone, found in the vicinity, and consists of ten or twelve substantially built houses, arranged in a semi-circle, half enclosing a smooth, green lawn watered by a stream of water brought from the Red Butte Canyon. The elegant residence of the Colonel, the barracks, the hospital and other buildings make up quite an attractive place. A good band furnishes music every Sunday afternoon to visitors from the city. At the camp we fell in with an ex-cursion party of about one hundred persons from San Francisco, Oakland and Sacramento, who were sight-seeing in Zion. Returning to the city, we drove past the magnificent building on Main Street, which is the head-quarters of Zion's Co-operative Mercantile In-stitution, founded by Brigham Young and other leading Mormons in 1868. This building is one hundred feet wide, three hundred and eighteen feet long, and three stories high. The business done here is by wholesale and retail, and this is the center of a great mercantile system throughout Utah and the Mormon settlements in the adjacent States and Territories. This institution does a business amounting to four or five millions of dollars annually.

We visited the grave of Brigham Young, in a private cemetery on the bench of the mountains. He lies buried under a large, square stone, about a foot thick, on which (by his direction) there is no inscription.

We drove past the Salt Lake Theatre, and the new Walker Opera House. The former was erected by Brigham Young and is a capacious and well constructed building. Theatricals, as well as music and dancing were encouraged by the late "Prophet Brigham." He had his private box at the theatre, where he was often seen with some of his wives. At dancing parties he often took the lead in tripping the "light fantastic."

We next drove out past the residence of Feramorz Little, formerly Mayor of the city. He was quite a wealthy man; and his residence and grounds would compare favorably with the best in our eastern cities. He was a Mormon and a polygamist, or had been, I have been told, but I have forgotten how many wives he has had. I had a conversation with him in the fall of 1882, while the registration of voters was going on ; and he complained bitterly that some Mormons were not allowed to register or vote, "although they were living pure and virtuous lives in the holy order of celestial marriage, while Kate Flint and her suite of painted Jezebels had walked up with brazen impudence and been registered as voters." (Kate Flint was the Gentile proprietress of a *maison de joie* in the city.) Woman suffrage was then allowed by law in Utah; but it was abolished by act of Congress, March 3, 1887.

Salt Lake City, originally called "Great Salt Lake City," had three years ago a population of about thirty-five thousand, and the census of 1890 shows about fifty thousand. It covers about six square miles, and is beautifully situated near the base of the Wasatch range of mountains. The northern portion of the city is on the bench (or a plateau) of the mountains, and this part of the city is considered the most eligible for residences. It is in this quarter of the city that Brigham Young and divers members of his family, and high dignitaries of the Church established their palatial residences, eastward of the Temple Block.

The whole city is laid off in blocks of ten acres each, so that in walking around a block you travel exactly half a mile. Each block is divided into eight lots of an acre and a quarter each. The streets are very wide, one hundred and thirty-two feet, including the sidewalks, which are each sixteen and a half feet wide. One of the pleasing features of the city is the great number of shade trees along the sidewalks of all the streets, and the fruit and ornamental trees, gardens and lawns of English grass that everywhere abound. But the great charm of the city, that formerly excited the admiration of all tourists and sojourners, were the streams of pure, clear water running along the edge of the sidewalks on all the streets. The water is brought down from the mountain canyons near the city, the principal supply being from City Creek Canyon.

These streams are fed by the melting of the snow high up in the mountains, and the water comes dashing and foaming down the canyons.

City Creek is dammed up at several places, and the water is carried around the sides of the mountains in ditches and flumes, to the higher parts of the city, and thence it is conducted east, west and south to all parts of the city, and is used for irrigating the trees, grass and gardens.

To pass along Main Street, which has a considerable descent to the south, on a hot July day and see the clear, cold water dashing rapidly along, is a grateful and novel sight.

The water thus carried to every man's door was used by the Mormons in the pioneer days for drinking and other purposes. But with the growth of the city, water works have been established, and water is now brought down in pipes from City Creek for domestic use, for irrigating lawns and for the fire department. This city has all the modern improvements—gas, electric lights, telephones, bicycles, skating rinks, theaters, race courses, street railroads, four daily newspapers, fire companies, etc.

There are also many saloons, gambling houses, and a few years ago there were several gilded palaces of sin, for all of which the Mormons say the city is indebted to the influx of Gentile population.

One of the attractions of Utah is the Great Salt Lake, or "Dead Sea of America," and I will now give an account of a visit to this great inland sea, which is about twelve miles from the city at its nearest point, but the two most noted bathing resorts are "Garfield Beach," on the southern end of the lake, about twenty miles west of the city, and "Lake Park," on the eastern side about sixteen miles distant.

We take the train at the Utah & Nevada Railroad for Garfield Beach at 8 o'clock a. m., and reach the lake in about one hour. At the western limits of the city we "cross over Jordan," a river that flows from Lake Utah, or Timpanogos, in the south, to Great Salt Lake, a distance of forty or fifty miles.

For a short distance from the city we pass through cultivated farms, and the air is laden with the delicious odor of the purple blossoms of alfalfa ; but for the greater part of the way the land is uncultivated and is white with alkali.

Arrived at Garfield Beach, we have a fine view of the lake. It looks a good deal like Lake Michigan ; except that the view here is obstructed by islands on the right and the left ; but directly to the north the vision extends unobstructed as far as it can reach.

The first mention of Great Salt Lake was by the Baron La Hontan, in 1689. He had gathered some vague notions of the lake from the Indians. In 1833, Captain Bonneville, of the United States Army, sent a party from Green River to make a circuit of the great lake, but when they struck the " Great Desert" on the northwest they lost their way and wandered off into southern California at Monterey.

In 1842 Col. John C. Fremont, on his exploring expedition to Oregon, visited the lake and spent a night on one of its islands. On the 22nd of July, 1847, the Mormon pioneers first caught a view of the great lake and valley from an elevated plateau at the mouth of Emigration Canyon, as they emerged from the Wasatch Mountains. Two days later (July 24th) they came down into the valley and camped near where the great temple is now located.

The lake is about eighty or ninety miles long and forty or fifty miles wide. It has a number of islands, the largest being Antelope (or Church) Island, Stansbury and Fremont.

Several hundred persons go to these bathing places from the city every day on excursion trains during the summer.

The water is very clear and so dense that a person cannot sink in it. Lying down on the water, one floats like a chip, and keeping one's self in a vertical position he cannot sink lower than the top of his shoulders. It is a hard place to make much headway in swimming, because it is so difficult to keep the feet under water. It has been poetically observed that the albatros sleeps on the wing; a fact however, which is not sustained by writers on natural history. Yet I have no doubt that a man could go to sleep and float on the surface of Great Salt Lake, if he would rig up some contrivance to rest his head on and keep from turning over.

There appears to be no danger of drowning in the ordinary way. But in 1882, a leading merchant of Salt Lake City went in bathing with a large party. He stayed in longer than the others, until a strong wind sprung up. He was missed by the party after the train started for the city; and although a large reward was offered, nothing was ever seen or heard of him, until, after the lapse of many months, the body was found at the southwest shore. One of the searchers told me that he had killed a large dog and thrown him into the lake to see if he would float, and found that he did float like a piece of timber.

But while one will not drown, in the ordinary sense of the word, yet it is exceedingly dangerous to swallow the salt and acrid water. Even a small quantity, not over a spoonful taken into the throat almost strangles a person, and I have no doubt that a larger quantity of the water would destroy life or render one insensible in a short time. It is supposed by some persons that the missing man became strangled in this way and floated off to the desert shore of the lake.

We all went into the lake and had a fine time. Several little children were in, floating around like ducks. Commonly there are many sea-gulls on the lake, and they are very tame. The Mormons appear to have great respect for them. In the pioneer days their fields and gardens were ravaged by grasshoppers and crickets, until "the Lord sent the gulls" and destroyed them by millions.

A number of rivers flow into the lake, the principal of which are, the Jordan from the south, the Weber
from the east, the Bear and Ogden from the north.
None of these "rivers" are large and would be called
"creeks" by the natives of Indiana.   There is no outlet
to the lake, and it was once supposed .that there was,
somewhere, a subaqueous vortex that served as an outlet to the water.   This idea is now exploded ; and indeed
the rivers that flow into the lake are so inconsiderable
that it will be readily conceived that the equilibrium is
maintained by the rapid evaporation in this high altitude,
there being such a vast surface exposed to the rays of
the sun.   Large as this great inland sea now is, it is
evident that it was many times larger in some remote
geological era, and that it once covered the whole of this
great valley, stretching. from the Wasatch range of
mountains on the east to the Oquirrh range on the south
and west.   All around on the sides of the mountains can
be seen several hundred feet above the level of the lake,
a horizontal bench or water-mark, plainly indicating that
this was once the surface of the lake or ocean.

The surface of the Great Salt Lake is more than
four thousand feet above the level of the Pacific Ocean,
with which geologists suppose it once communicated to
the north, along the Snake and Columbia river regions.

The water of the lake is very salt, containing about
twenty per cent., a much larger proportion than is contained in the water of the ocean.   Salt for domestic use is
obtained by boiling and skimming the water.   A large
quantity of crude salt is obtained by evaporation, the low
lands being inundated and then cut off from the lake by
dams, where the water is allowed to stand until it
evaporates, leaving a stratum of salt on the ground.
The crude salt obtained in this way is used in immense

quantities in this and other territories as a flux in smelting lead, silver and other ores.   In the southern part of Utah there are great banks or mountains of solid salt.

On the borders of the lake where herbage or shrubs are growing close to the edge of the water, they become encrusted with crystalized salt, resembling branches of coral or white rock candy.   Some of these are very beautiful.

There is no animal life in the lake except an infintesimally small animalcule, like a wiggletail, to which the naturalists have given a very long Greek name, which I have forgotten, as I have no faculty for remembering names of sesquipedalian length, for little creatures no larger than a gnat.   Efforts have been made to propagate fish, oysters, etc., in the lake, but without success.   They all die.

The mean depth of the lake is some twenty feet, and in its deepest places not over sixty feet.

There are no large crafts navigating it, but some years ago there was a pretty good-sized steam boat which was called the "General Garfield," used for excursion parties and transporting timbers to the Central Pacific railroad, north of the lake.   But persons desiring an excursion can hire a sail boat, or take passage on a little steamer.

While at the lake we had a cool breeze from the north, which made it very comfortable.   We started back at two p. m., and found it quite warm as we approached the city and again crossed over Jordan into the city of the Saints.   It was very curious to witness the wilderness of flowers and fruits and blossoming lucern of the modern Granada, and then to lift the eyes and see the clear cut and rugged peaks of the snow-clad mountains which half encircle the city on its eastern side.

We will not now dwell longer on the picturesque scenery of the Rocky Mountains, but will turn our attention to some of the remarkable phases of human character and society which we find in the heart of the continent between the Rocky Mountains and the Sierra Nevadas. I refer particularly to the Mormons, or Latter-day Saints.

The people called Mormons, have, during the last half century, been more talked and written about in books, pamphlets, magazines, brochures and newspapers than, perhaps, any other people, of no more considerable numbers, in modern times.

Many large volumes and other less pretentious have been published. Tourists, statesmen, savants and *literateurs* from all parts of the civilized world have visited Utah to learn something of those peculiar people, inhabiting the valleys of the mountains. I will not attempt to give anything more than a general outline of the history of the Mormons, with a brief account of some of the peculiarities of their creed.

The founder of Mormonism was Joseph Smith, who was born in Windsor County, Vermont, in 1805; he removed with his father's family to New York, when he was quite young. He was poor, illiterate, and, according to Gentile testimony, of an unsavory reputation.

In 1820, he claimed to have supernatural visions; these were repeated in 1823. In 1827, he claimed to have received the plates of the Book of Mormon, which was first published in 1830.

On April 6th, 1830, at Fayette, Seneca County, New York, he organized the "Church of Jesus Christ of Latter-day Saints," embracing only six persons.

Having made a considerable number of converts,

THE PROPHET JOSEPH SMITH.

the Mormons gathered to Kirtland, in the northern part of Ohio, where they built a temple and flourished for a while.

While their headquarters were still at Kirtland, in 1831, the land of Zion in Jackson County, Missouri, was consecrated for the gathering of the Saints, and they immigrated to Missouri in great numbers. In 1839, they were driven out of Missouri by mob violence, and took refuge in Illinois, where they built a city which they called Nauvoo. In 1844, Joseph Smith and his brother Hyrum were murdered in jail by a mob. The Mormons were driven from Nauvoo and commenced their exodus in 1846; and their advanced company of pioneers reached Salt Lake Valley in July, 1847, after a march of eighty days on foot, more than a thousand miles from the Missouri River. From that time they have gradually increased in numbers until the present population of Utah is estimated at about 250,000, three-fourths of whom are Mormons. The total number of the sect throughout the world, is estimated at over two hundred thousand.

We will now take a diversion, from this outline of events, to say something of the creed and peculiar institutions of this singular people. The Mormons believe in the Old Testament, the New Testament and a great deal besides; namely, the "Book of Mormon," and in divers revelations which they claim have been from time to time received by Joseph Smith, and his successors, Brigham Young, John Taylor and Wilford Woodruff, each of whom having been at the head of the Church, under the name and style of "Prophet, Seer and Revelator, and President of the Church of Jesus Christ of Latter-day Saints in all the world." Most of these so-called revelations are recorded in a volume, called the

"Book of Doctrine and Covenants;" and among them is one in favor of a plurality of wives.

Besides the views held by the Mormons in common with other denominations, there are some peculiar features, most of which they claim to be founded upon passages in the Old or New Testament. They have a hymn which will be found on page 349 of the "Sacred Hymns and Spiritual Songs for the Church of Jesus Christ of Latter-day Saints," that will serve to illustrate some of those peculiarities. It is modeled after the song and sung to the air of "The Rose that all are Praising, Is not the Rose for me." The whole of this singular composition I will now repeat with comments on each stanza.

> "The God that others worship is not the God for me:
> He has no parts nor body, and cannot hear nor see;
> But I've a God that reigns above—
> A God of power and of love—
> A God of revelation—Oh, that's the God for me!
>   Oh, that's the God for me!
>   Oh, that's the God for me!"

The Mormons believe in a personal God—that he is an actual personage, an individual, with body, limbs, features, etc., like a man, but with every faculty and attribute in the fullness of perfection. They refer to the passage in Genesis: "God made man in his own image."

A God of *revelation*. They believe not only that God revealed himself in ancient times to Moses and the prophets, and later in the days of our Savior to the apostles and disciples, but that He continues to make revelations in these latter days through Joseph Smith, Brigham Young and their successors, as prophets, seers and revelators. They also claim that each individual Saint may receive revelations pertaining to himself.

"A Church without a Prophet, is not the Church for me;
It has no head to lead it; in it I would not be:
But I've a Church not made by man,
Cut from the mountain without hand ;
A Church with gifts and blessings, O, that's the Church for me ;
	Oh, that's the Church for me !
	Oh, that's the Church for me !''

The Mormons esteem the President of the Church as a Prophet of the Lord after the order of Melchisedek.

A church of gifts and blessings. This is suggestive of some of the most remarkable phases of the Mormon religion. They claim that they are the Latter-day Saints, just as the disciples of Christ and His apostles were Saints in the former days, and that the Latter-day Saints have the same gifts and blessings that were enjoyed by the first Christians, as recorded in the New Testament, namely, the gift of the Holy Ghost, by the laying on of hands, followed by the gifts of prophecy, healing, visions, miracles, power over evil spirits, speaking in tongues and the interpretation of tongues. The Mormons claim that these gifts were common among the first Saints, and that they are enjoyed in different degrees by the Saints or (Mormons) at this day. They quote Acts viii: 14, 19; Acts xix: 6; II. Timothy, i: 6; John xiv: 26; xvi, 13; Gal. v: 22, 23; I. Cor. xii: 4–11.

"A Church without Apostles is not the Church for me;
'Tis like a ship dismasted, afloat upon the sea;
But I've a Church that's always led,
With the twelve stars around her head ;
A Church with good foundation, Oh, that's the Church for me;
	Oh, that's the Church for me !
	Oh, that's the Church for me !''

The Mormons have twelve living apostles, as a part of their Church organization, and some of these twelve may be seen on any Sunday afternoon sitting on elevated seats in the Tabernacle in Salt Lake City. In the autumn of 1882 it was gravely announced in the *Deseret News*, the official organ of the Mormon Church, that, in order to fill vacancies, "the Lord, by revelation, through His servant, President John Taylor, designated by name, Brothers George Teasdale and Heber J. Grant, to be ordained to the apostleship."

> "The hope that Gentiles cherish, is not the hope for me;
> It has no faith nor knowledge! far from it I would be:
> But I've a hope that will not fail;
> It reaches far within the veil.
> Which hope is like an anchor, Oh, that's the hope for me;
> > Oh, that's the hope for me!
> > Oh, that's the hope for me!"

There is no particular observation to be made on this stanza; unless it be that the Mormons consider all Christians and others who are not of the Mormon faith, as Gentiles; in Utah, even a Jew is a Gentile.

> "The Heaven of Sectarians, is not the Heaven for me;
> So doubtful its location, neither on land nor sea,
> But I've a Heaven upon the earth—
> The land and home that gave me birth;
> A Heaven of light and knowledge—Oh, that's the Heaven for me;
> > Oh, that's the Heaven for me!
> > Oh, that's the Heaven for me!"

This stanza appears to me, somewhat mixed, I suppose it refers to Zion, or the Kingdom of God on earth, and the state of the Saints on earth after the first resurrection. It would seem from a passage in one of Brigham Young's Thanksgiving Proclamations that one of the Mormon heavens is on a planet, which is unknown to other astronomers. He says, "Finally I say unto you, let the same process be continued from day to day, until you arrive at one of the days of *Kolob* (whose days are one thousand of our years) the planet nearest unto the habitation of the Eternal Father ; and if you do not find peace and rest to your souls, by that time, in the practice of these things, and no one else shall present himself to offer you better counsel, *I will be there* and *knowing more*, will tell you what to do next."

"A Church without a *gathering* is not the Church for me,
The Savior would not own it, wherever it might be;
But I've a Church that is called out
From false tradition, fear and doubt,
A gathering dispensation—Oh, that's the Church for me ;
    Oh, that's the Church for me !
    Oh, that's the Church for me !"

"Gathering" is a favorite expression among the Mormons. This "gathering place" is now the valleys of the mountains in Utah, but it is finally to be in Jackson County, Missouri.

There is another singular feature in the Mormon creed and practice, and that is baptism for the dead. They believe that the living relatives of the dead may be baptized in their stead, and that this vicarious baptism will work to their salvation. I imagine that this is the chief reason why the Mormons are so curious and careful as to matters of geneaolgy. I have noticed that they take great pains to find out the names, births, marriages and deaths of their relatives to remote branches.

They claim authority for this custom in 1 Corinthians xv: 29. These baptisms are by immersion, and must be administered *seriatim*, that is, there must be a separate immersion for each dead relative. An old Scotch

Mormon named Aird told me that he had been baptized for his dead, at the Temple in Logan City, one hundred and forty-four times, and that it took two weeks to get through; which would average ten a day.

Jesse N. Perkins was baptized one thousand one hundred times, which, at ten immersions per day, would take one hundred and ten days. The following curious account of his career and extraordinary baptisms is taken from an obituary notice in the *Deseret News:*

DIED.

PERKINS.—At Taylor, Apache Co., Arizona, March 2nd, 1883, at his own home, at 12:15 p. m., Friday, of smallpox, Jesse N. Perkins, Sen., son of Reuben and Elizabeth Pittillo Perkins.

Deceased was born February 19, 1819, in Jackson Co., Tenn., moved to Missouri in 1838, was married to Rhoda C. McClelland Jan. 13, 1842, was baptized into the Church of Jesus Christ of Latter-day Saints February 19, 1848, by Andrew H. Perkins, and was mobbed from his home in about fourteen days after his arrival at the camp of the Saints, about March 15; was ordained an Elder about the 10th of June, by Andrew H. Perkins, remained there until the following spring, and succeeded in getting his father's family to gather with the Saints in the mountains; crossed the plains in 1849 in Captain A. H. Perkins' 100, in Captain Allred's 50, and Captain Absalom Perkins' 10; arrived in Salt Lake City, Utah, Oct. 20, 1849, and remained there during the winter; moved to Bountiful, Davis County, the spring following; was called on a scouting party against the Indians, under Captain Robert T. Burton, served his time out and was honorably discharged; received his endowments February 2nd, 1852; was ordained a Seventy about the same time under the hands of Jedediah M. Grant; made a trip south with President Young and company in the fall of '54, and was called on a Lamanite mission in '55, which he performed to the entire satisfaction of those who called him; assisted in bringing in the Handcart Company in '56; went out under Major R. T. Burton in August, '57, against Buchanan's raiders, and discharged his duties to the entire satisfaction of those placed over him; returned home late in the fall; moved south in '58, and returned home in the latter part of the season; was called on a mission to the United

States, with Elder John Stoker, in '69; he labored in the State of
Virginia, and removed much prejudice from the minds of the people
concerning the Gospel, and returned home in the spring of 1870; was
called with his entire family, by President Brigham Young, to Southern
Utah in 1875, to assist in building up that country; was also called
by President Young to Arizona in 1877, with his family, which mission he has performed to the best of his ability; was ordained a High
Priest September 25th, 1880, under the hands of Apostles Brigham
Young and Erastus Snow; was called and set apart as one of the
High Council at the same time; had just returned from Saint George,
with four of his family, where he was baptized for 1,100 of his dead
and received 104 endowments. He has been a very honest, honorable
and upright man all his life, always been respected and on hand to
perform his duties in the Church; was a kind husband and father.
He retained his proper mind to the last moment, had full confidence
in the revelation of God, and in His servants that the Lord has called
to lead His people, and that he would come forth in the first resurrection and inherit a celestial glory in the Kingdom of God.   He gave
many good instructions to his family, who feel that he has finished his
work on earth, and that he has been called home to a greater field of
labor.

POLYGAMY.

A notice of the Rocky Mountain Saints which omits
to mention their peculiar creed and practice concerning
the marital relation would be like the play of Hamlet
with the Prince of Denmark left out.   It is this, more
than anything else, that has attracted so much curiosity;
and brought upon the Mormons repressive legislation
by the United States Government.

Polygamy is a sort of annex to the original Mormon
creed.   Indeed, the Book of Mormon condemns it in the
strongest language.   But the Mormon faith, being progressive in its nature on account of the vicissitudes of continuous and successive revelations (as before stated), Joseph
Smith as Prophet, Seer and Revelator, in the year 1843,
at Nauvoo, Illinois, claimed to have received a new revelation sanctioning polygamy and celestial marriage.

This manifestation of the Divine will came near being thwarted by the stubborn machinations of Mrs. Emma Smith, the "elect lady" and lawful spouse of the Prophet Joseph.

With that predilection for hyperbole and grandiloquence which is characteristic of the Mormons, they had bestowed upon her the name of "the Elect Lady," borrowed from the second epistle of John. With that feminine curiosity which was first conspicuously manifested in Eden's rosy bowers, she got to rummaging among her husband's papers, where she found the delectable revelation in favor of celestial marriage and a plurality of wives; and having a prejudice against possessing only a vulgar fraction of the Prophet's affections, she incontinently burnt up the revelation.

But the Prophet of the Lord, having been warned, no doubt, in a vision, had prudently guarded against such diabolical machinations; and had caused the revelation to be written out in duplicate; and so, one copy was preserved, to become, in future years, the beacon-light of the Rocky Mountain Saints. This is the account generally given by Gentile writers. At Nauvoo, this was kept a secret from the rank-and-file of the Mormons; but it was known and practiced by some of the leading elders at that time. In July, 1852, this dogma was publicly read to the people at Salt Lake City, and promulgated by President Young as a Divine revelation. At first a considerable number of the Mormons were shocked, and were disposed to recalcitrate. A few apostatized, but so great was the authority of the head of the Church, and so strong was the faith of the people in him as a Prophet, Seer and Revelator of the Lord, that they gradually gave in their adhesion to the new doctrine.

It was not long, however, until polygamy became the chief corner-stone of the Mormon structure in Utah. Brigham Young set the example by marrying a number of wives, and in four or five years all Utah went crazy on the subject of polygamy, blood atonement, etc. This was at a period of what the Mormons, by a ludicrous mis-nomer, call the "Reformation in Utah." The leading men of the Church seemed to vie with each other in the number of wives they should marry, and many of the common people, some of them very poor, took from two to half a dozen wives, as a means of securing exaltation in the world to come, both for themselves and their plural wives.

Brigham Young had twenty-five wives, and left fifty-four children surviving him. Heber C. Kimball had eighteen wives, and many other Mormons had from six to eighteen.

The singular notion of the Mormons in regard to marriage is in part illustrated by letters received by the Utah Commission. But in giving one of them to the reader, I must explain, that by the local laws of Utah prior to March 3, 1887, women could vote; and that by a law of Congress no man is allowed to vote who has more than one wife.

"PLAIN CITY, WEBER COUNTY, UTAH.
"May 21st, 1883.

"*Hon. Utah Commission,*

"GENTLEMEN:—I wish to present to you my case, and inquire whether or not I have been unjustly dealt with, by being prevented at the last election from voting. I married a second woman March 26, 1857. Not that she should be as a wife, for she was aged, but that she might be a married woman.* She lived with us till she died, October 12, 1866. Consequently I consider (conscientiously) that I have

---

* In order to be "exalted" in the hereafter.

never violated a United States law, nor do I intend to.   I have voted
the Republican ticket for many years, and my father voted it for many
years before me.   I would like to vote, and if I can, or cannot, please
send a line answering my inquiry.

                    "Yours to serve truly and humbly,

                              "WILLIAM W. MEGUIRE."

It is a noteworthy commentary on Senator Benton's
apothem that "the common sense of the common people
is often an over-match for book-learning"—that while the
Utah Commission and the federal judges of the Supreme
Court of Utah decided against all persons in the condition of William W. Meguire—that they had no right to
vote, yet the Supreme Court of the United States decided that the astute Commissioners and the erudite
Judges in Utah were wrong, and that the illiterate Mormons were right in contending that they "had been unjustly dealt with."

While on this topic, I want to call your attention to
a curious inscription which I copied from a tombstone in
the Mormon cemetery in Salt Lake City, showing the
career of another *very married man :*

"In memory of George Albert Smith, born at Potsdam, St. Law-
rence County, New York, June 26th, 1817.   Died at Salt Lake City
Utah Territory, September 1st, 1875, aged 58 years, 2 months and 5
days.

"NAMES OF ANCESTORS.

"George A., Son of John and Clarissa L. Smith, who was the
son of Asael and Mary D. Smith, who was the son of Samuel and
Priscilla G. Smith, who was the son of Samuel and Rebecca C. Smith,
who was the son of Robert and Mary Smith, who came from England
and was among the founders of Topsfield, Essex County, Massachusetts.

"NAMES OF HIS WIVES.

" Bathsheba W. Smith,
" Nancy C. Smith,

" Zilpha S. Smith,
"Sarah A. Smith,
"Hannah M. Smith,
"Susan E. Smith.

" NAMES OF HIS CHLDREN.

"George A. Smith, born July 7, 1842.
"Mary A. Smith, born February 11, 1852.
"Bathsheba W. Smith, born August 14, 1844.
"Sarah M. Smith, born July 1, 1850.
"Zilpha A. Smith, born March 21, 1846.
"Clarissa W. Smith, born April 21, 1846.
"Nancy A. Smith, born March 21, 1846.
"Eunice A. Smith, born March, 6, 1860.
"John Smith, born April 4, 1847.
"George A. Smith, born April 7, 1862.
" Don C. Smith, born July 21, 1847.
"Margaret W. Smith, born December 6, 1862.
"John H. Smith, born September 18, 1848.
"Grace L. Smith, born May 11, 1865.
" Charles W. Smith, born January 16, 1849.
"Susan E. Smith, born Sept 28, 1866.
"Joseph Smith, born January 12, 1850.
" Priscilla A. Smith, born June 11, 1869.
"Annie Smith, born August 6, 1850.
" Emma B. Smith, born April 19, 1871.

"He was baptized a member of the Church of Jesus Christ of Latter-day Saints: was ordained a member of the Seventies March 1, 1835. A High Priest June 28, 1838. One of the Twelve Apostles April 26, 1839. Appointed First Counselor to Brigham Young October 7, 1868, and Trustee-in-Trust for the Church April 8, 1873. He was cousin to the Prophet Joseph Smith; his personal attendant in Zion's Camp, possessing his unbounded confidence and love until the Prophet's death. He planted the first potato in Salt Lake Valley; was a member of the Senate of the Provisional State of Deseret; was commissioned Colonel of cavalry in the Mormon army November 25, 1851; was elected Historian to the Mormon Church in 1854. He was appointed aide-de-camp to the Lieutenant-general of the Nauvoo Legion April, 1866."

In the stanzas I already quoted you have a specimen of Mormon poetry. I will give you one more example.

In the rural districts of the Mormon-land they have a sort of folk-song, a fragment of which I have preserved:

> "The Mormon father loves to see
> His Mormon family all agree,
> With prattling children on each knee,
> Saying, 'Daddy, I'm a Mormon!'
> Hey the merry, aye the merry,
> Hey the happy Mormon!
> I never knew what joy was
> Till I became a Mormon!"

It must not be supposed, however, that these are the best specimens of Mormon poetry. It will be seen hereafter that they have some authors of real merit, both in prose and verse.

Questions are often asked by outside barbarians: "How do the Mormons get along with their numerous wives and children? How do the wives agree? How do they manage their domestic affairs?" etc. To answer these and like questions fully would take a great deal of time, and in some particulars might provoke a smile from the young and a blush from the fair. I may say, however, that in former years they often accompanied their numerous wives in public, at the tabernacle, the theater and at parties. But under the restraint of the Acts of Congress they now seldom appear in public with more than one wife. In some instances they lived with several wives in the same house. In other cases they had a separate dwelling house for each wife and her children, and their liege lord spent his time with them in rotation, generally a week at a time.

Of course there was more or less of jealousy,

A SHOSHONE FAMILY.

bickering and quarreling, but in some cases these were somewhat subdued by an intense fanaticism and a conviction that they were doing the will of God, and were "bearing the cross that they might wear the crown."

Another question is often asked, "Do Mormons really believe in this monstrous delusion?　Are they honest and sincere in the profession of their so-called religion?"

The answer must be in the affirmative, as to the generality of the Mormon people.　As to the leading men, many of whom have more than ordinary intelligence, it is hard for a novice to believe that they are sincere. But, on the other hand, it must be borne in mind that many of these leaders have been born, or brought up from childhood in the Mormon faith, and all experience teaches us that men of ordinary good sense sometimes believe in the most absurd religious creeds in which they were born and brought up.　Besides, a curious and not uncommon phase of self-delusion is thus delineated in the "Veiled Prophet of Khorassan :"

> " Dark tangled doctrines, dark as fraud can weave,
> Which simple votaries shall on trust receive,
> And wiser fain belief till they believe."

In order to bring this preliminary sketch within reasonable limits, we must proceed rapidly in redeeming our promise to go with the reader to the Pacific shore.

Passing through the State of Nevada, where we see at every station squads of Shoshone and Piute Indians, in feathers, paint and red blankets, we reach the summit of the Sierra Nevada Mountains in California, and looking down to the right we see the noted Donner Lake, where, in the pioneer days, Captain Donner's company of nearly one hundred emigrants froze and starved to death.

Here we see many pine and fir trees cut off ten or fifteen feet from the ground, and learn that these trees were cut down for fuel and habitation by the Donner party, standing on the surface of the deep snow in their desperate struggle with death.

Leaving the summit, we rapidly descend from the deep snows of the mountains to a semi-tropical clime, in the midst of vineyards and groves of oranges, lemons and almonds, and among green lawns, beautiful flowers, and humming bees. It is a strange transition to pass, in three or four hours, from the snowy crags of the Sierra Nevadas to the lovely gardens, decked with Marechal Neil roses and geraniums seven feet high.

Arrived at Oakland, on the bay of San Francisco, "the, sweetest dimple on ocean's cheek," we cross by steamer to the great metropolis of the West, the tawny lion's whelp, that lies crouching by the sea, in fierce, barbaric beauty, the warder of the setting sun.

In an hour more we are seated at the Cliff House, watching the white surf break against the gray old rocks, and noting the uncouth gambols of the sea-lions upon the adjacent islands.

We see the stately ships coming into the Golden Gate, or sailing out to India or Cathay, and the uttermost parts of the earth.

We must defer our visit to the wonders of the Yosemite, and the renowned Big Trees, those giants of the forest that were standing in the Sierras when Cæsar was slain in the Senate, and our Savior was a babe in the manger. And now we must bid adieu to the "glorious climate of California;" and returning to the Great Basin, we will resume, in the second part of these sketches, our narrative of what we saw in "Zion" in wrestling with the "Mormon Problem."

PART II.

THE UTAH COMMISSION.

"I have passed manye landes and cherched manye full strange places, wherein dwell strange men and women. Now I am comen home, and thus recordynge the tyme passed, I have putte hem wryten in this boke as thynges would come into my mynde." [Sir John Maundeville, A. D. 1356.]

ON MARCH 22, 1882, an act was passed by Congress entitled, "An Act to amend Section 5352, of the Revised Statutes of the United States, in reference to bigamy and for other purposes," commonly known as the " Edmunds anti-polygamy Act," the full text of which is given in the third part.

Under the ninth section of the act, President Arthur, by and with the advice and consent of the Senate, made the following appointments to constitute the Board of Commissioners to execute the law, viz. : Alexander Ramsey, of Minnesota ; Algernon S. Paddock, of Nebraska ; Geo. L. Godfrey, of Iowa ; James R. Pettigrew, of Arkansas, and Ambrose B. Carlton, of Indiana. Their commissions reached them in July, and at the request of the Chairman, a preliminary meeting was held in Chicago on the 17th of that month. At the suggestion of the President of the United States, the salary was raised by Congress to $5,000 per annum. The Appropriation Bill for executing the law and paying expenses was not passed by Congress until some time in August.

On the 15th of August, all the members of the

Commission met at Omaha, Nebraska, and on the 18th they arrived at Salt Lake City. One of the members of the Commission, who had been in Salt Lake City before, informed us that in the discharge of our official duties we would be "between the devil and the deep sea." What he meant by this began to dawn on us very soon after our arrival, and was fully confirmed by the sequel.

It was stated in the two reports made to the Secretary of the Interior for August 31st and November 17th, that the Commission encountered "complications and embarrassments" from the outset. The diplomatic reserve proper for a State paper forbade the Commission to set forth in their reports all the details and causes of "the complications and embarrassments" referred to. Some of these it is now proposed to set forth more fully.

In the first place it should be known that there was an intense feeling of hostility between the Mormons and a portion of the Gentiles. The latter charged the Mormons with being disloyal to the government of the United States, and with all manner of crimes and immoralities ; while the Mormons charged that those Gentiles who are making war upon them are a predatory band of adventurers and carpet-baggers, actuated by no higher motive than "to oppress the Mormons with a view to driving them to desperation, so as to steal the Mormon property." The daily newspapers in Salt Lake City, two on the Gentile side, and two on the Mormon side, were doing their part in fanning the flames of discord. Such was the community to which the Commission was sent ; the Mormons expecting the Commission to deal harshly with them, under a law of Congress which they declared to be cruel and unconstitutional ; while on the other hand, a portion of the Gentiles—the most active and demonstrative among them—seemed to act on the theory that a Mormon "had no rights which others are bound to respect."

In the first session of the Forty-seventh Congress the ultra Gentiles of Utah had labored 'for the passage of extreme measures against the Mormons, the leading idea of which was the abrogation of local self-government in Utah, the abolition of their Legislative Assembly, and the establishment of a "legislative Commission," to be appointed by the President, to enact and revise laws for the Territory.

Congress was unwilling, thus totally to destroy local self-government; and enacted the Edmunds Bill, which did not go far enough to please the ultra Gentiles, and went too far to please the Mormons. Another unpleasant feature of the situation, to some of the Gentiles, was, that the President appointed all five of the Commissioners from states outside of Utah, rejecting the slate that was telegraphed from Salt Lake City, by Governor Murray, consisting of rabid Mormon eaters of Utah.

The five Commissioners selected by the President, were, or had been practicing lawyers; and two of them had been members of the United States Senate, and had filled other high positions in public life.

The law of Congress was the charter of their authority—and they were not the kind of men to ignore or wilfully violate the law, and take a town-meeting view of the subject.

The Commission arrived at Ogden, Utah, on the 18th of August. At Ogden we were met by a large deputation of leading citizens from Salt Lake City, about half-and-half Mormons and Gentiles, among them Governor Murray, (Gentile) and Mayor Jennings (Mormon). Arrived at Salt Lake City the citizens gave the members of the Commission a public reception at the Walker Opera House. A large crowd assembled—numbering perhaps one or two thousand—made up of Mormons as well as Gentiles.

All seemed lovely—and reminded one of the "lion and the lamb," and the harmless cockatrice and all that. But, as we more than suspected at the time, it was only the "torrent's smoothness ere it dash below."

Very soon after our arrival in Salt Lake City we were kindly invited by the leading Gentile paper "to take a walk," in other words it was politely intimated that we might look around a few days and go back to where we came from. We were told that we couldn't hold an election under the law; and afterwards long dissertations followed, showing to the Mormons, the Commissioners, and all other anxious enquirers, that there were insuperable difficulties in the way of the Commission doing anything. But we had read the memorable anti-climax:

> The King of France, with forty thousand men,
> Marched up the hill and then marched down again.

But we did not care to follow the illustrious example of the valorous grand monarch. We thought that we could legally hold the election; and we did.

After resolving to proceed with the election, we prepared printed "Rules and Regulations." The Mormons thought that some of these rules were harsh and beyond the law, particularly those requiring an oath of every person seeking to be registered; and also our ruling extending the disfranchisement by reason of polygamy back to 1862, and even beyond. The reasons which the Commission thought justified these rules under the law are pretty fully set forth in our second report, and need not be repeated or enlarged upon here.

This action gave great offense to the Mormons, and was correspondingly pleasing to the ultra Gentiles. "A Daniel come to judgment, yea, a Daniel." But their exultation was short-lived. It was dashed to pieces by our ruling on the "Woman Suffrage" question. The Gentiles sent a deputation of lawyers, who made elaborate arguments to induce us to hold the Woman Suffrage Act of Utah to be invalid, and to make an order forbidding the women to be registered. It should be stated that the Gentiles in Utah had comparatively few women among them; so that to eliminate the whole female vote would have been a great loss to the Mormons at the elections. The Commission heard the arguments patiently and then unanimously decided against the motion. We had no authority to make new laws, nor to abrogate old ones. Woman suffrage had been established by law in Utah, with the implied approval of the Congress of the United States for twelve years. Besides, the Supreme Court of Utah had decided that it was a valid law.

This afforded a subject for adverse criticism. The courts of Utah were then appealed to. They decided the law to be valid, and the judges were abused and criticised.

The "Liberals" (or Gentiles) nominated for delegate to Congress Philip T. Van Zile; and the "People's Party" (or Mormons) nominated John T. Caine. The campaign was a spirited contest. The candidates both made good speeches, and were assisted "on the stump" by other speakers on each side. Mr. Van Zile was a good speaker, and spoke as conservatively as he well could, but he was handicapped from the start by the resolutions of the convention which nominated him.

They declared, among other things, substantially

that the Mormon leaders were tyrants and impostors, and the rank and file of the Mormon people were tools and slaves, not fit to vote or hold office ; therefore Congress should abolish local self-government in Utah, and establish a legislative commission to make laws. As the qualified Mormon voters were largely in the majority in the Territory, it seemed that the platform was cunningly devised to repel every Mormon in the Territory from the support of the Liberal ticket, for the express purpose of having it overwhelmingly defeated in order to show to Congress that there was no hope in anything except the most radical repressive measures.

Caine was elected by a large majority; and nothing else could have been expected under the circumstances. Mr. Caine was re-elected as delegate to Congress in 1884, 1886, 1888 and 1890.

But little more remains to be said concerning the first three months' service of the Commission in Utah. Notwithstanding Mr. Caine was elected by an immense majority, an effort was made to have the Commission decide that he was not entitled to a certificate of election, not because he had ever had more than one wife, but because he was a Mormon, and the Mormons *believed* in polygamy. But the Commission unanimously decided the other way; in which they were fully sustained by Senator Edmunds, the author of the bill.

This afforded another occasion for the clique of Gentile agitators to denounce and criticise the Commission ; and it soon began to appear, as was afterwards clearly demonstrated, that no federal official could receive the commendation or avoid the venomous abuse of that coterie except by the most abject and servile submission to their dictation.

The general reader, the scholar and the *litterateur*

wish to know more of a strange people and a strange country than what is usually presented in official communications, handicapped by official dignity and diplomatic generalities.

Who are the Mormons?   What is their genesis? What manner of bipeds are they?   Are they Anthropophagi?   Christians or pagans?   Are they a civilized people?   And if yea, how did they come to embrace polygamy in this enlightened age and country?   What kind of a country do they live in?   These and similar questions are often asked; and I propose in the following pages to give the result of my observations on some of these topics.

When I first learned that I was to go on an official mission to the Mormon-land I knew but little about the people of that Territory.   I had heard of the " Mormon War," the " Mountain Meadows Massacre," the " Danites" and the "Avenging Angels," and I had read some pages in sensational books like the "Crimes and Mysteries of Mormonism."   I had read some accounts more favorable to the "Saints," but on the whole I had the same ill opinion of them that is generally entertained by the " Gentiles."   However, I determined to divest myself as far as possible of all prejudice and investigate for myself.

On our arrival at Salt Lake City, carriages were in waiting to convey us to the Continental Hotel.   After supper, having been shown to my room and being ready to retire, I carefully examined the door and window fastenings, from a half-defined apprehension that some Mormon " Danite " might make me a victim of blood-atonement as an official persecutor of the Saints.   But my sleep was sweet, sound and secure; and after that night I was not long in discovering that one was as safe in Salt Lake City, by day or by night, as in any other city in the United States.*

The day following our arrival was spent in receiving information from Gentiles and Mormons—more or less reliable and disinterested—all of which we received with the modesty and docility so becoming to a "tenderfoot." We also took a look at objects of interest in the city, and watched the people on the streets.

There was nothing very unique in their appearance —nothing suggestive of the Orient. Instead of turbaned Turks with flowing robes and long black beards, we found the Utah polygamists arrayed in plug and Derby hats and Prince Albert coats. Instead of the fascinating beauties of the harem, as described by Byron and Moore, we saw modest looking Mormon girls in silks, satins and brocades. Instead of the dancing girls of the Orient with cymbals and tinkling bells, pirouetting to the "lascivious pleasing of a lute," we saw serious Mormon women in plain attire pleading for polygamy as a revelation from the Lord.

It was during that or the succeeding autumn that I first met John W. Young, a son of Brigham Young. Having heard that he had a plurality of wives, I had (I trust) a pardonable curiosity to learn what manner of man such a "very married man" might be. I found him to be very intelligent, urbane, well-dressed and good looking. He is a practical business man, with no outward indication of the religious fanatic ; but when you get him started he can quote Scripture and defend the Saints

---

* Later I ascertained that if a man should be sand-bagged, robbed or have his house burglarized, the chances were ten to one that the perpetrator would be an " outsider" and not a Mormon. It is a fact, shown by statistics, that while only about one-fifth of the population of Utah are Gentiles they contribute at least four-fifths of the crimes of a heinous character. The same proportion will hold good as to misdemeanors —excepting of course polygamy and cohabitation.

with as much zeal and earnestness as any other Mormon.

A natural inquiry arose in my mind: "Are the Mormons really devout? Do they really believe in the creed which they profess? And what are the peculiarities of their creed?"   In order to satisfy my mind on these questions, I often attended their religious meetings at the great Tabernacle, the Assembly Hall, the ward meeting houses and at funerals. I will now give some account of these meetings, written at the time, with the impressions then made on my mind.

Meeting in the Assembly Hall.   On Sunday, May 6th, 1883, attended services at the Assembly Hall (in which meetings are held in cool weather instead of the Tabernacle).   This hall holds three or four thousand people, and every seat was occupied. It has a fine organ, which with a choir of sixty or seventy singers rendered very fine and impressive music.

About twenty-five dignitaries of the Church, including Apostles, Counselors, Elders and so forth, were seated on elevated seats in front of the organ and choir. In front of these stood eight deacons or elders behind a long table, who, after the services began, stood up and were engaged a long time in breaking bread into small pieces and putting them into silver-looking baskets.

The services were begun by music and prayer, after which a sermon was preached by Apostle Brigham Young, one of fifty-four children of the late President of the same name. Brigham Young is a heavy, thick-set, broad-shouldered man, and in some respects he is a chip of the old block. He is credited with having only two wives. His discourse consisted in giving an account of his missionary labors the past winter among the Lamanites (or Indians) of Arizona, Colorado and New Mexico.

After he concluded, another hymn was sung, and then a sermon was delivered by a young elder apparently about twenty-five years old. He had recently returned from the Sandwich Islands, whither he had been sent as a missionary four years before. He gave an account of his labors in proselyting the natives to the Mormon faith. He appeared to be a Swede or Dane, and I understood him to say that he had just learned one [the English] language, when he had to begin to learn another—the native language of the Sandwich Islanders. Among other things, he spoke of the labors of the Mormon elders among the lepers of those Islands, of whose horrible condition he gave a graphic description, many of them being distorted out of human shape and resemblance, their eyes protruding from their sockets, their faces swollen and seamed with ghastly cracks, and their hands, fingers and toes twisted and knotted. [There is a settlement in Salt Lake City, near the Warm Springs, of about fifty or sixty natives of these Islands, who have been converted to the Mormon faith, and have "gathered to Zion."]

During the preaching by Apostle Young and the young elder, the bread and water (instead of wine) were passed around among the congregation. During the whole of the meeting there was a look of devout reverence and childlike faith on the face of each member of the congregation. They all listened with fixed attention to all that was said in the sermons. After benediction the vast throng dispersed, and I had an opportunity of closely observing their dress and demeanor. They were all in their best Sunday clothes, and appeared as serious and decorous as any other religious congregation.

A WARD MEETING: SPEAKING IN TONGUES—HEALING THE
SICK.

By "a ward meeting" no reference is intended to those convocations where "the boys" meet in a city to fix up a political State for a municipal spring election ; but to a feature of the Mormon ecclesiastical polity.

The city of Salt Lake is divided into twenty-two wards. This is a religious rather than a civil division. The whole Territory of Utah, and other regions inhabited by the Mormons, are also divided into wards. Each ward in the city and the country is presided over by a bishop.

On every Sunday night religious meetings are held in all these wards, each one having a meeting-house. Tonight (April 29th) I attended services at the 14th Ward meeting-house. I found the room already full of Mormon worshipers, and being about to retire, I was politely shown to a seat by one of the brethren. My attention was divided between a careful listening to the discourse of the preacher, and an observation of the demeanor and appearance of the congregation. They were very quiet and orderly throughout the meeting ; all looked steadfastly at the preacher and listened intently to all that was said. They had an organ, and a choir that sang very well. On this night the sermon was delivered by Joseph F. Smith, one of the "First Presidency." He is a son of Hyrum Smith, the brother of Joseph Smith, the Prophet, who were both murdered by a mob in the jail at Carthage, Illinois. He spoke fluently and well, and readily and accurately quoted many passages from the Old and New Testaments. By the way, this is characteristic of all the Mormon preachers (and the men are nearly all preachers or priests). They know more scripture and can quote more "off-hand" than any other people I ever saw.

During the greater part of the meeting there was nothing in the sermon or services that was peculiar. And if a good Baptist or Campbellite brother had happened to step into the meeting, not knowing that it was held by the Mormons, he would have had his "spiritual strength renewed," and would have been much edified by the greater part of the sermon, especially those parts of it advocating immersion as the only true baptism, and opposing infant baptism. But toward the close of the sermon the preacher struck the question of "polygamy," claiming plural or celestial marriage to be a divine revelation to the Latter-day Saints, and supporting his views by various passages in the Old Testament and by physiological and philosophical considerations.

At the conclusion of the sermon the choir sang a hymn very beautifully. The bishop of the ward then made some announcements as to persons to be baptized and confirmed, and a young elder pronounced the benediction.

The congregation then dispersed very quietly, the males keeping their heads uncovered while passing out—just like the Gentile Christians. At the meeting-house door I was invited by a Mormon elder to his house. I accepted, and while smoking a cigar I continued my quest for information.

Question. "Joseph F. Smith is one of your best preachers, isn't he?"

Answer. "Yes, he is; but we have many as good as he is. But our people take a great interest in him because he is a son of the martyred Hyrum Smith."

Q. "Do your people know, before going to church, who is going to preach?"

A. "No, sir. After the congregation meets, sometimes one and sometimes another is called up to speak to the people. Our men are nearly all elders or priests (I suppose there are not two hundred exceptions in all Utah), and we have no difficulty in having sermons enough preached."

Q. "Do your people have prayer meetings, and so forth, during the week like the Methodists and others?"

A. "Not exactly that. But on the first Thursday in every month we assemble at fast-meetings at all our meeting-houses. At this meeting every one is expected to give to the poor an amount equal to the value of one day's sustenance. For example, if my board costs me $1.20 per day, I would give that amount to the poor. This donation, however, is not compulsory, but is pretty generally observed."

Q. "Did you ever witness a 'speaking in tongues' at the Mormon meetings?"

A. "Oh, yes, often; but it does not occur now as often as in former years."

Q. "Will you describe it to me?"

A. "Yes. These fast-meetings of which I have spoken are occasions where the speaking in tongues often occurs. A person in the congregation gets up suddenly and unexpectedly and talks in a tongue unknown to himself and the congregation. After he sits down some one in the congregation gets up and gives an interpretation of the speech, translating it into English."

Q. "What authority have the Mormons for this 'speaking in tongues?'"

A. "In the New Testament, among the gifts and blessings vouchsafed to the disciples, are the 'speaking in tongues' and 'the interpretation of tongues.'"

Q. "Why is this not so much in vogue now as formerly?"

A. "Our people discourage it; because, as you heard Brother Smith say tonight, in full one-half of the cases of the speaking in tongues, it is *the work of the devil.*"

Q. "Were you ever a witness to a speaking in tongues when the devil got his work in?"

A. "Yes. At a meeting in the 13th Ward there was a woman of a rather low character and forbidding aspect got up and spoke in tongues. The whole congregation felt and knew that it was the work of the devil, and were much agitated. The Bishop stated that it was the work of the devil, and said, 'I rebuke thee, Satan,' and immediately all was calm and quiet."

On another occasion I had a conversation with the same Mormon elder concerning healing the sick by the laying on of hands. In answer to a question he said he had seen a great deal of it during his long residence in Salt Lake City.

"How is it done?"

"We anoint the sick person and then the Elders lay hands on him for a few minutes, and rebuke the sickness in the language of the New Testament."

"Does this always effect a cure?"

"It generally cures or improves the condition of the patient, but not always; sometimes it is not the will of the Lord that the person should recover."

"Do you believe in this thing?"

"Believe? Yes, I *know* it. I want to tell you a circumstance. Here a few years ago I was called into the house of Zina Young Williams, whose child was very sick and on the point of death. I found there besides the child's mother, Aunt Zina Young (one of Brigham's widows), who was in great distress and wanted me to lay hands on the child. I declined at first because I was the only Elder present, and the scriptures speak of the Elders (in the plural) laying on hands to heal the sick. But I finally told Aunt Zina that I would wait ten minutes to see if it was the will of the Lord to send another Elder to assist me. I took out my watch and held it in my hand to see when the ten minutes should be up."

"You were timing the Lord by a stop-watch."

"You are making light of serious things. I am telling you facts. Before the ten minutes were out Bro. Johnson came in and I knew the Lord had sent him. He was hauling a load of wheat into the city on Main Street, and when he got opposite the door of Sister Zina's house the horses suddenly stopped and would not go any further, and so he came in, and we all knew that it was the work of the Lord. We anointed the child and laid hands on it, rebuking the illness, and straightway the child was cured."

"Don't you think that it was animal magnetism?"

"You may call it what you please. I am telling you the truth. I call it the influence of the Holy Ghost. Other people besides the Mormons heal the sick by the laying on of hands and by prayer. But our Elders are more powerful in this way than others, because of the great faith of the Elders and the patient. Much depends on the degree of the faith of the sick person."

"Where do you get your authority for this sort of healing, and for speaking in unknown tongues, and the like?"

"From the New Testament, in a great many passages. Among others the 16th chapter of St. Mark, where it says, 'These signs shall follow them that believe, they shall cast out devils, they shall speak with new tongues ; they shall lay hands on the sick and they shall recover.' "

" Why do you have one person to speak in tongues and another person to interpret ? "

"Because that is according to the scripture: "If any man speak in an unknown tongue, let it be by two, or at most by three, and that by course ; and let one interpret.'—II. Cor. chapter 14. This speaking in tongues," continued the Elder, "was very common in the meetings of the former-day saints, as will readily be seen by any-one who will look through the New Testament."

"But haven't these things been done away with? "

"That's what is claimed by the sects, but there is no scripture to show that such things have been done away with ; and the Latter-day Saints hold that the gifts and blessings that were conferred on 'them that believe' were not only for the primitive believers, but for those of after times as well. Why should there be any discrimination? "

FUNERAL OBSEQUIES.

May 20th, 1883. Attended religious exercises at the 14th Ward Assembly Hall (or meeting house), the occasion being funeral services for James W. Cummings, who died yesterday morning. Cummings had been a Mormon for forty years and had been with the Saints at Nauvoo and ever since.

A very large crowd assembled, and the exercises were similar to those of other religious denominations, consisting of singing, prayers, sermons and benediction.

As is usual at the Mormon funerals, a number of discourses were delivered, the speakers being Elder Campbell, Lorenzo D. Young (a brother of the late Prophet Brigham Young), Brigham Young, one of the

THE TABERNACLE.

Twelve Apostles and a son of the late Brigham Young, Angus M. Cannon and Bishop Taylor. A long benediction was delivered by Daniel H. Wells. The corpse, in a fine casket covered with wreaths of flowers, was borne into the meeting house, followed by three widows of the deceased and many children and other relatives. Several of the speakers invoked the blessings of heaven on the "wives, children and grand-children of our departed brother."

The congregation contained quite a number of well dressed people. Everything was quiet and orderly, which I have noticed at all the Mormon meetings. I suppose that I was the only Gentile in the congregation.

Later in the afternoon I attended services at the big

TABERNACLE.

This tabernacle is an object of curiosity to all strangers and tourists, who avail themselves of the opportunity of attending religious exercises here when they stay over on Sunday. On this occasion Senator Davis of Illinois, and his bride were in attendance. It was a beautiful day, and there were probably twelve thousand persons in the congregation. Elder C. W. Penrose spoke. He is one of the best speakers among the Mormons, and he was probably put forward to deliver the discourse on account of the presence of the distinguished Senator. The music of the choir and organ was very fine. A further description of the Tabernacle is given in another place.

INTERVIEW WITH AN "APOSTATE."

I have taken a great interest since I have been in Utah in conversing with Mormon "apostates," etc., to try to "get the hang" of their mental operations.

Today, June 30, Mr. Stephen Hales, one of our registration officers, called at the Commission rooms. He lives in Bountiful, Davis County, twelve miles north of Salt Lake City. He is an "Apostate Mormon"—that is, he was born, baptized and brought up as a Mormon, by Mormon parents, but he is now an "infidel."

Question. "Are your people all Mormons?"

Answer. "Yes; my father is dead, but he was a good Mormon and a sincere believer. My mother is living yet. She and all my brothers and sisters are Mormons. So is my wife. Before I was married, while I was 'sparking' her, she told me that she wouldn't marry me unless I would be willing to take other wives, if I should get a 'recommend.'"

Q. "What would she say now if you proposed to take another wife?"

A. "She would kick against it. She thinks I am not religious enough to have more than one wife. But if I was a good Latter-day Saint I am satisfied that she would be willing for me to take plural wives."

Q. "How many children have you?"

A. "I have four, three besides this little fellow (referring to his little son, about eight years old, who came in with him)."

Q. "Are your children Mormons?"

A. "Yes, their mother has brought them up that way. I have a little girl, six years old, who came home from school the other day crying because some of the school children had called her a 'Liberal.'" (The Gentiles here have assumed the party name of "Liberals.")

Q. "Have your children been baptized into the Mormon Church?"

A. "Yes, one of them has. I don't believe in any sort of religion myself, but I allow my wife to have her own way with the children. My wife is a very religious woman, and very strict. This boy I have here with me is a little past eight years old, and he wants to be baptized."

I then spoke to the boy: "My son, are you a Mormon?"

Boy (whimpering). "Yes, sir."

Q. "Do you want to be baptized?"

Boy. "Yes, sir."

Q. "Do you think the Gentiles are bad people?"

Boy (crying). "Yes, sir."

Resuming my conversation with the father:

Q. "Do you know Eliza R. Snow, the poetess, and why she is sometimes called Eliza R. Snow Smith and sometimes Eliza R. Snow Young?"

A. "She was 'sealed' to Joseph Smith at Nauvoo, and after his death she was 'sealed' to Brigham Young. My grandmother (my mother's mother) was 'sealed' to Joseph Smith in celestial marriage at Nauvoo. She was to remain the wife of my grandfather in this life, and was to be the wife of the Prophet in the eternal life."

Q. "What did your grandfather do about it?"

A. "He raised the devil about it."

Strange as this statement may appear, concerning the request made by Hales' girl when he was "sparking" her, it is a fact that in former years there were instances where Mormon wives, under the influence of religious fanaticism, implored their husbands to take plural wives.

THE GENESIS OF MORMONISM.

What were the circumstances under which Mormonism had its origin, and in its early years had such a rapid and phenomenal growth?

The student of church history will bear in mind that

the first three or four decades of the present century was a period of great religious awakening and revivals in the United States, especially in what was then known as "The West." This was the period of camp meetings and the "jumping" and "barking" exercises at Cain Ridge in Kentucky. Itinerant preachers, such as Lorenzo Dow, fired with all the zeal and fanaticism of Peter the Hermit, traversed the country and harrangued the people. In this "awakening" there was a general disposition to break away from established creeds and church organizations in the search for "new light." At this juncture "the fullness of the new dispensation," presented by "Joseph, the Prophet," was attracting popular attention in Western New York and Northern Ohio. Several eloquent and popular preachers, in search of "new light," such as Sidney Rigdon, Orson Pratt and Parley P. Pratt, became converts to the new faith, and the proselyting progressed rapidly.

The original Articles of Faith of the Mormon Church, instead of being repulsive, were such as to meet with favor among the people. They are the following, as published by Joseph Smith:

1.   We believe in God, the Eternal Father, and in His Son, Jesus Christ, and in the Holy Ghost.

2.   We believe that men will be punished for their own sins, and not for Adam's transgression.

3.   We believe that, through the atonement of Christ, all mankind may be saved, by obedience to the laws and ordinances of the gospel.

4.   We believe that these ordinances are: First, Faith in the Lord Jesus Christ; second, Repentance; third, Baptism by immersion for the remission of sins; fourth, Laying on of hands for the Gift of the Holy Ghost.

5.   We believe that a man must be called of God, by "prophecy, and by the laying on of hands," by those who are in authority, to preach the gospel and administer in the ordinances thereof.

6.   We believe in the same organization that existed in the primitive church, viz.: apostles, prophets, pastors, teachers, evangelists, etc.

7.   We believe in the gift of tongues, prophecy, revelation, visions, healing, interpretation of tongues, etc.

8.   We believe the Bible to be the word of God, as far as it is translated correctly; we also believe the Book of Mormon to be the word of God.

9.   We believe all that God has revealed, all that He does now reveal, and we believe that He will yet reveal many great and important things pertaining to the Kingdom of God.

10.   We believe in the literal gathering of Israel and in the restoration of the ten tribes.   That Zion will be built upon this continent.   That Christ will reign personally upon the earth, and that the earth will be renewed and receive its paradisic glory.

11.   We claim the privilege of worshiping Almighty God according to the dictates of our conscience, and allow all men the same privilege, let them worship how, where, or what they may.

12.   We believe in being subject to kings, presidents, rulers and magistrates, in obeying, honoring and sustaining the law.

13.   We believe in being honest, true, chaste, benevolent, virtuous, and in doing good to *all men;* indeed, we may say we follow the admonition of Paul, "We believe all things, we hope all things;" we have endured many things, and hope to be able to endure all things.   If there is anything virtuous, lovely, or of good report, or praiseworthy, we seek after these things.

How other doctrines, such as baptism for the dead, and a plurality of wives were evolved from the foregoing principles may be readily understood, by a brief explanation.   Given: a living "Prophet, Seer and Revelator" on whose divine mission the people had unbounded confidence, and the further doctrine of "continuous revelation," it will be seen how a credulous and intensely devotional people were led by degrees to accept the revelations in favor of polygamy, etc.   The Mormon doctrine in regard to "continuous revelation," as I understand it, is something like this: They say that there has been a long line of prophets revealing the divine will, from time to time, during many centuries, beginning with Moses and Aaron (or perhaps going back to Abraham.) Then, at different times came the prophets Samuel, Isaiah, Daniel, Joel, Jeremiah, Nahum and many others. Afterwards, nearly nineteen centuries ago came new revelations through Jesus Christ, His apostles and disciples. The Mormons contend that it is not in accordance with the divine will, that revelations should have been confined to any one age or people of the world; or, that in these "latter-days" the people should be shut in, as with a canopy of brass, barring all further revelations from the Creator to His creatures. That the people had gone so far astray, and there had arisen such a great number of sects, groping in the dark, the new revelations in the "fullness of this dispensation" were necessary for the salvation of the people. And so a "youth" in the state of New York, Joseph Smith, by name, was inspired by divine authority as a "Prophet, Seer and Revelator" to restore the true religion. To the objection that Smith was a poor and illiterate country lad, they reply that Moses was a foundling, Jesus was cradled in a manger, and David was a shepherd boy. I give this explanation as I have read it in their doctrinal books, and have heard it often expounded by the elders in their preaching.

What manner of people are the Mormons? Are they as bad as they are generally represented? If they are not, why is there such a general concensus of ill-opinion concerning them, both as to the present and past? They were run out of Ohio, Missouri, and Illinois; and have given the government a deal of trouble since they settled in the valleys of the Rocky Mountains. How could all this be, unless they are a very bad people?

At first blush this seems to settle the question against the Mormons.

But here comes the puzzle. In nearly seven years' experience and careful observation, I, in common with many other disinterested observers, have found the Mormons, with rare exceptions, to be honest, industrious, sober, hospitable, kind and peaceable, as well as singularly devotional in their religious duties and observances. Where are the Danites, the Destroying Angels and the perpetrators of "blood-atonement?"

That some of the outrages imputed to the Mormons in former times did actually occur, may be possible. Religious enthusiasts, as well as some cranks and fanatics "gathered" to the Mormons from many quarters of the globe. In such a heterogeneous gathering, there were some bad men who joined them as a city of refuge; and there were some religious fanatics whose heads were shaped wrong *ab initio*, and who, though intensely devout, could not be good men, because they were not "built that way." A few men of this sort can give a bad name to a whole community.

This seems to me to account in a large measure for the conflict of opinions, charges and denials, affidavits and counter-affidavits concerning the conduct and character of the Mormon people.

But there is another consideration not to be overlooked in accounting for the antipathy of several communities where the Mormons had their "gatherings." Their claims of having a living "prophet" receiving almost daily revelations from the Lord—was offensive to the other religious denominations; and the *odium theologicum* was supplemented by the anger of worldlings and sinners who thought they discerned an "imperium in imperio" on the claim of Christ's Kingdom on Earth;"

and, accordingly, it was no uncommon spectacle in the troubles in Missouri, to see a Methodist or "Campbell-ite" preacher, with rifle in hand, at the head of an armed mob of "border ruffians," pursuing the "Saints" with horn and hound, and with fire and sword. Many of the Mormon leaders being of New England birth, the charge that they were "abolitionists" found a ready lodgment in the minds of the Missouri crusaders. Also the theocratic nature of the creed and practice was urged as a reason of their being dangerous to the government.

Recurring to the condition of affairs in Utah, it is curious to observe the opposing views of different writers. A stranger or sojourner in Salt Lake City is surprised to find nearly everything apparently very different from what he had heard or read. Generally, while in Utah, he gets his information at second-hand, one side painting the Mormons very black, and the other side defending and recriminating. Information derived in this way should be carefully sifted, and this is never done by such writers as are more desirous of relating a blood-curdling and sensational story, than to make a reliable narrative. Hate, like charity, is very credulous. It hopes all things and believes all things against its adversaries. As a devoted lover sees "Helen's beauty in a brow of Egypt," so a good hater sees only deformity in the objects of his dislike, and among his adversaries he "sees more devils than vast hell can hold."

Accordingly, if a stranger believes all that the two factions in Utah allege against each other, he will conclude in the language of Milton, that "all hell is broke loose" in Utah, and that no self-respecting man or pure woman would want to stay there any longer than until the departure of the next train. But, bye and-bye, the candid inquirer will learn that, with a modicum of truth, there is a vast amount of falsehood and exaggeration, and that among the Gentiles as well as the Mormons a great majority are good people. Of course, there are exceptions. The Mormons have suffered in reputation by the example of some bad men among them. And the Gentile population have suffered in like manner. There is a pretty general opinion that the Gentile population of Utah is largely made up of outlaws, adventurers and refugees from justice. This does a majority of them great injustice ; but there can be no doubt that there are too many men there of this description ; and the good and respectable Gentiles of Utah are much to blame for allowing themselves to be dominated by a few unconscionable and mendacious agitators.

These " Sketches of the Mormons " are necessarily fragmentary, and are intended to represent their characteristics, their creed and their way of life, and no attempt is made toward a regular chronological history. A work of that sort, with reasonable fullness of detail, would fill more than a thousand octavo pages of closely printed matter. But an account of the expulsion of the Mormons from Illinois is of such thrilling interest, and so well suited to illustrate the character of this strange people, that I will venture to devote a number of pages to this extraordinary event.

THE MORMON EXODUS.

Early in February, 1846, a council was held in Nauvoo to make arrangements for a speedy departure to the West. Captains of Hundreds and Fifties were chosen, and on the 5th of February the first company crossed the Mississippi River on the ice. On the next day the main body of the Mormons began to move, and some twelve hundred wagons were transported to the Iowa shore in the month of February. The weather was cold, and the homeless exiles lived in their wagons and tents.

Brigham Young was chosen leader, and early in March, began that wonderful exodus, without a parallel in modern times. By the 15th of May, not less than sixteen thousand Mormons, had abandoned Nauvoo and its vicinity, and were making their way toward the Missouri River, where they were to have a temporary halting place, near where Council Bluffs now is.

About one thousand Mormons had been left at Nauvoo, mostly on account of sickness and poverty, and some to dispose of property and settle the affairs of the Church.

Some of the Gentiles took measures to get up a new quarrel with the Mormons. In September, under various pretexts, the anti-Mormons, numbering about eight hundred men, laid siege to Nauvoo,—which was defended by one hundred and fifty Mormons. The contest was kept up for three days, the anti-Mormons being headed by one Thomas S. Brockman, who is described by Governor Ford as a "Campbellite preacher, nominally belonging to the Democratic party, a large, awkward, uncouth, ignorant *semi-barbarian*, ambitious of office, and bent upon acquiring notoriety."

But few persons were killed on either side; the Mormons were, of course, overpowered. The chivalrous bearing of Brockman and his men, and the result of the siege, are thus chronicled by Gov. Ford:

"The constable's *posse* marched in with Brockman at their head, consisting of about eight hundred armed men, and six or seven hundred unarmed, from motives of curiosity to see the once proud city of Nauvoo humbled and delivered up to its enemies and to the domination of a self-constituted and irresponsible power. When the *posse* arrived in the city, the leaders of it erected themselves into a tribunal to decide who should be forced away, and who remain. Parties were despatched to search for Mormon arms and for Mormons, and to bring them to the judgment, where they received their doom from the mouth of Brockman, who then sat, a grim and unawed tyrant for the time. As a general rule the Mormons were ordered to leave within an hour, or two hours ; and by rare grace some of them were allowed until next day ; and in a few cases longer.

"The treaty specified that the Mormons only, should be driven into exile. Nothing was said in it concerning the new citizens who had with the Mormons defended the city.

" But the *posse* no sooner obtained possession, than they commenced expelling the new citizens. Some of them were ducked in the river, being in one or two instances actually baptized in the name of the leaders of the mob; others were forcibly driven into the ferry boats to be taken over the river, before the bayonets of armed ruffians ; and it is asserted that the houses of most of them were broken open and their property stolen during their absence.   *   *   *   *   *

"The Mormons had been forced away from their houses unprepared for a journey. They and their women and children had been thrown houseless upon the Iowa shore, without provisions or the means of getting them, or to get to places where provisions might be obtained. It was now the height of the sickly season, Many of them were taken from sick beds, hurried into the boats and driven away by the armed ruffians now exercising the power of government. The best they could do, was to erect their tents on the banks of the river and there remain to take their chances of perishing by hunger or by prevailing sickness. In this condition, the sick, without shelter, food, nourishment, or medicine, died by scores. The mother watched her sick babe without hope, and when she sank under accumulated miseries, it was only to be quickly followed by her other children, now left without the least attention; for the men had scattered out over the country seeking employment and the means of living." [See Governor Ford's History of Illinois.]

At this juncture a distinguished citizen of Pennsylvania, Colonel Thomas L. Kane, appeared upon the scene. In a lecture before the Historical Society of Pennsylvania, he gave the following graphic account:—

"A few years ago, ascending the upper Mississippi in the autumn when its waters were low, I was compelled to travel by land past the region of the rapids. My road lay through the Half-Breed Tract, a fine section of Iowa, which the unsettled state of its land-titles had appropriated as a sanctuary for coiners, horse-thieves and other out-laws. I had left my steamer at Keokuk, at the foot of the Lower Fall, to hire a carriage, and to contend for some fragments of a dirty meal with the swarming flies, the only scavengers of the locality. From this place to where the deep water of the river returns, my eye wearied to see everywhere, sordid, vagabond and idle settlers; and a country, marred without being improved by their careless hands.

"I was descending the last hill-side upon my journey, when a landscape in delightful contrast broke upon my view. Half encircled by a bend of the river, a beautiful city lay glittering in the fresh morning sun; its bright new dwellings, set in cool, green gardens, ranging up around a stately dome-shaped hill, which was covered by a noble marble edifice whose high tapering spire was radiant with white and gold. The city appeared to cover several miles; and beyond it, in the background, there rolled off a fair country, chequered by the careful lines of fruitful husbandry. The unmistakable marks of industry, enterprise and educated wealth everywhere, made the scene one of singular and most striking beauty.

"It was a natural impulse to visit this inviting region. I procured a skiff, and rowing across the river, landed on the chief wharf of the city. No one met me there. I looked and saw no one. I could hear no one move; though the quiet everywhere was such that I heard the flies buzz, and the water-ripples break against the shallow of the beach. I walked through the solitary streets. The town lay as in a dream, under some deadening spell of loneliness, from which I almost feared to wake it; for plainly it had not slept long. There was no grass growing up in the paved ways; rains had not entirely washed away the prints of dusty footsteps.

"Yet I went about unchecked. I went into empty workshops, ropewalks and smithies. The spinner's wheel was idle; the carpenter had gone from his workbench and shavings, his unfinished sash and casing. Fresh bark was in the tanner's vat, and the fresh-chopped light wood stood piled against the baker's oven. The blacksmith's shop was cold; but his coal heap and ladling pool and crooked water-horn were all there, as if he had just gone off for a holiday. No work-people anywhere looked to know my errand. If I went into the gardens clinking the wicket latch loudly after me, to pull the marigolds, heartsease and lady's-slippers and draw a drink with the water-sodden well-bucket and its noisy chain; or knocking off with my stick the tall, heavy-headed dahlias and sunflowers, hunted over beds for cucumbers and love apples, no one called out to me from any opened window, or dog sprang forward to bark an alarm. I could have supposed the people hidden in the houses, but the doors were unfastened; and when at last I timidly entered them, I found dead ashes white upon the hearths, and had to tread on tip-toe as if walking down the aisle of a country church, to avoid rousing irreverent echoes from the naked floors.

"On the outskirts of the town was the city graveyard, but there was no record of plague there, nor did it in any wise differ much from other Protestant American cemeteries. Some of the mounds were not long sodded; some of the stones were newly set, their dates recent, and their black inscriptions glossy in the mason's hardly dried lettering ink. Beyond the graveyard, out in the fields, I saw in one spot hard by where the fruited boughs of a young orchard had been roughly torn down, the still smouldering remains of a barbecue fire, that had been constructed of rails from the fencing around it. It was the latest sign of life there. Fields upon fields of heavy-headed yellow grain lay rotting ungathered upon the ground. No one was at hand to take in the rich harvest. As far as the eye could reach, they stretched away—they sleeping, too, in the hazy air of autumn.

"Only two portions of the city seemed to suggest the import of this mysterious solitude. On the southern suburb, the houses looking out upon the country, showed, by their splintered wood-work, and walls battered to the foundation, that they had lately been the mark of a destructive cannonade. And in and around the splendid temple, which had been the chief object of my admiration, armed men were barracked, surrounded by their stacks of musketry, and pieces of heavy ordnance. These challenged me to render an account of myself, and why I had the temerity to cross the water without a written permit from the leader of their band.

"Though these men were generally more or less under the influence of ardent spirits, after I had explained myself as a passing stranger, they seemed anxious to gain my good opinion. They told the story of the dead city: that it had been a notable manufacturing and commercial mart, sheltering over 20,000 persons; that they had waged war with its inhabitants for several years, and had been finally successful only a few days before my visit, in an action fought in front of the ruined suburb; after which they had driven them forth at the point of the sword. The defense, they said, had been obstinate, but gave way on the third day's bombardment. They boasted greatly of their prowess, especially in this battle, as they called it; but I discovered that they were not of one mind as to certain of the exploits that had distinguished it; one of which, as I remember, was, that they had slain a father and his son, a boy of fifteen, not long residents of the fated city, whom they admitted to have borne a character without reproach.

"They also conducted me inside the massive sculptured walls of the curious temple, in which they said the banished inhabitants were accustomed to celebrate the mystic rites of an unhallowed worship. They particularly pointed out to me certain features of the building, which, having been the peculiar objects of a former superstitious regard, they had, as a matter of duty, sedulously defiled and defaced. The reputed sites of certain shrines they had thus particularly noticed; and various sheltered chambers, in one of which was a deep well, constructed, they believed, with a dreadful design. Besides these, they led me to see a large and deep chiseled marble vase or basin, supported upon twelve oxen, also of marble, and of the size of life, of which they told some romantic stories. They said the deluded persons, most of whom were emigrants from a great distance, believed their Deity countenanced their reception here, of a baptism of regeneration, as proxies for whomsoever they held in warm affection in the countries from which they had come. That here parents went into the water for their lost children, children for their parents, widows for their spouses, and young persons for their lovers; that thus the great vase came to be for them associated with all dear and distant memories, and was therefore the object of all others in the building, to which they attached the greatest degree of idolatrous affection. On this account the victors had so diligently desecrated it as to render the apartment in which it was contained too noisome to abide in.

"They permitted me also to ascend into the steeple to see where it had been lightning-struck on the Sabbath before; and to look out east and south on wasted farms like those I had seen near the city, extending until they were lost in the distance. Here in the face of the pure day, close to the scar of the Divine wrath left by the thunder bolt, were fragments of food, cruses of liquor and broken drinking-vessels with a brass drum and a steamboat signal-bell, of which I afterwards learned the use with pain.

"It was after nightfall when I was ready to cross the river on my return. The wind had freshened since the sunset, and the water beating roughly into my little boat, I hedged higher up the stream than the point I had left in the morning, and landed where a faint glimmering light invited me to steer.

"Here, among the docks and rushes, sheltered only

by the darkness, without roof between them and sky, I
came upon a crowd of several hundred human creatures,
whom my movements roused from uneasy slumber, upon
the ground.   Passing these on my way to the light, I
found it came from a tallow candle in a paper funnel
shade, such as is used by the street vendors of apples
and peanuts, and which, flaming and guttering away in
the bleak air off the water, shone flickeringly on the
emaciated features of a man in the last stage of a bilious
remittent fever.   They had done their best for him.
Over his head was something like a tent, made of a
sheet or two, and he rested on a but partially ripped
open old straw mattress, with a hair sofa-cushion under
his head for a pillow.   His gaping jaw and glazing eye
told how short a time he would monopolize these luxu-
ries; though a seemingly bewildered and excited person,
who might have been his wife, seemed to find hope in
occasionally forcing him to swallow awkwardly sips of
the tepid river-water, from a burned and battered bitter-
smelling tin coffee-pot.   Those who knew better had furnished the apothecary he needed; a toothless old bald-
head, whose manner had the repulsive dullness of a man
familiar with death scenes. He, so long as I remained,
mumbled in his patient's ear, a monotonous and melancholy prayer, between the pauses of which I heard the
hiccup and sobbing of two little girls, who were sitting
upon a piece of drift-wood outside.

Dreadful, indeed, was the suffering of these for-
saken beings; bowed and cramped by cold and sunburn
alternating as each weary day and night dragged on,
they were, almost all of them, the crippled victims of disease.   They were there because they had no homes, nor
hospital, nor poor-house, nor friends to offer them any.
They could not satisfy the feeble cravings of their sick;

they had not bread to quiet the fractious hunger-cries of their children. Mothers and babes, daughters and grand-parents, all of them alike, were bivouacked in tatters, wanting even covering to comfort those whom the sick shiver of fever was searching to the marrow.

" These were Mormons in Lee County, Iowa, in the fourth week of the month of September, in the year of our Lord 1846. The city—it was Nauvoo, Illinois. The Mormons were the owners of that city, and the smiling county around. And those who had stopped their plows, who had silenced their hammers, their axes, their shuttles, and their work-shop wheels, those who had put out their fires, who had eaten their food, spoiled their orchards, and trampled under foot their thousands of acres of. unharvested bread—these were the keepers of their dwellings, the carousers in their Temple, whose drunken riot insulted the ears of the dying.

"I think it was as I turned from the wretched night-watch of which I have spoken, that I first listened to the sounds of revel of a party of the guard within the city. Above the distant hum of the voices of many, occasion-ally rose distinct the loud oath-tainted exclamation, and the falsely intonated scrap of vulgar song: but lest this requiem should go unheeded, every now and then, when their boisterous orgies strove to attain a sort of ecstatic climax, a cruel spirit of insulting frolic carried some of them up into the high belfry of the Temple steeple, and there, with the wicked childishness of inebriates, they whooped, and shrieked, and beat the drum that I had seen, and rang in charivaric unison their loud-tongued steamboat bell.

"There were, all told, not more than six hundred and forty persons, who were thus lying on the river flats. But the Mormons in Nauvoo and its dependencies, had

been numbered the year before at over twenty thousand. Where were they? They had last been seen, carrying in mournful train, their sick and wounded, halt and blind, to disappear behind the western horizon, pursuing the phantom of another home. Hardly anything else was known of them; and people asked with curiosity, 'what had been their fate—what their fortunes?' * * *
They began their march in mid-winter, and by the beginning of February, nearly all of them were on the road, many of the wagons having crossed the river on the ice.

"Under the most favoring circumstances, an expedition of this sort, undertaken at such a season of the year, could scarcely fail to be disastrous. But the pioneer company had set out in haste, and were very imperfectly supplied with necessaries. The cold was intense. They moved in the teeth of keen-edged northwest winds, such as sweep down the Iowa peninsula from the ice-bound regions of the timber-shaded Slave Lake and the lake of the woods ; on the bald prairie there, nothing above the dead grass breaks their free course over the hard rolled hills. Even along the scattered water courses, where they broke the thick ice to give their cattle drink, the annual autumn fires had left little wood of value. The party, therefore, often wanted for good camp fires, the first luxury of all travelers ; but to men insufficiently furnished with tents and other appliances of shelter, almost an essential to life. After days of fatigue, their nights were often passed in restless efforts to save themselves from freezing. Their stock of food, also proved inadequate ; and as their systems became impoverished, their suffering from cold increased. Sickened with catarrhal affections, manacled by the fetters of dreadfully acute rheumatism, some contrived for a while to get over the shortening days' march, and drag along some other. But the sign of an impaired circulation soon began to show itself in the liability of all to be crippled. The hardiest and strongest became helpless. About the same time, the strength of their beasts of draught began to fail. The small supply of provender they could carry with them had given out. The winter bleached prairie straw proved devoid of nourishment; and they could only keep them from starving by seeking for the brouse, as it is called, a green bark and tender buds and branches of the cottonwood, and other stinted growths of the hollows.

"The spring came at last. It overtook them in the Sac & Fox country, still on the naked prairie, not yet half way over the trail they were following, between the Mississippi and Missouri Rivers. But it brought its own share of troubles with it. The months with which it opened proved nearly as trying as the worst of winter.

"The snow and sleet and rain which fell, as it appeared to them, without intermission, made the road over the rich prairie soil as impassable as one vast bog of heavy black mud. Sometimes they would fasten the horses and oxen of four or five wagons to one, and attempt to get ahead in this way, taking turns; but at the close of a day of hard toil for themselves and their cattle, they would find themselves a quarter or half a mile from the place they left in the morning. The heavy rains raised all the water-courses; the most trifling streams were impassable. Wood fit for bridging was often not to be had, and in such cases, the only resource was to halt for freshets to subside—a matter in case of the head-waters of the Chariton, for instance, of over three weeks delay.

"The frequent. burials made the hardiest sicken. On the soldier's march it is a matter of discipline, that after the rattle of musketry over his comrades' grave, he shall tramp it to the music of some careless tune, in a lively quick-step. But, in the Mormon camp, the companion who lay ill and gave up the ghost within view of all, all saw, as he stretched a corpse, and all attended to his last retiring place. It was a sorrow, too, of itself, to simple-hearted people, the deficient pomps of their imperfect style of funeral. The general hopefulness of human—including Mormon—nature, was well illustrated by the fact that the most provident were found unfurnished with undertaker's articles; so that bereaved affection was driven to the most melancholy makeshifts.

"The best expedient, generally was, to cut down a log of some eight or nine feet long, and slitting it longitudinally, strip off its dark bark in two half-cylinders. These placed around the body of the deceased and bound firmly together with withes made of alburnum, formed a rough sort of tubular coffin which surviving relations and friends, with a little show of black crape, could follow with its enclosure to the hole, or bit of ditch, dug to receive it in the wet ground of the prairie. They grieved to lower it down so poorly clad, and in such an unheeded grave. It was hard. Was it right, thus hurriedly to plunge it in one of the undistinguishable waves of the great land-sea, and leave it behind them there, under the cold north rain, abandoned to be forgotten? They had no tomb-stones; nor could they find rocks to pile the monumental cairn. So, when they had filled up the grave, and over it prayed a *miserere* prayer, and tried to sing a hopeful psalm, the last office was to seek out land-marks, or call in the surveyor to help them to determine the bearings of valley, bends, head-lands, or fork and angles of constant streams, by which its position should in the future be remembered and recognized. The name of the beloved person, his age, the date of his death, and these marks were all registered with care.   This party was then ready to move on.   Such graves marked all the line of the first year of the Mormon travel—dispiriting milestones to failing stragglers in the rear."

REMY AND BRENCHLEY ON THE MORMONS.

A great many books and pamphlets have been published concerning the Mormons, one of the most remarkable of which is "A Journey to Salt Lake City [1855] by Jules Remy and Julius Brenchley," two French *litterateurs* who made a long sojourn in Utah for the express purpose of seeing and judging for themselves ; and they have given their impressions with French naivete and freshness.   From this work I give the following extracts :

"The invincible repugnance we have to the polygamic doctrine, the profound disgust we entertain for the practices to which it has given rise, and for those attributes to it, with or without reason, must not prevent our saying that the Mormons appeared to us less licentious than we were naturally inclined to suppose.   *   *   *
Personally, during our stay in Utah, we saw scarcely anything which seemed to be at variance with the strictest morality.   No question, polygamy is extensively practiced by the Mormons, and we believe it to be a bad and horrible thing ; still, if we trust exclusively to our own observation, we are in no position to condemn the practice however ruthlessly we may persist in rejecting the theory.   Love of truth compels us to say that we were, generally speaking, edified with all that we saw, and that, as far as external appearances go, Utah is the most moral country in the world.   All the males in it are usefully employed ; we met with neither sluggards, idlers,

gamblers nor drunkards.   The polygamous Saints, almost without exception, left upon us the impression of being good fathers and husbands.   All that passed under our eyes was decorous, and we have a decided objection to supposing that we had to deal only with hypocrites. Besides, how are we to reconcile their industry, their love of work, their continued occupation with the debauched habits that are ascribed to the Mormons?   Experience has sufficiently proved that the industrious man is not thinking of what is evil.   Polygamy,—we cannot repeat it too often,—is a detestable thing; but these men have embraced it in all sincerity, and we have had the opportunity of ascertaining that they observed it with chastity and propriety as a divine command.   *   *   * We are satisfied that the Mormons are, in general, better than their system, and in our appreciation of them we must make a large allowance for fanaticism, and acknowledge that a majority of them are honest men, entitled to our esteem on more grounds than one, in spite of what is revolting and absurd in some of their superstitions.   *   *   *   The Mormon women surpass in fanaticism any thing we could have possibly conceived. In emphatically declaring that they are pious, modest, chaste, faithful, devoted, sincere, laborious, honest, honorable in all respects, it is satisfaction to find ourselves agreeing with every traveler, who, like us, has spent some time on the borders of Salt Lake.   *   *   * It results from what has been said that the sincerity of the Mormons is beyond all question, and this alone would screen me, if it were necessary, from the reproach of having wasted so much time upon them, and of too indulgently handling their extravagance.   Had I found them cheats and hypocrites, I should have felt for them nothing but disgust, and should have been content to denounce and brand them, but I discovered them to be dupes, more deserving of pity than blame, upright minds that have fallen into an abyss, from which God alone can rescue them."

CACHE VALLEY—VISIT TO THE RURAL DISTRICTS.

In the autumn of 1882, in company with Commissioner George L. Godfrey, I made a visit to Logan City, in Cache County, bordering on the Idaho line, ninety or a hundred miles north of Salt Lake City. Our object was to see something of the Mormons in the rural districts. We found Logan to be a very pretty little city of four or five thousand inhabitants, most of the population being Mormons.

At the hostelry where we stopped we met a very irate saloon keeper. He boasted of being "an American." "The d——d Mormons," said he, "are trying to break up my business. They have passed an ordinance against selling liquor in Logan, but I will beat the d——d fanatics. They have fined me in a good many cases, but I have appealed to the United States Court in Ogden and I will beat them there."

During the day we called at the residence of Moses Thatcher, one of the "Twelve Apostles." We found him to be a rather good-looking and well-dressed man. In conversation he told us a good deal about the city and republic of Mexico, where he had resided in the interest of his Church.

Two years later I made another visit to Logan and Bear Lake in company with Hon. Alexander Ramsey, then Chairman of the Utah Commission, and Arthur L. Thomas, the Territorial Secretary. We sent a spring-wagon and team with a driver from Salt Lake City, and on the next afternoon we went by rail to Brigham City, about sixty miles north of Salt Lake City. Our driver had arrived with the wagon and team, and we stopped that night with a Welsh widow lady, who occasionally entertained travelers, there being no regular inn in the town. Our hostess was a Mormon, as were nearly all the people of the town, which had a population of two or three thousand. As in nearly all the Mormon dwellings, the walls were adorned with portraits of Brigham Young and Joseph and Hyrum Smith, the two martyrs, dressed in the height of fashion of their day, with swallow-tailed coats, high rolling collars, &c. On a table among the books were a Bible, the Book of Mormon, Doctrine and Covenants, Parley P. Pratt's "Voice of Warning," and a song book with music for Sunday school children.

We rose very early next morning and looked around the town. It was a perfect wilderness of fruit and flowers. Here comes a man on horseback, accompanied by a couple of stump-tailed dogs. He is lustily winding a horn, a veritable cow's horn. What does this mean? It is soon explained when we see several hundred cows coming toward him from all directions. He is the town herdsman, and his business is to drive all the cows of the city to the grassy plain below the city every morning and bring them back to be milked every evening. We resumed our journey next morning in the wagon, going in a circuitous way round the point of the mountains. At noon we stopped to feed our horses with a man who kept a little saloon and grocery. He told us that he had been a Mormon, but the Church had "cut him off" for selling liquor. In the afternoon, passing over "the divide," we began to descend into Cache Valley. Here we found a large building, with many fine fat cattle in the vicinity. This was the "Church Dairy." After drinking freely of the rich milk, from the hands of a Scandinavian "Maud Muller," we went on our way, and came down into the valley at Mendon, thence to Wellsville, where we passed the night. Next day across the valley to Hyrum. We overtook a little girl with a basket of eggs.

"Won't you get in, little girl, and ride?"

"Yes, sir, thank you."

"What are you going to do with your eggs?"

"I am taking them to the Tithing House."

"Do you go to school?"

"Yes, sir, I go to the Primary and to Sunday school."

Arrived at Hyrum we found that our coming had been anticipated, and we were welcomed by the mayor and other leading citizens. They had a brass band and a large American flag on a huge pole. They kindly pressed us to stay over night; but we were obliged to decline, as our itinerary fixed Logan City as our stopping place for that night.

Passing through two or three other towns we arrived at Logan City—a very handsome place. In the evening at the hotel we had a number of callers, and later a serenade from a band. Chairman Ramsey being called out by the large crowd who had assembled, advanced to the middle of the street, and with hat in hand addressed the audience in a forcible and eloquent speech in which he said—nothing. I followed and succeeded equally well in the result. Cache Valley is one of the most lovely and fertile spots in the Rocky Mountain region, I suppose it is about thirty miles long and fifteen miles wide. A fine view is had from the top of the Mormon Temple on the mountain side in the eastern part of the city. Logan City lies before us, while eight or ten other towns and cities are plainly seen. A high range of mountains is on the east, while snowy peaks are seen far up in Idaho, (July 19th.)

The next morning we left Logan for Bear Lake. To get there we had to go through one of the canyons of the Wasatch range, and we selected Blacksmith's Fork canyon, near the head of which is Curtis' ranch which we proposed to reach by the middle of the afternoon, and to remain there until the next morning.

A "tender-foot" might imagine that the "ranches" of the "cattle kings," and sheep men of the western plains and Rocky Mountain valleys are something grand; like a Spanish-American hacienda ; but he will find them nearly all like that of Mr. Curtis—a low, one story dwelling house, built of small, round logs of pine and aspen, with two or three rooms—outbuildings to match, a corral of stone or logs—a stack of hay or lucern, etc. Mr. Curtis was expecting our party and he and Mrs. Curtis gave us kind and hospitable entertainment. We had killed some grouse and other birds coming up the canyon, and caught some mountain trout at the ranch. These added to Mrs. Curtis' fare, made a very good supper and breakfast for hungry travelers. How sweet is game when it is " the spoil of one's own bow and spear!" After supper we chatted with Mr. Curtis until a late hour. He said he had emigrated from Indiana. Gov. Ramsey inquired: " I suppose you are disfranchised Mr. Curtis?" "They say so," replied Mr. C., which, being interpreted, meant that he had more than one wife, and was therefore under the law of Congress, not allowed to vote or hold office. It was understood that he had one wife living at the ranch and another living down in the valley at Hyrum. He told us of the great number of rattle-snakes and bear that had been killed in that neighborhood. A few years before he found a valuable cow close to his house, that had been killed by some wild animal. He cut out a piece of the cow's flesh and put strychnine on it, placing it on a little stake, close by the carcass. The next morning he found there a dead grizzly bear of huge size that would weigh 1800 pounds.

Our worthy host being the husband of two wives and the father of eighteen children, and having a large flock of sheep, is, no doubt, in favor of encouraging " home industry."

In the canyon stream near Curtis' ranch we found a beaver dam, composed of logs, brush and clay, that had become as hard as stone or hard-pan. Here it is said John Jacob Astor's men had trapped for beaver, nearly eighty years ago. This is quite probable from the line of travel of the expedition as related in Irving's Astoria.

Off next morning for Bear Lake. Winding our devious way over the mountains, gradually ascending to the " divide," then descending into the valley, we came in sight of Bear Lake, a beautiful body of water, elliptical in shape, and about thirty miles long by fifteen miles wide. At the southern end of the lake we reached Laketown, about 2 o'clock in the afternoon. It being Sunday we all went to the Mormon meeting house where services were going on. After dinner we took a look at the lake. It is full of trout—and in a stream flowing into the lake our host took a large number of fish with a pitchfork.

Started next morning for Evanston in Wyoming, fifty miles away. Ascending a canyon from the lake we came to a vast plateau 7000 feet above the level of the sea. From this elevation we could see in nearly all directions, snow-covered ranges of mountains, eighty or a hundred miles away.

At Woodruff we stopped for dinner with Judge Walton, with whom we were acquainted. He was a Mormon, and was holding the position of Probate Judge of the County. He is a native of Maine, the son of the Chief Justice of that State. Some years before he started from home, with some other young men, to go around the world by way of San Francisco. Arrived at Salt Lake City he was taken sick, and while convalescing he became a convert to the Mormon faith and married a Mormon girl. So his trip around the world ended in obscurity and oblivion in a ranch of aspen poles on a wind-swept plateau of Utah. But he appeared to be contented, cheerful and firm in the faith. We arrived that evening at Evanston, and on the next day took the train and reached Salt Lake City at 8 o'clock.

During our sojourn in Utah we made many trips of this kind to various places in the Territory. The incidents were similar to those here recorded, and everywhere we were received with every appearance of respect, kindness and cordiality.

SPRINGVILLE—STRAWBERRIES—CHILDREN CELEBRATING BRIGHAM YOUNG'S BIRTHDAY.

One of these excursions was of peculiar interest, illustrating Mormon ways through Utah. On June 1, 1888, in strawberry time, the Commissioners were the guests of Hugh M. Dougall, an ex-Mormon at Springville, in Utah County, one of the prettiest towns in the Territory, with a population of about 2,500. We were royally entertained by our host, his wife and their lovely daughter. At dinner we had the finest strawberries—as well as the largest I ever saw. Our host told us, that if we wanted to see something which was probably new to us, he would take us out to Bishop Packard's grove where the children of the " Primary School" were celebrating Brigham Young's birthday. We accepted the invitation and arriving at the grove we found that the celebration had already commenced by prayer and singing. About four hundred children were present all dressed in their "Sunday's best." The exercises consisted in recitations, songs and instrumental music by the children, together with a catechism by one of the teachers, in which she would ask questions, to which all the children would respond in unison, like this:

" What day of the month is this?"

"June 1st."

" Whose birthday do we celebrate today?"

" President Brigham Young's."

Then followed other questions and answers concerning " Joseph the Seer," and the creed and discipline of the Mormons. We were introduced to several persons, among others, Mrs. Presendia Kimball, and Mrs. A. K. Smoot, who seemed to be some sort of officers of the primary associations. Both made short and appropriate speeches to the children, speaking with ease and fluency as if they were accustomed to it. Mrs. Smoot is one of the wives of A. O. Smoot, president of the " Utah (County) Stake of Zion." She is a Norwegian by birth—a tall, stately and rather handsome brunette. Mrs. Kimball was past 82 years old, but she was large, strong and vigorous, and was no doubt a beauty in her youth. I asked her " Were you related to the apostle Heber C. Kimball?"

"I am proud to say that I was one of his wives," was her answer, as she drew herself up to her full stature.

We were also introduced to a little *wearish*, thin old man who looked like " the last leaf," Philo Dibble by name. He was proud of having "seen Joseph," and that he was the thirty-first member of the Mormon Church. By the way all the old Mormons are very proud of having known Joseph in the early days—and they are fond of making it known in their discourses and conversation.

All the people old and young, sat down to an elegant dinner. I sat beside Mrs. Kimball, who undertook to edify me with the "fullness of the everlasting gospel in these the latter days." I listened patiently and without contradiction. It seemed to do her good and did me no harm.

THE "HELL-POTS" OF MIDWAY.

"Like a hell-broth boil and bubble."
—*Macbeth*.

There are many thermal springs in Utah; among them the Warm springs and Hot springs near Salt Lake City and the Hot springs, north of Ogden. It is claimed that these springs have excellent curative qualities for rheumatism and other ailments. But of all the thermal springs which the writer has seen, the most curious are the "Hell-pots of Midway," in Wasatch County about forty-five miles south-easterly from Salt Lake City. In the summer of 1888, in company with two other commissioners and two young men, we made a visit to Heber City, Midway and the Hell-pots. Heber City is the county seat of Wasatch County, and is a very pretty town, built principally of red sandstone, which is found in abundance in the immediate vicinity. We stopped at an inn kept by John Duncan—a one-eyed and one-legged man—who, notwithstanding his disadvantages, stumped around with great activity and energy. He did not appear to be a very devoted Mormon, from his conversation, but Mrs. Duncan was evidently a zealous Latter-day Saint. We were well entertained in every way, especially by the vivacious conversation of our hostess. She was a good looking English woman, with the English complexion, but dark brown eyes—which being remarked as unusual by one of the company, she said that dark eyes were characteristic of the Tudors—and she then informed us that she was a descendant of the royal House of Tudor. She was a sort of doctor, and drove around in her buggy in the practice of a certain branch of the profession.

The hell-pots are about an hour's drive from Heber City, near the Provo River. We examined twelve or fifteen of these, and saw several others at a distance.

A description of one of them, will give an idea of all, but they differ in size and other respects. A mound of calcareous substance, 25 to 40 feet in diameter, with a hole generally circular, at the top. Ascending the mound and looking down into the hole, we find clear hot water—sometimes level with the surface of the mound and sometimes 5 to 10 feet below. The inside of the pot is concave like the inside of a jug, with the top broken off. Some of these pots have gone dry and some have hot water, some tepid and some cold. The largest mound is three or four hundred yards in circumference at the base. The water in it is very warm, and flush with the top of the crater, from which it overflows and runs in a small stream down the side of the mound.

The hot water and the crater-like mounds, are suggestive of volcanic action, but on examination and reflection, we came to a different conclusion. That whole region is a calcareous formation. The soft porous limestone cropping out in many places. And it seems that these mounds were formed by the deposition of carbon-

AN INDIAN CRADLE.

ate of lime, which is thrown up by the springs; and that the water is heated by chemical action.

The commissioners had a pleasant visit at Heber City.

Abram Hatch, the " President of the Stake" and "funny man" of the Legislature, was absent from home, but from his two sons we received very kind and courteous attention.

In the early morning we saw something new in the street—a drove of milk-cows and young cattle, of improved stock, each with a fine toned bell around the neck; and being of different sizes and tones, there was a sort of chime of " sweet bells jangled and out of tune."

We were told that these cattle belonged to the " President of the Stake."

While we were in Heber we met with a " young buck and his squaw"—to use the elegant language of the miners and cowboys of the West—meaning a noble red man and his spouse. They had with them a beautiful little girl, and the trio presented a picture for a painter. The "buck" was a handsome athletic young fellow, while the woman reminded us somewhat of our youthful conceptions of the fair Indian maidens of the story books. The young men of our party engaged in a shooting match with the "buck," and it was a pleasing sight to see the young wife with the beautiful child in her arms, watching with triumphant smile, the superior skill of her liege lord.

A CELESTIAL PANTHEIST.

It was a festival given by the good ladies of the Congregationalist Church of Salt Lake City, in honor of their Celestial converts. Among the guests were the

Governor of Utah, the Utah Commissioners, and a promiscuous assemblage of Jews, Gentiles, Mormons and Congregationalists with six or eight of their Chinese wards.

The decorations were striking and unique. There were big fans and little fans and all manner of Chinese bric-a-brac. There were pictures and effigies of impossible fishes and preposterous birds, with grotesque quadrupeds and reptiles such as never were seen on land or sea. There were dragons, chimeras and octopeds, quadrupeds with wings, and birds with duck bills, web feet, four legs and hair like a possum. There were green pots of plants like onions to bloom on the Chinese New Year, whose only nutriment was little stones and water. These curios had been furnished by the ex-heathens to add to the attractiveness of the festival.

Prominent among the Celestials, was one Wong Lee. I say *one*, advisedly, because there are thirty or forty millions of people, of the same name in the Flowery Kingdom.

Wong had a good voice for singing, and played exquisitely on a little instrument with three strings. I asked Wong one day, to tell me the name of this sweet little instrument, and he answered "Moosic," (music).

On repeating my question, he said, "Tinkee-tinkee velly good music." I was not satisfied with this meagre information, but I continued my quest for information in the ornithological line and calling Wong's attention to a gorgeous bird with brilliant plumage, green, red, and golden, with a tail like that of a bird of Paradise, I wanted to know its name. He answered "Cheekin" (chicken).

Recurring to Wong's music, it must be admitted

that his performance on the "tinkee-tinkee" was well received by the audience, and they were thrilled with delight when he added the music of his voice in those sweet guttural sounds such as clang, clung, clong, oolong, etc.

But music of the highest order, is like Limburger cheese, frogs legs and other delicacies. It requires cultivation to properly appreciate them. Some people, at first, are not fond of this Chinese music, but when they get used to it they find that it is a great deal better than it sounds.

But behold Wong Lee and his companions! Solomon in all his glory was not arrayed like one of these Cathayans at this memorable festival! Wong had doffed his blue cotton overshirt and his white trousers, and now bloomed like a bed of tulips, arrayed in a satin gown, a veritable coat of many colors, with voluminous trousers of blue silk. His dainty feet were encased in embroidered shoes of black cloth, with wooden soles as white as chalk. The front part of his head was shaved as smooth as a billiard ball, and his queue hung down his back nearly to the floor.

The lovely Christian ladies wore their best attire and sweetest smiles, as they dispensed the delicious strawberries and ice-cream to saint and sinner alike. But they were especially charming and Madonna-like in their attentions to the new converts. *Eureka*! We all felt happy. Repeal the Exclusion Acts! Let the Chinese come, and thus be brought under Christian influences, sandwiched with fair women, strawberries and ice-cream.

How happy the converts looked in their new-born faith and zeal, Wong Lee, Ah Moo Long, Lung Sing, Sam Sing and the rest of the quandam pagans.

Near the quarters of the Utah Commission, on West Temple Street, Wong kept a laundry. Now, it is well-known that the Chinese, like the quadrumani, are very imitative, and that the Celestials are quick to learn the arts and artifices of the "Melican man," in drawing custom, "If you have a good thing, let the people know it." Accordingly our friend displayed the following sign, deftly painted by himself:

WonG LEE

GooD LaUNdRy.

One morning, soon after the festival, I called as a teacher in the ward, to have an interview with the regenerated heathen; with the following result:

"Wong, do you believe in the religion of Christ?"

"Clist velly good man."

" Have you given up the Chinese religion?"

" No—that is velly good too."

" What do you think of Joseph Smith, the Prophet?"

" Velly good ploffet."

" What do you think of the Jews?"

" No sabe—Pleachy say they killed Melican man's god."

" Do you belong to the Liberal Party or the People's Party?"

" Me washee washee."

Adopting and adapting the language of Goldsmith, the "inspired idiot," I propounded the following interrogatory, to be answered positively and without evasion or mental reservation:

" Do you believe that the concatenation of fortuitous circumstances, proceeding in a reciprocal duplicate and geometrical ratio will produce a theoretical and theological dialogism, establishing the doctrine of justification by faith alone ?"

"*No sabe.*"

I repeated the question distinctly and with an oro rotundo voice ; but such was Wong's opaque ignorance, or guile, that he either did not understand or pretended not to understand what I said ; and then for the first time in all my acquaintance with the amiable and child-like people, I saw a slight shadow of displeasure on a Chinaman's face, as he replied :

" Melican man too much talkee talkee—dammee—too much 'lidgion—me washee washee."

My learned friend, Mr. Eli K. Horniday, formerly a worthy citizen of the good county of Pike in the State of Missouri, who had gone West with Johnston's army, as a teamster during the " Mormon war"—-and had diligently studied the Chinese character at the Sand-lots in 'Frisco—under the tuition of Dennis Kearney—having overheard my conversation with the Chinaman, stoutly maintained that Wong had understood what I said well enough.   " Them Chinese," said he, "are all that way whenever they are up to some devil*ment* or shy-*keen*-ery, they always pretend they *no sabe.*"

For the benefit of my musical readers, I give Wong Lee's favorite aria as performed by him one hundred con-secutive nights with great applause from Ah Moo, Ling Lee, Ah Sin and other admiring friends :

GRAND BALL AT BEAVER CITY.

There was a sound of revelry by night."
                              —*Lord Byron.*

" Tripping as they go
On the light fantastic toe.''
                              —*John Milton.*

It would, no doubt, be "caviare to the general" to inform them that the above fantastic couplet was written by such an austere and sublime poet as John Milton. And yet, as the Mexicans say : "*Quien sabe.*" Who knows what the grave and reverend signiors of the Utah Commission, Judge Williams, Mr. Arthur L. Thomas (not to mention the Chairman) may do on the light fantastic toe, when they are "romancing" in the rural districts ? And yet, it would be an unpardonable omission, if, in these fragmentary and veracious sketches, no mention should be made of the visit of the Utah Commission to Beaver City in June, 1888. By the kindness of Hon. John Sharp, superintendent of the Utah Central Railroad we were furnished with his private car, in which we traveled south some two hundred miles or more, to Milford. Here we took passage in wagons, stopped at Minersville for dinner, with Mr. Du Paix a very fine specimen of a Frenchman. I think it is safe to say than in this half day's travel we saw at least five thousand jack-rabbits—many of which were shot by the boys, who accompanied us in the expedition. From Milford to Minersville, we passed through a valley of surpassing loveliness in appearance, but it was a delusion. There was no cultivation whatever. It was a desert for the want of water. We reached Beaver City late in the afternoon, and were informed that a reception was to be given that evening at the Mormon meeting house. When we arrived at the Church, we found the large auditorium, as well as the galleries, jammed and crammed with people, and a brass band and one or two choirs of singers, in full blast. The whole town, saints and sinners, Mormons and "Jack-Mormons," appeared to have turned out; while the most pronounced anti-Mormons mingled with the throng. Speeches were made by Mayor Emerson (Mormon), Rev. J. D. Gilliland, of the Methodist mission, James Low, Esq., J. R. Murdock, President of the Beaver Stake of Zion, and others.

The Commissioners being vociferously called for, also spoke; but 'twere long to tell, and not worth the telling what we had to say. Mr. Clarence W. Hall, responding for himself and Mr. Jas. Adams, Charles C. Carlton and Willie Godfrey, the young men who were attaches of the Commission, made a neat little speech, which was well received. If he "keeps on" he is likely to become the Columbian orator of the Rocky Mountains.

On the next day the Commissioners and their attaches went a fishing—up in a canyon stream, toward the snow-capped Mount Baldy—all but the chairman, the author of these veracious pages—who stayed down in town, and, like Falstaff, took his ease in his inn, wisely playing croquet with the girls under a spreading box-elder tree, and, at supper, wisely eating his full share of the fine mountain trout, which the other fellows had caught.

The members of the Commission and their friends partook of an excellent dinner at the residence of Mr. Thompson; and in the evening attended a grand ball at a public hall given in their honor. There was a large attendance, Mormons, Gentiles, Saints and Sinners, mingling together. There was not much swallow-tail style, nor any lavish display of diamonds ; but all were well dressed, and everything was carried on in an orderly and good humored manner. Bishops, elders and deacons joined in the dance. The Mormons have always been fond of music and dancing. All four of their prophets, Joseph Smith, Brigham Young, John Taylor, and Wilford Woodruff would occasionally join in the dance. As to music, there is scarcely a town or village in Utah but has one or more brass bands ; and in Salt Lake City there are probably fifteen or twenty. But we must bid adieu to the lovely town of Beaver City, which will long be remembered by "the boys," the old boys and the young boys, for the *Angel-ic* charms of the ladies, as well as the hearty hospitality of the masculine Saints and Sinners. Amongst the many who contributed to the entertainment of our party, we remember especially, Mr. Du Paix, Ed. Thompson, Dr. George H. Fennimore, Mayor Emerson, the reverend Mr. Galliland, Dr. Christian, Major Lowe, President Murdock, and a perpetual-motion genius whose Christian or heathen name, as well as his patronymic I have happily forgotten.

THE UTAH COMMISSION—BETWEEN SCYLLA AND CHARIBDIS.

The Utah Commission reassembled in Salt Lake City in the spring of 1883. From that time to the present it has been between two cross-fires with occasional intermissions. The ultra-Gentiles charged that it was inclined to stretch or override the law against them.

How far the charge that the Commission was "too conservative and favorable to the Mormons" is sustained by the real facts will appear by the following orders :

OATH REQUIRED TO BE TAKEN BY VOTERS UNDER THE RULES ADOPTED BY THE UTAH COMMISSION.

TERRITORY OF UTAH,   } ss.
  COUNTY OF

I.... .being duly sworn, (or affirmed) depose and say, that I am over twenty-one years of age, and have resided in the Territory of Utah for six months, and in the precinct of............ ... .. one month immediately preceding the date hereof, and (if a male) am a native born or naturalized (as the case may be) citizen of the United States, and a tax payer in this Territory, (or if a female), I am native born or naturalized citizen of the United States ; and I do further solemnly swear (or affirm) that I am not a bigamist or polygamist ; that I have not violated the laws of the United States prohibiting bigamy or polygamy ; that I do not live or cohabit with more than one woman in the marriage relation, nor does any relation exist between me and any woman which has been entered into, or continued in violation of the said laws of the United States prohibiting bigamy or polygamy ; (and if a woman) that I am not the wife of a polygamist, nor have I entered into any relation with any man in violation of the laws of the United States concerning polygamy or bigamy.

Subscribed and sworn to before me this. . day of . ...188.....

--------------------- --   ....

Registration Officer ..   ..Precinct.

ORDER OF THE UTAH COMMISSION, ADOPTED FRIDAY, SEPTEMBER 1, 1882.

Wm. A. C. Bryan, Registration Officer for the County of Juab, having submitted to this Commission the following question for our decision :

"If, in any case, a man has violated the laws of the United States, prohibiting bigamy or polygamy, and is not at the time he may apply to be registered as a voter, actually living with two or more wives, should he, or should he not, be deemed a legal applicant for registration ?"

"The Commission, after due consideration, made the following order:

That any person, male or female, who, in violation of the Act of Congress, approved July 1st, 1862, (sec. 5352, Revised Statutes, United States), or who, in violation of section 1 of the Act of Congress, approved March 22nd, 1882, entitled "An Act to amend Section 5352 of the Revised Statues of the United States, in reference to bigamy, and for other purposes," has entered into any of the relationships described in section 8 of said last-named act, is not a legal voter, and cannot be registered.

And the Secretary of this Commission is directed to communicate this order to Mr. Bryan; and all other Registration Officers will take due notice of this order.

NOTE.—The following is section 8 of said act:

That no polygamist, bigamist, or any person cohabiting with more than one woman, and no woman cohabiting with any of the persons described as aforesaid in this section, in any Territory or other place over which the United States have exclusive jurisdiction, shall be entitled to vote at any election held in any such Territory or other place, or be eligible for election or appointment to or be entitled to hold any office or place of public trust, honor or emolument in, under or for any such Territory or place under the United States.

ORDER OF THE UTAH COMMISSION, ADOPTED JUNE 13, 1883.

William Jennings having appeared before the Commission on Monday, June 11th, 1883, and made the following statement:

"I decided not to register last year, but appeared before the Deputy Registrar of the Third Salt Lake City Precinct, on Saturday, June 9th, 1883, and took the oath prescribed by Rule 2 of the rules defining the duties of the Registration Officers, and was duly regis-

tered.   Subsequently I received notice from the Deputy
Registrar that my name had been stricken from the list
of voters of said precinct by the direction of Thomas C.
Bailey, Registration Officer of Salt Lake County.   I
entered into a polygamous relation prior to July 1st,
1862, and continued in that relation until about the year
1871, at which date my first wife died, and I have since
lived and cohabited with but one wife.   I, therefore,
claim that I have not entered into any marriage relation
in violation of law, and that I am entitled to have my
name appear on the list of registered voters of said
precinct, and ask that the action of the Registration Officer for said county be reversed, and my name restored
to the list of voters of said precinct."

After due consideration by the Commission it is
ordered "that said William Jennings is within the meaning of Section 8 of the Act of Congress of March 22nd,
1882, disqualified as a voter, and is therefore not entitled to register or vote."

The Mormons earnestly protested against these
rulings, as being unjust and unwarranted by the law.

Finally they brought the question before the United
States Judges of Utah, who decided against them.   The
latter appealed to the Supreme Court of the United
States, where it was decided that the Mormons were
right in their view of the law, and that the Federal
Judges and the Commission in Utah, were wrong.   [See
Jesse J. Murphy vs *Alexander Ramsey* ET AL, October
Term, 1874, of the Supreme Court of the United
States.]

After the decision of the Supreme Court, the Commission prepared a Circular for the information of Registration officers, in which scrupulous care was taken to
conform strictly to the law as interpreted by that tribunal, so that little or no objection was made by either
side.

So matters went on—without anything of much interest to the general reader until the spring of 1887.

The writer arrived in Salt Lake City on the 23d of February of that year. Found many of the "Liberals" or Gentiles in a great state of excitement, concerning the "Edmunds-Tucker bill." [See this Act in Part III.] This bill had passed both houses of Congress, but had not yet been approved by the President, who allowed it to become a law without his approval, by lapse of time, under the Constitution. The bill as it passed the House of Representatives, among many other provisions, authorized the President of the United States to appoint the members of the Council of the Legislative Assembly, and also the Judges of the Probate Courts and the county selectmen. It also authorized the Governor to appoint most of the other officers in the Territory. Delegate to Congress and members of the House of the Legislative Assembly were still left to election by the votes of the people. But in conference committee all those parts of the bill which authorized the President to appoint the twelve members of the Legislative Council, and authorized the Governor to appoint certain officers, were stricken out; and in this shape the bill became a law. When the text of the law became known in Utah, some of the "Loyal Leaguers" became perfectly furious at what they called the "emasculation" of the bill.

The "Loyal League" was an anti-Mormon organization, more or less secret in its character, with branches in many parts of the Territory. Some of its more hot-headed members denounced the President in unmeasured terms. He was a "Jack Mormon;" so were Lamar, Garland and Teller; and Edmunds and Ingalls were not much better, for either suggesting or acquiescing in the aforesaid "emasculation." Crimination and recrimination amongst the Gentile leaders, were the order of the day, and of course the Utah Commission, especially its chairman, received a large share of abuse.

Another trouble, was, that the "registration oath" as it was worded in the bill when it became a law, was not as sweeping and comprehensive as was expected and desired. On the 4th of March, it was learned by telegraphic correspondence with Attorney General Garland, that the bill had become a law.

On the following Monday, March the 7th, there was to be a municipal election held in Brigham City in Box Elder County, and it was the duty of the Commission to make preparation for that election, by formulating the necessary oaths of the judges of election and of voters as required by the new law. During the day (March 4th) while engaged in this business, a number of the federal office-holders, the Governor, two of the judges and two other officers called to consult with the Commissioners in regard to the new law, and the form of the oath for officers and voters. The form which we had prepared was exhibited, and it was conceded that it contained all that the law required; but the question was suggested whether certain expletives and amplifications might not be inserted in the oath. After an informal talk of some length, the general conclusion was that it was best to follow the form which we had prepared.

Another question was: "Does the law requiring an oath of office-holders apply to those already commissioned, or only to those who may hereafter be commissioned?" And further does the law apply to the Judges, Commissioners and other federal office-holders?

The Utah Commission were of the opinion that the law requiring the oath applied to federal as well as local officers, but that it had no application to those already commissioned. In this opinion the Attorney General of the United States concurred, in an official opinion published sometime afterwards. Meantime several of the federal officers took the oath, one of the judges adopting the Commission's form of oath, and another swearing to all that the law required, and a great deal besides.

On the 19th of March, all the Commissioners (except Mr. Thomas) viz: McClernand, Williams, Godfrey and Carlton, being present, we completed our "Circular for the information of Registration officers," under the new law, and soon afterwards it was printed and circulated all over the Territory. Soon after this we heard rumors of war from the "Loyal League."

The parts of the circular which gave special offense, were, first, the form of the registration oath (which we had formulated strictly according to law, and which any reader can verify by comparison;) second, the clause which specified all the disqualifications of voters under the laws of Congress, and concluded with these words: "No *opinions* which they (the voters) may entertain on the subject of religion or church policy, should be the subject of inquiry or exclusion of any elector."

On the 21st of April two gentlemen of the "Liberal Party," called at the Commission office, one in person, and the other by proxy, to insist upon a change in the registration oath. The result of this interview is shown in the following communication:

CORRESPONDENCE.

Salt Lake City, Utah, April 22, 1887.
Messrs. R. N. Baskin and J. E. Dooly, Esqs.

GENTLEMEN :—Yesterday I received from each of

you a manuscript form of a registration oath, both forms being substantially the same. That which was furnished by Mr. Dooly is given below (the other has been mislaid).

"That I will support the Constitution of the United States and will faithfully obey the laws thereof; that I will obey the acts of Congress prohibiting polygamy, bigamy, unlawful cohabitation, incest, adultery and fornication; that I will not *hereafter, in any Territory of the United States, at any time, in obedience to any alleged revelation, or to any counsel, advice, or command, from any source whatever, or under any circumstances, enter into plural or polygamous marriage, or have or take more wives than one*, or cohabit with more than one woman; that I will not *at any time hereafter*, directly or indirectly, aid or abet, counsel or advise, any person to have or take more wives than one, or to cohabit with more than one woman, or to commit incest, adultery or fornication; that I am not a bigamist or polygamist; that I do not cohabit polygamously with persons of the other sex; and that I have not been convicted of any of the offenses above mentioned."

I understand that the purpose for which these forms have been furnished, is to suggest to the Utah Commission, the propriety of our changing the form of the registration oath—heretofore prepared by the Commission, by interpolating the words which I have put in *italics*. Besides other changes have been made. In regard to this proposition I desire to say, in the most respectful manner, that I cannot see the necessity or propriety of making such change.

About a month ago, the form of the oath was promulgated by the Commission in a "Circular for the *information* of registration officers." These have long ago been transmitted to all the deputy registrars of the Territory, and later, printed oaths to the number of 35,000 have been distributed all over the Territory; still this would not be an insuperable obstacle to a change of the form, if we should be satisfied that by mistake or inadvertence, we had violated the law. After careful consideration, we are thoroughly satisfied that in suggesting this form of oath we have made no mistake—in other words, that the oath which we have formulated is *in accordance with the law.* I believe that this is conceded on all hands; but the contention is that we might go further and keep within the law—that there might be interjected into the oath certain expletives, adjectives, circumlocutions and amplifications within the limits of the law, which might have the effect of preventing certain classes of persons from registering and voting.

The answer to this is that if we follow the form and pursue the language of the *law,* we *know* we are right, if we depart from this rule, we are then in a labyrinth of conflicting opinions. For, if the registrars are to depart from the language of the law, and each man of the 270 deputies may prepare an oath to suit himself, the result will be that every man's right to vote (a right hitherto held sacred in all American communities) will depend on the arbitrary will, caprice, or prejudice of the registration officers, who in this as well as other communities, are mostly men of little or no learning in the law. I believe that to allow this would be contrary to law, and a bad precedent that would meet with the condemnation of the Executive Government and of all enlightened jurists who took part in the passage of this law.

Similar suggestions have frequently been made to our Commission, both orally and in writing, by registrars and election judges. This was the occasion of our inserting in our circular to registration officers a brief statement enumerating ALL the disabilities of voters, under the law of Congress, adding the following paragraph:

"The Commission is of the opinion that the above specifications include all the disabilities to which electors are subject, under the laws of Congress, and that no opinions which they may entertain upon questions of religion or church polity should be the subject of inquiry or exclusion of any elector."

The following specifications include all the disabilities

to which voters in Utah are subject under the laws of Congress:

No polygamist, bigamist, or any person cohabiting with more than one woman, shall be entitled to register or vote at any election in this Territory ; nor any person who has been convicted of the crime of incest, unlawful cohabitation, adultery, fornication, bigamy or polygamy ; nor any person who associates or cohabits polygamously with persons of the other sex ; nor can any person register or vote who has not taken and subscribed the oath prescribed by the Twenty-fourth Section of the Act of Congress of March 3, 1887; nor can any woman register or vote.

The converse of the proposition is, that, (conceding all the local salutary qualifications, as to age, residence, citizenship, etc., every male person is entitled to register and vote if he is not a bigamist or polygamist, nor cohabiting with more than one woman ; does not associate or cohabit polygamously with persons of the other sex ; has not been *convicted* of incest, fornication or adultery, and is willing to *take and subscribe* to the oath as prescribed by the Twenty-fourth Section of the Act of Congress.

[As to those in polygamy, or unlawful cohabitation, they are disqualified whether they have been convicted or not.]

The oath is to be "subscribed," and therefore it is to be a written or printed affidavit, that it should contain no more nor no less than what is provided in the act.

The oath prescribed by Congress (as to its material parts) is entirely *promissory* in its character, having reference to the future, the affiant swearing not as to what he *does* or has done, but what he *will*, or *will not do*. Whether he is willing or not to take the oath, is a matter addressed to his own conscience—and is binding only *in foro conscientiae*. The duties of the officer in making the registration and administering the oath are purely ministerial in their character, and he has no right to inquire into any man's motives, nor to catechise him as to his opinions on matters of religion, tithes, or other church contributions, or his church membership.

It was evidently the intention of Congress to allow all male persons of proper age, etc., to vote if they are not disqualified by polygamy, etc., provided they are willing to take the prescribed oath.

An inquisitorial catechism of a metaphysical character by the registrars, as to whether the party might some time in the future change his mind and go into polygamy, or under certain seductive temptations might commit fornication or adultery, is in my opinion not authorized by law. The same remarks will apply to the registration officer on a proceeding to strike off names on the registry list. In such a proceeding he may investigate the questions whether a party is under any of the disabilities provided by Territorial law or the Acts of Congress— these last are : Is he in fact a polygamist ? Is he living in unlawful cohabitation ? Is he associating or cohabiting polygamously with persons of the other sex? Has he been *convicted* of bigamy, polygamy, unlawful cohabitation, incest, adultery or fornication? Has he taken the oath prescribed by the Act of Congress? The enumeration exhausts ALL *the disqualifications* provided by Congress. Further than this (except as to local statutory qualifications) the registrar cannot go. The same principle will apply to judges of election upon a challenge at the polls.

The law of Congress provides that no person "otherwise eligible to vote," shall be excluded from the polls "on account of any opinion such person may entertain on the subject of bigamy or polygamy." The debates in Congress, especially in the Senate, plainly show that the advocates and champions of the bill, regarded it as not interfering with any man's religious opinion, or church membership.

The duty of this Commission and the registration and election officers, is not to make, but to execute the law, such law as Congress has given us. We must execute it *as it is*, not as we might *wish* it to be.

In conclusion it may not be deemed superfluous to say, that our Commission does not claim authority to *instruct* anybody—as has been asserted. But from the time of our first appearance in Utah we have annually issued a circular for the information of registrars, and another to the election judges. The necessity of this arose from the fact that we have been, and still are, constantly receiving inquiries from such officers and others in regard to the interpretation of the law and the course of procedure. This course has, heretofore, been approved or acquiesced in, in the very quarter from which objections now come. We submit that the propriety of giving such information, is now more plainly demonstrated than at any previous time, by reason of the exasperated condition of public feeling now existing in Utah. Very respectfully yours,

A. B. CARLTON,
Chairman of the Utah Commission.

After the expression of these views, the Commission were surprised to receive a visit shortly afterwards from a committee of seven representatives of the " Liberal," or "Loyal League" party, who again argued in favor of a change in the oath. The result was, that all the Commissioners present, McClernand, Godfrey, Thomas and Carlton, the chairman, agreed to the following communication :

OFFICE OF THE UTAH COMMISSION,
SALT LAKE CITY, April 28, 1887.

Hon. C. W. Bennett:—

DEAR SIR: In response to a request by a committee of gentlemen that called on this commission several days ago, in reference to a change of the form of registration oath which has been furnished to the registration officers throughout the Territory, we would respectfully say that we are not convinced of the propriety, or necessity of making such change, for a number of reasons, among others:

1st. Because we are satisfied that the oath furnished by us is in accordance with the law.

2nd. The modifications proposed by you, if equivalent to the language employed by the act of Congress, are unnecessary; and if not in accordance with the act, they are illegal.

The law is one declaring the political disfranchisement of the citizen under certain conditions. We hardly need add that such laws, as a rule, are viewed critically and construed strictly by the courts, in favor of political manhood.

3rd. The request comes at such a late day (the registration beginning May 2d), and so long after the printed forms of affidavits to the number of 35,000 have been distributed over the Territory, that the proposed change would occasion much delay and great unnecessary expense.

4th. Plainly, it is not the intent of the law to prescribe any religious creed to the citizen, but to prescribe a rule of action, irrespective of his present or future secret intentions or convictions, or the change of any of them. The oath we have formulated in the terms of the law is but auxiliary to the enforcement of the actua observance of the law, and the rule of action prescribed by it; hence, as a conclusion, it is equally plain to us, that whosoever takes the oath and transcends the rule it prescribes by perpetrating a prohibited and punishable crime, thereby, incurs not only the stain of moral perjury, but liability to legal punishment for the commission of any such prohibited crime; and this consequence would as logically and necessarily follow the infraction of the form of oath which we have furnished as the interpolated form which has been proposed.

5th. The fact that Congress has prescribed the oath is, in itself, an assumption by that body that the oath will not be in vain, but be practically binding upon conscience and useful. Otherwise, why the legal re-

quirement of the oath? Nor is this construction inconsistent with either the municipal or moral law, which
respectively presumes the honesty and innocence of the
individual, until that presumption is overcome by competent proof.

6th. Since the interview with the Committee at
our rooms, we were advised that a written communication was to be presented by the Committee, and after-
ward we received information that it would not be presented. We therefore make this reply, desiring to be
entirely courteous to the Committee, apprehending that
further delay might be misconstrued.

By order of the Commission.

W. C. HALL, Sec'y.

It will scarcely be believed by persons outside of
Utah, that this action of the Commission provoked
another war against them. Some of the Loyal League's
exponents poured out the vials of their wrath, yea,
bottles and demi-johns of wrath, upon the devoted heads
of the Commission, especially the chairman. A stranger
reading those philipies might have supposed that we had
committed some awful crime, like the hay-market atrocity
in Chicago, or Guy Fawkes' gunpowder plot, instead of
having administered the law fairly, justly and conscientiously.

The cause of this tempest in a teapot can be explained in a few words:—The agitators wanted the Commission to act the part of offensive partisans, and they
refused to be used in that way. A large portion of the
Gentile population of Utah are good men and pure
women ; but, it is to be regretted that many of them
allow themselves to be influenced by a small clique who
really care nothing for polygamy except as a means for a
certain end. This coterie, I am thoroughly satisfied,
would be delighted to see a "polygamic revival" amongst

the Mormons, for the reason that this would afford an excuse for additional congressional legislation, that might enable the clique to dominate the Territory, and ultimately pose as United States Senators, Representatives in Congress, Governor, etc.

What a strange and funny world this is!   Here the Commission had performed certain official duties under the law, fairly and justly.   We can imagine each of these officials saying to himself with a natural and excusable pride, "This is right—this is well done—this is good for time and eternity—it commends itself as good law, to all good lawyers and all just and fair men!"

And then, to find himself abused, stigmatized, as if he were a gorgon, an octopus, an anthropohagous monster—an embodiment of the doctrine of metempsychosis, whereby he has inherited all the wicked and infamous characteristics of Judas Iscariot, Nero, Caligula, Anacharsis Cloots, Guy Fawkes, Benedict Arnold and Aaron Burr!

With all this, a "tenderfoot" would become indignant ; but a philosopher of the school of Democritus will find rather a theme for fun and laughter, to see a lot of grotesque little bipeds standing on their heads in a moral mirage and malaria, and in whose jaundiced vision truth herself looks mean, sneaking and pusilanimous. *Vive la bagatelle.*

A SWELL-AFFAIR—WINING AND DINING WITH PROPHETS, APOSTLES AND SAINTS.

These "sketches" are swelling on my hands to such a degree—beyond my original intention—that I must omit many things that would make a connected narrative ; and I come down to the anti-polygamy movement

among the monogamous Mormons in 1887.   But I will premise by saying that Governor Ramsey the first Chairman of the Commission and myself, were to a certain extent "running mates."   We often traversed the city together and made visits to the Saints in the rural districts; and on all proper occasions we gave our advice to the Mormons that they ought to abandon the practice of polygamy.   For the same philanthropic purpose, we even had the temerity to except an invitation to a "swell" dinner at the country residence of George Q. Cannon, one of the Mormon magnates, where we met among many other leading men John Taylor, Prophet, Seer and Revelator, and President of the Church of Jesus Christ of Latter-day Saints in all the World." *   Several ladies in handsome costumes also graced the occasion.

We sat down to a very excellent dinner—with flowers, wine, and all that.   It should be stated, however, that the Mormon dignitaries did not partake of the the wine.   We did not, like Macbeth, "break the good meeting with most admired disorder" by introducing ghosts and the like; but privately we gave some good advice, which may possibly have borne fruit in the sequel. Not having asked permission from some of the leading Gentiles to attend this reception, the Commission were duly criticised for thus associating with the Saints; and we found out that it was not considered *en regle* for federal officers to have any thing to do with Mormons in a social way.

At the dinner I sat between two of the fair daughters of Israel, well-dressed and handsome young ladies.   At

---

* The Apostle Brigham Young, Jun., with one of his wives, Wm. H. Hooper, formerly Utah delegate to Congress, Counselor Joseph F. Smith, Mayor William Jennings. Gen. Daniel H. Wells and other leading Mormons were also present.

first they seemed a little nervous, doubtless on account of the presence of supposed persecutors of the Saints. But we soon came to a better understanding, and they conversed in an interesting and piquant manner. One of them, I believe was daughter of Gen. Wells, and the other a Miss Cannon.

Roaming around Salt Lake City, with Gov. Ramsey, we met Bishop Weiler of the Third Ward. He was a native of Pennsylvania and had been with the Mormons from an early day. He had a strong cast-iron face and a massive, protruding jaw. We "tackled" him in an argument to convert him to our sort of religion. At the conclusion, he very mildly and coolly and smilingly, showing his big white teeth, said : "Gentlemen, I am very sorry for you, that you cannot see these things as I do."

After we separated from the bishop, I said to Gov. Ramsey : "Do you remember those big granite boulders we saw in Little Cottonwood Canyon? You had as well talk to one of them as to try to change Bishop Weiler." The Governor replied with his Pennsylvania-Dutch and-Scotch shrewdness : "A constant dropping will wear away *stones.*"

As the reports of the Commission will show, we had confidence, that ultimately the enforcement of the laws, and other influences would bring about the desired result. We occasionally heard rumors and law indications that the Mormons were contemplating the abandonment of the practice of polygamy.

On June 30th, 1887, a constitutional convention was held in Salt Lake City, composed of delegates from nearly all the counties, for the purpose of prohibiting and punishing polygamy, and asking admission as a state of the Union. The full particulars of this movement will be found in the annual official report of Commissioners Carlton and McClernand for the year 1887, printed in Part III. of this volume. In this place I only wish to note a curious feature of the situation in Utah : and that is, that many of the Gentile leaders in Utah do not want the Mormons to abolish polygamy, but they dread it above all things. The reasons are quite obvious.

The movement among the Mormons in Utah, to get rid of polygamy struck consternation into the extremists among the Gentiles. That which they greatly feared was coming to pass. They had hoped that the Mormons would continue obstinate and stiff-necked until Congress should be induced to disfranchise the whole Mormon population, or enact such extreme legislation as would have the effect of driving them out of the Territory, so that the minority should have political control. The Utah Commission had been reluctant to advise such legislation, and had used their official and personal influence to induce the Mormons to abandon polygamy. This, in a nut-shell, was the cause of the so-called Gentile "indignation" against the Commission, which was wired from Utah. I was then and am now thoroughly satisfied that the monogamous Mormons of Utah (comprising more than three-fourths of the Mormon population) earnestly desire that polygamy shall be abandoned; and I think that in their efforts in this direction they ought to be encouraged and not spurned by the Government of the United States.

It is superfluous for me to say that I regard many parts of the Mormon creed, especially their modern "revelations" as the merest *bagatelle*. But I have no commission, nor has the United States government any authority, to punish, by pains, penalties or disfranchisement any portion of the people for errors of creed and opinion.   Punish for criminal or wrongful *actions*, but religious *opinions*, never.

EVOLUTION—ARE THE MORMONS INCORRIGIBLE?

"The leading strings of the past are dropping from you; they are dropping from the world, not wantonly or by chance, but in the providence of God. All things change, creeds and philosophers and outward systems—but God remains!

—*Robert Elsmere.*

In the official report of Messrs. McClernand and Carlton of Sept. 29, 1887, the following language is employed :

Now, while the great mass of the Mormon people are making an effort for the abandonment of the practice of polygamy, we are asked to recommend further legislation of a hostile and aggressive character, almost, if not entirely, destructive of local self-government, thereby inflicting punishment on the innocent as well as the guilty.   Our answer is, we cannot do so ; we decline to advise Congress to inflict punishment by disfranchising any portion of the people of Utah on account of their religious or irreligious opinions.

In Utah there are persons of multifarious religious creeds, and some with no religious belief at all.   Some prominent and enterprising citizens believe in the revelations of the *Old* Testament and reject those recorded in the *New*, while a large majority of the people of the Territory profess a belief in the Old Testament, the New Testament, and divers modern "revelations" besides.   Those who accept the revelations of the Bible are divided into many separate church organizations by reason of diverse interpretations.   Then, in the close of the most enlightened century in the tide of time, shall we invoke legal coercion over the consciences of men and resort to the pains and penalties inflicted in former times for recusancy, non-conformity, and heresy?

In this age the world moves, and even religious fanatics must keep pace with progress. The Utah of to-day is not, and never can be again what it was when Brigham Young, as prophet, seer, and revelator, dominated over his devoted followers, isolated from all the world, in the secluded valleys of the Rocky Mountains ; nor, in our opinion, can that fading and dissolving specter of the past be justly or properly invoked as excitative to legislation proscriptive of religious opinion. The railroad and the telegraph, free speech and a free press, are there now. Schools and colleges and churches of many denominations are found in all parts of the Territory. The people are no longer isolated, but are now in communication with all the world; and Salt Lake City is one of the most cosmopolitan places on the continent, a resort for tourists, savants, statesmen, and scholars from abroad. Under such circumstances is it not morally impossible that Utah shall ever become subject to that church domination and oppression which are now imputed by some persons as an existing reality against the "Mormon hierarchy ?"

Churches and creeds are subject to the laws of evolution, and Mormonism must yield to the inexorable logic of civilization. Polygamy must go, and its abrogation will, sooner or later, be an accomplished fact. Other objectionable features are gradually giving way ; and we are thoroughly satisfied that whatever the Federal authorities can rightfully accomplish in the way of reform can be done without resorting to the total overthrow of local self-government.

To use a clerical phrase, the writer will make an "improvement" on the statement in the last paragraph which I have put in *italics.* But to avoid all controversy, I had better put it in this way : All churches and creeds except the orthodox—that is *our* church—are subject to changes and modifications. For example : the Calvinistic doctrines of "predestination" and its correlative, " reprobation"—with the logical consequences—are not now received in the same strict sense they formerly were. The *Methodists,* now a very respectable and numerous body of Christians have undergone, in the last century a very great change from those "methods" which once distinguished them and gave them their name. A "new church organ" would not now break up the church as it would have done in former times. A comely damsel or even an elderly sister in Israel would not now, as formerly, be "cut off" from the church for wearing jewelry or flowers. Another evidence of the evolution of liberal views among the orthodox Christians is that Unitarians and even Universalists are beginning to be considered as component parts of the great Christian family instead of cousins-german to Atheists and Infidels. So the world *does* move! And *mirabile dictu!* it is now said by Gladstone and other eminent Christians, that the "Salvation Army" is doing much good, and is worthy of encouragement and toleration! How the world *does* move!

Another instructive consideration concerning religous evolution is this: Many sects once despised, contemned, persecuted and ridiculed—are now eminently and justly considered respectable and conservative.

Some of these sects were not much more respected in the first decades of their work than the "Salvation Army."

One trouble about the Mormons is that they are too primitive. They have gone back to the infancy of the Christian faith and organization, and fanatically hold on to a literal interpretation of what the Christians generally treat as "figurative," or, as having gone into "innocuous desuetude." But, unless the Mormons are anamolies in human nature, evolution will affect them as it has other sects. Human nature is the same in all countries and all ages.

As, with a smile of derision, we read about the

bombards, stone cannon-balls, catapults, cross-bows, arquebusses and other implements of medieval warfare, —so many ministers and laymen at this day, look upon the fervent zeal, the undoubting faith and literal interpretation of the good old days—and all those comforting doctrines of predestination and reprobation—as so many antique curiosities.

Now, the Mormons, although they do not in all cases, stand up for a literal interpretation of the scriptures, yet, in general they lay great stress upon the primitive creed and practice of the "former-day Saints," and however peculiar or absurd some of their tenets or religious customs may seem, they can readily turn to chapter and verse in the Old or New Testament, that support their view as they claim. They declare that in the valleys of the Rocky Mountains, Zion has been established, and there the primitive religion of Christ, the faith as it was delivered to the Saints, is preserved in its original purity and integrity. So the elders preach wherever they go; and descanting on the want of "spiritual-mindedness" among the "sects" and the wickedness of "Babylon"; together with the beatitudes of their Zion, they make several thousand converts every year.

With each remove from the Catholic Church—first "the Reformation"—and then the successive branches, off-shoots, scisms and sects, the zealous propagandist of each new faith devoutly maintains that there is nothing new about it—it is only a restoration of primitive Christianity. So the Mormons claim that they have the genuine article of religion; that they are the true Church of Jesus Christ and are the Saints in these latter-days."

But "Saints" and "Sinners" in these "latter days," when irreverent scientists or scholars will look into the mouth of antiquity with no more ceremony than a jockey will look into a horse's mouth, must, perforce, keep step with progress, and the Mormons are advancing with the rest.   In the days of Dr. Johnson and Goldsmith, it was customary for the literary wits and playwrights, to ridicule the "snivelling Methodists and Puritans"; but evolution has done away with all this. And now the "Salvation Army" with their flame-colored toggery, tambourines and braying trumpets are brought upon the mimic stage for the contempt and ridicule of the groundlings ; but this will not be so, if the "Salvationists" become rich and strong, with cushioned pews and gilt-edged prayer books.   Such is "evolution !" This view of the evolution of churches and creeds may be illustrated by the history of witchcraft.   It has been estimated by a well-known author that during a period of four hundred years down to the close of the Salem witchcraft atrocities in 1692, at least *nine millions* of human beings had been put to death for witchcraft in the different countries of Christendom.   At Salem, in Massachusetts, a large number were executed for witchcraft.   And many others under the preaching of the Reverend Cotton Mather were put to death for denying the reality of witchcraft.   A respectable minister of the gospel swore that he saw Moll Flanders enter a copse clad in old clothes, and that he saw her come out of the copse a ravenous wolf that proceeded at once to devour flocks of sheep.   This evidence was corroborated by a respectable farmer.   As a matter of course Moll Flanders was found guilty of witchcraft, and incontinently executed. Betty Coyne was accused of riding on a broomstick from Boston to New York, making the trip in a few moments.   The fact was proved by the incontestible evidence of three ministers of the. gospel, ten farmers, and six merchants, and the wretched old woman was bound hand and foot and was cast into the water and drowned. Old Giles Cory, seeing that conviction was certain, refused to plead and *was pressed to death*.

The people of New England have long since ceased to burn and hang witches and Quakers ; and no one would now think of holding the "advanced thinkers" of Boston or Salem responsible for what was done by their "pious ancestors," before the day of religious evolution had set in.

Are the Presbyterians of the present day, to be held responsible for the burning of Michael Servetus at the instigation of John Calvin?   Are the Protestants of this age to be held responsible for the extravagances of the Anabaptists, or the decision of Luther, Melancthon and Bucer, allowing the Landgrave of Hesse to go into polygamy?*   [See Spalding's History of the Reformation, and Boswell's Life of Johnson."]

Those fading and dissolving spectres of the past may no longer be invoked to excite prejudice against genuine Christianity; and fair play to the Mormons commends them for their efforts for reformation, instead of holding them as incorrigible anomalies, "dragons, gorgons and chimeras" outside of the pale of humanity.

It is germane to this topic to consider briefly the crimes and fanatical extravagances imputed to the Mormons.

---

*One of the most remarkable curiosities in literature is the document signed by Martin Luther, Philip Melancthon, Martin Bucer, Antony Corvin, Adam, John Leningue, Justus Wintfertes and Denis Melanther, leaders of the Reformation in Germany giving permission to their brother in the gospel, Philip, the Landgrave of Hesse to enter into a secret polygamous marriage with Margaret de Saal, the lawful wife of said Philip, Christiana by name, being still alive and undivorced. A full account of this transaction is given in Baylis' celebrated Dictionary. It is adverted to by Dr. Johnson as a well-known historical fact and is conceded to be authentic by Hallam in his Constitutional History of England. In Spaulding's History of the Reformation, Vol. I. pp. 147-149, and in Note C. at the end of the volume a full account of the whole proceedings and the contract of marriage are fully set forth *verbatim et literatim*.

Supposing these accounts to be true—and probably some are true—while others are exaggerated and some wholly false—the sojourner in Utah now sees nothing, and hears nothing of the kind.   He remains in Utah six or seven years, and still no destroying angels, Danites, or "blood atoners" are known to "materialize"; but instead, he finds the people as quiet, peaceable, orderly, industrious, honest and temperate as any people he has ever known.   Upon inquiry he finds that the same condition has existed for at least two decades.   The conclusion is, "these are not bad people; if reports are true of the past, there has been a wonderful change for the better.   But perhaps the generally-accepted accounts are not true, or true only in part."   Or perhaps the philosophical inquirer may find the true solution in an hypothesis like this: "that the crimes imputed to the Mormons at an early day were the result of that religious fanaticism or frenzy, which is near akin to insanity, and which has characterized many of the sects in the early or formative stage of their existence."   Besides, "Reformations" are often attended with very singular ethical notions, for example, John Balfour, and his Presbyterian associates who assassinated the Archbishop of St. Andrews, in Scotland, expressed the belief that "they were doing the will of the Lord who had delivered the prelate into their hands.

But times change, and men change with them.   The Mormons are not now what Gentile writers have represented them to have been thirty or forty years ago; and the atrocities imputed to them in former times will not again be repeated any more than the Presbyterians would now murder an Archbishop of the Established Church, or the Catholics would repeat the massacre of St. Bartholomew's day, or the people of New England

PRESIDENT JOHN TAYLOR.

would repeat the hanging and burning of witches and Quakers.

DEATH OF JOHN TAYLOR.

Among the notable events that occurred during our sojourn in Utah, was the death and funeral of John Taylor, the head of the Church, or, according to Mormon nomenclature : "Prophet, Seer and Revelator, and President of the Church of Jesus Christ of Latter-day Saints in all the world." He died on the 25th of July, 1887.

The funeral took place on the 29th of July, in the presence of a vast concourse of people, in the Tabernacle. The writer was present and viewed the remains. The body lay in a casket of Utah pine, stained in accordance with the wishes of the deceased. The handles and ornaments were of silver. On the plate was engraved :

PRESIDENT JOHN TAYLOR.

DIED JULY 25TH, 1887.

Aged 78 years, 8 months, and 24 days.

Upon a smaller plate, near the foot of the coffin, were the words :

HOLINESS TO THE LORD.

Rest in Peace.

A floral anchor at the foot and a plain bouquet were the only flowers on the coffin.

A great crowd had assembled from all parts of the Territory, and at 6:30 a.m. they began to pass through the Tabernacle. It was estimated that 18,000 people viewed the remains. At 12 o'clock the services began, the great organ pealing out "Angels ever bright and fair." The congregation was called to order by Angus

M. Cannon, "President of Salt Lake Stake of Zion," who read the following instructions that had been written by President Taylor:

SALT LAKE CITY,
NOVEMBER 13th, 1873.

President B. Young,

DEAR BROTHER:—Being asked to give a written account of the way I wish to be buried, I present the following.

I have no desire for any particular formula; but I should wish my body to be washed clean; to be clothed in clean white linen garments and robes, with shoes, apron, cap, etc.; to be laid in a coffin sufficiently large to contain my body without pressure.

Should I die here, let me be buried in my own lot in the graveyard. Let the coffin be neat and comely, but plain and strong; made of cedar or redwood, or of our own mountain pine; if of the latter, colored or stained, and placed in an outer strong box, with a light cotton or woolen mattress or bed, and a convenient pillow for the head.

The services, such as prevail at the time among the Saints. A plain slab may be placed over the body, and a stone at the head and feet; on the headstone to be given an account of my name, age and birth, as shall suit the feelings of my family.

Should I die in Jackson County, Mo., let the above directions be carried out, as far as practicable.

Respectfully, your brother,
JOHN TAYLOR.

The funeral exercises were similar to those of other religious congregations. There were prayer, hymns and several sermons or funeral discourses. The singing by the choir of over one hundred voices, was accompanied by the great organ and an orchestra of instrumental music.

CASTLE GATE.

RAINBOW FALLS.

From the discourses delivered on this occasion I select those of Apostles Snow and Richards, and this will answer, in some measure the queries propounded to the writer of these Sketches. "What do the Mormons believe?"—"What is their style of preaching?" "Have they any men of ability among them?" etc.

Audi alteram partem is a good maxim; and it is but fair to allow the exponents of a religious creed to speak for themselves.

APOSTLE LORENZO SNOW.

A passage of Scripture has occurred to my mind that, I think, is quite appropriate and applicable on the present occasion, which I will read. It will be found in the Second Epistle of Paul to Timothy, the last chapter, the 6th and 7th verses:

For I am now ready to be offered, and the time of my departure is at hand.

I have fought a good fight, I have finished my course, I have kept the faith.

I desire, while I occupy a few moments, to have the undivided attention of this vast assembly, also the benefit of your prayers, that such things may be offered as shall be suitable to the occasion.

Paul, whose remarks I have read in your hearing, was an Apostle of the Lord, our Savior. The individual whose remains now lie before us was an Apostle of the Lord and Savior Jesus Christ, the Son of the living God. And as Paul made this statement in regard to himself, so also could be made a statement similar by President Taylor, whose remains lie before us this afternoon.

Paul, during his life, struggled and contended for the faith which was once delivered to the Saints—those principles which pertain to the life and salvation of the human family; and he was willing to make any sacrifice and go through every scene of difficulty and trouble, in order to accomplish this object, that his testimony in regard to the Son of God and those principles that he had espoused might be carried forth to the nations of the earth—to the whole human family. He suffered imprisonments; he suffered the lash of his persecutors; he suffered every indignity, and finally died a martyr to those principles that he so laboriously and so effectually carried forth among the human family.

So also, we can say of President Taylor. Those principles that had been made known to him by the revelations of the Son of God as being of a divine nature—principles that pertained to the interests and salvation and exaltation of the human family—he carried forth to the various nations of the earth; and he heeded not the difficulties that ensued or that were in his path of progress. He has shown to the world, he has shown to the Latter-day Saints, he has shown to angels and to the Lord our God, his willingness, his determination, his resolution to do all in his power to carry out and accomplish the work of the Most High God. This he has done, and there lie his remains. He has left this world of sorrow, of trials, of afflictions of every nature that the Saints have to endure. He has gone to a better world. And it may be said of him truthfully, as was announced to John, the Revelator, when upon the Isle of Patmos, who was commanded to write what he heard by a voice from the eternal worlds:

Blessed are the dead which die in the Lord from henceforth. Yea, saith the spirit, that they may rest from their labors; and their works do follow them.

In a few verses before those that contain this vision it says, an angel was seen passing swiftly through the midst of eternity, coming down to earth, bearing the Gospel of the Son of God, to be declared unto every nation, kindred, and tongue, and people. This message our dear beloved brother has sought, during a part of his life covering a period of over fifty years, to carry forth to the nations of the earth. And during this period it is well known to the Latter-day Saints, whose history is before them, the sufferings, the trials, the afflic-tions, and the blood that he spent in announcing and carrying forward these principles of life and salvation to the world of mankind. He truly fought a good fight. He has finished his course; "and henceforth," his spirit could well proclaim, if he were here before us, "there is laid up for me a crown of righteousness, which the Lord, the righteous judge, shall give me at that day; and not to me only, but unto all them also that love his appear-ing."

Of course we feel the affliction; we feel the sad stroke. The Latter-day Saints feel that we have lost a friend; that we have lost a mighty counselor; that we have lost one of the greatest men that have stood upon the earth since the days of the Son of God—a man whose virtue, whose integrity, whose resolution to pur-sue the path of righteousness is known, and well known, and is profoundly understood and comprehended deeply. Now, we could apply this passage of Scripture to many others who have gone before: they have fought the good fight and kept the faith to the end; they have finished their course, and they now sleep in peace in the spirit world, and the influences of their grand doings and great accomplishments in the path of righteousness extend over the land of Zion. The Latter-day Saints feel those beautiful and glorious influences. Our hearts are made glad to coutemplate their virtues, their fidelity, their faithfulness, their glorious integrity.

This our beloved brother has not only been a father and friend to his wives and to his children and his numer-ous family; he has been a faithful friend to the world of mankind, which at some future period, though it may not be for a thousand years to come, they will distinctly under-stand. He has stood firm to those principles that are a light to the world, that are a light to the human family.

And did the world understand President Taylor and his motives during the last fifty years of his pilgrimage among the children of men, they would feel differently towards him than they now do. Those who put themselves in the attitude of enemies towards the Latter-day Saints and the servants of God, do so because they don't comprehend us; they don't understand our hearts, and don't understand our willingness to sacrifice in order to lay a plan or to carry out measures by which salvation may come to them also. We dedicate our lives which we hold as not dear to us, in order that the world may understand that there is a God in the eternal worlds; in order that they may understand that God has something to do at the present time with the affairs of the children of men. The world is passing into feelings and opinions of infidelity. Even among the Christian portions of the human family, thousands and tens of thousands, though they are not willing to confess it because of being unpopular, do not believe that God has anything to do with the children of men. We have to stand forth and make sacrifices in order that that belief and knowledge may come to the children of men. That is the case with our beloved brother, President Taylor. He has shown himself willing to make sacrifices before he would deny or turn his back upon those principles that, when people understand them, lead them to the path of knowledge, of salvation, and of immortality.

Well, it is so ordered that one man's death, or the death of a dozen, though they stand in high positions in the Church, do not stop this work. The Latter-day Saints have advanced to that wisdom, and that intelligence, and that understanding that this does not materially affect their interest. The Kingdom of God moves forward. It is not dependent upon one man or half a dozen men. It was thought by some in the days of Joseph that this Church could not prosper except Joseph guided its destinies, and when the time came when he was to pass away from this world as a martyr into the spirit world, the Saints throughout the Kingdom of God were greatly agitated. It was something unexpected. They hardly knew how things would then move. The responsibility then devolved upon the Quorum of the Twelve Apostles; and through the blessings of God upon them and the spirit of inspiration that dwelt in their bosoms, and under the guidance of the Almighty, the Kingdom moved forward. And so in regard to the time when our beloved brother Brigham Young was called from this state into the spirit life. He passed away almost unexpectedly. The Saints were hardly prepared for it. And yet the Kingdom of God moved forward. The duties of guidance were still upon the Quorum of the Twelve Apostles.

The Lord has now seen proper to call our beloved brother, President Taylor, away from these scenes of suffering, these scenes of martyrdom ; and the Church still moves forward. Notwithstanding the duties and the obligations devolve again upon the Quorum of the Twelve Apostles for the third time, through the blessing of the Almighty and the spirit of inspiration that will be upon them, as always has been, the Church will move forward. We are gaining that experience that each man and each woman knows what his or her duty is ; and they know the foundation upon which this Kingdom and Church is founded. They know the foundation upon which each individual is established ; and they know that God reigns over the children of men and over the affairs of the Latter-day Saints. They feel now, perhaps, different from what they generally feel when circumstances of this kind occur. They feel more calm, more assurance in the providences of the Almighty.

And so in regard to the beloved family of President Taylor. Of course, they cannot help but feel—and it is well that they do feel—that they have lost a parent, a father, a guide, to direct and to counsel. But still there is nothing in the way of their progress, any more than there is in the way of the progress of the Kingdom of God. They can move forward, and it is their duty to move forward in order that the word of the angel may be fulfilled, which said :

Blessed are the dead which die in the Lord from henceforth ; yea, saith the Spirit, that they may rest from their labors and their works do follow them.

And this family of President Taylor's, if they prepare themselves, can go onward notwithstanding they have lost their head.   The road is still clear.

They still have the counsels of the Holy Spirit, to which they are entitled, for guidance and direction, and they can move forward in the path of wisdom and knowledge, and in all those beautiful qualifications that make a Latter-day Saint ; and they can prepare themselves, so that the words of the angel may be fulfilled. Elder Taylor's works follow him.   His labors, so far as his family are concerned, follow him.

Well,. I have occupied sufficient time.   There are a number here that we wish to speak.   I ask God in His mercy to bless the family of President Taylor, that the Holy Spirit of Life may be upon them, and that they may have consolation in their hearts.   Their parent is now dwelling in glory, having a crown of righteousness upon his head ; and he will be there to welcome them as they pass off one after another from this into the next world and to take them by the hand.   God bless the family of President Taylor.   God bless the Latter-day Saints.   God bless the Quorum of the Twelve Apostles, on whom rests the responsibility of moving forward the interests of the Kingdom of God.   God bless all the authorities of the Latter-day Saints, and bless the honest in all the world of mankind, is my prayer in the name of Jesus.   Amen.

APOSTLE FRANKLIN D. RICHARDS.

Beloved fellow-mourners : On occasions of this kind, when the great men whom God has raised up for our guidance, are released from their labors in this low estate and called to another of a higher and more glorious character, it appears to me suitable that we should spend a little time and dwell upon their virtues, their excellent examples, and those high dignified traits of character which they have shown forth unto us as the exemplars of that which is right and proper before all good people, and which is most acceptable to God and the angels of heaven.

We are called to part with one of God's noblemen —a brother, a father, a husband and a true friend to all that is excellent and praiseworthy among mankind. Many of the points of his character and of the transactions of this great and good man, have already been noticed in the prints, and it is to be hoped that a correct, competent and creditable biography of his life may be given to the Saints and to the world, that his true character as a man of God may be known as a standing and abiding testimong to the whole human family. I, therefore, cannot, neither can any of us today—enter largely into a consideration even of the most important features of the busy and very profitable life which he has spent. But I wish to notice two or three of the prominent points or traits of his character which, as a fellow-laborer in the Gospel, I have come personally to know.

President Taylor was a man that could not get down to grovel with the low-lived, the vicious, the ribald, nor any who indulged in the follies and vanities of mortal life. When the Gospel first found him, he was aspiring from the measure of grace that existed among the most devout religious worshipers, and hungering and thirsting for something nobler and better, and the testimony of the glorious truths again revealed came to his ears by the Elders of the Church and soon by the blessed testimony of the Prophet Joseph.

Brother Parley P. Pratt had the distinguished honor to sound the Gospel of Jesus Christ in his ears. He was the instrument to lead him into the Church of Christ. Brother Pratt found in him that right heart and that open hand by which he was led to go right forward in the truth, and the new wine in the old vessel did not harm. President Taylor was a man bold and daring for the truth. He knew no fear. I recollect well when he and I were on our missions in Europe together. He labored in France—on the coast of infidel France—if I mistake not, in Havre. He labored in that vicinity diligently; and at one time a number of religious divines combined together to put down this heresy, as they termed it. President Taylor, with that boldness which ever characterized him consented to meet a whole pack of them, all that were willing to conspire together to silence and turn away the testimonies from reaching the hearts of the people. I recollect well my feelings when in Liverpool at the time. Morally speaking it was like Paul when he writes about fighting the beasts at Ephesus. He withstood them and he brought forth the truth and souls were given him as the result of his labors ; an interest was awakened, and some were gathered out. His labors were continued and incessant until he obtained a translation of the Book of Mormon in the French language. President Taylor was a man who, in his bearing and nature was onward and upward. Who that is before me ever heard him indulge in ribaldry or light and trifling and vain conversation? He was always looking forward from the moment he embraced the Gospel, for a higher platform upon which he could climb and rise until he could go back, a son of God, and associate, as he did here on the earth, with the Prophets of the Most High. There were but very few men that attained the warm personal relation that he attained to and maintained most successfully with the Prophet Joseph Smith till he died, and then the story of that personal affection was consummated by the bullets he received in Carthage jail with the Prophet when he was slain. President Taylor himself was disabled. In the scene that he then passed through he experienced all that pertains to martyrdom. He never suffered greater pain or more severe pain than he experienced in the jail with the Prophet Joseph. But it was not appointed for him to give up the ghost then. He had to wait another 40 years so that he might show forth his magnanimity, his priesthood and his fervor, and be a blessing to God's people in these valleys of the mountains. At another time when President Taylor was laboring in New York he went to work and with faith and the co-operation of such brethren as he could find, established a paper, and published it in New York

—one of the most successful enterprises of the kind that was ever undertaken in the last days. Some of the papers of New York undertook to run him out, thinking New York belonged to them. They dared President Taylor to an investigation. He proposed to meet as many of them as pleased to attend ; but he met them with so magnanimous a heart and so full a hand, that they declined the opportunity to meet him. I cite these instances of the high moral bravery that President Taylor possessed anywhere, everywhere and at all times in behalf of the truth while traveling and laboring in various countries. This has been his spirit and feeling. And while he has been of this magnanimous character, he has always entertained the most profound regard for legitimate authority. No man delighted more to receive and obey the counsel of those over him. This he did with the Prophet Joseph, although some of the counsels given him tested him and many of his brethren to the innermost soul and to the veritable life itself. President Taylor always delighted to serve the people. It was a notable trait in his character that he was not addicted to hankering after money. Many men could see a sovereign or a half eagle a long way farther off than he could. He sought for the riches of eternal life. Blessed be God he is rich in the possession of the knowledge he attained, and the skill and integrity which he exercised and the authority with which he was entrusted, until he has taken his departure and gone hence. President Taylor entertained the most profound regard for the superiority of the principles of the American government as embodied in the holy constitution and the just laws of the land. I recollect well when the news arrived of the passage of those laws which have lately engaged the attention of the people, how with what consideration he sat down and conversed with myself and others upon that subject, and how he carefully and prayerfully adjusted the affairs of his household in a way that, in the honesty of his heart and the magnanimity of his soul, he felt no man nor no government could take exceptions to.   He felt to place himself in conformity with the law. He would rather do that than that any issue should arise.   He therefore gladly bade family, kindred and friends adieu and went into retirement, went where under certain circumstances, he could still serve his brethren, still counsel them in the ways of life, still advise them as a man who was entrusted with the keys of eternal life to the human family, and this he did, blessed be God! until the day of his death.   And it will be pleasant to some who are present to know that President Taylor has not died of organic disease.   He has died from the legitimate consequences of confinement, of limitation from exercise, just as everybody else would do if they were limited and could not get exercise.   Their candle would go out for want of oil; the fires of their life would go out for want of fuel.   He has attained to the age of four score, and the Lord has permitted him to finish his days in this, and to a degree, happy manner, notwithstanding the unfavorable circumstances which surrounded him. When we recount the activity of his life, when we contemplate the dignity of his character and of his course, and how exceptional it has been, what an example it is for us!   Should we not be tending upward too, and continually so?   But President Taylor, by the blessing of God, was placed in a position where he was not only a father and protector to his family, but God made him a great benefactor to many of the human race.   There are numbers here to-day before me who have been brought from distant lands—lands where poverty and want looked them in the face, and they have been brought to this land where there is room for enterprise and industry, whereby multitudes of the poor have come to have homes and the comforts of life around them.   President Taylor has exercised this discretion and this authority with a liberality that was becoming a Saint of God, and there are few in the Church more intimately acquainted with these facts than myself, and I wish to testify of them.   A great man and a good man has fallen—fallen not from grace, not from any virtue or any adornment of mortal life, but his mortal body is laid down that his spirit may go hence. And while we are together in meeting we are in his presence though we may not discern it. God is bringing to light many wonderful developments of science, so much so that men are constructing eyes by which they can look at the distant planets and tell their surface and tell their distances, and comprehend those things that lie at very remote distances in space. And these things are made after the pattern of the human eye. Shall He who made the human eye not see? We are taught by the revelations that some men can see into the future. But God is able and He has power to see us continually. We are in His presence continually, and we ought never to forget it. He who has made the ear, shall he not hear? Behold! men are already learning to talk to each other at a distance of many hundred miles. If men can do this by the limited knowledge they possess, is it not true that greater things shall yet be revealed? Jesus said to marvel not at certain things ; for the day should come when all they that are in their graves shall hear His voice and live.

We lay our bodies down, but it is as true to science as it is to revealed religion that these bodies shall be brought forth by the power of that resurrection which was attained to by Jesus ; and though the wicked may scoff and the fool may say in his heart there is no God, the Saints know their foolishness. Now, then, my dear friends, my brethren and sisters—friends and relatives of President Taylor—I feel thankful that I have been favored with an acquaintance of so great and noble a household. There are few households indeed in. Israel or on the earth that are as honorable as that of President Taylor. My dear young brethren and sisters, endeavor, and ask God to help you to strive to emulate those glorious qualities of your dear father, who has gone before you, as he has written in the song. For President Taylor, be it known, was a writer, he was an author and a poet, and there are very few productions more exalted and ennobling and dignified than the one which he composed, and which he used to sing with great eclat :

> "The Seer, the Seer, Joseph the Seer,
> I love to dwell on his memory dear,
> The chosen of God and the friend of Man."

He who had all these qualifications as a man here on the earth among us, is a great exemplar to all Israel and a worthy instructor to my young brethren and sisters. I beg you to heed the counsels he has given, heed the testimonies he has left on record and strive to follow the same, so that bye and bye, when you return to clay, he will be ready to welcome you on Zion's shore. He has gone to prepare a place for you. Be not discouraged. Be not afflicted. We mourn President Taylor's absence. We will lose his counsel. We cannot well spare such men. We need such men in the Church to establish righteousness and preach the gospel, and build up Zion on the earth. You and I feel his loss. All Israel feels it. We are all mourners on this occasion. I feel to say then, that while we bid President Taylor adieu, let us send him congratulations. Oh what a joyful reception will be given him yonder, when he will strike hands with Joseph again, with Hyrum and Brigham, with Parley and Orson, and George A. and Willard, and all of the brethren of the Twelve! Why, there is nearly a quorum of the Twelve Apostles to establish and carry on the work which we here but begin. My dear brethren and sisters, may the spirit of the Gospel, the spirit of the Gods be with all those who seek to know and obey the Gospel of the Lord Jesus Christ, and to keep His commandments, and to walk in his statutes and ordinances continually. May the Lord help us to cultivate and to follow the examples of so great and glorious men. May we acquire their virtues and like them seek more abundantly to become Saints of God; seek to stand without rebuke in this untoward generation; seek to overcome all evil, that we may ultimately gain the reward of the faithful. This is my desire, my purpose and my labor with you all, in the name of Jesus Christ. Amen.

THE TWENTY-FOURTH OF JULY—PIONEER DAY.

This day being the anniversary of the arrival of the pioneer Mormons in Salt Lake Valley, has for many years, until recently, been celebrated throughout Utah with great pomp and ceremony, including street processions headed by brass bands, public addresses, religious exercises and amusements. Of late years these public demonstrations on a large scale have been suspended; still the day is observed in most parts of the Territory in a different way. On July 24th, 1888, I attended one of these celebrations at the Tabernacle in Salt Lake City. The exercises consisted in a number of addresses by the old pioneers and others. Music by the choir and organ, songs, recitations, etc. The most interesting part of the performance, was the singing by some five hundred Sunday School children in the auditorium of the great building. They sang in concert under the lead of a musical director on the stage. A great crowd of people were present, filling the auditorium and galleries.

Such demonstrations as this suggest to the thoughtful mind a theme for serious reflection. Here is a vast concourse of people (with similar ones all over the Territory) devoutly earnest in their religious faith, and for sixty years their children have been taught and trained the same as these five hundred Sunday School children. Not only in Sunday School, but in primary schools, "Mutual Improvement Associations," Ward meetings, Fast meetings, Conferences, Pioneer Celebrations, funerals, and Tabernacle meetings; the children are taught that the "Latter-day Saints" are the true Church to whom the "fullness of the everlasting Gospel" has been revealed.

Now arise the queries: "What *is* the Mormon Problem?" "What *is* the thing that is to be solved?" "Granted that the government may rightly punish polyg-amy, and that its practice must be abrogated, and there is no doubt that it is rapidly going into desuetude. But polygamy out of the way, what next? These are con-siderations that naturally arise. At present I only sug-gest them, and may make further observations on these topics in another place.

SILVER LAKE, AT BRIGHTON'S.

At the head of Big Cottonwood Canyon, thirty or thirty-five miles from Salt Lake City, there is some of the wildest and most picturesque scenery to be found anywhere in the West. The best way to get there, is to go by the Denver and Rio Grande railway and tram-way up Little Cottonwood Canyon to Alta, thence on horse-back over the "divide" to Brighton's at Silver Lake, three miles, they say, but it seems much further over the steep and almost impassible road. Arrived at the divide, the backbone between the two canyons, and look-ing down into the Big Cottonwood Canyon, the beauti-ful lakes at its head, and the high and rugged mountains shutting in valleys and lakes, while "peaks on peaks and Alps on Alps arise"—a panorama is presented to the enraptured vision that cannot be surpassed. The writ-er's first visit to Brighton's was about the middle of the month of July. Passing over the "divide," and begin-ning to descend, the Mormon boy who was my guide dis-mounted from his horse.

"Are you going to walk down?" I asked.

"No I am going to "cinch" the saddles "(*Anglice*, tighten the saddle girths.) Both saddles having been "cinched," we continued on the steep descent, standing in the stirrups and leaning back as far as possible.

"What's that ahead of us?"

"It is snow."

"How deep is it?"

"About twenty feet."

"How will we get over it?"

"It is packed down so we can ride over it."

So we rode over this and other banks of snow, and arrived at Brighton's at Silver Lake in about two hours' ride from Alta.   Brighton keeps a hotel there; and while it is not as stylish as some of the Caravansaras at Saratoga or Manitou Springs, there is always enough to eat, including fresh mountain trout from Silver Lake.   This valley is about 8,000 feet above the level of the sea. Nearly half the year it is covered with snow eight or ten feet deep, so that no one can live there.   But in the summer time it is covered with luxuriant grass and a wilderness of wild flowers.   In hot weather there are generally sixty or eighty persons here, chiefly from Salt Lake City.   Some at the hotel and others camping in tents or shanties among the groves of pine and aspen trees. Further up the canyon two and a half to three miles are the "Twin Lakes," "Mary's Lake" and others. "Mary's Lake" with its surroundings, its shores of granite, and the lofty mountains looking down upon it, is greatly admired, and has been painted by Bierstadt and other artists.

But neither the pen of the ready writer, nor pen of the skillful artist can do justice to this wonderful scenery. When you see it you are loth to go—and departing, you turn and look again and again, that "you may call it up when far away."

At Brighton's, even in July and August we have to

sit by a roaring fire of nights and mornings ; but when the sun gets up it is pleasant enough.

In the summer of 1887, the writer was sojourning again at Silver Lake with General McClernand and Chief Justice Zane. We were foolish enough to go on foot to Mary's Lake ; but we had the good fortune to have a charming young lady as our cicerone, Miss Godbe, of Salt Lake City. The alleged two-and-a-half miles appeared to us to be about five, but the young lady scaled the steep mountain acclivities, and bounded from rock to rock like a chamois of the Alps. She was more accustomed to it than we were, and besides she was only about twenty, and we were perhaps over—say fifty—or the rise. Arrived at the lake we parted company, the gallant Chief Justice and the young lady going one way, and the General and myself making a " circumbendibus " around the lake, over big rocks, fallen trees, and gushing streams. We finally succeeded in making the circuit, completely tired out. I doubt if the General, in any two hours of battle, ever had a more tiresome struggle. The Chief Justice did not fare much better, being on the side of the mountain, among ten thousand huge broken stones, he slipped and fell with his head down hill, and his foot fast in a crevice between the rocks ; but the young lady as quick as lightning rescued him from his perilous situation.

Coming down the defile of the mountains, we thought we saw a grizzly bear, but I guess we didn't. It was only a *bete noir* or optical illusion. And, sooth to speak, I am bound to confess, that in all my wanderings in the Wild West, I have never seen an (uncaptured) elk, grizzly, cinnamon or black bear, mountain lion, wild-cat, buffalo, panther, murderous Indian, blood atoner,

Danite or Avenging Angel. 'Tis distance that lends enchantment, as well as terror to the view.

Mr. Brighton, the proprietor of the hotel and grounds, is a Scotchman, and a Mormon. He has a rough exterior but a kind and hospitable disposition. He is no fool either, and like all the Scotch he is fairly educated. He was fond of repeating lines from Robert Burns, and it was a theme for curious reflection, that the winged seeds of the peasant poet's fame had been wafted over seas and plains and mountains and sown by the fair minds in these rugged solitudes of the Wild West!

While at Silver Lake, on another occasion, I met another Scotch Mormon. He appeared to be about fifty years of age, and was born in Ayrshire. He said he had never gone into polygamy and never expected to do so, but he defended the institution, and said he thought it was all right where all the parties were consenting.

I asked, "Doesn't this plurality of wives result in quarrels and troubles among the women?"

"Yes," said he, "sometimes, but a good and devout religious man can get along all right with many wives, or only one wife. But," said he, "don't you have quarrels, divorces, suicides, and uxoricides in the monogamic condition? How many a monogamic husband can appreciate the lines of Robert Burns":

> First when Maggie was my care,
> Heaven, I thought was in her air;
> Now we're married; spier na mair—
>   Whistle o'er the lave o't.
>
> Mag was meek, and Mag was mild;
> Bony Mag was Nature's child:
> Wiser men than me's beguiled:
>   Whistle o'er the lave o't.

> Wha I wish were maggot meat,
> Dished up in her winding-sheet,
> I could write, but Mag maun see't—
> Whistle o'er the lave o't.

Silver Lake is surrounded on all sides, except down the canyon, with high mountain walls and peaks. One of these to the eastward, I ascended, one day in August, in company with a young companion. We started on a couple of broncos with Mexican saddles tightly "cinched." The top of the mountain appeared to be about a mile away, but we found it to be at least three miles.

We wound our devious way along a log-road among forests of pine and aspen trees and little streamlets trickling through the melting snow. Zig-zagging to right and left, up, up, we went, until the ascent became so steep we had to dismount and lead the horses. We were aiming for a ridge or "hog-back" that connected with the peak we intended to ascend. With much difficulty we reached the ridge where we tied the horses to little trees; and then following the ridge with an easy ascent for four or five hundred yards we reached the steep and rugged acclivity. Here was hard climbing for an hour, over a chaos of broken rocks of all sizes and shapes. Now we come to a huge mass of high rocks that seem to bar all further progress. But " excelsior " is the word and we find a way around on the rugged stones crawling on hands and knees. So we go on till we come in full view of the rocky summit. So we thought. But on reaching it we find the real summit a thousand feet higher ! We reach it at last completely tired out. We sit down to rest on a big rock. We have no shade, but none is needed in the cool breeze ten

thousand feet above the sea.   Here in a crevice of a
rock I found some beautiful little flowers " wasting their
sweetness on the desert air."

One of these I gathered and sent to my little
daughter with the lines :

Ten thousand feet above the sea,
This little flower was plucked for thee.
Enduring as these granite hills,
 And pure as are these mountain rills,
O such is now my love for thee,
Ten thousand feet above the sea.

Here we had one of the grandest views that can
anywhere be seen.   To the east are to be seen, perhaps
fifteen miles away the lovely little town of Heber City,
with five or six other towns and villages in that beautiful
Provo Valley in Wasatch County.   To the north we see
the smoke of the great Ontario Mines at Park City, with
other works of the silver mining industry of that district,
seven or eight miles away.   We see many beautiful little
lakes nestled at the foot of the mountains, with hundreds
of little yellow mounds on the mountain sides—where
the adventurous prospectors have been at work.   To
the west we see Silver Lake with its surroundings of
pines and aspens and white granite cliffs.

Jefferson says, in his " Notes on Virginia," " that
the mountain scenery at Harper's Ferry is worth a trip
from Europe to see."   But if the sage of Monticello
could return and see the wonderful scenery at the head
of Big Cottonwod Canyon, he might well say that it
would repay a trip from " the Orient and the farthest
Ind."

"SEGREGATION"—THE UTAH JUDICIARY, ETC.

FIRST CLOWN.—But is this law ?
SECOND CLOWN.—Aye, marry, crowner's—guest—law.
—Hamlet.

The Mormons complain that many of the federal officers in Utah have treated them wrongfully and unjustly, and that the Courts in some instances have perverted law and justice in order to "cinch" them. Amongst others they particularly animadvert on the decision of the Federal Judges of the Supreme Court of Utah, in 1885 in what is known as the "Segregation Doctrine." A few words will suffice to explain this extraordinary judicial ruling :

The law of Congress provides that any one who shall unlawfully cohabit with two or more women shall be fined not more than $300 ; and imprisoned not exceeding six months. But the Utah judges decided that when a man had been living in unlawful cohabitation continuously with two or more women as his wives, say for twelve months, the time might be divided up into successive periods, and a number of indictments might be found, and the defendant might lawfully be convicted on each one for the full punishment provided by law, and that the terms of imprisonment and the fines were cumulative.

That is to say, in legal effect, if a man were indicted for cohabiting with more than one woman for three years, (the period of limitation), he might be indicted and punished for each day, that is one thousand and ninety-five times for one offense ; and might lawfully be fined $328,500 and imprisoned in the penitentiary five hundred and forty-seven years and six months. The Mormons bitterly complained of these rulings ; but their complaints were unheard and unheeded, until the Supreme Court of the United States came to their relief, and decided unanimously that the decision of the Supreme Court of Utah was erroneous.

The court says, that "it (unlawful cohabitation) is inherently a continuous offense, having duration, and not an offence consisting of an isolated act. * * The division of the two years and eleven months is wholly arbitrary. On the same principle, there might have been an indictment covering each of the thirty-five months, with imprisonment for seventeen years and a half, and fines amounting to $10,500, or even an indictment covering every week, with imprisonment for seventy-four years, and fines amounting to $44,400 ; and so on, *ad infinitum*, for smaller periods of time. * * No case is cited where what has been done in the present case has been held to be lawful. But the uniform current of authority is to the contrary both in England and the United States."—*In re* Snow, 120 U. S. Supreme Court Reports, p. 275.

Meantime, for nearly two years prior to this decision of the Supreme Court of the United States, many indictments were found under this "segregation" doctrine ; in consequence of which a large number of Mormons "took to the underground," as it was termed ; that is to say, they fled from the Territory, or concealed themselves rather than to take the chances of going to the penitentiary during their natural lives. Some of the defendants escaped the extreme penalty by promising to obey the law as interpreted by the Court; while others declined to make such promise on the ground that they would prefer to submit to the full measure of punishment "rather than to openly repudiate those wives (with their children) with whom they had entered into covenants many years before."

Another extraordinary decision was made in the First District Court of Utah, in 1888, in the case of Hans Neilson, *Habeas Corpus.*

The substance and legal effect in this decision, as appears by the petition and demurrer admitting the facts to be true as alleged, was, that where a man has been living continuously in unlawful cohabitation with two women as his wives, for a given length of time, (say from Oct. 15th, 1885, up to the time of the finding of the indictment on September 27th, 1888,) the District Attorney and the Grand Jury might bring in two indictments, one for unlawful cohabitation, and another for adultery, or, for that matter an unlimited number of indictments for the latter offense. The ingenious device for thus multiplying punishments, was, for the District Attorney to select an arbitrary date, the 13th of May, 1888, as the alleged termination of the unlawful cohabitation, although it was a fact as shown by the proof that it continued up to the finding of the indictment; and then at the same time to have the Grand Jury bring in another indictment for adultery, alleged to have been committed the 14th of May, that is the next day.

The effect of this decision, if correct, would be that when a man had been living in unlawful cohabitation for three years before the finding of the indictment, he might at the same time be charged and convicted for cohabitation for the first year, and a number of times for adultery committed with the same plural wife during the last two years.

This *pious* fraud, was however effectually punctured by the Supreme Court of the United States, in May, 1889, deciding that the decision of the Court in Utah, was a violation of the principles of the Constitution providing that no one shall be punished twice for the same offense.

The decisions above referred to, were made by judges that are gentlemen of good character and standing. How do they come to make such decisions?

But Utah has often been cursed by other judges of quite a different character, whose examples were not well calculated to reform the polygamous Saints. Among them was Judge Drummond, who years ago administered justice in Utah, and lectured the polygamists, while a prostitute, whom he falsely claimed as his wife, sat by his side on the bench.

The miserable death of this judge in a low saloon is recorded in the Chicago Inter-Ocean of November 21st, 1888.

Before closing these "sketches," I wish deliberately to record my conviction that the Mormons have been worse misrepresented and lied about than any people I have ever known.

Lies about them have been made out of whole cloth; venial faults and weaknesses have been magnified into gross and monstrous offences, and innocent or indifferent actions have been misinterpreted. I have been an eye-witness to transactions, in which the Mormons were cruelly and outrageously abused for conduct that was just, right and honorable. I have read what purported to be Mormon sermons, that were purely fictitious ; one in particular, a very few years ago, a brutal, blood-thirsty, disloyal harrangue, alleged to have been delivered by " Bishop West at Juab," on a certain day, whereas in truth and in fact no such sermon had been delivered at any time or place, and it was acknowledged afterwards to be a pure and simple fabrication ; but not

until it had gone abroad as evidence of the disloyalty of
the Mormons. Every now and then lies are set afloat
that the Mormons are about to rise in armed insurrec-
tion|; when, in truth, I can say after nearly seven years
observation, that there is no community on the civilized
globe less liable than the Mormons to take up arms
against the government or its officers. Polygamy aside,
the Mormons have been more sinned against than sin-
ning.

MORMON POETRY.

In Part I of this volume a Mormon hymn, with an
exegesis is published ; also a fragment from a doggerel
folk-song said to have been formerly sung in the rural
districts. In justice to the Mormons it should be stated
that writers among them have produced some poetical
performances that are quite creditable. Among them
may be mentioned Mrs. Eliza R. Snow, who died in 1888,
in her 83d year. She had been with the Mormons from
an early day, and was regarded as a sort of poet laureate
among them. One or more volumes of her poems, hand-
somely printed and bound, have been published.

Bishop O. F. Whitney—more able and distinguished
as a prose writer and a preacher than a poet, has contributed some poetical effusions that are highly esteemed by
the Mormons. Below specimens of the writings of each
are given.

O MY FATHER THOU THAT DWELLEST.

By Eliza R. Snow

O my Father, thou that dwellest
  In the high and glorious place !
When shall I regain thy presence,
  And again behold thy face ?

In thy holy habitation,
    Did my spirit once reside?
In my first primeval childhood
    Was I nurtured near thy side?

For a wise and glorious purpose
    Thou hast placed me here on earth,
And withheld the recollection
    Of my former friends and birth;
Yet oft-times a secret something
    Whispered, You're a stranger here;
And I felt that I had wandered
    From a more exalted sphere.

I had learned to call thee Father,
    Through thy Spirit from on high;
But, until the Key of Knowledge
    Was restored, I knew not why.
In the heavens are parents single?
    No; the thought makes reason stare!
Truth is reason; truth eternal
    Tells me, I've a mother there.

When I leave this frail existence,
    When I lay this mortal by,
Father, mother, may I meet you
    In your royal court on high?
Then, at length, when I've completed
    All you sent me forth to do,
With your mutual approbation
    Let me come and dwell with you.

THE MOUNTAIN AND THE VALE.

By Bishop O. F. Whitney.

There's a mountain named Stern Justice,
    Tall and towering, gloomy, grand,
Frowning o'er a vale called Mercy,
    Loveliest in all the land.

Great and mighty is the mountain,
    But its snowy crags are cold,
And in vain the sunlight lingers
    On the summit proud and bold.

11

There is warmth within the valley,
    And I love to wander there
'Mid the fountains and the flowers,
    Breathing fragrance on the air.

Much I love the solemn mountain;
    It doth meet my sombre mood,
When, amid the muttering thunders,
    O'er my soul the storm-clouds brood.

But when tears, like rain have fallen
    From the fountain of my woe,
And my soul has lost its fierceness.
    Straight unto the vale I go;

Where the landscape, gently smiling,
    O'er my heart pours healing balm,
And as oil on troubled waters,
    Brings from out its storm a calm.

Yes, I love both vale and mountain,
    Ne'er from either would I part,
Each unto my life is needful,
    Both are dear unto my heart;

For the smiling vale doth soften
    All the rugged steep makes sad,
And from icy rocks meander
    Rills that make the valley glad.

CASTLE GATE—BLACK CANYON—MARSHALL'S PASS, GRAND CANYON OF THE ARKANSAS—ROYAL GORGE, MANITOU, ETC.

The rolling stream, the precipice's gloom,
The forest's growth and Gothic walls between,
The wild rocks shaped as they had turrets been
In mockery of man's heart;   *   *   *
All that expands the Spirit, yet appals,
Gather around these summits, as to show
How Earth may pierce to Heaven, yet leave vain man below.
           —*Childe Harold's Pilgrimage.*

In Part First of these sketches, some account is given of the picturesque canyons and other wonderful scenery in Utah. It is proposed now to introduce the reader to new features of the "Wonderlands of the Wild West," along the line of the great "Scenic Route," the Denver and Rio Grande Railway, between Ogden, Utah, and Denver, Colorado.

Leaving Ogden in the forenoon, we run in a southerly direction about 36 miles, skirting the Great Salt Lake, near its eastern shore, we reach Salt Lake City about 11 o'clock a. m. Still continuing south for fifteen or twenty miles we reach the Jordan River and follow up along its tortuous windings till we reach Utah Valley. We stop for dinner at Provo, a beautiful little city of five thousand inhabitants, built on a great fertile plain between bold and lofty mountains on the east, and Utah Lake on the west. In this lovely valley we pass by fields of wheat, oats, barley and potatoes in great abundance, and thousands of fat cattle and horses are feeding on the luxuriant grass. Five miles from Provo we pass through the pretty town of Springville, in the same valley. Leaving the town of Spanish Fork to our right, and running in a south-easterly direction we enter the mouth of the Spanish Fork Canyon, and follow it up for many miles in order to get over the Wasatch range of mountains. And now for five hundred miles running in an easterly direction we are in the mountains, for the most part a dreary and desolate region, with few inhabitants, and no cultivation except in a few spots at long intervals, but relieved of its monotony by some of the grandest scenery to be found anywhere in the world. The first object of great interest is " Castle Gate," at the lower end of Price River Canyon. This, so-called " Gate " is constituted of two large pillars of rock on each side of the railway, the one on the left (as you go east) being 500 feet high, and the one on the right 450 feet. These pillars are not exactly opposite to each other, but they so appear at a little distance, and therefore they have the appearance of a " gate."

The pillar on the left is very remarkable. It is perpendicular on the east and west sides as well as the thin edge projected to the south toward the railroad track. The train always stops here a few minutes for the passengers to take a look at the pillars of the "Castle Gate."

SOLITUDE.

"O, Solitude! where are the charms
That sages have seen in thy face?"
COWPER.

A few miles east of Green River, there is a railway station named "Solitude." There is no office there, no dwelling, no building of any sort, no cattle chute or corral, no telegraph station, no switch, no sidetrack, no Y; nothing but a painted board with the strange device:

And such a solitude! No tree, no shrub, no grass, no flower, no water, no soil, no beast or bird, no noise of any living thing; nothing but Solitude! The barren and undulating ground is colored and wrinkled like an elephant, and seamed and scarred with deep and crooked gullies. Those who are fond of solitude can find it here in perfection. It would have been a paradise to the her-

BLACK CANYON OF THE GUNNISON.

mits of the Thebaid, or the "Pillar Saints" of Asia Minor. But it is apprehended that most readers will agree with the writer: Give Diogenes his tub, St. Simon his pillar, the anchorite his cave, but commend me to the soliloquy of Alexander Selkirk:

> "O, Solitude! where are the charms,
>   That sages have seen in thy face?
> Better to dwell in the midst of alarms,
>   Than to reign in this horrible place!"

In the Rocky Mountain states and territories there are many vast expanses of barren and desolate tracts like this, having the appearance, to the unscientific eye, of an old and wornout portion of the earth—or an unfinished creation with the top-dressing left off. Such are the vast alkali plains of the "bad lands" and the "bitter creek" regions, amounting to millions of acres.   •

The "Black Canyon of the Gunnison" is the next object of interest. The head-waters of the Gunnison River, starting at the continental "divide" flowing westerly into the Gunnison, thence into Grand River, which with its confluence with Green River forms the "Colorado of the West," find their way into the Gulf of California and the Pacific Ocean.

On the eastern side of the divide (at Marshall Pass) are the head-waters of the streams that flow into the Arkansas River.

· Now to construct a railroad on a straight line across the Rocky Mountains, for a distance of five or six hundred miles would be a difficult, not to say, an impossible undertaking. Therefore the engineers follow up the streams on the west of the divide as far as they can, and when they can go no further in this way, they go over the divide in many a "winding boot," until they reach the other side and then they follow the little streams that finally find their way into the Arkansas River, and thence down this river into the plains of Colorado.

Following up the Gunnison River, to find a pass over the mountains we come to the renowned "Black Canyon." This is a very long canyon, I know not how long, whether fifteen, twenty or thirty miles. It is so deep, so grand, so silent, so dark, and we feel so like mere *homunculi*, that we take no note of time or space. In many places the walls of this canyon are two or three thousand feet high, and they are so precipitous and the gorge so narrow that for unknown ages the sun has never shone upon the fast-rushing river that flows between the dark-colored rocky walls.

There are many sharp curves in the railway following up the course of the crooked stream, and disclosing to the view numerous steep crags and awful side-gorges with silvery cascades dancing down the black rocks from a thousand feet above. Among a vast multitude of grotesque rocks on either side of the great chasm the most noted is "Currecanti Needle," a very high and sharply pinnacled crag, or rather mountain of rock. It is of red sand-stone and presents a very beautiful and graceful appearance. It has been compared to the Cleopatra Needle; but this does "Currecanti" injustice, the latter being of such huge proportions in comparison with the Egyptian obelisk.

About nine o'clock a. m., twenty-four hours out from Ogden, we began the ascent of the renowned "Marshall Pass."

Ever since we crossed Grand River in the western part of Colorado, we have been gradually ascending for over two hundred miles, following up the general course of the Gunnison River, and then up a small tributary called the Tomichi. We have now reached a

THE CURRECANTI NEEDLE.

point eight or ten miles west of the back-bone of the Rocky Mountains. We can follow up the streams no longer, and now we have to surmount those mountain heights many of whose peaks are capped with perpetual snow (August 6th). We cannot go in a straight line, for it would cross innumerable acclivities, gulches and gorges. The grade is becoming steeper, and an additional locomotive is put on. Slowly we move upward. the two stalwart little engines laboring, puffing and blowing, turning and winding to every point of the compass. The road is becoming more and more tortuous, and the grade is becoming steeper.

Governor Ramsey, of Minnesota, then Chairman of the Utah Commission, was my traveling companion on this trip.

"Do you think," said he, when we began the ascent, "that Marshall Pass is equal to the 'Horse-shoe Bend' on the Pennsylvania Road?"

"Wait and see," was the answer, "You will find that Marshall Pass will make fifty of such horse-shoes with plenty of material left over."

Up, up we go, winding now to the right, now to the left in a circle, now describing an attenuated ox-bow, now a series of double S's and sometimes something almost as crooked as an antique character &. Looking back from the rear end of the Pullman car, we see, far below several railroad tracks apparently of different roads running in many directions; and here close by us but 300 feet below, across a deep gorge is the track we passed over some time ago, and we have traveled at least a mile to gain three hundred feet in altitude, and not over three hundred feet in distance. These several tracks we see are the one road we have passed over.

Looking forward up the mountains, we see many snow sheds and railroad tracks; while "peaks on peaks and Alps on Alps arise" before us.

"That snow-shed up there is the summit, isn't it?"

"No, we are not more than half way up."

"Good Lord, I give it up, the Pennsylvania Horse Shoe Bend is not a circumstance compared to Marshall Pass."

Finally the summit is reached.   The train stops ten minutes, to have the drivers and truck wheels and Westinghouse brakes examined.

The passengers get out and take a look at the scenery, from an elevation of 10,858 feet above the sea. Mt. Ouray is to our left, and the serrated and snowy range of the Sangro de Cristo Mountains are seen to the right.   Standing here on this continental "divide" the imagination naturally goes to the Gulf of Mexico at the Balize, and the Pacific Ocean at the Gulf of California toward one or the other of which the waters must flow from this spot.

The descent on the eastern side of the divide, is very similar to the ascent on the other side.

Following down the mountain streams that flow into the Arkansas, we reach that river at Salida where the train stops for dinner.   About the middle of the afternoon we reach the "Grand Canyon of the Arkansas." This canyon is not so long as the Black Canyon, but it is generally considered more attractive, especially that part of it called the "Royal Gorge."   This gorge is so narrow that in one place an iron bridge is suspended from iron rafters the feet of which rest on the sides of the cliffs on each side.

The general features of these Rocky Mountain canyons, are so much alike that a description of one like the Black Canyon, will in the main answer for all.

MARSHALL'S PASS.

THE ROYAL GORGE.

But it must not be supposed that the few objects which I have attempted to describe, are the only ones of interest in these canyons and elsewhere along this route. In addition to them, there are thousands of objects of curiosity in these awful chasms; grotesque rocks shaped like monsters of the world of fable, castles, battlements, buttresses, fortalices, huge walls that look like the masonry of Titans, grottoes and drawbridges. Here and there are lateral gorges, or canados, down which, for thousands of feet streams are dashing and cascading to join the main canyon stream below. No matter if the traveler, like the writer of these sketches, has passed through these canyons a dozen times, he will lay aside his newspaper or novel and take another long look. Time cannot abate one's delighted curiosity, nor "custom state the infinite variety" of these wonderful works of nature.

Our traveling companion, after we reached Canyon City and left this wonderful scenery of the Rockies behind us, enthusiastically declared that he had visited the most noted scenery in the Alps and elsewhere in Europe, and that there was nothing there so grand and picturesque as what he had seen on this route.

Just below the eastern end of the Grand Canyon, we find "Canyon City," the seat of the State Prison of Colorado. Here the valley of the Arkansas River widens out. We have left the Rocky Mountains to our rear, and looking easterly before us, lie the great plains stretching six or seven hundred miles to the Missouri River. Here were the great pasture lands, where years ago, hundreds of thousands of buffalo roamed and fed.

Running down the Arkansas River, we find a large number of oil wells between Canyon City and Pueblo.

From the last named city we run nearly north to Denver about 120 miles. About midway between these two cities are Colorado Springs and Manitou and Pike's Peak, a few miles to the west. A lateral railway five or six miles long runs out to Manitou, the "Saratoga of the West." It is a handsome little town with several large hotels and many boarding houses for those who visit the Springs for health or pleasure. The attractions about Manitou are Pike's Peak, the Ute Pass, Williams Canyon, the Cave of the Winds, the Rainbow Falls and the "Garden of the Gods," which is not a garden at all; but the soil is red and looks like disintegrated red sandstone. The "Garden" is filled with many curious rocks, and at its entrance there are two immense sandstone rocks of a deep red color. At Manitou and its vicinity the soil is all of this deep red color, and I suppose that is what gave the name of "Colorado" (red) to the Territory and State, this spot being well known long before Denver was located. In fact, at an early day, before there were any white settlers west of the Missouri River, Major Pike, of the United States army marched up the Arkansas River, on an exploring expedition with a detachment of soldiers. A hundred miles away he caught a glimpse of a snow capped peak, and he determined to go to it. Leaving the river and marching in a north-west direction, the party, after three or four days' travel, camped at Manitou at the foot of the great mountain which received its name from that of the leader of the expedition.

Manitou and the "Garden of the Gods" according to the guide books, like all mineral Springs, have a wonderful legendary and exceedingly apocryphal Indian history; but I will not trouble the reader with such hazy and doubtful narratives.

THE NEEDLE MOUNTAINS

THE MOUNTAIN RECLUSE.

Contributed by C. C. C.

The nooks and corners of these far western mountains furnish retreats for some queer characters. Here
are found a motley collection of unfortunates. There
are refugees from justice, and from all kinds of adversity
and sorrow—all social outcasts. They dwell in these
secluded spots and, like the poor souls on the banks of
Lethe, drink oblivion of their former lives, trusting
time to "raze out the written troubles of the brain"—
to "pluck from the memory its rooted sorrows."

A queer character I have in mind lives up in the
towering snow-topped mountains that environ Salt Lake
City on the east side. The deep chasm in which he lives
bears the name of Big Cottonwood Canyon. Its width is
only sufficient for the occupancy of its mountain torrent,
a stream which has its fountain-head at the summit of
the range, and fed by melting snows and innumerable
springs, goes tumbling, dashing and roaring down
through the canyon and empties into the Great Salt
Lake—the Dead sea of America. Now and then the
canyon widens and forms miniature valleys, lovely little
parks, with green grass and flowers in the summer time,
and all surrounded by towering and precipitous crags
and battlements. In such a spot, my eccentric individual,
poor soul, has lived for fourteen years, among the
flowers, the blue jays and chip-munks.

My friend came from Virginia fourteen years ago
and commenced boring into the hillside in search of gold,
and though he has taken none from his mine as yet, lives
in great hopes, confidently expecting each stroke of his
pick to reveal to him the hidden treasures of the earth.
He has been advised time and again that all of his labor

is likely to be in vain ; but with obstinate pertinacity clings to the belief that the " Dolly " will be the greatest mine in the world ! So he lives here in serene contentment, borne up by a faith in his mine, that is almost pathetic. Like many another miner, imbued with and upheld by that wonderful leavener of depressed spirits —hope—which alone, of all the contents of Pandora's jar, escaped not, but remained as a compensation for the escaped multitude of plagues for helpless man. If you ask this man what his vocation in life is, he will say he is a " rustler." He is the *Pooh-Bah* of the district, being postmaster, recorder of claims, registrar, notary public, justice of the peace and judge of election. He does his own cooking, and it is a comical sight to see him in his flannel shirt with his pants tucked in his boots, washing dishes. An absurd-looking cat is the recipient of most of his affection, though the blue-jays and chip-munks come in for a share of his attention, so tender that it would seem to be impelled by a belief in the doctrine of metemsychosis.

The only person ever known to invade his domain, and contest his proprietorship of the " flat " was (as told by the boys) a kind-faced old lady who appeared one morning in spring and essayed to keep boarders, thinking thereby to put money in her purse; but her attempt was abortive. Posterity will never know what happened between them, but the same morning " the old hen fled" precipitately down the mountain side, with Jimmy after her, and went cackling away into the dim, shadowy distance. He keeps her market basket as a trophy of the chase.

The advent and egress of this kind old lady, marks a new epoch in his chronology. From this occurrence he dates and ante-dates all the happenings of his life. A semi-weekly mail brings him a letter—in the summer-time by a carrier on horseback; in the winter, when the snow is piled many feet deep, by a carrier on snow shoes. The " boys " say that this letter is from his old mother, away down in old Virginia, and that he invaria-bly keeps this letter unopened until night time and then, when all is quiet, reads it by candle-light. For fourteen years the gray-haired mother has been writing to him to " come back," but he says " I aint going back till I get rich!"

No doubt the mother of this bundle of eccentricities has put away in the bureau drawer, a little pair of baby shoes, or some other trifle over which she cries, like any other mother, when she thinks of a long absent child. As for " Jimmy " he'd be afraid to " blubber;" some of the boys might be peeking in through the window at him.

Many occurrences incident to his quiet life serve to remind him of old Virginia. The wild roses that grow beside his cabin door

> " Are kinder pale and faded,
>   And there's not much style about 'em
> But they kinder set him thinkin
>   Of the ones that used to grow
> And climb in thro' the chinkin
>   Of the cabin, don't you know."

I happened in upon him, unawares, one day, and he was playing " I Wish I Was in Dixie" upon an old comb with paper stretched over it.

The first time I ever saw him he was seated on a beer keg in his kitchen, in shirt sleeves and bare feet, making some entry pertaining to the functions of justice of the peace, smeared with ink from head to feet, and had been wiping his red-ink pen in his curly blonde hair, so that he presented a horrible spectacle. His signature was embellished with many frills, furbelows and curly " Q's", the whole surrounded with red-ink quotation marks.

Notwithstanding the manifold duties that would seem to devolve upon him by virtue of his numerous offices, he seldom comes into contact with his fellow beings; but election day he celebrates with great pomp and splendor. On such occasions he is the only candidate in the field, and is duly elected to all the offices within the gift of his constituents. On election day the "boys" from the Maxfield mine troop into Jimmy's place and after they have elected him to all the offices they are entertained by him in royal style in witness whereof a big pile of beer kegs appears in front of his door the next morning. Thus the day is given up to merriment, and toward night the kitchen floor is strewn with many snoring forms.

As I was passing by his house one day I dismounted, tied my horse and went around to his kitchen, as usual, and found it full of miners. The " election " had just taken place, and now they were having a "rastling bee." The recipient of so many political honors being the only thoroughly sober man in the company, was selected as referee, and announced as he took his seat on the bench *i. e.*, his beer keg, that as justice of the peace it was his duty to see fair play. Said he (with a wise look) "Mickey, I swear you in as constable, plenipotentiary." Mickey evidently thought he understood. Perhaps he had a vague idea that it had something to do with the penitentiary. He seized a table-leg and entered upon the duties of his office at once in answer to a verbal warrant from his honor, who said : "I think Johnson is drunk enough to arrest." The unfortunate Johnson was therefore dragged out and locked up in the cellar.

What an incongruous assemblage! Imagine the sublime spectacle of justice, seated upon a beer keg, refereeing a wrestling match! When one of the boys, in the fullness of his heart (or his stomach), wished to attest his appreciation of Jimmy's entertainment, with a slap on the back and the exclamation that "Our able J. P. is the boss feller, you bet!" he resented the familiarity and threatened to arrest the offender for contempt of court.

Jimmy prides himself on being something of a philosopher, too. Perched upon his kitchen table, this mountain oracle has descanted to me, for a whole afternoon, upon political economy, ethics, psychology, and the Chinese question. In conversation he passed easily from one topic to another. " Now here are these durned anarchists," said he "raising h—ll in Chicago. Now, I ask you, what are we all coming to? I ask you this now: Has a Chinaman any right to be killed because he can live on ten cents a day?"

He continued in this strain : " I'm no fool. I never had much education. I just come by it naturally. I tell you, it's in a man. When I was a little kid my mother used to remark that I was bucket-headed. She always thought I'd make a genius—bless her old heart. Now, here's this tariff question"——

At this point he seized a rusty old gun and creeping to the window peeked cautiously out. After a moment he returned, put up his shooting iron, heaved a sigh of relief and whispered, "That was a narrow escape!" He told me that the man who had just passed by was his worst enemy, and had sworn to have his life at first sight of him. I knew that all of this was intended to impress me with an idea of his great prowess ; or else, becoming conscious of his danger in tackling the tariff question, thus sought a diversion.

To those who contemplate moving to "Argenta" to grow up with the country I will say that as yet she is only a poor little town, with one inhabitant, and he is in fact the mayor, common council, police force and fire department. I can't describe her "mild and equable climate," and her "splendid railroad facilities," because she has none. I can't even say that her citizens are "public spirited," there being only one ; but one of these days some miner will strike it rich in Argenta's vicinity, and she will have a "boom." She will have a hotel, a store, a blacksmith shop, a faro-bank, and if she be but patient she shall have an "Excelsior saloon" with deer horns over the door. Some quack will come along and open a doctor shop, and some broken down lawyer, who has been run out of Nevada by the vigilantes, will open a law office. I say open an office ; but more likely he will insert an advertisement in the *Daily Snorter*, informing the public that " William Blackstone, attorney at law, and notary public (formerly chief justice of Kentucky), can always be found at the Excelsior saloon."

Thus will Argenta boom, in the fashion peculiar to mining camps, when, some morning, the mines will "peter out." Then there will be a mighty exodus from Argenta. The once flourishing town will fade into insignificance and finally be blotted from the face of the earth as completely as if she had never been. And all this while Jimmy will be bucking in his tunnel.

Well, bound away, old boy. Likely you will pass in your checks before you strike gold ; but, then, no matter ; the boys will have a funeral worthy of their

CANYON OF RIO LAS ANIMAS.

great publicist—their able J. P. Maybe Burns would furnish some appropriate music, as on the occasion of the death and burial of "Sweet William" Smith, when, seated upon the top of a flour-barrel, Burns wafted Sweet William's soul out into the great unknown, upon the doleful strains of a wheezy old accordion. And then they will carry you and lay you "in your mother's lap." They will strew your grave with mineral specimens in lieu of flowers ; and it will be a nice place to sleep, after life's fitful fever, up there in the quiet canyon, among the flowers and blue-jays, until Gabriel blows his horn on resurrection morn, and shouts : "Get up, Jimmy! here's gold for you. Struck it rich at last, old bucket-head."

THE ARGONAUTS—THE NOVUS HOMO—ODD CHARACTERS IN THE WEST.

Among the Argonauts and their successors, many strange characters are to be found, who have drifted from California or the East, into all the mining camps of the Sierras and the Rocky Mountains. A volume could be filled with authentic anecdotes of the "newly rich."

There was Pat McC. a broad-shouldered, handsome, rollicking Irishman. He had "struck it rich," and was almost a millionaire, but his good fortune did not entirely make a fool of him. He still wore the slouched hat, the woolen shirt, and his pantaloons stuffed into the tops of his high boots. However, he indulged in one article that was an evidence of wealth and luxury, a splendid gold watch with a heavy chain to match. Now, Pat's early education had been somewhat neglected; in fact he could no more read the figures on his time-piece than he could decipher the hieroglyphics on his Chinese laundryman's bill. The boys in the camp knew of this, and took a delight in asking "Pat, what time a day is it?" But he soon "tumbled to that racket," and would hold his watch to the eyes of the anxious enquirer, saying: "Look for yourself; if I tell you, you'll think I'm lyin' to you."

Another man in a western city who kept a little grocery and supply store, furnished a prospector with a "grub stake," on shares. A rich mine was struck, and the grocery man became immensely rich, built the finest hotel and opera house in the Rocky Mountain region, and boasted that his night shirts cost him five hundred dollars each. He divorced his plain old wife, and married a fashionable woman. He won *golden* opinions from all sorts of men and became a United States Senator for thirty days! Thus verifying the Spanish proverb: "There is no lock, but a golden key will open it."

But these instances of sudden wealth, are exceptional. For every success, there are hundreds and thousands of failures.

Among the Argonauts of '49, mostly young men, "as gallant a host as ever trooped down the startled solitudes of an unpeopled land," there was many a bright eyed youth, upon whose face a razor had never come, who had left father and mother, brother and sister, and perhaps a dearer one, full of dreams of glory and honor, riches and renown, in the El Dorado of the West ; who can now be found wrinkled and gray, in some wild canyon solitude of Utah or Colorado, working as a common laborer at a "concentrator," or with pick and shovel in the tunnel. He has been beaten in the game of life, and he has thrown up his hand.

In one of my rambles in Southern Utah, at the miserable little mining town of Milford, in Beaver County, I met with one of these "Forty Niners." He had been brought up in Ohio, started to California at the age of twenty-one, had made two hundred and fifty thousand dollars, had lost it all, then drifted, as a prospector to Nevada, and then to Utah; and he was now keeping a little eating house. But he still retained something of the old grandios California style ; for, he charged fifty cents for a cup of black coffee, a fried egg and a piece of stale bread.

"Have you ever gone back to your old home in Muskingum County?" I asked.

, " Yes, once, after I had been gone for twenty years; but I didn't enjoy it much. It seemed lonesome-like. So many more dead and gone, and everything and everybody were so changed that I was almost sorry that I ever went back."

I questioned him no further. I imagined the rest. It was the old, old story of blighted hopes, of strangled affections; the flowers had turned to dust and ashes in his grasp, and the lovely mirage of his youth had been lifted from the arid and desolate desert of life. And then, I thought, perhaps it was better, after all, that, after twenty or thirty years of exile from the home of his childhood and youth, the wanderer should pursue his lonely journey to the end, among the mountains and valleys of the West. Better to cherish the sweet and tender memories of the Long Ago, than to break the spell of enchantment with the hard and cold realities of the present. Better to sit on a granite boulder or the mountain side, while the moaning winds are playing melancholy music among the lofty pines overhead, and dream of youth, and love, and beauty, than to go back, a pilgrim gray, with nothing to show but a blank in the lottery of life!

And O, such dreams as the old prospector may have! He wanders back to the village school. He remembers *one* with soft blue eyes and peach-blow cheeks, and feels again on his sun-browned cheek the delicate brush of her sunny hair. Is it not better, thus to cherish her memory as it has haunted him in all these years like some wild, sweet melody, than to see her now, a sad-faced matron with furrowed brow and sunken cheeks?

If the old miner returns to his old home, he will find everything changed, everything turned topsy turvy ; the hills do not look so high, the streams are not so wide, but worse than all the people are changed. The old men are dead, and the little boys have grown to stalwart manhood, "full of strange oaths and bearded like the pard." They look upon the old prospector with no more regard, than they would a grizzly bear or a coyote. The whirligig of time has produced many changes, not all, but many like these. The town-drunkard's son has been elected to Congress, and the preacher's boy has been sent to the penitentiary. The village belle has run off with a gambler, and the bound girl has married the banker.

The " aristocratic " family of the town, so considered because they lived in a two-story brick house, and the old man kept a store, exchanging dry goods and groceries for feathers, beeswax, and ginseng have " broke up " and moved off to " the Ioway."

The timid school-boy who broke down while reciting a speech "On the Evils of Intemperance " has become an inmate of an inebriate asylum !

How changed, too, was the old prospector ! The mother that bore him would not recognize her boy in the grizzly biped from the mountains. But no matter—she is dead. Long ago she folded her poor, thin hands upon her withered breast and passed away with the wanderer's name upon her dying lips: "Write to my boy Eddie to come home."

I will attempt to delineate one more unfortunate, among the many who have been stranded on the lee shore of adversity in the Far West.

Colonel S——— was a native of Massachusetts, but I am sorry to say that he had but little of that odor of sanctity that perfumes the memory of the *Mayflower* and Plymouth Rock. Why they called him "Colonel," I never knew, for I have never heard that at any time, in peace or war, he had "set a squadron in the field." But this goes for nothing ; for we find plenty of "Colonels," "Majors" and "Captains" who never smelt gunpowder, everywhere between the two oceans.

Our "Colonel" was something of a *litterateur* and scientist ; and would, no doubt, have made a good poet, his organs of invention and imagination were so largely developed. His hair-breadth escapes from grizzly bears, Indians and Danites, would raise your scalp-lock like porcupine quills.

But his chief peculiarity was in his facility for "workin up the briny." When he was drunk he could shed tears at will, and was then fond of quoting Scripture and talking of religion.

"On account of this wild way of life in the west," said he, "and reading Tom Paine and Bob Ingersoll, I would have become an infidel if it hadn't been for a lock of my Christian mother's hair which I always carry with me." Here he made profer of the precious locket while a big tear started down his rubicund cheek. But the boys from the "Blazing Star" district said that this "Christian mother racket," was an old fake of the Colonel's—and the locket was a gift from "Eureka Sall," the braid of hair having been deftly plaited from her lovely auburn tresses, brown in the shade and gold in the sun.

The lady designated by the aforesaid ungallant soubriquet was never called by any other name, and was well-known in all the mining camps thereabout. She belonged to that enterprising class, that, like the adventurous bee and the festive beer keg, are always found in the vanguard of civilization in the wild west.

"Eureka Sall," like many other good and worthy residents of Utah, had patriotically emigrated from the State of Nevada for her country's good. She was a fugitive from justice, or rather from the vigilantes.

Some said she had salted a mine; others declared that she had killed her husband ; but the gallant Colonel S———, who was "her friend," loyally insisted that she had only killed a d——d Chinaman, who ought to have been killed for insulting a respectable white woman ! "The Chinese must go," said he, "and the quicker the better, you bet !"

"As to salting the Blue Hoss mine in the Eureka district," said he, "Sall had no interest in the job, she only gave a helping hand to the boys to fix the mine so as to cinch them bloody Hinglish tenderfeet. Sall did her part jam up. She got a basketful of the best ore from the two hundred foot level of the Lucky Boy—that would run two thousand to the ton, and glued them onto the rocks in a stope of the Blue Hoss ; that was a good joke on them Frisco experts. They reported two millions in sight ! O, I tell you, Sall was a good one in them days !"

Now, it is not improbable that this glowing eulogy on the exploits of my lady was all a lie. But the Colonel meant no harm by it. On the contrary, according to his confused ideas of morality he thought he was paying her a high compliment.

The Colonel had an "affidavit face" and an innocent and child-like smile that would soften the heart of a police judge. He took a good look at the five Commissioners and sized them up. He selected his quarry with all the skill of a trained falcon—*which* one it boots me not to say—but he was so innocent-looking and guileless that he suspected no guile in others.

The Colonel's "main holt" was to work the anti-Mormon racket. Time and again he would descant on the wickedness of the Mormon leaders and bewail the condition of "the poor little sin-branded children" of Mormon parents. Here another big tear would start, crawl slowly down his cheek, and then halt for the observation of the sympathetic beholder. Then the gallant Colonel would express his great satisfaction with the wisdom of the government in selecting Commissioners of "talent, character and experience."

And so he would go on, from day to day, between drinks, occasionally interlarding his conversation with the technics of geology and mineralogy. But the "Mormons" were the chief source of his inspiration. He actually declared that he had seen more than a dozen hair ropes (or lassoes) that had been made of the hair of the women who were massacred at Mountain Meadows!

Sequel—The guileless Commissioner lost a small sum of money and a friend at the same moment. The lachrymos Colonel incontinently cut his acquaintance, and the Commissioner heard no more from him about "sin-branded children," Danites, or "hair ropes." At last accounts the Colonel was in jail, afflicted with a complication of charges for offenses against the peace and dignity of the United States, and the People of the Territory of Utah.

Poor devil! Let him have our sympathy and pity. Most likely he is not a bad man at heart, and under more auspicious stars and a kindlier smile of fortune, he would have been a respectable and honored member of society. *Quien Sabe?* Let us draw the mantle of charity over his faults and misfortunes as I have done over his name!

In closing this sketch I wish to enter my caveat against the conclusion that the pariahs and outcasts I have attempted to portray shall stand as representatives of the mining class in general. On the contrary I take pleasure in bearing my testimony to the high sense of honor, sterling business qualifications, and gentlemanly deportment of very many mining men in Utah and elsewhere in the West.

GENERAL CONFERENCE OF THE MORMONS—CEREMONIES IN SUSTAINING A NEW "PRESIDENT, PROPHET, SEER AND REVELATOR," ETC.

On Saturday, April 6, 1889, the Mormons held their fifty-ninth general annual conference at Salt Lake City. Several days before the day of meeting the people began to flock to the city, so that on Sunday, the second day of the conference, a vast throng from all parts of Utah and the adjacent territories had assembled.

In company with General McClernand I went in the afternoon to the Tabernacle, where the conference was held. But the great building was already full, and there was not even standing room, while many thousands were on the outside in the Temple Block and on the streets. Besides the residents of the city, there were probably

twenty thousand Mormons attending the conference from other parts of this Territory, Idaho and Arizona.

We passed some time in moving around among the vast crowd on the outside, in order to observe the manners, dress and appearance of the people. They were all respectably, and many were well dressed. Their deportment, without a single exception, was perfectly decorous, quiet and good-natured. Among them were three stalwart Indian Mormons, standing in a row on a bench.

The conference continued its session for three days. There were on the stand, of the Council of the Twelve Apostles: Wilford Woodruff, Lorenzo Snow, Franklin D. Richards, George Q. Cannon, Moses Thatcher, John Henry Smith, Heber J. Grant and John W. Taylor; of Counselors to the Twelve, Daniel H. Wells; Patriarch, John Smith; of the Presiding Council of the Seventies, Henry Harriman, Jacob Gates, Abraham H. Cannon, Seymour B. Young, John Morgan; of the Presiding Bishopric, William B. Preston, Robert T. Burton, John R. Winder. There were also present a large number of Presidents of Stakes.

The exercises consisted of singing, prayer, sermons, and business appertaining to Church organization. Sermons, or "discourses," as they are commonly called among the Mormons, were delivered by President Wilford Woodruff, the Apostle Heber J. Grant, Elder Charles W. Penrose, the Apostles Moses Thatcher, John W. Taylor, George Q. Cannon, Lorenzo Snow, Franklin D. Richards, Francis M. Lyman, John Henry Smith, and Bishop O. F. Whitney.

But the most interesting part of the proceedings was the installation of a new President, Wilford Woodruff—the order of succession from the beginning being Joseph Smith, Brigham Young, John Taylor, and Wilford Woodruff.

The Priesthood were arranged and seated in quorums according to the following order:

The members of the Council of the Twelve Apostles, and Counselors to the Twelve, in the two upper seats of the center of the stand.

On the south wing of the stand were the Patriarchs—the Patriarch of the Church in front—Presidents of Stakes, their Counselors, and High Councilors.

The High Priests in the north center of the body of the hall, the quorum presidents in front of them.

The Seventies in the south center and south division of the body of the house, the first seven presidents and members of quorum councils in front.

The Elders were located in the rear of the High Priests.

On the north wing of the stand were the Bishops and their Counselors, with the Presiding Bishopric in front.

On the extreme left of the body of the hall were the Lesser Priesthood—Priests, Teachers, and Deacons—with the quorum presidents in the front.

The general congregation were seated in those portions of the body of the building not occupied by the Priesthood, and in the gallery.

APOSTLE GEORGE Q. CANNON.

" The object in arranging the Priesthood as they are this afternoon in their several quorum capacities, is to form a general assembly of the Priesthood of the Church of Jesus Christ of Latter-day Saints; and in presenting the authorities of the Chnrch they will be presented to each quorum separately, for each quorum to vote by a rising vote and by lifting up their right hands.   If there be any who object to any name that is presented, they will have the privilege of making manifest their objections.   After one name is presented and it is carried by all the Priesthood, they will then sit down, and it will be submitted to the entire congregation, including the Priesthood, who will rise with the Saints in the galleries and elsewhere, to their feet, and vote as a congregation upon the names that shall be offered.

" The first quorum to vote will be the quorum of the Twelve Apostles.   Then the Presidents of Stakes, or rather the Patriarchs, the Presidents of Stakes and their Counselors, and the High Councils.   Then the High Priests will vote; then the Seventies, then the Elders, then the Bishops and their Counselors, and then the Lesser Priesthood, including the Priests, Teachers and Deacons, after which the body of Saints and Priesthood will be called separately to vote."

Apostle George Q. Cannon presented the general authorities, which were voted upon by the different divisions of the Priesthood, in the order given above, each division acting separately by rising and holding the right hand toward heaven.   After the vote of each quorum or division was obtained upon the name of each individual presented, the action by vote of the whole assembly was taken.

The following is the order in which the authorities were presented, the vote in each instance being unanimous.

Wilford Woodruff, as Prophet, Seer and Revelator and President of the Church of Jesus Christ of Latter-day Saints in all the world.

George Q. Cannon as First Counselor in the First Presidency.

Joseph F. Smith as Second Counselor in the First Presidency.

Lorenzo Snow as President of the Twelve Apostles.

As members of the Council of the Twelve Apostles—Lorenzo Snow, Franklin D. Richards, Brigham Young, Moses Thatcher, Francis M. Lyman, John H. Smith, George Teasdale, Heber J. Grant, and John W. Taylor.

Counselors to the Twelve Apostles—John W. Young and Daniel H. Wells.

After the above named were voted upon and unanimously sustained, for the positions mentioned, the voting was done by the general assembly only, and not by quorums on the following:

The Twelve Apostles with their Counselors, as Prophets, Seers and Revelators.

Patriarch to the Church, John Smith.

First Seven Presidents of the Seventies; Henry Harriman, Jacob Gates, Abraham H. Cannon, Seymour B. Young, C. D. Fjeldsted, John Morgan and B. H. Roberts.

Wm. B. Preston as Presiding Bishop, with Robert T. Burton as his First, and John R. Winder as his Second Counselors.

Franklin D. Richards as Church Historian and general Church Recorder.

From the official report of the proceedings of this Conference, as well as the accounts in the City newspapers. it appears that nothing was said on the subject of polygamy, either advocating or opposing it.   This is strongly in contrast with what might have been heard at similar convocations, some years ago, when polygamy was publicly approved and sometimes commanded. This affords additional evidence of the progress of "evolution" on which I have commented in another part of this work, and which is admitted by the leading anti-Mormon newspapers of Utah, in the conclusion of an article on the proceedings of the conference:—

"There are but two things that can crush what is illegal in such an institution as the Mormon system. One is force; one is light.   Our people and our country are so free that they recoil against using force.   The sentiment of the Nation is that the proper cure for Utah, while enforcing the laws, is to enlighten the people. That enlightenment is coming.   We cannot note it from day to day, but we can from year to year.   Things have changed within six years, yes, within four years: yes, later still."   *Tribune, April 10th, 1889.*

This is in accordance with the view of every fair and impartial observer; and the conviction is fast gaining ground, that the " Mormon Problem " is already substantially settled, or at all events, its obnoxious features put into the condition of ultimate extinction.

"THE MORMON PROBLEM."

What is the Mormon Problem? and what is its proper solution?

The avowed purpose of the Edmunds Act of 1882 was the suppression of polygamy.   This accomplished, the "Mormon question" is no more a "problem" so far as the government is concerned, than the Catholic Problem, or the Presbyterian Problem, or the Methodist Problem.   In matters of religious faith "error is to be tolerated when truth is free to combat it."

If you are a Christian man, you cannot wholly condemn the faith of the Mormons; for they believe all that you do, and a good deal besides. They believe in the Old and the New Testaments; in the Father, Son and Holy Ghost ; in baptism, repentance and atonement; in short, they are so far from being infidels or skeptics, that they believe in these doctrines with all that undoubting faith and devotion that are going out of fashion with many advanced thinkers and "progressive Christians." As to those "latter day" vagaries resulting from "continuous revelation," and an intense belief in the influence of the Holy Ghost, we may confute, deride and ridicule them;—but if the Mormons conduct themselves as good citizens and obey the laws, there is an end of the argument. It is a dangerous ground to assume that any people shall be punished for their religious errors or vagaries. Such an assumption would rekindle the fires of Smithfield and relegate us to the thumb-screws and red-hot pinchers of Torquemada, and the massacre of St. Bartholomew's day.

This is no new doctrine; for it has been sealed with the blood of martyrs, and crystalized in the constitution.

Religious *liberty*—not *toleration*—is the American doctrine. Toleration is a mere concession, that which is borne or graciously permitted by the sovereign authority— czar, emperor, king or republic. Toleration implies a religion established by law—a despotism over the consciences of mankind, whereby dissent is tolerated, limited and regulated.

But in the lexicon of American constitutional liberty the word *toleration* is unknown. It is a hateful word—a relic and a badge of the spiritual slavery of other ages and other nations. It is a word which implies authority in the civil government to prescribe a religious creed for the people and to enforce its decrees with pains and penalties. The world has had enough of this.

MEMBERS OF THE COMMISSION.

The present members of the Utah Commission

(April, 1889) are Gen. John A. McClernand, of Illinois, A. B. Carlton, of Indiana, George L. Godfrey of Iowa, A. B. Williams of Arkansas, and Arthur L. Thomas, now residing in Salt Lake City, formerly of Pennsylvania. William C. Hall, Territorial Secretary, is *ex-officio* Secretary of the Commission. Of the Commissioners originally appointed, only two remain, Messrs. Godfrey and Carlton. Gen. McClernand was appointed in the Spring of 1886, vice Alexander Ramsey resigned. Judge Williams was appointed in October, 1886, vice James R. Pettigrew, deceased, and Mr. Thomas was appointed in December, 1886, vice A. S. Paddock resigned.

[Since the foregoing was written, A. B. Carlton resigned the Chairmanship, and in April, 1889, Geo. L. Godfrey was elected in his stead. In May, 1889, Messrs. Thomas and Carlton resigned from the Commission, and Hon. Alvin Saunders of Nebraska, and Hon. Robert S. Robertson of Indiana were appointed by President Harrison, to fill the vacancies.]

RIDING A BRONCHO—BOOMING WITH A BRASS BAND.

"Cromwell, I charge thee, fling away ambition.
By that sin fell the angels."
Henry VIII.

Jefferson Davis Clark is the colored *valet de chambre* to his excellency, the Governor of Utah. He came into the government headquarters· the other morning, in a breathless state of excitement, to inform the boys that he had purchased a broncho. He pictured in such glowing colors the many fine points about his animal that we all resolved to go down and see him. Accordingly at 4 o'clock p. m. we made our way to the stable where he was kept. Jeff. promised that each of us should ride him; he said that he was as gentle as a lamb. He hadn't ridden him himself as yet, but then, you know, he hadn't had time.

The brute was finally led out to be saddled and bridled. It became noised about that somebody was going to ride a broncho. Hostlers and stable-boys appeared as if by magic, from stable-lofts and stalls. The crowd that gathered around the broncho attracted others and soon assumed gigantic proportions. Stable boys, jockeys, and men and boys of all sizes and colors assembled to see the fun. A group of Chinamen stood chattering in their heathenish gibberish, and a big buck Indian with three squaws and a whole army of papooses squatted themselves in a corner of the lot and waited expectantly. Even the girls from the city bakery came out.

Everybody had something to say about the broncho. Said one: "He looks kind enough out of the eyes."

"Oh, he is kind," said another.

In fact there were so many asseverations as to the brute's honesty, and kindly feeling for mankind in general, that I became suspicious, and was glad that Hall, of Kentucky was to ride first.

"Is that the feller that is going to ride him?" asked a big cow-boy of me.

"Yes," said I, "and he is a rider, too."

I told the crowd that Hall was raised among horses, —that he could ride anything on four legs.

I continued to extol my Kentucky friend's accomplished horsemanship and the crowd looked at him admiringly, while Hall tried to assume an air of nonchalance; but I saw him grow a little pale, as he overheard a big cow-boy say to another, "I feel sorry for the poor devil."

After the honest little broncho had kicked three boards from his stall, he was finally saddled and bridled and led out into the stable-yard.

"I don't much like the way he kicks," said Hall.

"Oh that's just a way he has. He's a little bit green yet."

The crowd insisted that Hall should take off his overcoat; but he kept it on, I think for the purpose of breaking the force of the fall.

Hall walked "with a firm step and a pale face" like a convict to the gallows.

The accomplished Kentucky horseman tried to mount from the wrong side. The honest little broncho was evidently unused to such proceedings, for he jumped over a stile and butted his head up against a brick wall.

Hall retired from the field, and whispered to me that I ought to try him. He argued that honor demanded that I should make an attempt. What would the crowd think of me if I declined? But I wisely resolved that discretion was the better part of valor, and like Falstaff, soliloquized: "Yes, honor sets me on. But how if it sets me off when I come on? How then? Honor has no skill in surgery."

Then there were loud cries for "Broncho Bill." Did anybody know where he was? But Bill had just stepped out to see a man.

There were a dozen professional broncho riders who would ride if it were not for this, that and the other. One wanted a snaffle bit and another a different saddle, etc., but finally Jeff himself was prevailed upon. Said the crowd to him: "You bet, now, if *we* had paid forty-five dollars for a horse, *we* would ride him." So Jeff after making repeated efforts to get into the saddle, finally succeeded, and had hardly got his feet into the stirrups, and was engaged in patting his broncho's neck and was mumbling, "Wo! horsy, nice little horsy!" when the honest little broncho arched his back and the son of Ham shot upward like a glass ball out of a trap, and fell to earth with a dull, sickening thud.   As he picked himself out of the mud, he said: "I will trade that horse for a city lot.   A man offered me one for him this morning."   At this, the crowd grew facetious. Said one fellow with fine irony; "Yes, I *would* trade him if I was you.   You might be able to *ride* a city lot."

Hall, of Kentucky was invited to make a second attempt, but with a grim smile declined, asking a stableman if he had a nice old white mare.   As for Adams, of Maryland, a nice gentle buggy was good enough for him.

Jeff, according to his announcement, traded the beast to a real estate man for a lot in "Forest Grove" sub-division.   It may be stated that the inducement which impelled him to dicker for a lot in this locality, appeared in the shape of a brass band which paraded the streets, in a wagon drawn by four milk-white horses, with banners advertising the unrivaled attractions of "Forest Grove" sub-division.   Jeff's eyes bulged nearly out of their sockets as he read the inscriptions on the banners:

"The Great Forest Grove sub-division; A Paradise on earth!"

"An abundance of water!"

"The garden spot of the world!"

Jeff followed the band around a whole morning, waiting to get to see the business manager of the company, that he might be able to secure a city lot before they were all gone.

A few days ago I took a drive out to Forest Grove, in company with Jeff and his attorney, Clarence W. Hall. We found, much to our dismay, that Jeff's lot, and in fact the whole of "Forest Grove" sub-division was under the Hot Springs lake!

Jeff's countenance fell. Said I: "Jeff, that fellow was right, when he said you might be able to ride a city lot. There's a boat for you!"

Jeff stood looking at the expanse of water. Suddenly he broke out with: "Cap, that bannah tole the truth."

"Why, how is that Jeff?"

"It said that Forest Grove sub-division was well watered."

THANKSGIVING PROCLAMATION BY BRIGHAM YOUNG.

A curious and characteristic proclamation by Brigham Young in 1851, when he was civil Governor of Utah as well as the head of the Church, was found by the writer of these sketches, in one of the executive record books in a beautiful hand writing:—

TERRITORY OF UTAH.

Proclamation for a Day of Praise and Thanksgiving:

It having pleased the Father of all good to make known His mind and will to the children of men, in these last days, and through the ministration of His angels, to restore the Holy Priesthood unto the sons of Adam, by which the gospel of His Son, has been proclaimed and the ordinances of life and salvation are administered, and through which medium the Holy Ghost has been communicated to believing, willing and honest minds, causing faith, wisdom and intelligence to spring up in the hearts of men, and influencing them to flow together from the four quarters of the earth to a land of peace and health; rich in mineral and vegetable resources; reserved of old in the councils of eternity for the purposes to which it is now appropriated; a land choice above all other lands; far removed from the strife, contention, divisions, moral and physical commotions, that are disturbing the peace of the nations and kingdoms of the earth.

I, Brigham Young, Governor of the Territory aforesaid, in response to the time-honored custom of our fathers of Plymouth Rock, by the Governors of the several States and Territories, and with a heart filled with humiliation and gratitude to the Fountain of all good, for His multiplied munificence to His children, have felt desirous to, and do proclaim Thursday, the first day of January, eighteen hundred and fifty-two, *a day of praise and thanksgiving*, for the citizens of this, our peaceful Territory; in honor of the God of Abraham, who has preserved His children amid all the vicissitudes they have been called to pass; for His tender mercies in preserving the Nation undivided, in which we live; for causing the gospel of His Kingdom to spread and take root upon the earth, beyond the power of men and demons to destroy; and that He has promised a day of universal joy and rejoicing to all the inhabitants who shall remain when the earth shall have been purified by fire, and rest in peace.

And I recommend to all the good citizens of Utah, that they abstain from everything that is calculated to mar or grieve the Spirit of their Heavenly Father on that day; they rise early in the morning of the first day of the New Year and wash their bodies with pure water; that all men attend to their flocks and herds with carefulness; and see that no creature in their charge is hungry, thirsty or cold; while the women are preparing the best of food for their household, and their children ready to receive it in cleanliness; then let the head of each family with his family, bow down upon his knees before the God of Israel, and acknowledging all his sins, and the sins of the household, call upon the Father in the name of Jesus for every blessing that he desireth for himself, his kindred, the Israel of God, the universe of man; praying with full purpose of heart and united faith that the union of the United States may be preserved inviolate against all the devices of wicked men until truth shall reign triumphant, and the glory of Jehovah shall fill the earth; then in the name of Jesus, ask the Father to bless your food; and when you have filled the plates of your household, partake with them, with rejoicing and thanksgiving; and if you feel to make merry in your hearts, sing a song of thanksgiving, and lift up your hearts continually in praise and acknowledgment of the unbounded mercies you are momentarily receiving. I also request of all good and peaceful citizens, that they abstain from all evil thinking, speaking, and acting on that day; that no one be offended by his neighbor; that all jars and discord cease; that neighborhood broils may be unknown; that tattlers and strife may not be remembered; that evil surmising may be forgotten; that all may learn the truth and have no need of priests to teach them; that all may be well, and have no need of doctors; that all may cease their quarrels and starve the lawyers; that all may do as they would be done unto, so that perfect love which casteth out all fear may reign triumphant, and there shall be nothing to disturb the quiet of an infant in all the Territory of Utah; that there be no contention in the land; and that the same peace may extend its influence to the utmost bounds of the everlasting hills, and from thence to the habitation of every man and beast, to the end of the earth, till the leopard shall lie down with the kid, the lion shall eat straw like the ox, and the babe shall lay its hand upon the cockatrice's den, and find peace to its soul. I further request, that when the day has been spent in doing good; in dealing your bread, your butter, your beef, your pork, your turkeys, your molasses, and the choicest of all the products of the valleys of the mountains at your command, to the poor; that you end the day in the same order and on the same principle that you commenced it; that you eat your supper with singleness of heart, as unto the Lord, after praise and thanksgiving, and songs of rejoicing, remembering that you cannot be filled with the Holy Spirit, and be preparing for celestial glory, while the meanest menial under your charge or control, is in want of the smallest thing which God has given you power to supply, remembering that that menial is dependent on you for its comforts, as you are dependent on your God for your constant support. Retire to your beds *early*, that you may be *refreshed*, and arise early again and so continue until times and seasons are changed; or finally, I say unto you, let the same process be continued from day to day, until you arrive unto one of the days of Kolob (whose day is one thousand of our years) the planet nearest unto the habitation of the Eterna Father; and if you do not find peace and rest to your souls by that time, in the practice of these things, and no one else shall then present himself to offer you better counsel, I will be there, and knowing more, will tell you what you ought to do next.

Done at the Executive Office, Great Salt Lake City; in witness whereof I have hereunto set my hand, and caused the seal of the Territory to be affixed, this nineteenth day of December, A. D. one thousand eight hundred and fifty-one, and of the Independence of the United States the seventy-sixth.

{ SEAL }

BRIGHAM YOUNG.

By the Governor:

W. RICHARDS, Sec. pro tem., appointed by the Governor.

THE YOSEMITE—"THE BIG TREES"—THE YELLOWSTONE NATIONAL PARK.

Next to the Grand Canyon of the Colorado of the West, the scenery of the Yosemite in California is probably the most picturesque, to be found in North America. It is situated in the Sierra Nevada mountains about 160 miles in a direct line from San Francisco. This noted valley at its bottom is about 4,000 feet above the level of the sea, it is several miles in length and in many places so narrow that the Mexicans would call it a canyon. It is hemmed in on each side by immense mountain walls, with many objects of interest,—great precipitous granite masses, lofty peaks, and beautiful water falls. A volume would not contain a description of all the wonderful views of the Yosemite. One of the most noted is El Capitan, an immense block of granite, rising 3,300 feet above the valley, presenting an almost vertical face toward the valley.

On the other side of the canyon, is the "Bridal Veil Fall" a beautiful sheet of water which is precipitated into the Yosemite in a single leap of 630 feet. But this is not all, the water here strikes on a shelving slope of loose rocks, and then dashes down the mountain side in a number of cascades, till it reaches the valley, so that, from a distance, it appears to be a single fall of 900 feet perpendicular.

Another wonderful cascade is called "The Yosemite Fall." First a vertical fall of 1,500 feet to a shelving plateau. From this point the water dashes down in a series of cascades, making a descent equal to 626 feet perpendicular; next a final leap of 400 feet, giving a total of 2,526 feet.

There are many other interesting objects here; and one of the grandest views to be found anywhere, is to be had from some one of the mountain heights overlooking the valley. The valley is so far below, and the view is so nearly vertical that the beholder is filled with that mixed feeling of awe and delight which every one has experienced, who has looked down from a great height; the Washington Monument for example; but consider that here at Yosemite, you are looking down from an altitude *six times as great as the Washington Monument.*

Looking down into the valley everything has dwindled into Lilliputian proportions. The river seems like a thread. There are but few objects of animated nature to be seen, a few cattle and horses and now and then a solitary horseman—but everything looks so small as to seem ridiculous.   Just above the top of El Capitan a solitary eagle is winging his lordly flight.   No doubt he is taking a birdseye view of the Yosemite Valley and the Pacific Ocean from the west.

> He clasps the crag with hooked hand ;
> Close to the sun in lonely lands,
> Ring'd with the azure world he stands.
> The wrinkled sea beneath him crawls ;
> He watches from his mountain walls,
> And like a thunderbolt he falls.
> *—Tennyson.*

Not far from the Yosemite are some of the Big Trees (*sequoia gigantea*) the Mariposa grove.   There are eight or more distinct patches or groves of these trees in California, all in the region of the Sierra Nevada.   In order, as you go south, they are first the Calaveras ; second, the Stanislaus ; third, Cram Flat ; Fourth, Mariposa ; fifth, Fresno ; sixth, King's and Kaweah Rivers ; seventh, North Fork Tule River ; eighth, South Fork, Tule River.   The whole area covered by these groves will probably not exceed fifty square miles.   The best of these groves are those of Calaveras and Mariposa.

Several of the big trees are over three hundred feet high—and seventy, eighty, ninety, and one hundred feet in circumference, with bark eighteen inches thick.   One tree still standing, has had a tunnel cut through it at its base through which a stage coach drawn by six horses is driven.   A tree between King's and Kaweah Rivers, which had fallen, and had been burned hollow was so large that three horsemen could ride abreast thirty feet into the cavity, which at seventy feet from the entrance was yet eight feet in diameter.

THE YELLOWSTONE NATIONAL PARK,

from the number and variety of its attractions is perhaps the most noted among the wonders of the west. It is now easily accessible by the Northern Pacific Railway, as well as branches of the Union Pacific. This celebrated park is fifty-five by sixty-five miles square, and lies in the north-west corner of Wyoming, lapping over slightly into the adjacent Territories of Idaho and Montana. It is a government reservation, and by act of Congress it has been dedicated forever to the people of the United States as a national park, and it is cared for and controlled under the authority of the United States government.

Leaving Salt Lake City on the Union Pacific or Denver and Rio Grande Western railroad, we run north to Ogden thirty-six miles; here we take the Utah and Northern division of the Union Pacific for Pocatello and Beaver Canyon, two hundred and seventy-one miles. From this point we go to the Park by stage about ninety miles to Fire-hole Basin, the whole distance from Salt Lake City to the Park being three hundred and ninety-seven miles. From this point may be seen columns of mist or clouds rising from the geysers and hot springs. The nearest geysers are about two miles away, at "Geyser Meadows" throwing their waters twenty to twenty-five feet high. In this vicinity are the Fairy Creek Falls with a descent of two hundred and fifty feet. Five miles from Fire Hole Basin, the Midway Geyser Basin is reached, and here are the grandest hot springs that have been discovered on earth. The Great Spring is two hundred and fifty feet in diameter, and is surrounded by a wall twenty-five or thirty feet high. The surface of the water is in a constant ebulition with a scalding steam rising to a great height.   Only a few feet away there is a spring of cold water of great depth, twenty-five feet in diameter.   The chalk vats close by, are boiling with a mush-like substance varying in color from a pure white to a delicate pink.

The Geysers of Iceland, so well-known for many years, are quite insignificant in comparison with some of the spouters of the National Park.   Ten of the largest geysers that have ever been discovered are in the Upper Geyser Basin.   One of these is called "Castle Geyser." A part of the time it is inactive, but anon it begins to make a noise like muffled thunder, the precurser of an eruption, gradually increasing from a small spurt until with a trembling of the earth and a poluphloiscal, rumbling sound, the rushing waters, in volume like a river mount upward, overflowing many acres around. "Old Faithful" is a periodical worker.   Every fifty-seven minutes this geyser throws a large stream to the height of two hundred feet.   The " Bee Hive " also throws a stream two hundred feet high.   The "Giantess" with a crater fifteen or twenty feet in diameter, throws up a large volume of water two hundred and fifty feet.

There are many other geysers in this park, which need not be here described ; also many fine waterfalls and picturesque canyons.   The Yellowstone canyon being regarded by many as the finest canyon in the world.   At the head of the canyon are the Upper Falls of the Yellowstone, three hundred and ninety-seven feet high.

BRIGHAM YOUNG'S WILL.

The following document, executed by a "very married man," is presented as a legal and literary curiosity ; the like of which was never before, and will probably never again be seen in America.

In the name of God, Amen : I, Brigham Young, Sen., of the city of Salt Lake, in the county of Salt Lake, in the Territory of Utah, being of the age of seventy-two years and of sound mind and memory, do make, publish and declare this to be my last will and testament :

2.   I direct my funeral expenses and debts to be paid, and for this purpose as well as for the payment of legacies and the full settlement of my estate, I authorize and empower my acting executors, the survivor, or survivors of them, to sell at private or public sale my real estate, and to convey to purchasers a good title therefor in fee simple, without liability on their part ; to see to the application of the purchase money, part whereof may be secured by bond and mortgage of the premises sold.

3.   I give and bequeath to each of the mothers of my children named in the following classes, twenty-five dollars, or that amount that may be necessary to defray the expenses of the month, to be paid to them within one month after my decease.

4.   All my estate, real and personal, whatsoever and wheresoever, after payment of all debts and all legacies, and delivery of real estate, devised, given or made either by this will, or any codicil thereto, I give and devise to my executors who shall act under this will, and to the survivors or survivor of them and their and his heirs, with the power of sale aforesaid, upon the trusts following :   In trust, to take and hold the same, and to pay over the net rents and income thereof to and for the use and benefit of the persons named in the following classes, in the manner and proportion and for periods of time hereafter expressed, and to make distribution of the principal and proceeds of sale thereof as hereinafter directed, excluding any child or children for bad conduct

as the mother shall exclude them, as hereinafter provided.

5. Class One shall be: Mary Ann Angell Young, (daughter of James W. and Phœbe Morton Angell, deceased,) now residing at Salt Lake City, the mother of my following named children, to wit:

Joseph Angell Young, now aged 39 years; Brigham Young, Jr., now aged 36 years; Alice Young Clawson, now aged 34 years; Luna Young Thatcher, now aged 31 years; John Willard Young, now aged 29 years.

6. Class Two shall be: Lucy Ann Decker Young, (daughter of Isaac and Harriet Decker, late of Salt Lake City, deceased,) now residing at Salt Lake City, the mother of my following named children, to wit:

Heber Young, now aged 28 years; Fannie Caroline Young Thatcher, now aged 24 years; Ernest Irving Young, now aged 22 years; Shamira Young, now aged 20 years; Arta de Crista Young, now aged 18 years; Feramorz Little Young, now aged 15 years; Clarissa Hamilton Young, now aged 13 years.

7. Class Three shall be: Emeline Free Young, (daughter of Absalom P. and Betty Free, of Salt Lake City,) now residing at Salt Lake City, the mother of my following named children, to wit:

Ella Elizabeth Young Empey, now aged 26 years; Marinda Hyde Young Conrad, now aged 24 years; Hyrum Smith Young, now aged 22 years; Emmeline A. Young McIntosh, now aged 20 years; Louisa W. Young Ferguson, now aged 19 years; Lorenzo D. Young, now aged 17 years; Alonzo Young, now aged 15 years; Ruth Young, now aged 12 years; Adela Elona Young, now aged 9 years.

JOSEPH F. SMITH,
D. McKENZIE, } BRIGHAM YOUNG, SR.
JAMES JACK,

[End of first page.]

8. Class Four shall be: Emily D. Partridge Young, (daughter of Edward Partridge, late of Ohio, deceased, and Lydia Partridge, of Salt Lake City,) now

residing at Salt Lake City, the mother of my following named children, to wit:

Emily Augusta Young Clawson, now aged 24 years ; Caroline Young Croxall, now aged 22 years ; Joseph Don Carlos Young, now aged 18 years ; Miriam Young, now aged 16 years ; Josephine Young, now aged 13 years.

9. Class Five shall be : Clara Decker Young, (daughter of Isaac and Harriet Decker, late of Salt Lake City, deceased,) now residing at Salt Lake City, the mother of my following named children, to wit:

Jennette Richards Young Snell, now aged 23 years ; Nabby Howe Young, now aged 21 years ; Charlotte Talula Young, now aged 21 years.

10. Class Six shall be : Lucy Bigelow Young, (daughter of Nathan Bigelow, late of Davis County, deceased, and Mary Gibbs Bigelow, of St. George,) now residing at St. George, Utah Territory, the mother of my following named children, to wit:

Dora Young Dunford, now aged 21 years ; Susa Young Dunford, now aged 17 years ; Rhoda Mabel Young, now aged 10 years.

11. Class Seven shall be : Eliza Burgess Young, (daughter of James and Betty Burgess, deceased,) now residing at Provo City, Utah Territory, the mother of my following named child, to wit:

Alfales Young, now aged 20 years.

12. Class Eight shall be : Margaret Pierce Young, (daughter of Robert Pierce, of Salt Lake City, and Hannah Pierce, deceased) now residing at Salt Lake City, the mother of my following named child to wit:

Brigham Morris Young, now aged 19 years.

13. Class Nine shall be : Zina D. Huntington Young, (daughter of William and Zina Baker Huntington, deceased), now residing at Salt Lake City, the mother of my following named child, to wit:

Zina P. Young Williams, now aged 23 years.

14. Class Ten shall be : Harriet E. Cook Young, (daughter of Archibald Cook Campbell, deceased, and

Elizabeth M. Campbell, of Saquoit, Oneida County, New York), now residing at Salt Lake City, the mother of my following named child, to wit:

Oscar Brigham Young, now aged 27 years.

15.   Class Eleven shall be: Harriet Barney Young, (daughter of Royal and Sarah Bowen Barney, of Salt Lake City), now residing at Salt Lake City, the mother of my following named child, to wit:

Phineas Howe Young, now aged 11 years.

16.   Class Twelve shall be: Mary Van Cott Young, (daughter of John and Lucy Lavinia Van Cott, of Salt Lake City), now residing at Salt Lake City, the mother of my following named child to wit:

Fannie Van Cott Young, now aged 3 years.

17.   Class Thirteen shall be: Susannah Snively Young, (daughter of Henry and Mary Snively late of Pennsylvania deceased), now residing in Salt Lake City, and my following named adopted child to wit:

Julia Young, now aged 20 years.

JOSEPH F. SMITH,
D. MCKENZIE,   } BRIGHAM YOUNG, SR.
JAMES JACK,

[End of second page.]

18.   Class Fourteen shall be: My daughters Elizabeth Young Ellsworth, now aged 48 years, and Vilate Young Decker, now aged 43 years, being the children of Miriam Works Young, deceased.

19.   Class Fifteen shall be: My daughters Mary E. Young Croxall, deceased; represented by her children, Mary Eliza and Willard Croxall, aged respectively seven and five years, my daughter Maria Young Dougall, now aged 23 years, my son Willard Young, now aged 21 years; and my daughter Phœbe Young Beatie, now aged 19 years, being the children of Clara Ross Young, deceased.

20.   Class Sixteen shall be: My daughter Evaline L. Young Davis, now aged 23 .years: and my son Mahonri Moriancumr Young, now aged 21 years, being the children of Margaret Alley Young, deceased.

21.   Class Seventeen shall be the following named persons, to wit:

Eliza R. Snow Young, now aged 69 years; Naoma K. J. C. Twiss Young, now aged 52 years; Martha Bowker Young, now aged 51 years.

And my executors shall pay to each of them, during the term of their natural lives, from any rents or income accruing from my estate, such a sum annually, payable in monthly installments, as may be necessary for their comfortable support, and as shall be in proportion to the amounts paid to other individual members of my family; and they together with Clara Decker Young, Harriet Cook Young, Susannah Snively Young, Eliza Burgess Young, and Margaret Pierce Young, have my dwelling known as the Lion House, situated in Lot two (2,) in Block eighty-eight (88) Plat A, Salt Lake City Survey, as their place of residence during their natural lives.

22.   Class Eighteen shall be: Harriet Amelia Folsom Young, now aged 35 years, to whom my executors shall pay during the term of her natural life, from any rents or income accruing, from my estate, such a sum annually payable in monthly installments, as may be necessary for her comfortable support; and as shall be in proportion to the amounts paid to other individual members of my family; and she, with Mary Ann Angell Young, shall have a residence during their natural lives in my dwelling known as the Gardo House, situated in Lot six (6) in Block seventy-five (75) Plat A, Salt Lake City Survey.

23.   Class nineteen shall be: Augusta Adams Young, now aged 70 years, to whom my executors shall pay, during the term of her natural life, from any rents or income accruing from my estate, such a sum annually, payable in monthly installments, as may be necessary for her comfortable support, and shall be in proportion to the amounts paid to other individual members of my family.

24.   The divisions of such shares of rents and in-

come, shall be apportioned and paid to each class in the proportion the number of mothers and children in each class, shall bear to the whole number in all the classes, and any child born to either mother within nine months after my decease, shall be taken to be one of her class and have all the share and rights of a child born in my life time; and as the number of each class shall be at the commencement of each year, so shall the apportionment be; but a mother or children married, shall cease on marriage to have any share of rents and income, and the earnings of minors shall go to increase the share of their class ; and also, the earnings of children of lawful age, who shall continue to live with their class at the homestead, shall contribute rateably to the common support; otherwise they shall cease to have a right to reside in the homestead and to share the income.

JOSEPH F. SMITH,
D. McKENZIE,   } BRIGHAM YOUNG, SR.
JAMES JACK,

[End of third page]

25.   The classes shall continue to occupy the homestead in which they shall have been left by me without charge, they paying the taxes thereon, and the repairs thereof until the decease or marriage of their mother, and one year longer, and minors until of lawful age; but until her death, the whole income shall be paid to the mother, to be applied in her discretion for the use of her children. Provided that if the share of the whole estate shall have been set off to the children of a deceased or married mother, the executors shall still be the trustees of minors, and make compensation for their maintenance and education; and also for the proper maintenance of those of age who shall be incompetent to take care of themselves, at their original homestead, or at other suitable place. But in no instance is any child to have more than his or her proper equal share of income, or principal, out of the joint trust estate.

26.   Should any mother fail to do her duty in contributing with others the proper proportion of her clas

toward the common expenses of the household in which they may be, the executors shall have power to make payment of a due share of income directly to that object; and they shall have a discretionary power to settle all differences between the members of families, and be pacificators among them, and their decision shall be final. "

27.   If the mother of a class shall be deceased at my death, or shall thereafter die or marry, and as often as one shall die or marry, there shall be within one year thereafter, or as soon as may be practicable, a valuation made of all my real and personal estate by the executors acting, and as many other competent persons as there may be executors, to be appointed by a majority of the mothers then living, a majority of which valuers shall make a final division and allotment of the shares of the real and personal estate (or of either,) which shall be set off as, and for the proper and equal share of the children of the deceased or married mother; and such share shall be taken rateably by them for their full share of my estate; and they, as they shall be or become of lawful age and receive the possessions of their respective portions thereof shall give full releases and acquittance to the executors, of all claims and demands, and of all right and title in and to my undivided estate, in form to be placed on record.

28.   If any child of any mother shall be dead at the time of making payment of rents and income, or if dividing the estate, leaving issue then living, said issue shall be counted as one, in place of their parent in the proper class, to receive rateably by representation the share their parents would have received if living; that is, a share of the rents and income if living at the homestead, and of the principal wherever living when payable as aforesaid; but no payments of principal shall be payable to a minor during minority, but rents and income of their allotted shares may be applied to and for their maintenance and education.

29.   All payments made to the mothers of the respective children, for their maintenance and education, shall be valid payments, and the mothers' receipts shall be

complete discharges and releases to the executors; but the mothers may appoint a receiver or treasurer for the family, if more convenient and so many as constitute him or her their agent shall be bound by his or her receipts.

30.   Should a mother, son or daughter, marry at a proper age, or a son go into business after twenty-one years of age, the trustees may make a payment to such mother of a sum of One Hundred dollars, and to a son or daughter a sum of Five Hundred dollars, to be charged in the division without interest, as follows: The payment to the mother to be charged to the whole fund of her class, and the payments to the children to be charged to their respective portions thereof.

31.   The homestead and its furniture, bedding and household utensils, shall be the last to be sold for payment of debts or legacies, or to make division among said classes: but if they must be sold for any of said purposes, the proceeds left shall be invested in a safe manner, on bond and mortgage, for the advantage of those entitled as aforesaid, and the executors shall have power if deemed best, to raise money by mortgage of the real estate to pay off debts, legacies or shares on division, and this from time to time.

32.   The provisions hereby made for the mothers of my children, shall be in lieu of all dower, or other legal claim, upon my estate.

33.   Should one or more of my acting executors die, resign or become incapable of acting in the trust, I authorize the majority of the mothers of my children living at the time, to appoint by writing, under their hands and seals, another, or other trustees to act in his or their place, in whom the title of said estate shall become vested, as if he or they were originally appointed by this will; and he or they shall have all the rights and powers therein expressed; and I direct the surviving or continuing trustee and executor, or trustees and executors, to convey the estate to a third party, who shall re-convey the same to them and the new appointees in fee jointly upon all and singular the trusts of this will, with all the

powers and authority, and subject to the duties therein contained; but if this power be not exercised, the acts of the surviving or

JOSEPH F. SMITH,
D. McKENZIE,   } BRIGHAM YOUNG, Sr.
JAMES JACK.

[End of fourth page.]

continuing executors, or executor, shall be as valid as if this power to fill vacancies did not exist.

34.   To avoid any question, the words married or marriage, in this will shall be taken to have become consummate between man and woman, either by ceremony before a lawful magistrate or according to the order of the Church of Jesus Christ of Latter-day Saints, or by their cohabitation in conformity to our custom.

35.   The mother and trustees, and executors, shall have power to determine whether any child she may have, shall have a right of residence in the homestead, and shall have power to remove any one, or more, for disobedience or vicious conduct, or bad habits; and the mother may appoint what would otherwise be the share of any such child, or children, to his or her issue, or to said mother's other children or their issue, and her determination by writing, to take effect in her life, or by will, shall be binding: but on full reformation she may revoke such writing, made to take effect during her life.

36.   I appoint to be executors and trustees under this will, George Q. Cannon, Brigham Young Jr., and Albert Carrington, with all the authority therein contained; and I authorize them to take as their joint commission three per cent. on principal passing through their hands, to be charged but once on the same principal, and five per cent on income; but they shall make no charge as on a rent for any homestead occupied by my legatees.

37.   I authorize my executors and trustees with the consent of the said mother, or mothers surviving, and of all their children of the age of twenty-one years, to wind up and close the entire trust of my estate, reserving and

keeping at interest the shares of all minors, until they shall respectively arrive at said lawful age; and the acquittances of said legatees shall be a full discharge to the executors and trustees; and every trust shall be closed within twenty-one years after the decease of the surviving mother of my children aforesaid.

38. I authorize my executors to settle all trusts wherein I am trustee, and to pay any debts I may owe in respect to the same, and to recieve whatever claims may be due my estate therefrom; and to make conveyance and assignment to the proper party, or parties, of the trust estate, and to make proper indemnity and security as to all outstanding liabilities I may be under for such trust estate, so that my private estate shall suffer no loss by reason of my liabilities for such debts.

39. To prevent any failure of trustees, should a surviving executor, or trustee, original or substituted, die leaving executors, or an executor, they, or he, and the survivors or survivor, of them shall be the executors, or executor, or trustees, or trustee, to complete the trusts of this will, with all the authority and powers therein stated ; and should the surviving executor, or trustee, have left an executor, or should he, or they, die before the complete execution of this trust, they, the executors, or the survivors, or survivor, of the executors of my will, or substituted trustee, who shall have next before died, shall be the executors, or executor, of my will; and so back until an executor or some executor of my will, or trustee, shall be obtained, if any exist, who shall have the authority and powers aforesaid, so that no vacancy in the trust may happen.

40. In testimony whereof, I have hereunto set my hand and seal, this fourteenth day of November, 1873.

BRIGHAM YOUNG, SEN. [L. S.]

Signed, sealed, published and declared by Brigham Young, Sen., to be his last Will and Testament in our presence, and we have at his request, in his pre-

sence, and in the presence of each other, subscribed
our names as witnesses thereto.

JOSEPH F. SMITH,
D. MCKENZIE,
JAMES JACK.

[End of fifth page.]

First codicil to my foregoing will:

1.   I hereby annex a schedule of property, with its
value attached, which I have given to the mothers of my
children, and to my children, and which I direct my executors to charge to each in the manner described hereinafter;

2.   To Mary Ann Angell Young, and her heirs and
assigns of Class One in my foregoing Will, I have
deeded through a deed to George A. Smith, dated July
29, 1873, Lots 7, 8 and 9, in Block 1, Plat I, Salt Lake
City Survey, being 234 feet front on South Temple street,
and 20 rods deep, valued at $20,000, which amount I
authorize and request my executors in the division of my
estate to charge to the principal of her class without interest.

3.   To Lucy A. Decker Young, and her heirs and
assigns, of Class Two in my foregoing Will, I have
deeded through a deed to Feramorz Little, dated July
29, 1873, part of Lot 1, in Block 88, Plat A, Salt Lake
City Survey, commencing at a point 2 rods east of the
southeast corner of said Lot; thence running north 16
rods, thence west 94 feet and 8 inches ; thence south 16
rods; thence east 40 feet 8 inches, to the place of
beginning, with the buildings thereon, valued at $50,000.
Also through a deed to George Q. Cannon, dated July
29, 1873, part of Lot 3, in Block 70, Plat A, Salt Lake
City Survey, commencing at the southwest corner of said
Lot; thence running east 96 and 9-12 feet to the southwest corner of Commercial street; thence 97 feet bearing 1¼ degrees east on the west line of Commercial
street; thence west 99 feet, more or less, to the west line
of said Lot 3; thence south 97 feet, to the place of beginning, valued at $80,000.   This amount I authorize and

request my executors in the division of my estate to charge to the principal of her class without interest.

4.   To Emeline Free Young, and her heirs and assigns, of Class Three in my foregoing Will, I have deeded through a deed to James Jack, dated June 24, 1873, part of Lot 7, in Block 75, Plat A, Salt Lake City Survey, commencing at a point 26 feet due north from the southeast corner of said Lot; thence running north 69 feet; thence west 10 rods; thence south 69 feet; thence east 10 rods; to place of beginning, with the building thereon, valued at $20,000.   Also through a deed to George Q, Cannon, dated July 29, 1873, parts of Lots 5 and 6, in Block 70, Plat A, Salt Lake City Survey, commencing at a point 7½ feet west of the northwest corner of said Lot 5; thence running south 100 feet; thence east 7½ feet; thence north 2 feet; thence east 110 feet, more or less, to the west line of Commercial street, 98 feet to a point 53 feet west of the northeast corner of said Lot 6; thence west 119½ feet, to place of beginning, valued at $40,000.   The above named two pieces of land, with the buildings thereon, are valued in the aggregate at $60,000.

JOSEPH F. SMITH, ⎫
D. McKENZIE,   ⎬ BRIGHAM YOUNG, SR.
JAMES JACK.   ⎭

[End of sixth page.]

This amount I authorize and request my executors in the division of my estate to charge to the principal of her class without interest.

5.   To Emily D. Partridge Young, and to her heirs and assigns of Class Four in my foregoing Will, I have deeded Lot 7, in Block 62, Plat B, Salt Lake City Survey, with the buildings thereon, valued at $12,000, which amount I authorize and request my executors to charge to the principal of her class without interest.

6.   To Clara Decker Young, and her heirs and assigns of Class Five in my foregoing Will, I have deeded through a deed to Joseph F. Smith, dated July 29, 1873, part of Lot 3, in Block 70, commencing at a point 97 feet

north from the southwest corner of said Lot; thence running east 99 feet, more or less, to the west line of Commercial street; thence 150 and 9-12 feet north, bearing 1½ degrees east; thence west 102⅓ feet, more or less to the west line of said Lot 3; thence south 150 and 6-12 feet, to the place of beginning, valued at $30,100. Also through a deed to Feramorz Little, dated July 29, 1873, Lot 18, in Block 1, 10 by 10 rods, Plat I, Salt Lake City Survey. Also all that certain piece or parcel of land known and described as follows: Part of Lot 2, in Block 14, Plat D, Salt Lake City Survey, commencing at a point 5 rods west of the southeast corner of said Lot 2 ; thence running west 6 feet; thence north 10 rods; thence east 7 feet; thence south 10 rods, to place of beginning; which with the above mentioned Lot 13, are valued at $5,200; the above named pieces of land are valued in the aggregate at $35,300. This amount I authorize and request my executors to charge to the principal of her class without interest.

7. To Zina D. Huntington Young, and her heirs and assigns of Class Nine in my foregoing Will, I have deeded the south half of Lot 4, in Block 56, Plat A, Salt Lake City Survey, with the buildings thereon, valued at $16,000, which amount I authorize and request my executors in the division of my estate to charge to the principal of her class without interest.

8. To Mary Van Cott Young, and her heirs and assigns of Class Twelve in my foregoing Will, I have given through a deed to her father, John Van Cott, part of Lot 3, in Block 76, Plat A, Salt Lake City Survey, commencing at the southeast corner of said Lot; thence 63 feet west: thence 100 feet north; thence 63 feet east; thence 100 feet south to place of beginning, valued at $18,000, which amount I authorize and request my executors in the division of my estate to charge to the principal of her class without interest.

9. To my son, Heber Young, I have deeded Lot 1, in Block 14, Plat D, Salt Lake City Survey, with the buildings thereon, valued at $15,000. I authorize and re-

quest my executors to deduct $5,000, and in the division of my estate to charge the balance, $10,000, without interest, to his portion in his class.

10.   To my son Hyrum S. Young, I have deeded a strip of land 1 foot wide, commenc-

JOSEPH F. SMITH,
D. McKENZIE,   }   BRIGHAM YOUNG, SR.
JAMES JACK,

[End of seventh page.]

ing at the northeast corner of Lot 5, in Block 78, Plat A, Salt Lake City Survey, and running south 10 rods, and part of Lot 6, in the aforesaid Block, commencing at the northwest corner of said Lot; running thence south twenty (20) rods; thence east seventy-three (73) feet to the place of beginning, with the business thereon, valued at fifteen thousand dollars ($15,000) from which I authorize and request my executors to deduct five thousand ($5,000) dollars, and in the division of my estate charge the balance, ten thousand ($10,000) dollars, without interest, to his portion in his class.

11.   To my son Ernest I. Young, I have given five thousand ($5,000) dollars, in cash, which I authorize and request my executors to charge without interest, in the division of my estate to his portion in his class.

12.   To my daughter, Elizabeth Y. Ellsworth, I have deeded Lot 6, in Block 74, Plat A, Salt Lake City Survey, with the buildings thereon, valued at twenty thousand ($20,000) dollars; also part of Lot 6 in Block 70, Plat A, Salt Lake City Survey, commencing at a point ninety-eight (98) feet south of the northwest corner of said Lot six (6), thence running south seventy-four feet and nine inches (74 9-12), thence east one hundred and eight feet (108), more or less, to the west line of Commercial street, thence seventy-four feet and nine inches (74 9-12) north, bearing one and one-quarter (1 ¼) degrees east, on the said west line of Commercial street at its junction with First South street; thence west one hundred and ten (110) feet, more or less, to the

place of beginning, valued at $14,940.   The above named two pieces of land, with the buildings, are valued in the aggregate at $34,750.   This amount I authorize and request my executors, in the division of my estate, to charge without interest, to her portion in her class.

13.   To my daughter, Vilate Y. Decker, I have deeded Lot 6, in Block 63, also 10 rods by 11 rods, south of and adjoining the above Lot, being part of Lot 3, in the aforesaid Block, Plat B, Salt Lake City Survey, with the buildings thereon, valued at $15,000 ; also part of Lot 7, in Block 70, Plat A, Salt Lake City Survey, commencing at a point 172 9-12 feet south of the northwest corner of said Lot 6 ; thence running south 74 9-12 feet ; thence east 106 feet, more or less, to the west line of Commercial street ; thence 74 9-12 feet north bearing 1 1/4 degrees east on the said west line of Commercial street, to a point 172 9-12 feet south from the northwest corner of Commercial street, at its junction with First South street ; thence west 108 feet more or less, to the place of beginning valued at $14,950.   The above named two pieces of land with the buildings thereon, are valued in the aggregate at $29,950.   This amount I authorize and request my executors in the division of my estate to charge without interest to her portion in her class.

14.   To my daughter, Alice Y. Clawson, I have deeded part of Lot 7, in Block 75, Plat A, Salt Lake City Survey, commencing at the northeast corner of said lot ; thence running south 70 feet ; thence west 10 rods ; thence north 70 feet ; thence east 10 rods to the place

<table>
<tr><td>Joseph F. Smith,
D. McKenzie,
James Jack,</td><td>}</td><td>BRIGHAM YOUNG, Sr.</td></tr>
</table>

[End of eighth page.]

of beginning, with the buildings thereon, valued at $10,000, which amount I authorize and request my executors in the division of my estate to charge without interest to her portion in her class.

15.   To my daughter Luna Y. Thatcher and her

heirs and assigns, I have given through a deed to her husband, George W. Thatcher, 6 rods fronting south, extending north, 10 rods of the west end of Lot 1, in Block 67; also 1½ rods fronting south, extending north 10 rods, off the east end of Lot 2, in the aforesaid Block, Plat A, Salt Lake City Survey, with the buildings thereon, which I value at $7,500. This amount I authorize and request my executors in the division of my estate to charge without interest, to her portion in her class.

16. To my daughter Fanny Y. Thatcher and her heirs and assigns, I have deeded the east half of Lot 2, in Block 14, Plat D, of Salt Lake City Survey, with the buildings thereon, valued at $7,500, which amount I authorize and request my executors in the division of my estate, to charge without interest to her portion in her class.

17. To my daughter Ella E. Y. Empey and her heirs and assigns, I have deeded the northeast corner of Lot 8, 5 rods by 5 rods, in Block 74, Plat A, Salt Lake City Survey, with the buildings thereon, valued at $10,000, which amount I authorize and request my executors, in the division of my estate, to charge without interest to her portion in her class.

18. To my daughter Emily A. Y. Clawson and her heirs and assigns, I have deeded Lot 5, in Block 1, Plat I, Salt Lake City Survey, 112 feet front by 10 rods deep, valued at $5,000, which amount I authorize and request my executors to charge, without interest, in the division of my estate, to her portion in her class.

19. To my daughter Miranda H. Y. Conrad and her heirs and assigns, I have deeded Lot 2, in Block 1, Plat I, Salt Lake City Survey, 7 rods by 10 rods, valued at $5,000, which amount I authorize and request my executors, in the division of my estate, to charge without interest to her portion in her class.

20. To my daughter Maria Y. Dougall and her heirs and assigns, I have deeded part of Lot 8, in Block 76, Plat A, Salt Lake City Survey, commencing at a point 3 rods north of the southeast corner of said Lot;

thence running north 55 feet ; thence west 10 rods ; thence south 55 feet ; thence east 10 rods to place of beginning, valued at $11,000 which amount I authorize and request my executors in the division of my estate, to charge without interest to her portion in her class.

21.   To my daughter Jeanette R. Y. Snell and her heirs and assigns, I have deeded Lot 3, in Block 14, Plat D, Salt Lake City Survey, 10 rods by 10 rods, valued at $5,000, which amount I authorize and request my executors, in the division of my estate, to charge without interest, to her portion in her class.

22.   To my daughter Zina L. Y. Williams and her heirs and assigns, I have deeded Lot 10, in Block 8, Plat I, Salt Lake City Survey, valued at $5,000, which amount I authorize and request my executors in the

JOSEPH F. SMITH,
D. McKENZIE,   } BRIGHAM YOUNG, SR.
JAMES JACK,

[End of ninth page]

division of my estate, to charge without interest to her portion in her class.

23.   To my daughter, Evaline Y. Davis, and her heirs and assigns, I have deeded Lot one, in Block 2, Plat I, Salt Lake City Survey, valued at $5,000, which amount I authorize and request my executors, in the division of my estate, to charge without interest to her portion, in her class.

24.   To my daughter, Caroline Y. Croxall and her heirs and assigns, I have deeded 5 rods front by 10 rods deep, being the northeast corner, Lot 7, in Block 47, Plat H, Salt Lake City Survey, valued at $3,000 ; also I have given her a note of hand given me by her husband, Mark Croxall, for money loaned by me to him, amounting to $3,133.91, which amount being in all $6,133.91.   I authorize and request my executors, in the division of my estate, to charge without interest to her portion in her class.

25.   To my daughter, Nabby Howe Young and her

heirs and assigns, I have deeded Lot 11, in Block 1, Plat I, Salt Lake City Survey, valued at $5,000, which amount I authorize and request my executors in the division of my estate, to charge without interest to her portion in her class.

26. To my daughter Dora Y. Dunford and her heirs and assigns, I have deeded Lot 8, in Block 3, Plat I, Salt Lake City Survey, valued at $5,000, which amount I authorize and request my executors, in the division of my estate, to charge without interest to her portion in her class.

27. To my daughter Emeline A. Young McIntosh and her heirs and assigns, I have deeded parts of Lots 7, and 10 feet fronting east on north side of Lot 8, both pieces running 20 rods deep, with the buildings thereon, valued at $3,000, which amount I authorize and request my executors, in the division of my estate, to charge without interest to her portion in her class.

28. To my daughter Shamira D. Young and her heirs and assigns, I have deeded Lot 3, in Block 2, Plat I, Salt Lake City Survey, valued at $5,000, which amount I authorize and request my executors in the division of my estate, to charge without interest to her portion in her class.

29. To my daughter Phœbe Y. Beatie and her heirs and assigns, I have deeded a part of Lot 8, in Block 86, Plat A, Salt Lake City Survey, commencing at a point 104½ feet north from the southeast corner of said Lot; thence running 80 feet north; thence west 10 rods, thence south 80 feet; thence east 10 rods to the place of beginning, with the building thereon, valued at $16,000 which amount I authorize and request my executors, in the division of my estate, to charge without interest to her portion in her class.

30. To my daughter Susa Y. Dunford and her heirs and assigns, I have deeded Lot 9, in Block 3, Plat I, Salt Lake City Survey, valued at $5,000, which amount I authorize and request my executors, in the division of

my estate, to charge without interest to her portion in her class.

Joseph F. Smith,
D. McKenzie,   } BRIGHAM YOUNG, Sr.
James Jack,

[End of tenth page.]

31.   To my daughter Louisa W. Y. Ferguson and her heirs and assigns, I have deeded the south half of Lot 4, in Block 73, Plat A, Salt Lake City Survey, valued at $10,000, which amount I authorize and request my executors in the division of my estate, to charge without interest to her portion in her class.

33.   To my daughter, Clarissa H. Young and her heirs and assigns, I have deeded part of Lot 4, and all of Lot 7, in Block 2, Plat I, Salt Lake City Survey, being 6 rods by 13¾ rods, valued at $5,000, which amount I authorize and request my executors, in the the division of my estate, to charge without interest to her portion in her class.

34.   To my daughter, Josephine Young, and her heirs and assigns, I have deeded Lot 2, in Block 42, Plat D, Salt Lake City Survey, valued at $5,000, which amount I authorize and request my executors in the division of my estate, to charge without interest to her portion in her class.

35.   To my daughter, Ruth Young and her heirs and assigns, I have deeded Lot 2, in Block 4, Plat I, Salt Lake City Survey, valued at $5,000, which amount I authorize and request my executors in the division of my estate to charge without interest to her portion in her class.

36.   To my daughter, Charlotte Talula Young and her heirs and assigns, I have deeded Lot 3, in Block 2, Plat I, Salt Lake City Survey, valued at $4,000, which amount I authorize and request my executors to charge without interest to her portion in her class.

37.   To my daughter Rhoda Mabel Young, and her heirs and assigns, I have deeded Lot 10, in Block 3, Plat A, Salt Lake City Survey, valued at $5,000, which

amount I authorize and request my executors in the division of my estate to charge without interest to her portion in her class.

38.   To my daughter Adelia Young and her heirs and assigns, I have deeded Lot 1, Block 4, Plat I, Salt Lake City Survey, valued at $5,000, which amount I authorize and request my executors in the division of my estate, to charge without interest to her portion in her class.

39.   To my daughter, Fanny Van Cott Young and her heirs and assigns, I have deeded Lot 9, in Block 2, Plat I, Salt Lake City Survey, valued at $5,000, which amount I authorize and request my executors in the division of my estate to charge without interest to her portion in her class.

40.   To my daughter, Mary Y. Croxall's children, Mary Eliza and Willard Croxall and their heirs and assigns, I have deeded Lot 3, and 4, in Block 3, Plat I, Salt Lake City Survey, valued at $5,000, which amount I authorize and request my executors in the division of my estate, to charge without interest to Mary Y. Croxall's portion in her class.

<table>
<tr><td>Joseph F. Smith,
D. McKenzie,
James Jack,</td><td>}</td><td>BRIGHAM YOUNG, Sr.</td></tr>
</table>

[End of eleventh page.]

41.   To my adopted daughter, Julia Young and her heirs and assigns, I have deeded Lot 3, in block 43, Plat D, Salt Lake City Survey, valued at $5,000, which amount I authorize and request my executors in the division of my estate to charge without interest to her portion in her class.

42.   Provided, that if in the division of my estate, my executors shall find that any of the above named property, deeded to my children or to their mothers, shall have at that time a greater or less value than is placed upon it in this, my will, and injustice will thereby be done to any of the classes, then the executors are

hereby authorized to value the same in the manner provided in paragraph 21 of my foregoing will, and to charge the amount at which it is newly valued instead of the amount herein mentioned to the principal of the class without interest ; but if any of my children or the mothers of my children shall have received by my gifts of property before mentioned, more than the value of the share coming to them from my estate, they shall not be required to refund such excess—it shall be charged to them or their class as their full share of my estate, and they, if of lawful age, or as they become of lawful age, shall give full release and acquittance to the executors of all claims and demands, and of all right and title in and to my undivided estate in form to be placed of record.

43. No charge shall be made against any of my children or the mothers of my children, for any gifts which I have given them previous to the date of my will, which are not mentioned in this will and schedule.

44. I furthermore countermand, revoke, annul and make void my former will executed by me on the seventeenth day of August, A. D. one thousand eight hundred and seventy-one, and all other wills, or parts of wills, heretofore made or executed by me.

45. In testimony whereof, I have hereunto set my hand and seal this fourteenth day of November, 1873.

BRIGHAM YOUNG, Sen.   [L. S.]

Signed, sealed, published and declared by Brigham Young, Sen., to be his last will and testament, in our presence, containing with the schedule, twelve pages, and we have, at his request, in his presence, and in the presence of each other, subscribed our names as witnesses hereto.

JOSEPH F. SMITH,
D. McKENZIE,
JAMES JACK.

In the name of God, Amen: I, Brigham Young, of Salt Lake City, in the county of Salt Lake, Territory of Utah, being of the age of seventy-four years on the first day of June, 1875, next ensuing, and being of sound mind and memory, do make, publish and declare this to be my last will and testament.

I do hereby give and bequeath unto my children and their mothers, as hereinafter described, that certain piece or parcel of land, for a burial ground forever, known and described as follows, to wit: Lot No. 12, Block 1, Plat I, Salt Lake City Survey, containing 100 square rods, or 10 rods square, being situated and bounded as follows, to wit: Having Clara Decker's Lot on the east, Nabby Young's Lot on the west, Le Grand Young's Lot on the south and the street on the north, together with all the hereditaments appertaining; to have and to hold the premises above described for a burial ground forever, as aforesaid, to my children and their mothers, as follows, to wit: to my daughters by Miriam Works, to wit: Elizabeth Ellsworth and Ann Decker; to Mary Ann Angell and my sons and daughters by her, to wit: Joseph A. Young, Brigham Young, Jr., John W. Young, Alice Y. Clawson and Luna Y. Thatcher; to Lucy Decker and my sons and daughters by her to wit: Heber Young, Ernest Young, Arta D. Crista Young, Feramorz Young, Fanny Y. Thatcher, Shamira Young and Clarissa H. Young; To Clara Decker and my daughters by her, to wit: Jeanette Y. Snell, Nabby Young and Charlotte Talula Young; to Emeline Free and my sons and daughters by her, to wit; Hyrum S. Young, Lorenzo O. Young, Alonzo Young, Ella Y. Empey, Miranda Y. Conrad, Emeline Y. McIntosh, Louisa Y. Ferguson, Ruth Young, and Della Young; to Harriet Cook and my son by her, to wit: Oscar Young; to my sons and daughters by Clarissa Ross, deceased, to wit: Willard Young, Mary Y. Croxall, Maria Y. Dougall, and Phœbe Y. Beatie; to my sons and daughter by Margaret Alley, deceased, to wit: Mahonri Morancumr Young and Eva Y. Davis; to Emily Partridge and my sons and daughters by her, to wit: Don Carlos Young, Emily Y. Clawson, Caroline Y. Croxall, Miriam Young and Josephine Young; to Zina Huntington and my daughter by her, to wit: Zina P. Young Williams; to Margaret Pierce Young and my son by her, to wit: Brigham

Morris Young; to Lucy Bigelow and my .daughters by her, to wit: Elvira Y. Dunford, Susa Y. Dunford and Mabel Young; to Elizabeth Burgess and my son by her, to wit: Alfales Young; to Harriet Barney and my son by her, to wit: Phineas Howe Young; and to Mary Van Cott and my daughter by her, to wit: Fanny Young; and also to my other wives who have been sealed to me and who are hereinafter named, I do give and bequeath the before described piece and parcel of land for a burial place for themselves, their names being as follows; Augusta Adams, Eliza R. Snow, Susan Snively, Nahamy Curtin, Martha Bowen and Harriet Amelia Folsom; to all the above named persons as my children, to their descendants and to my children's mothers as hereinbefore named, and to my other wives, who have been sealed to me (but have no children,) and who have been before named, I do give and devise the herein described piece or parcel of land for themselves as a burial place forever.

In testimony whereof, I have hereunto set my hand and seal this eighth day of February, 1875, (February 8th, 1875.)

BRIGHAM YOUNG, Sen.

The foregoing instrument, consisting of one sheet, was signed, sealed and published and declared by Brigham Young to be his last will and testament in our presence, and we have in his presence, and the presence of each other subscribed our names as witnesses thereto this 8th day of February, 1875.

James G. Bleak,
Wm A. Rossiter,
John Webster Watson.

———

Territory of Utah, County of Salt Lake, In the Probate Court for said county.

In the matter of the estate of President Brigham Young, deceased.

Certificate of proof of will and facts found.

I, Elias Smith, Probate Judge for said county, hereby

certify that on the 19th day of September, A. D. 1877, the annexed instruments were admitted to probate as the last will and testament of said Brigham Young, deceased, and codicil thereto, and from the proofs taken and the examination had therein the Court finds: that the said Brigham Young died on the 29th day of August, A. D. 1877, in the city and county of Salt Lake, Territory of Utah, of which place he was a resident; that the said annexed will and first codicil thereto were duly executed by said decedent in his lifetime in this city, county and Territory aforesaid, and was signed by the said testator, in the presence of Joseph F. Smith, David McKenzie and James Jack, the subscribed witnesses thereto; that he acknowledged the execution of the same in their presence, and declared the same to be his last will and testament and first codicil thereto, and the said witnesses attested the same at his request, in his presence and in the presence of each other.   That the said second codicil to said will was duly executed by the said testator on the 8th day of February, A. D. 1875, at the city of St. George, county of Washington, Territory aforesaid, and was signed by the said testator in the presence of W. A. Rossiter, James G. Bleak, and John W. Watson, the subscribing witnesses thereto that he acknowledged the execution of the same in their presence, and declared the same to be a codicil to his last will and testament; and the said witnesses attested the same at his request in his presence, and in the presence of each other.

That said decedent, at the time of executing said instruments, and each of them, was over the age of seventy years, of sound mind, and not under any restraint, undue influence or fraudulent misrepresentation, nor in any respect incompetent to bequeath and devise his estate,

In testimony whereof I have signed this certificate, and caused the same to be attested by the [SEAL.] clerk of said court, under the seal thereof, this 19th day of September, A. D. 1877.

Attest: E. SMITH, Probate Judge.
                              D. BOCKHOLT, Clerk Probate Court.

CENTENNIAL OF WASHINGTON'S INAUGURATION.

Some time prior to the 30th of April, 1889, the following notice was published in the *Deseret News* and other Mormon papers in the Territory.

CENTENNIAL INAUGURATION DAY.

In response to the Proclamation of Benjamin Harrison, President of the United States, and of Caleb W. West, Governor of the Territory of Utah, we deem it proper that Tuesday, the 30th of April, 1889, be observed by the Latter-day Saints as a day of thanksgiving to the Almighty for the establishment of this Republic, and of prayer for the perpetuation and extension of civil and religious liberty. We therefore request the Presidents of Stakes and the Bishops of the several wards to co-operate in making arrangements for the holding of public services, in their various Stakes or wards, as will be most convenient, that the centennial anniversary of the inauguration of the first President of the United States may be appropriately commemorated throughout this Territory and in all the Stakes of Zion.

WILFORD WOODRUFF,
GEORGE Q. CANNON,
JOSEPH F. SMITH,

Presidency of the Church of Jesus Christ of Latter-day Saints.

Pursuant to this notice, a large concourse of people assembled in the Tabernacle, in Salt Lake City. I attended the meeting as a looker-on in Zion.

The exercises were opened with a prelude on the big organ, followed with a song by two or three hundred children.

The orator of the day was Lieutenant Richard W. Young of the United States army, a grandson of Brigham Young. It was a creditable and scholarly performance, and was delivered in quite an oratorical manner. Instrumental and vocal music followed, and then short speeches were delivered by Franklin S. Richards, George Q. Cannon and President Woodruff. All the speakers were emphatic in their praise of the principles of republican government and the Declaration of Independence. "The Constitution of the United States," they declared was inspired from on high. That although in some instances the Constitution had been violated, this was the fault of erring man, and these abberrations ought not to destroy or impair the respect of the Latter-day Saints for that sacred instrument, which is the heaven-inspired chart of the best government on earth and the palladium of civil and religious liberty."

After the speeches the children sang "Hail Columbia" in an animated manner, each one of the two or three hundred little singers keeping time by waving a small American flag. After a benediction by Elder C. W. Penrose, editor of the *Deseret News*, the great crowd quietly dispersed.

MINES AND MINING IN UTAH.

Prior to 1869, there were comparatively few "Gentiles" or non-Mormons in Utah, and the people were generally engaged in agricultural pursuits and stock-raising on the ranges. Brigham Young in his day discouraged and discountenanced the mining business, upon the ground that it was less conducive to the substantial prosperity and happiness of the people, than agriculture. Besides he thought that the opening of the mines of precious metals would bring into Utah an undesirable population. But after the completion of the trans-continental railroad through Utah, an impetus was given to the mining business, and a large number of Gentile miners poured into the Territory from California, Nevada, Idaho and other quarters.

The principal mines now worked are in Beaver, Juab, Summit, Salt Lake, Tooele and Washington Counties. From 1871 to 1887, both inclusive, the total output was as follows:

Gold, 148,316 fine ounces, at $20 67	$ 3,065,692 72
Silver, 65,226,753 fine ounces, commercial value	73,201,966 51
Lead, 689,630,705 pounds, commercial value	33,799,599 17
Copper, 19,044,995 pounds, commercial value	3,003,889 21
Total	$ 113,071,147 61

The most valuable mine in the Territory is the Ontario, at Park City, in Summit County, about thirty-two miles south-easterly from Salt Lake City. Some idea of this great mine may be formed from the following extract from an official statement in the report of the Governor of Utah for 1888.

There are more than 20 miles of openings in the Ontario. About 130,000 cubic yards have been stoped out. The plant of mine and mill cost $2,570,000 ; over four hundred men are given employment year after year at an average wage of $100 per month.

The total output of the mine to the end of the past year is, in round numbers, $19,300,000, rating silver at its commercial value. Its monthly dividends are 139, aggregating $8,825,000. Rating the silver at its coining value would increase the output to $23,000,000 and the dividends to $12,525,000. On the 4,500 feet of vein there are three shafts, Nos. 1 and 2, in Ontario Gulch ; No. 3, 1,100 feet further west. The latter, through which 28,500 tons of ore were raised the past year, has rested for three years past on the tenth level. About 37,000 tons of ore were extracted in 1887, altogether, from which the company realized in gross and in round numbers $1,860,000, and paid $900,000 in dividends.

Shaft No. 2 has recently been sunk to the twelfth level. The sixth-level drain tunnel three years ago ran 6,300 gallons a minute, of which 2,400 were lifted from the levels below the sixth by the pumps. Now the tunnel runs 5,900 gallons per minute, and the amount raised from the levels below is 2,050 gallons. This drain tunnel has been extended to a connection with the Daly workings, which it drains to the eighth level, that mine being higher than the Ontario. Many of the levels of the two mines have been run together, the respective shafts being 3,300 feet apart.

There are many other good mines in the Territory, among them the Eureka Hill, the Bullion-Beck, the Mammoth and the Northern Spy, in Juab County; the Horn Silver in Beaver County; and the Crescent, the Daly, the Anchor and others in Summit County. A number of valuable mines are also worked in the Bingham Canyon district, and also in the Big Cottonwood and Little Cottonwood Canyons, twenty or thirty miles from Salt Lake City. The mines in Tooele County near Stockton are also said to be doing well.

PART III.

"THE MORMON PROBLEM"—THE QUESTION OF STATEHOOD FOR UTAH.

By the census of 1890 it appears that the population of Utah is 206,498, an increase during the last ten years of 62,538, or 34-44 per cent. The population of Salt Lake City is now 45,025, and that of Ogden 14,919, both of which cities have more than doubled their population in the last decade. The extraordinary increase in population of these two cities, is principally due to immigration of non-Mormons or Gentiles; so that the municipal governments of these two most important cities in Utah, are under the political control of the non-Mormon party. A number of liberals or Gentiles have also been elected to the Legislative Assembly. In consequence of these changes the complaint heretofore made, whether well or ill-founded, that theMormons exercised an undue political influence in the Territorial, County and City governments, will be entitled to little or no consideration.

Whatever interested or prejudiced parties may say, there is no doubt about the fact that the practice of polygamy in Utah, has practically gone into desuetude. That is to say, new plural marriages are now and for several years have been rare occurrences, not more frequent than bigamist marriages elsewhere, and there is reason to believe that when the present marital relations of the older Mormons will close with the death of the parties, Utah will practically be in accord with public sentiment of the country at large in this respect, and material prosperity being unquestioned, the Territory, in these respects is ready for admission into the Union as a State. Several attempts for admission, notably that of 1887, have been made, by a majority of the people, an account of which is given in the subjoined report of 1887. It will be seen that the author of this work, while occupying the position of an election and registration officer under the United States government, declined to make himself a party to either side of the acrimonious controversy.

The people of the Territory are in the habit of claiming that it is the *duty* of Congress, under certain conditions, to admit them as States. But it is evident that this is a duty of imperfect obligation, because if Congress for any reason, or no reason, declines to admit a Territory into the Union as a State, there is an end of the argument. There is no appeal from the authority of Congress. This, however, does not militate against the idea that there is a moral obligation, on the part of Congress to extend a fostering care to the people of the Territories, and ultimately to admit them as States of the Union under proper conditions.

The condition of Utah is peculiar. About three fourths of the white people are Mormous. Hitherto their maintenance of polygamy has made them obnoxious to Congress and the people of the United States. I have no doubt that this incubus on the fair fame and prosperity of Utah, is rapidly and certainly going into "innocuous desuetude," and that it will ere long be a thing of the past. My reasons for this conclusion are set forth in the Reports referred to, and it is fully con-
ed by subsequent observation and investigation.

But the contention of the Gentile politicians is, that even if polygamy is abandoned, Utah ought not to be admitted, so long as a majority of the people are Mor-

mons and they are allowed to vote and hold office.
These agitators would be quite willing for the admission
of Utah, provided they could have it on their own terms,
namely, the disfranchisement of the whole Mormon population, leaving the governing power exclusively in the
hands of the Gentile minority, with all the offices at their
command, among others two United States Senators, or
two members of the House of Representatives in Congress, a Governor, State and County officers, etc. There
can be no doubt that this is the aim of those Gentile leaders who are endeavoring to incite Congress to further
extreme legislation in derogation of local-self government.
The result would be an anomalous sort of republican
commonwealth, whereby three-fourths of the white people would be in a condition of political slavery. If Utah
is not now in a proper condition for admission, let her
wait. Better keep the Territory out for the next fifty
years than to erect a State with a rapacious oligarchy to
rule over three-fourths of the whole people deprived of
all their political rights.

In 1887 and 1888 there was a difference of opinion
among the Commissioners in some respects, which led to
two separate reports for each year, one signed by Commissioners Godfrey, Thomas and Williams, and the other
by Carlton and McClernand. The reports of the first
named gentlemen were very voluminous, and largely
devoted to an argument against the admission of Utah
as a State; and urging additional legislation abridging
local self-government. These reports, as we thought,
represented Utah and the Mormons in very sombre
colors, which so far as they were correctly laid on, made
up a picture of the Past rather than the Present.

We were of opinion, too, that the legislation of
Congress was already quite stringent and had gone far

enough unless it was designed to utterly destroy the principles of local popular government. We thought, too, that while the great mass of the Mormon people were taking an attitude against polygamy, they ought not to be spurned by the officers of a just and generous government.

As to the question of statehood, that being a question of local politics, and acrimonious dispute, we thought it judicious to avoid taking sides, as that might seem to savor of "offensive partisanship."

The majority reports are too voluminous for publication here; and this explanation is given so that some parts of the "Minority reports" will be better understood.

MINORITY REPORT.

SAINT LOUIS, Mo., September 29, 1887.

SIR: Concurring in part in the majority report of our associates, but dissenting from it in other parts, particularly as regards its general animus and tone and the propriety of introducing a theological discussion into a secular document, we deem it advisable, in order to a clear and distinct expression of our views, to submit this our separate report.

Omitting the details of the Commissioners' mode of procedure, which have been heretofore set forth, we proceed at once to such matters as are more interesting to the government and the public.

At the election held on the 3d of November last for Delegate to the Fiftieth Congress, John T. Caine (Mormon) was elected by the following vote: Caine 19,605; William M. Ferry, 2,810; William H. Dickson, 34; scatter-

ing, 34; total, 22,483.   At this election the women voted
under the Territorial law, which has since been repealed
by Congress (March 3d, 1887.)

Early in February of the present year the Commission reassembled in Salt Lake City and prepared for certain municipal elections to be held in the spring.

The supplemental act of March 3d, 1887, materially
changed the law as to the qualifications of voters and
office-holders; and the Commission in pursuance of our
former usage in like cases issued a "circular for the information of registration officers," which was transmitted
to them throughout the Territory, the qualifications of
voters being thus set forth:

(1) No polygamist, bigamist, or any person cohabiting with more than one woman, shall be entitled to register or vote at any election in this Territory; nor any
person who has been convicted of the crime of incest,
unlawful cohabitation, adultery, fornication, bigamy, or
polygamy; nor any person who associates or cohabits
polygamously with persons of the other sex; nor can
any person register or vote who has not taken and subscribed the oath prescribed by the twenty-fourth section
of the act of Congress of March 3, 1887 ; nor can any
woman register or vote.

The Commission is of the opinion that the above
specifications include all the disabilities to which electors
are subject under the laws of Congress, and that no
opinions which they may entertain upon questions of
religious or church polity should be the subject of inquiry
or exclusion of any elector.

The oath proposed as a condition for the registration
of voters, following the language of the act of Congress
as closely as possible, was formulated as follows :

TERRITORY OF UTAH,
    County of ——— :

I, ———, being duly sworn [or affirmed], depose and say that I am over twenty-one years of age ; that I have resided in the Territory of Utah for six months last past, and in this precinct for one month immediately preceding the date hereof; and that I am a native-born [or naturalized, as the case may be] citizen of the United States ; that my full name is ——— ; that I am ——— years of age ; that my place of business is ——— ; that I am a [single or] married man ; that the name of my lawful wife is ——— ; and that I will support the Constitution of the United States, and will faithfully obey the laws thereof, and especially will obey the act of Congress, approved March 22, 1882, entitled *"An act to amend Section 5352 of the Revised Statutes of the United States in reference to bigamy and for other purposes,"* and that I will also obey the act of Congress of March 3, 1887, entitled : *" An act to amend an act entitled ' An act to amend Section 5352 of the Revised Statutes of the United States in reference to bigamy and for other purposes,' approved March 22nd, 1882,"* in respect of the crimes in said act defined and forbidden, and that I will not, directly or indirectly, aid or abet, counsel or advise any other person to commit any of the said crimes defined by acts of Congress, as polygamy, bigamy, unlawful cohabitation, incest, adultery and fornication.

Although the person applying to have his name registered as a voter may have made the foregoing oath, yet if the registrar shall, for reasonable or probable cause, believe that the applicant is then, in fact, a bigamist, polygamist, or living in unlawful cohabitation, or associating or cohabiting polygamously with persons of the other sex, or has been convicted of polygamy, unlawful cohabitation, incest, adultery, or fornication, in our opinion, the registrar may require the applicant to make the following additional affidavit :

Territory of Utah,
    County of ——— :

    I ———, further swear [or affirm] that I am not a bigamist, polygamist, or living in unlawful cohabitation, or associating or cohabiting polygamously with persons of the other sex; and that I have not been convicted of the crime of bigamy, polygamy, unlawful cohabitation, incest, adultery, or fornication.

Soon after the passage of the act of March 3, it was a common belief among the Gentiles that the Mormons, generally, would not take the oath; but it soon became apparent that there was a general disposition among them to take it. Thereupon the Commission was waited on by a committee representing the "Liberals" or "Gentiles," requesting a modification of the oath by interpolating certain expletives and amplifications. The Commission unanimously declined to accede to this request, for the reasons assigned in a written communication. (See Appendix, I.)

Quite a number of the Mormons, as well as the non-Mormons, declined to take the oath; the latter, as we were officially informed, objecting to the clause concerning adultery and fornication.

The general result of the election of August 1 may be stated as follows: Of the 36 members of the legislative assembly, the Mormons elected 31 and the Gentiles 5. Of the Territorial, county, and precinct officers, a large majority of those elected are Mormons, none of whom, however, are living in polygamy.

In former official reports the Commission several times expressed the opinion that the laws of Congress, in connection with other influences, were "setting strongly in the direction of reform" in Utah; and that at no distant day "this relic of Asiatic barbarism (polygamy) would be swept from the land." We have predicted from the beginning that the legal discrimination in favor of the monogamous Mormons against the polygamists would sooner or later be attended with good results. Early in the present year we thought we discerned a disposition among the Mormons to give up the practice of polygamy; and we wish to add that we have used our official and personal influence to induce the Mormons to take such a step.

Early in June of the present year we were gratified to learn that a general movement for the abrogation of polygamy was taking an organized form. The central committee of the "People's (Mormon) party" published a call in the newspapers for mass meetings of the legal voters to be held in all the counties of the Territory, to select delegates to a convention to be held in Salt Lake City, June 30, 1887, for the purpose of adopting a State constitution, and inviting all parties in the Territory to participate in those meetings. The other political parties in the Territory declined to participate in the movement.

The convention, with delegates from all or nearly all the counties in the Territory, met at the time and place designated and remained in session over a week. During their session the Commission received a communication from them requesting us to take charge of the election for the adoption or rejection of the proposed constitution by the legal voters, at the general election to be held August 1.

The Commission responded by disclaiming any express legal authority to take any official action in the premises, "but considering the fact as represented, that said proposed constitution would contain a prohibition of the institution and practice of polygamy, as well as a

prohibition of the union of church and state—the suppression of polygamy being contemplated by the acts of
Congress under which the Commission is acting," we
expressed a willingness "to recommend to the judges of
election that they might receive all the ballots which
should be cast by the qualified voters on said proposition, and deposit the same in separate boxes to be provided by the convention; and to canvass and make
return of the same to such authority as the convention
should provide."

This recommendation was printed in the form of a
resolution and sent by the Commission to the judges of
election throughout the Territory, prefaced with the
following preamble:

Whereas the prohibition of polygamy is the paramount
object of the special legislation of Congress as applicable to Utah, we are of the opinion that when the great
body of the legal voters of the Territory manifest a disposition to place themselves on record against polygamy,
in howsoever an informal manner, they ought to be
encouraged therein, the object of the Government being
not to destroy but to reform the Mormon people.

The convention concluded not to furnish the separate ballot-boxes, but to rely on the judges of election, or
some of them, to count the votes and make return of
the election on the adoption or rejection of the proposed
constitution.   This was done in nearly all the voting precincts, and the result was:

	Votes.
For the constitution	12,195
Against the constitution	505

But few of the Gentiles voted on this proposition,
and of the 504 negative votes probably about one-half

were cast by Mormons. The total vote for members of the legislative assembly was about 16,500, of which the Gentiles cast about 3,500; so it appears that about 95 per cent. of the Mormon voters cast their ballots for the constitution.

In this connection we wish to state that, in such action as the Commission has taken in regard to the vote on this question, we expressly disclaim any purpose of interfering in the question of statehood for Utah. But certainly, whether that Territory shall be admitted early, late, or never, a strong advanced position is gained when the great mass of the people are induced, either in a regular or informal and unusual manner, to place themselves on record in opposition to polygamy.

The provisions of the proposed constitution of the "State of Utah" upon the question under consideration are the following:

SECTION 3 (of Article I). There shall be no union of church and state, nor shall any church dominate the state.

SEC. 12 (of Art. XV). Bigamy and polygamy being considered incompatible with a "republican form of government," each of them is hereby forbidden and declared a misdemeanor.

Any person who shall violate this section shall, on conviction thereof, be punished by a fine of not more than one thousand dollars and imprisonment for a term of not less than six months nor more than three years, in the discretion of the court. This section shall be construed as operative without the aid of legislation, and the offenses prohibited by this section shall not be barred by any statute of limitation within three years after the commission of the offense; nor shall the power of pardon extend thereto until such pardon shall be approved by the President of the United States.

ARTICLE XVI.—*Amendments.*

SECTION I.   Any amendment or amendments to this constitution, if agreed to by a majority of all the members elected to each of the two houses of the legislature, shall be entered on their respective journals, with the yeas and nays taken thereon, and referred to the legislature then next to be elected, and shall be published for three months next preceding the time of such election, and if, in the legislature next elected as aforesaid, such proposed amendment or amendments shall be agreed to by a majority of all the members elected to each house, then it shall be the duty of the legislature to submit such proposed amendment or amendments to the people, in such manner and at such time as the legislature shall prescribe, and if the people shall approve and ratify such amendment or amendments, by a majority of the qualified electors voting thereon, such amendment or amendments shall become a part of the constitution : *Provided*, That section 12 of Article XV shall not be amended, revised or in any way changed, until any amendment, revision, or change as proposed therein shall, in addition to the requirements of the provisions of this article, be reported to the Congress of the United States and shall be by Congress approved and ratified, and such approval and ratification be proclaimed by the President of the United States, and if not so ratified and proclaimed said section shall remain perpetual.

Many of the Gentiles in Utah claim that this anti-polygamy movement among the Mormons is "all a sham." But we do not think so. After careful and impartial investigation and consideration, our conclusion is that, whatever may be their motives, and whether they are influenced by choice or necessity, the generality of the monogamous Mormons (who are more than three-fourths of the Mormon population) have deliberately and wisely resolved that their highest earthly interests, the prosperity and happiness of themselves and their posterity, and the avoidance of the odium which attaches to them throughout the civilized world, demand that polygamy shall be abolished.

The Mormons have been led to believe that if the practice of polygamy shall actually and in good faith be abolished, Congress will no further pursue them with hostile legislation, and that their religious faith will not be the subject of legal animadversion or discrimination. If the premises are granted (namely, the bona fide abrogation of polygamy), their conclusion is impregnable upon well settled principles and precedents.

The Supreme Court of the United States has declared that—

Laws are made for the government of *actions*, and while they cannot interfere with mere *religious belief*, they may with *practices*. * * * Congress can not pass a law for the government of the Territories which shall prohibit the free exercise of religion. The first amendment to the Constitution expressly forbids such legislation. Religious freedom is guaranteed everywhere throughout the United States so far as Congressional interference is concerned. (8 Otto, 145.)

Madison says, sententiously: "Religion, or the duty which we owe the Creator, is not within the province of civil government."

Jefferson says:

Believing that religion is a matter which lies solely between man and his God, and that he owes account to none other for his faith or his worship, that the legislative powers of the Government reach *actions* only and not *opinions*, I contemplate with solemn reverence that act of the whole American people which declares that their legislature should make no law respecting an establishment of religion or prohibiting the free exercise thereof.   (8 Jefferson's Works, 113.)

Upon the passage of the act of March 3, 1887, similar views were expressed by distinguished Senators from Vermont and Kansas.

Acting upon these fundamental canons, and in accordance with the acts of Congress, the Commission has from time to time, in official reports and otherwise, assured the Mormon people that the Government of the United States had no design to coerce them concerning their church membership or their religious opinions, and that all that was required, and all that could rightfully be required, was that they should come within the laws and abandon the practice of polygamy.   For example, in the Commission's first annual report, of November 17, 1882, it said: " The legislation of Congress, as we understand it, is not enacted against the religion of any portion of the people of this Territory.   The law under which we are acting is directed against the *crime of polygamy.*"

In its report of October 30, 1883, it is said that "by abstaining from the polygamic relation they [the Mormons] will enjoy all the political rights of American citizens."

In its last annual report (September 24, 1886) the following language was employed: "We recognize the obligation of the Government of the United States to protect the personal and property rights of the Mormon people and to deal with them as equals before the law, yet it is equally the duty of the Government to punish crime."

In its "circular for the information of registration officers," issued in March, 1887, after enumerating all the disqualifications of voters under the law, it added:

"That no *opinions* which they (the Mormons) may entertain upon questions of religion or church polity should be the subject of inquiry or exclusion from the polls," and the Edmunds act of 1882 declares that no person shall be excluded from the polls on account of any opinion he may entertain on the subject of polygamy or bigamy if he is otherwise eligible to vote.

Having received information that some of the registration officers were disregarding the principle thus settled and repeatedly announced, they were promptly removed from office by the unanimous vote of all the members of the Commission.

After such assurances have been held out to the Mormon people by the Supreme Court of the United States, by those eminent statesmen who championed the anti-polygamy legislation in Congress, and by the Commission, representing no party or faction, but the Government of the United States ; now, while the great mass of the Mormon people are making an effort for the abandonment of the practice of polygamy, we are asked to recommend further legislation of a hostile and aggressive character, almost, if not entirely, destructive of local self-government, thereby inflicting punishment on the innocent as well as the guilty. Our answer is, we cannot do so ; we decline to advise Congress to inflict punishment by disfranchising any portion of the people of Utah on account of their religious or irreligious opinions.

In Utah there are persons of multifarious religious creeds, some with no religious belief at all. Some prominent and enterprising citizens believe in the revelations of the *Old* Testament and reject those recorded in the *New*, while a large majority of the people of the Territory profess a belief in the Old Testament, the New Testament, and divers modern "revelations" besides. Those who accept the revelations of the Bible are divided into many separate church organizations by reason of diverse interpretations.   Then, in the close of the most enlightened century in the tide of time, shall we invoke legal coercion over the consciences of men and resort to the pains and penalties inflicted in former times for recusancy, non-conformity, and heresy?

In this age the world moves, and even religious fanatics must keep pace with progress.   The Utah of to-day is not, and never can be again, what it was when Brigham Young, as prophet, seer and revelator, dominated over his devoted followers, isolated from all the world, in the secluded valleys of the Rocky Mountains; nor, in our opinion, can that fading and dissolving specter of the past be justly or properly invoked as an excitative to legislation proscriptive of religious opinion.   The railroad and the telegraph, free speech and a free press, are there now.   Schools and colleges and churches of many denominations are found in all parts of the Territory.   The people are no longer isolated, but are now in communication with all the world; and Salt Lake City is one of the most cosmopolitan places on the continent, a resort for tourists, savants, statesmen, and scholars from abroad. Under such circumstances is it not morally impossible . that Utah shall ever again become subject to that church domination and oppression which are now imputed by some persons as an existing reality against the "Mormon hierarchy?"

Churches and creeds are subject to the laws of evolution, and Mormonism must yield to the inexorable logic of civilization.   Polygamy must go, and its abrogation will, sooner or later, be an accomplished fact.   Other objectionable features are gradually giving way; and we

are thoroughly satisfied that whatever the Federal authorities can rightfully accomplish in the way of reform can
be done without resorting to the total overthrow of local
self-government.

Polygamous marriages, in Utah are becoming less
frequent, as will hereinafter be shown.   No polygamist
votes, holds office, or sits on a jury.   The mass of the
Mormons have taken the test oath and voted against
polygamy.   The conclusion is that the present laws of
Congress are working successfully; that there is no
necessity of resorting to un-American plans of government; and that if, as we apprehend, the object of the
Government is to reform and not to destroy the Mormon people, they should be encouraged and not spurned
in their efforts for the abrogation of polygamy and for
reform.

During the last two years and a half there has been
no relaxation in the enforcement of the laws for the suppression of polygamy.   During that period there have
been about three hundred convictions to the penitentiary
for offenses against those laws, which, notwithstanding
the signs of reform, should continue to be enforced
against all persons violating them; no step backward
should be tolerated; at the same time the innocent should
be scrupulously protected.

In a larger view polygamy is adjudged by the most
enlightened nations to be a manifold evil.   It is the
parent of caprice, cruelty and license.   It enervates the
male and degrades the female.   Socially, politically, and
physically it is corrupting and deteriorating.   Despotic
in the family, it is the prototype of despotism in the
government.   It largely accounts for the differing characteristics of the Asiatic and European; for the indolence
and feebleness of the one, and the energy and enterprise

of the other. Inferiority is its badge. In the armed contests of rival civilizations, alike in ancient Greece and modern India, it succumbed to the superiority of monogamy. It is at variance with the divine economy in that originally God created but one man and one woman, Adam and Eve, each as the only partner in wedlock of the other. Logically, and as a consequence, it is irreconcilable to the idea of the marriage covenant as practiced and revered by the masterful Teuton, Celt and Anglo-Saxon. That covenant runs in these comprehensive and searching words:

Will thou have this woman to be thy wedded wife, to live together after God's ordinance in the holy estate of matrimony? Wilt thou love her, comfort her, honor her, and keep her in sickness and in health; and forsaking all other, keep thee unto her so long as ye both shall live?

Recognizing polygamy to be an evil and a bane, Congress has from time to time, enacted laws to eradicate it from Utah. One of them, known as the "Edmunds law," approved March 22, 1882, re-enacted and extended the provisions of those of earlier date. It declares polygamy a crime, defines the same, and punishes its commission by a fine not exceeding $500, and imprisonment not exceeding five years; declares cohabitation by a man with more than one woman a misdemeanor, punishable by fine of not more than $300, or by imprisonment for not more than six months, or by both in the discretion of the court, and allows a joinder of counts for polygamy and unlawful cohabitation in the same information or indictment;

Disqualifies any person from serving as a juror in any prosecution for polygamy or unlawful cohabitation who is, or has been, living in the practice of bigamy, polygamy, or unlawful cohabitation with more than one woman, or who believes it right for a man to have more than one living and undivorced wife at the same time, or who believes it right to live in the practice of cohabitation with more than one woman, upon his being challenged for any such cause;

Authorizes the President to grant absolute or limited or conditional amnesty to offenders against any such previously enacted laws;

Legitimates the issue of polygamous marriages, solemnized according to the ceremonies of the Mormon sect, who were born before the 1st day of January, 1883;

Disqualifies any polygamist, or other person cohabiting with more than one woman, from voting at any election, or for election or appointment to any office or place of trust, honor or emolument.

The last law on this subject, known as the "Edmunds-Tucker act," which took effect on the 3d day of March, 1887, is supplemental to the act of 1882, and is more comprehensive in its scope. It makes the lawful husband or wife (if consenting to testify) a competent witness in any examination, inquest or prosecution touching the other, under a statute of the United States forbidding any of the above-named offenses, except as to communications between each other deemed confidential at common law ;

Waives the original process of subpœna and authorizes an attachment for witnesses in any such criminal proceedings, upon cause shown by oath or affirmation;

Prescribes the rule determining the degrees of consanguinity, denounces incest, adultery and fornication, and prescribes the punishment therefor;

Vests the Commissioners who are or may be appointed by the supreme or district courts in the Territory, with the same powers and jurisdiction of justices of the peace in the Territory under the laws thereof; it also confers on such commissioners the same powers conferred by law on commissioners appointed by circuit courts of the United States;

Requires every ceremony of marriage performed in the Territory to be signed by the parties thereto, and by every officer, priest, or other person taking part therein; and that the same when thus authenticated, shall be filed in the office of the probate court of the proper county for record, and that the record thereof shall remain subject to inspection, and enforces the requirement by inflicting fine or imprisonment, or both, upon any willful violation thereof;

Incapacitates every illegitimate child in the Territory to take or receive by inheritance the estate or any part of the estate of his or her father, save such of them as shall have been born within twelve months after the passage of the act, or are legitimated by the act of 1882;

Dissolves the corporations known respectively as the "Perpetual Emigration Fund Company" and "the Church of Jesus Christ of Latter-day Saints," makes their renewal unlawful, and forfeits and escheats their property to the United States, subject to certain limitations and exceptions;

Regulates the right of dower; makes the judges of the probate courts appointable by the President, by and with the advice and consent of the Senate; abolishes female suffrage: requires the governor and secretary of the Territory together wih the Utah Commission, to redistrict the same, and to apportion the representation in the legislative assembly according to the numbers of the people in the Territory (exclusive of untaxed Indians and other non-citizens,) and the number of the members of the present legislative assembly, respectively;

Continues the powers and duties of the Utah Commission until the same shall be superceded by the legislative assembly of Utah and the subsequent approval of Congress;

Limits the right of suffrage to male persons, who as a precedent condition to the exercise thereof, shall have registered ·their names as voters, and subscribed an oath or affirmation that he is over twenty-one years of age, has resided in the Territory six months, and in the precinct of his residence one month; including in such oath or affirmation a statement according to fact, that he is a native born or naturalized citizen of the United States; and of his age, with his place of business, his status, whether single or married, and, if married, the name of his lawful wife; that he will support the Constitution of the United States and faithfully obey the laws thereof, especially the act of 1882, and this act in respect of the crimes in the same defined and forbidden, and will not directly or indirectly aid or abet, counsel or advise any other person to commit any of said crimes;·

More: It renders every person ineligible to serve as an officer or a juror in the Territory, who has not taken the oath therein set forth, similar in form, and absolutely disqualifies every person for such service, as also to vote in any election therein, who has been convicted of any crime in either of the acts mentioned, or who shall be a polygamist or in association or cohabitation polygamously with a person of the other sex;

Moreover, the act suspends the laws of the Territory providing for the method of electing and appointing the Territorial superintendent of district schools; abolishes that office, and devolves its powers and duties upon another officer, to be appointed by the supreme court of the Territory; restricts the quantity and mode of the tenure of the land which may be held by religious bodies, and annuls all local laws on that subject; provides that the militia of Utah shall be organized and subject in all respects to the laws of the United States regulating the militia in the Territories, and that the general officers of the militia shall be appointed by the governor of the Territory by and with the advice and consent of the council thereof.

The vigorous enforcement of these laws has resulted in a sense of disquietude and insecurity in the mass of the Mormon population, and, as we have before said, the indications of an important change are apparent. The truth of this statement is corroborated by the answers of the chief justice of the Territory and others, set forth in the appendix, numbered II, III, and IV, respectively, which are cited for what they express apart from any inference respecting further legislation.

It is admitted, however, that these answers designate no definite or approximate period when polygamy in Utah may be expected to cease; indeed it is deemed impracticable to do so. For ourselves we may repeat, that the practice of polygamy appears to be declining and in the course of ultimate abandonment, and that our observation leads us to believe that the present intention of the ascendent numbers of the monogamous Mormons is to compass and hasten that end.

The questions remaining relate to the admission of Utah as a State, and the consequent surrender of the power of Congress over the subject of polygamy under the existing Constitution of the United States. With respect to the first question, we have only to say that it appeals solely and properly to the sound discretion of

Congress, where we are content to leave it without further remark.

As to the second question, it evidently now engages earnest public attention and divides opinion. Considering these facts, and the importance of continuing the power of Congress over the subject of polygamy and of relieving the power from any question, we venture respectfully to recommend the adoption of an amendment to the Constitution of the United States, prohibiting the institution or practice of polygamy in any form in the States and in the Territories or other places over which the United States have exclusive jurisdiction, supplemented with appropriate power of legislation to carry it into full effect. This recommendation is in accordance with propositions which have already been submitted, respectively, in the Senate and House of Representatives, of which that in the House was supported by an able and elaborate report from its Judiciary Committee.

Such an amendment would put an end to special and provisional legislation, upon a disturbing question, which legislation, under the present Constitution, must cease to operate with the cessation of the territorial status. It would raise an implied and incidental power, primarily drawn from the power of Congress "to dispose of and make all needful rules and regulations respecting the territory or other property belonging to the United States," to the dignity of an express power embedded in that instrument itself.

Other considerations favor it. It would insure us a solemn and deliberate verdict of the American people against the practice of polygamy, either as a social institution or religious rite. It would serve as a rampart for the protection of monogamy, the bed-rock of American and European civilization, against the inroads of an

Asiatic vice.   It would be an authoritative notice to immigrants from all lands that the United States are dedicated to the virtues of monogamy, and, passing as a lesson into the common schools of the country, would form the minds of rising generations in harmony with its ideas and object.

Yours, respectfully,   A. B. CARLTON.
JOHN A. McCLERNAND.

Hon. L. Q. C. LAMAR,
Secretary of the Interior, Washington, D. C.

I.

OFFICE OF THE UTAH COMMISSION,
SALT LAKE CITY, May 2, 1887.

The following letter is published for the the information of the registration officers.

OFFICE OF THE UTAH COMMISSION,
SALT LAKE CITY, April 28, 1887.

Hon. C. W. Bennett.

DEAR SIR: In response to a request by a committee of gentlemen that called on this Commission several days ago in reference to a change of the form of the registration oath which has been furnished to the registration officers throughout the Territory, we would respectfully say that we are not convinced of the propriety or necessity of making such a change, for a number of reasons; among others:

(1.)   Because we are satisfied that the oath furnished by us is in accordance with the law.

(2.)   The modifications proposed by you, if equivalent to the language employed by the act of Congress, are unnecessary; and if not in accordance with the act, they are illegal.   The law is one declaring the political disfranchisement of the citizens under certain conditions.

We hardly need add that such laws, as a rule, are viewed critically and construed strictly by the courts in favor of political manhood.

(3.)   The request comes at such a late day (the registration beginning May 2nd,) and so long after the printed forms of affidavits to the number of 35, 000 have been distributed over the Territory, that the proposed change would occasion much delay and great unnecessary expense.

(4.)   Plainly, it is not the intent of the law to prescribe any religious creed to the citizen, but to prescribe a rule of action, irrespective of his present or future secret intentions or convictions, or the change of any of them.   The oath we have formulated in the terms of the law is but auxiliary to the enforcement of the actual observance of the law and the rule of action prsecribed by it; hence, as a conclusion, it is equally plain to us, that whosoever takes the oath and transcends the rule it prescribes by perpetuating a prohibited and punishable crime, thereby incurs not only the stain of moral perjury, but liability to legal punishment for the commission of any such prohibited crime; and these consequences would as logically and necessarily follow the infraction of the form of oath which we have furnished as the interpolated form which has been proposed.

(5.)   The fact that Congress has prescribed the oath is, in itself, an assumption by that body that the oath will not be vain, but be practically binding upon conscience and useful.   Otherwise, why the legal requirement of the oath?   Nor is this construction inconsistent with either the municipal or moral law, which respectively presume the honesty and innocence of the individual until that presumption is overcome by competent proof.

(6.)   Since the interview with the committee at our rooms, we were advised that a written communication was to be presented by the committee, and afterwad we received information that it would not be presented. We therefore make this reply, desiring to be entirely courteous to the committee, apprehending that further delay might be misconstrued.

By order of the Commission.

W. C. HALL, *Secretary.*

II.

From Hon. Charles S. Zane.

OFFICE OF THE UTAH COMMISSION,
SALT LAKE CITY, August 10, 1887.

Hon. Charles S. Zane,
(U. S.) Judge 3rd District U. T.:

DEAR SIR: In view of your great experience and eminent service as a judge in this Territory, I beg to ask of you brief answers as matter of useful information to the following questions:

1.   Whether, in your opinion, the existing laws, diligently and strictly enforced, may be reasonably relied on to work the cessation of polygamy as a practice?

2.   Whether any case originating in the commission of the crime of polygamy since the date of the Edmunds-Tucker act has come under your judicial notice?

3.   Whether, in your opinion, the alternative provisions of that act extending the electoral franchise to those complying with their conditions, and denying it to those not complying with them, or who are otherwise disqualified, have materially prompted the present movement for a constitutional inhibition of polygamy?

Your obedient servant,

JOHN A. McCLERNAND.

To the first question propounded within, I answer, yes.

To the second question, I answer, no.

To the third question, I answer, yes.

C. S. ZANE.

III.

From Hon. William G. Bowman.

OFFICE OF THE UTAH COMMISSION,
SALT LAKE, August 16, 1887.

Hon. Wm. G. Bowman,
    Surveyor-Gen. U. S. U. T.:

DEAR SIR: Permit me to inquire whether, from personal and official observation, you are of opinion that the laws of the United States are working with increasing and encouraging effect a reformation of the practice of polygamy in this Territory?

    Your obedient servant,

JOHN A. McCLERNARD.

SALT LAKE CITY, UTAH,
August 17, 1887

To Hon. A. B. Carlton and Gen. John A. McClernand:

MY DEAR GENERAL: My answer to above interrogation is a decided yes. The change in Mormon sentiment in the last year has been marked and encouraging on the question of the suppression and abandonment of polygamy.

    Truly your friend,

WM. G. BOWMAN,
U. S. Sur. Gen'l.

IV.

Letter of Hon. Hadley D. Johnson.

SALT LAKE CITY, UTAH.
September 1, 1887.

GENTLEMEN: Your esteemed note of August 17th has been at hand for some days, and after some delay, having been some what indisposed, I shall attempt a reply to your inquiry.   *   *   *

You ask me, "What, in your [my] judgment, wi be the efficacy of the laws of the United States, particularly the Edmunds-Tucker act, in putting a stop to the practice of polygamy in this Territory" (Utah)?   *   *

I have been somewhat acquainted with a good many of the Latter-day Saints, as they call themselves, since the year 1851, at which time I located at Council Bluffs, Iowa, at which time most of the inhabitants of that place and vicinity were of the Mormon faith, and, although never having been sufficiently intimate with them to become acquainted with the inside workings of their " peculiar institution," I have not been unobservant of its outside effects and influences.   *   *   *

The bill introduced into Congress providing for a Territorial government in Utah became a law in 1850, and from that time until 1862 Congress, although doubtless fully aware of the open practice of this offense (polygamy) in Utah, failed to   *   *   *   enact any law prohibiting the practice   *   *   *   in the Territory.   *   *   *   *   *   *   *   *

Even after the enactment   *   *   *   of 1862, no efforts of any importance seem to have been made to enforce it for many years, the Mormons claiming and no doubt believing the law to be unconstitutional, and remaining unmolested,   *   *   continued openly to avow their unlawful practices.   *   *

To test the constitutionality of the law of 1862, an appeal was taken to the Supreme Court of the United States, and that tribunal decided the law to be constitutional.   *   *   *   *   *   *

Recently, however,   *   *   there seems to have been a change in the nature of the efforts to punish violators of the law against polygamy and unlawful cohabitation.   By unyielding and determined, yet humane, efforts, the law is now being enforced to such an extent   *   *   (that) the open and avowed practice of polygamy is unknown here.   *   *   *

But you want my opinion.   *   *   Therefore, to be more explicit,   *   *   I will remark, that if judicious, legal, and humane efforts shall continue to be made

17

by those having authority to enforce the laws now in existence, in a spirit of fairness and without apparent or real malice, I am prepared to believe that the "peculiar institution" may be repressed in the not distant future, or, if not entirely suppressed, it will become so unpopular that the younger members of the church will repudiate the system,   *   *   *   and that as a tenet of the Mormon Church it will become obsolete and fall into a state of "innocuous desuetude."

As you are aware, at the late constitutional convention held in this city, among the provisions   *   *   * adopted by that body was one providing for a total prohibition of the practice of polygamy in the proposed State.   There are different opinions as to the good faith of the members of the convention—some people holding that the adoption of this provision was a mere sham, intended to deceive Congress and the people of the States, and by means of this deception to procure admission into the Union of the States, while others believe that the proposition was made in good faith, and that if the State should be admitted the provision   *   *   * would be carried out to the letter.   What might have influenced the majority of the convention   *   *   * I, of course, have no means of determining.   All that I know is that some of the members were and are sincerely desirous that the system of polygamy should be eliminated from the Mormon Church.   I say I *know* such to be the case, but, perhaps, it would be nearer the truth to say that I firmly *believe* it.   *   *   *

If statehood should be granted at once, or if those who clamor for a legislative commission succeed in their efforts, the result might be different.

From what I have said you may reasonably infer that I do not think any change is at present desirable in the laws of Congress on this subject.   Let the Government persist in a just and vigorous effort to enforce existing laws, and I believe a change will take place for the better—one which will redound to the interest and peace and happiness of the people of Utah,   *   *   * and in time, when they become reconciled, they will be permitted to assume and enjoy the inestimable blessings of statehood."

Very sincerely, your friend,

HADLEY D. JOHNSON.

[NOTE.—The author of the letter containing the foregoing extracts was an early and prominent actor in public affairs successively in Indiana, Iowa, Nebraska and Idaho, and is now and has been for years a resident of Salt Lake City.]

MINORITY REPORT.

CHICAGO, ILL., September 24, 1888.

SIR: Former reports of this Commission have been so full and elaborate as to supersede the necessity of any particularity of detail at this time. It may be stated generally that the reform in Utah is progressing favorably, far beyond our most sanguine anticipations when we first entered upon our official duties. Utah is forging to the front among the Rocky Mountain States and Territories, and may be compared favorably with any of them in the enterprise of her citizens, the fertility of her valleys, the richness of her mines, and the flourishing conditions of her cities and towns.

A great deal of capital is being invested in Utah by non-Mormons in city lots, farming lands and mining property. Such investments are as safe there as in any other State or Territory; that is to say, there is not the slightest danger of armed insurrection, nor, in our opinion, is there any danger of adverse legislation that will jeopard personal security or property rights. Apart from sexual offenses (which are decidedly on the decrease) the Mormon people of Utah will compare favorably with other communities for peace, good order, sobriety, honesty and industry. In this respect we concur in the opinion of our three associates of the Utah Commission as expressed in their report of September 30, 1887:

The majority of the Mormons are a kindly and hospitable people. They possess many traits of character which are well worthy of emulation by others. In their local affairs they strive to suppress the vices which are common to settled communities. In matters of religion they are intensely devotional, rendering a cheerful obedience to their church rules and requirements. They possess many of the elements which under a wise leadership would make them a useful and prosperous people.

Either this "wise leadership" or the voluntary action of the people appears to have been asserted within the last eighteen months in ways that are commendable. Within that time the mass of the Mormon voters have taken the registration oath, swearing that they will not go into polygamy, and 95 per cent. of them voted in August of last year for the adoption of a constitution prohibiting and punishing the offense. Subsequently the legislative assembly of Utah, composed of thirty-one Mormons and five non-Mormons, on March 8th, 1888, passed a very well-considered and efficient marriage law, providing, among other things, severe penalties against clerks who issue licenses for plural marriages, and officers, priests and preachers who solemnize such unlawful marriages. The act also declares all polygamous marriages null and void.

The same legislature also adopted a resolution in relation to polygamy and other sexual offenses under the laws of Congress that—

This assembly is in favor of a just, humane and im

partial enforcement of said laws of the United States in the same manner that other criminal laws are enforced, under the Constitution and laws of our country, to the end that such offenses may be effectually prohibited.

In the city of Salt Lake, one of the most beautiful and flourishing cities in the Rocky Mountain region, the non-Mormons constitute about one-third of the population. Among them are many strong, energetic and prosperous citizens.

Formerly, under the law, the aldermen and councilmen were elected by the voters at large, of the whole city. The result was that the Mormons being in the majority, elected all their candidates. But at the municipal election of this year, in February, the Mormons proposed to the "Gentiles" that they select four of their best men as candidates, to put on a ticket with eleven Mormons, for aldermen and councilmen. This proposition was accepted by a portion of the non-Mormons; and this fusion ticket was elected by a large majority. In this connection it is proper to add that the last legislative assembly enacted a law for the election of members of the city governments by wards.

The import of these facts is emphasized in a remarkable manner by what is now transpiring in the courts in Utah. Within a few days past a number of Mormons, charged by indictment with sexual offenses and who had been evading trial, came into open court, waived trial, voluntarily pleaded guilty to the indictments and received sentence of fine and imprisonment. Among the number so doing were one or more leading men. We repeat that this example is, in our opinion, pregnant with significance, and that it will be followed by other like examples; that the hindrance which has hitherto impeded the course of law and justice, is giving way as a raft before the steady and increasing current of the rising stream. It is hardly to be supposed that they or other men in the same category would voluntarily take such steps, with the purpose to repeat and continue to repeat them. On the contrary, rationally, they conduct to a different conclusion, namely, a disposition on the part of the Mormons to abandon the commission of sexual offenses and to yield obedience to the law. Yet the laws should continue to be vigilantly and strictly enforced against all violating them. No step backward in this regard should be sanctioned. Let the laws be executed.

The facts above set forth with others that have fallen under our observation confirm the opinion that a great majority of the Mormons have wisely resolved that the practice of polygamy should be abandoned.

Our view that polygamy is on the decline in Utah, is supported by an eminent Methodist minister, who for many years has been in charge of the " Methodist mission in Utah," and who has mingled with the people in all parts of the Territory. He is credibly reported as having stated in conference, at Cincinnati, early in this month, " that notwithstanding reports given out by the press in general, polygamy is on the decline," and that " in a few more years it will be driven out of Utah."

The chief justice of Utah, the Hon. C. S. Zane over a year ago expressed the opinion " that the existing laws, diligently and strictly enforced, might be reasonably relied on to work a cessation of polygamy as a practice," and about the same time the Hon. William G. Bowman, surveyor-general of Utah, stated that " the change in Mormon sentiment in the last year has been marked and encouraging on the question of the suppression and abandonment of polygamy."

The statement of the reverend gentleman, hereinbefore mentioned, suggests the remark that on account of the "peculiar institutions" of a portion of the people of Utah, "the reports given out by the press" are not only at present, but have been for years, of a sensational and highly colored character. That the condition of affairs has been improving in Utah for many years is evidenced by the following statement made about five years ago by the leading anti-Mormon newspaper of Utah:

Salt Lake City is so changed from the Utah of ten years ago that, could the old style of affairs be restored for a week, the old slavery, the old tyranny and the restrictions, the Mormon people themselves would rise up in rebellion. There are forces at work in Utah which are all-powerful, and which no artifice or restrictions, no falsehoods and no superstitions can resist.

The "forces at work" at that time have been supplemented by additional Congressional legislation, and such vigorous enforcement of the laws that there can be no doubt of a successful result in the near future.

There is a considerable "Gentile" immigration into Utah, and this is to be an important factor in the solution of the "problem." Utah has a mild and equable climate, and those who contemplate sojourning or settling there for health, pleasure, or business need not be deterred by sensational newspaper reports of "Mormon outrages." Much that is said concerning an unpopular and hated people should be received *cum grano*, for it is easy as well as agreeable for many persons to deal largely in hyperbole and fiction against those whom it is the fashion to despise.

It is obvious that the laws of Congress and of the Territorial legislature, the officers in charge of the execution of the Federal statutes, the people of Utah, including the Gentiles and the monogamous Mormons, with many other beneficent influences, such as railroads, telegraphs, schools, colleges, and the invincible progress of civilization, are rapidly and surely working out a reformation of the inhibited sexual offenses in Utah; and there does not now seem to be any necessity or propriety for further legislation restrictive of political rights in that Territory.

We are thoroughly satisfied that the work of reformation in Utah is progressing rapidly, and that it will soon result in a successful issue without a resort to legislation that is proscriptive of religious opinion.   Our view may be epitomized in a few words: *Punish criminal actions; but religious creeds, never.*

The present laws of Congress appertaining to Utah are very stringent, and they will accomplish all that can be reasonably required of legal coercion.   We are therefore unwilling to advise any further abridgment of local self-government in that Territory.

Without going into tedious detail, the general result shows gratifying progress in the enforcement of the laws in Utah.

All polygamists have been excluded from voting or holding office, and the laws for the punishment of polygamy and other sexual offenses have been ably and vigorously enforced, which fully appears by the following table prepared from information furnished by the United States district attorney in pursuance of a resolution of the House of Representatives   of   the   United States :

Number of convictions for polygamy, unlawful cohabitation, etc., under the acts of Congress of 1862, 1882, and 1887, in the Territory of Utah, with the amount of fines, etc.

Year.	Convictions.	Fines collected.	Costs collected.	Total amounts collected.
Under laws of 1862 and 1882.				
Polygamy:				
1875	1			
1879	1			
1884	3			
1885	2			
1886	4			
1887	4			
1888	1			
Under law of 1882.				
Unlawful cohabitation:				
1885	39	$4,500	$855.00	$5,355.00
1886	123	5,800	1,685.30	7,485.30
1887	228	13,175	4,260.50	17,435.50
1888	107	9,730	4,229.40	13,958.40
Under laws of 1887.				
Adultery:				
1887	4			
1888	4	25	21.90	
Fornication:				
1887	6	55	39.45	
1888	2			

The deputy registration officers of the whole Territory, having been requested to report the names of all persons who they had reasons to believe had gone into polygamy in their respective precincts during the year subsequent to the June revision of 1887, gave the names, in the aggregate, of twenty-nine men who, in their opinion, had entered into that relation during the year. Whether these opinions were based on evidence or mere conjectures we can not say. But allowing that they had good grounds for their opinions, this is a small showing compared with former times; and it is a noteworthy fact that, according to these reports, no cases of polygamy within the year had occurred in the more populous and enlightened portions of the Territory, such as the precincts of Salt Lake City, Logan City, Ogden City, Provo City, Fillmore City, and others.

This is another confirmation of our belief that polygamy can not stand up before modern civilization.

We will not call in question the good faith of the deputy registrars who reported the twenty-nine cases of supposed polygamy, but it is somewhat strange that there has only been one indictment found up to this time, for a polygamous marriage alleged to have occurred since the 3rd of March, 1887. This information we have officially from the clerks of the first and third district courts, which districts comprise about three-fourths of the population of Utah. From the second district we have no satisfactory report in consequence of the records having been destroyed by fire.

This year, in the real estate excitement in Utah, commonly called a "boom," the Mormons freely sold their city lots and other real estate to Gentiles as well as to others; and this, notwithstanding the general understanding that the Mormon Church leaders have deprecated and remonstrated against their people selling their land to Gentiles. This is another strong evidence of the the spirit of independence among the monogamous Mormons that is influencing young Utah, and of the general disposition to repudiate the authority of the Church leader, in secular and civil affairs. "Business is business," and it has a wonderfully cosmopolitan effect upon all classes of men, the Jew and the Gentile, the saint and sinner, the Catholic and the Puritan.

This potent factor of civilization, toleration and liberal thought has induced the hitherto opposing elements to unite in the institution of a chamber of commerce in Salt Lake City, which is in a very flourishing condition, where Mormons and Gentiles are working together for the common good. This, too, was accomplished by the people, notwithstanding considerable opposition or reluctance on the part of extreme men of both factions.

On the 4th of July of this year, as well as last year, the Gentiles and the Mormons cordially united in the celebration of Independence Day, and on each occasion there was a magnificent street procession, and patriotic speeches by Gentiles and Mormons.

From the foregoing statement of our views it will be readily seen why we can not concur in the report of our associates. For us to sign such a report would be wholly inconsistent with the principles and opinions avowed by us in our annual report of a year ago. We there stated that—

The conclusion is that the present laws of Congress are working successfully; that there is no necessity of resorting to un-American plans of government; and that if, as we apprehend, the object of the Government is to reform and not to destroy the Mormon people, they should be encouraged and not spurned in their efforts for the abrogation of polygamy and for reform.

The Commission has repeatedly announced the purposes of the Government.

On November 17, 1882, it said—

The legislation of Congress is not, as we understand it, enacted against the religion of any portion of the people of this Territory. The law under which we are acting is directed against the *crime of polygamy*.

On October 30, 1883, it said—

By abstaining from the polygamic relation they (the Mormons) will enjoy all the political rights of American citizens.

In our report of September 28, 1887, the following language was employed:

After such assurances have been held out to the Mormon people by the Supreme Court of the United States, by those eminent statesmen who championed the anti-polygamy legislation in Congress, and by the Commission, representing no faction or party, but the Government of the United States—now, while the great mass of the Mormon people are making an effort for the abandonment of polygamy we are asked to recommend further legislation of a hostile and aggressive character, almost, if not entirely destructive of local self-government, thereby inflicting punishment on the innocent as well as the guilty.   Our answer is, we can not do so.

If we should concur in the report of our associates we would seem to be entering "a new departure," a crusade against a church, and a raid for the destruction of political rights.   We do not understand that we have any commission for such purposes.

We renew the recommendation made by us in our last report:

Considering the importance of continuing the power of Congress over the subject of polygamy and of relieving the power from any question, we venture respectfully to recommend the adoption of an amendment to the Constitution of the United States prohibiting the institution or practice of polygamy in any form in the States and in the Territories or other places over which the United States has exclusive jurisdiction, supplemented with appropriate power of legislation to carry the amendment into full effect.

This recommendation is in accordance with propositions which have already been submitted, respectively, in the Senate and House of Representatives, of which that in the House was supported by an able and elaborate report from its Judiciary Committee. Such an amendment would put an end to special and provisional legislation upon a disturbing question, which legislation under the present Constitution must cease to operate with the cessation of the Territorial status. It would raise an implied and incidental power, primarily drawn from the power of Congress "to dispose of and make all needful rules and regulations respecting the Territory or other property belonging to the United States," to the dignity of an express power imbedded in that instrument.

Other considerations favor it. It would insure as a solemn and deliberate verdict of the American people against the practice of polygamy, either as a social institution or religious rite. It would serve as a rampart for the protection of monogamy, the bed-rock of American and European civilization, against the inroads of an Asiatic vice. It would be an authoritative notice to immigrants from all lands that the United States are dedicated to the virtues of monogamy, and, passing as a lesson into the common schools of the country, would form the minds of rising generations in harmony with its ideas and object.

The Commission was originally selected by President Arthur from five different States, on the theory, as we have been credibly informed, that non-residents would not likely be influenced by the passions and prejudices of the two factions in Utah.

Election and registration officers should be as free from prejudice and passion as the ermined judge on the bench.

As well from a sense of personal and official propriety, as in deference to the considerations understood to have influenced the President in selecting non-residents of Utah as Commissioners, we are forbidden from assuming an attitude of hostility toward any part of the people of Utah.

We have no commission to bring in or reject new States, nor to give unasked-for advice on such subject to Congress.

We are not under any obligation, nor have we any disposition, to defend the Mormons against all that has been alleged against them, but we believe that they are entitled to be treated with justice and humanity; that they are not incorrigible; that they are subject to be influenced by the same causes that have changed and ameliorated other peoples' churches and creeds. We also believe that they have got common sense, and by the exercise of this valuable attribute they have found out that polygamy must go.

We believe the great mass of the Mormon people are determined to go on with the reform, and that they will accomplish the work, in spite of the reported harangue of Rudger Clawson, and in spite of any influence that may be attempted to be exercised by a few fanatical old polygamists. Since the date of the Commission's last report a general election occurred in the Territory on the 6th of August ultimo pursuant to law. The election comprised county, district, and precinct officers, numbering in all 950. The agencies employed in connection with the election comprised 318 electoral registrars, 1,124 judges of elections, and a canvassing board of 5 members, all of whom were appointed by the Commission and took the prescribed test oath. There were also municipal elections in Salt Lake City and a number of other cities and towns. The elections were conducted satisfactorily, and transpired in a peaceable and orderly manner.

Passing to the subject of the social evils which prompted Congress to enact relevant, repressive laws, including the auxiliary provisions constituting this Commission and defining its powers and duties, we, as members of the commission, have just occasion to congratulate the Government and the public at large upon the efficacy of these agencies in promoting the work of reform. While the instances of polygamy have confessedly decreased since the enactment of the Edmunds law of March 22, 1882, the judicial convictions for that offense, owing to the activity and diligence of Federal officers, have been numerically increased.   These convictions outnumber all such convictions preceding that date; and since the date of the Edmunds-Tucker law of March 3, 1887, the same comparison applies to the instances of unlawful cohabitation and the convictions therefor.

The convictions for polygamy legally entailed imprisonment in the penitentiary not exceeding five years and a fine in each case not exceeding $500, and for unlawful cohabitation like imprisonment for not more than six months and a fine of not more than $300.   The fines and costs assessed and collected in the latter class of cases amount to the sum of $44,235.20.

These laws variously and powerfully re-inforced by the progress of ideas, intelligence and the modern agencies of communication and intercourse, as railroads, the telegraph and the press, have, in our opinion, struck a deadly blow at the institution of polygamy and the indulgence of sexual offenses in Utah.

On the other hand, individual instances of aberration from the general course of reform thus evidenced, have been cited.   We have no disposition to excuse or palliate these exceptions; on the contrary, we condemn them.   Yet in a large and philosophical view, they should not be deemed unnatural or strange.   Radical revolutions of opinions and habits, especially of religious convictions, usually if not universally encounter the friction of opposition and resistance. While the mass moves onward, minorities and individuals pull backward and secede. It has always been so, and, in the nature of things must continue to be so. The history of political and church government abundantly and alike illustrates this truth. Nevertheless, the revolution as the world, will move on, carrying the consenting with it and destroying the influence of the dissenters and obstructionists.

The revolution of opinion and conduct among the Mormons in Utah, particularly in the rising generation, is inaugurated and advancing with increasing momentum to the front and the control, and, in our opinion, it will irresistibly proceed until its mission is finished. Revolutions as a rule, do not retrograde.

Now that it is apparent that the practice of polygamy is passing away, another thing is made prominent and brought forward by non-Mormons in Utah as a justification for further hostile discrimination by the Government against the Mormons, namely, their religion and church government. On this subject we will repeat the language of our last annual report:

Now, in the close of the most enlightened century in the tide of time, shall we invoke legal coercion over the consciences of men and resort to the pains and penalties inflicted in former times for recusancy, non-conformity, apostasy and heresy?

In this age the world moves: and even religious fanatics must keep pace with progress. The Utah of to-day is not what it was when Brigham Young, as prophet, seer and revelator dominated over his devoted followers, isolated from all the world in the secluded valleys of the Rocky Mountains; nor in our opinion, can that fading and dissolving specter of the past be justly or properly invoked as an excitative to legislation proscriptive of religious opinions. The railroad and the telegraph, free speech and a free press are there now.   Schools and colleges and churches of many denominations are found in all parts of the Territory.   The people are no longer isolated, but are now in communication with all the world; and Salt Lake City is one of the most cosmopolitan places on the continent; a resort for tourists, savants, statesmen and scholars from abroad.   Under such circumstances is it not morally impossible that Utah shall ever again become subject to that church domination and oppression which are now imputed, by some persons, as an existing reality against the " Mormon hierarchy?"

In concluding this report we wish to say that we take our stand on the Constitution, the decisions of the Supreme Court, and the principles of civil and religious liberty as proclaimed by the fathers of the Republic, principles that should never be violated at the behest of popular prejudice against Jews, Catholics, Protestants or Mormons.

The Supreme Court of the United States has declared that—

Laws are made for the government of *actions* and while they cannot interfere with mere *religious belief*, they may with *practice*.   *   *   *

Congress can not pass a law for the government of the Territories which shall prohibit the free exercise of religion.   The first amendment to the Constitution expressly forbids such legislation.   Religious freedom is guaranteed everywhere throughout the United States, so far as Congressional interference is concerned (8 Otto, 145).

Madison says, sententiously:

Religion, or the duty which we owe to our Creator, is not within the province of civil government.

Jefferson says:

18

Believing that religion is a matter which lies solely between man and his God, and that he owes account to none other for his faith or his worship ; that the legislative power of the Government reaches *actions* only, and not *opinions*, I contemplate with solemn reverence that act of the whole American people which declares that their legislature should make no law respecting an establishment of religion or prohibiting the free exercise thereof. (8 Jefferson's Works, 113).

In the discharge of our official duty relating to Utah we have endeavored to divest ourselves of all prejudice and animosity, and in a calm and judicial frame of mind to ascertain the truth.   Our conclusion, from all the evidence before us, including our personal observation, is that a radical reform in the near future is morally certain, and that "Young Utah" will stand forth redeemed, regenerated, and disenthralled from the heavy burden that has so long rested upon the people.

Yours, respectfully,

JOHN A. McCLERNAND.
A. B. CARLTON.

The SECRETARY OF THE INTERIOR,
Washington, D. C.

CONGRESSIONAL LEGISLATION.

AN ACT

To punish and prevent the Practice of Polygamy in the Territories of the United States and other Places, and disapproving and annulling certain Acts of the Legislative Assembly of the Territory of Utah.

Be it enacted by the Senate and House of Representatives of the United States of America in Congress assembled, That every person having a husband or wife living, who shall marry any other person, whether married or single, in a Territory of the United States, or other place over which the United States have exclusive jurisdiction, shall, except in the cases specified in the proviso to this section, be adjudged guilty of bigamy, and, upon conviction thereof, shall be punished by a fine not exceeding five hundred dollars, and by imprisonment for a term not exceeding five years: *Provided, nevertheless*, That this section shall not extend to any person by reason of any former marriage whose husband or wife by such marriage shall have been absent for five successive years without being known to such person within that time to be living nor to any person by reason of any former marriage which shall have been dissolved by the decree of a competent court; nor to any person by reason of any former marriage which shall have been annulled or pronounced void by the sentence or decree of a competent court on the ground of the nullity of the marriage contract.

SEC. 2. *And be it further enacted*, That the following ordinance of the provisional government of the State of Deseret, so called, namely: "An ordinance incorporating the Church of Jesus Christ of Latter-day Saints," passed February eight, in the year eighteen hundred and fifty-one, and adopted, reenacted, and made valid by the governor and legislative assembly of the Territory of Utah by an act passed January nineteen, in the year eighteen hundred and fifty-five, entitled "An act in relation to the compilation and revision of the laws and resolutions in force in Utah Territory, their publication, and distribution," and all other acts and parts of acts heretofore passed by the said legislative assembly of the Territory of Utah, which establish, support, maintain shield, or countenance polygamy, be, and the same hereby are, disapproved and annulled: *Provided*, That this act shall be so limited and construed as not to affect or interfere with the right of property legally acquired under the ordinance heretofore mentioned, nor with the right "to worship God according to the dictates of conscience," but only to annul all acts and laws which establish, maintain, protect, or contenance the practice of polygamy, evasively called spiritual marriage, however disguised by legal or ecclesiastical solemnities, sacraments, ceremonies, consecrations, or other contrivances.

SEC. 3. *And be it further enacted*, That it shall not be lawful for any corporation or association for religious or charitable purposes to acquire or hold real estate in any Territory of the United States during the existence of the territorial government of a greater value than fifty thousand dollars; and all real estate acquired or held by any such corporation or association contrary to the provisions of this act shall be forfeited and escheat to the United States: *Provided*, That existing vested rights in real estate shall not be impaired by the provisions of this section.

APPROVED July 1, 1862.

AN ACT.

In relation to courts and judicial officers in the Territory of Utah.

(COMMONLY DENOMINATED THE POLAND LAW.)

Be it enacted by the Senate and House of Representatives of the United States of America in Congress assembled, That it shall be the duty of the United States marshal of the Territory of Utah, in person or by deputy, to attend all sessions of the supreme and district courts in said Territory, and to serve and execute all process and writs issued out of, and all orders, judgments, and decrees made by, said courts, or by any judge thereof, unless said court or judge shall otherwise order in any particular case. All process, writs, or other papers left with said marshal, or either of his deputies, shall be served without delay, and in the order in which they are received, upon payment or tender of his legal fees therefor; and it shall be unlawful for said marshal to demand, or receive mileage for any greater distance than the actual distance by the usual routes from the place of service or execution of process, writ, or other paper, to the place of return of the same, except that when it shall be necessary to convey any person arrested by legal authority out of the county in which he is arrested, said marshal shall be entitled to mileage for the whole distance necessarily traveled in delivering the person so arrested before the court or officer ordering such arrest. Said marshal is hereby authorized to appoint as many deputies as may be necessary, each of whom shall have authority, in the name of said marshal, to perform any act with like effect and in like manner as said marshal; and the marshal shall be liable for all official acts of such deputies, as if done by himself. Such appointment shall not be complete until he shall give bond to said marshal, with sureties, to be by him approved, in the penal sum of ten thousand dollars, conditioned for the faithful discharge of his duties; and he shall also take and subscribe the same oath prescribed by law to be taken by said marshal, and said appointment, bond and oath shall be filed and remain in the office of the clerk of the supreme court of said Territory. In actions brought against said marshal for the mis-feasance or non-feasance of any deputy, it shall be lawful for the plaintiff at his option, to join the said deputy and the sureties on his bond with said marshal and his sureties. Any process either civil or criminal returnable to the supreme or district courts, may be served in any county, by the sheriff thereof or his legal deputy, and they may also serve any other process which may be authorized by act of the Territorial Legislature.

DUTIES OF UNITED STATES ATTORNEYS.

SEC. 2. That it shall be the duty of the United States attorney in said Territory in person or by an assistant, to attend all the courts of record having jurisdiction of offenses, as well under the laws of said Territory as of the United States, and perform the duties of prosecuting officer in all criminal cases arising in said courts, and he is hereby authorized to appoint as many assistants as may be necessary, each of whom shall subscribe the same oath as is prescribed by law for said United States attorney and the said appointment and oath shall be filed and remain in the office of the clerk of the supreme court of said Territory. The United States attorney shall be entitled to the same fees for services rendered by said assistants as he would be entitled to for the same services if rendered by himself. The Territorial Legislature may provide for the election of a prosecuting attorney in any county; and such attorney, if authorized so to do by such Legislature, may commence prosecutions for offenses under the laws of the Territory within such county, and if such prosecution is carried to the district court by recognizance or appeal, or otherwise may aid in conducting the prosecution in such court. And the costs and expenses of all prosecutions for offenses against any law of the Territorial Legislature, shall be paid out of the treasury of the Territory.

JURISDICTION OF JUSTICES', PROBATE AND DISTRICT COURTS.

SEC. 3.   That there shall be held in each year, two terms of the supreme court of said Territory, and four terms of each district court, at such times as the governor of the Territory may by proclamation fix. The district courts shall have exclusive original jurisdiction in all suits or proceedings in chancery, and in all actions at law in which the sum or value of the thing in controversy shall be three hundred dollars or upward, and in all the controversies where the title, possessions or boundaries of land, or mines or mining claims shall be in dispute, whatever their value, except in actions for forcible entry or forcible and unlawful detainer; and they shall have jurisdiction in suits for divorce. Probate courts, in their respective counties shall have jurisdiction in the settlement of the estates of decedents, and in matters of guardianship and other like matters; but otherwise they shall have no civil, chancery, or criminal jurisdiction whatever; they shall have jurisdiction of suits of divorce for statutory causes concurrently with the district courts;

but any defendant in a suit for divorce commenced in a probate court shall be entitled after appearance and before plea or answer, to have said suit removed to the district court having jurisdiction, when said suit shall proceed in like manner as if originally commenced in said district court. Nothing in this act shall be construed to impair the authority of the probate courts to enter land in trust for the use and benefit of the occupants of towns in the various counties of the Territory of Utah, according to the provisions of "An act for the relief of the inhabitants of cities and towns upon public lands," approved March second, eighteen hundred and sixty-seven, and "An act to amend an act entitled 'An act for the relief of the inhabitants of cities and towns upon the public lands,'" approved June eighth, eighteen hundred and sixty-eight; or to discharge the duties assigned to the probate judges by an act of the Legislative Assembly of the Territory of Utah, entitled "An act prescribing rules and regulations for the execution of the trust arising under an act of Congress entitled 'An act for the relief of the inhabitants of cities and towns upon the public lands.'" All judgments and decrees heretofore rendered by the probate courts which have been executed, and the time to appeal from which has by the existing laws of said Territory expired, are hereby validated and confirmed. The jurisdiction heretofore conferred upon justices of the peace by the Organic Act of said Territory, is extended to all cases where the debt or sum claimed shall be less than three hundred dollars. From all final judgments of justices of the peace an appeal shall be allowed to the district courts of their respective districts, in the same manner as is now provided by the laws of said Territory for appeals to the probate courts; and from the judgments of the probate courts an appeal shall lie to the district court of the district embracing the county in which such probate court is held in such cases, and in such manner as the supreme court of said Territory may, by general rules framed for that purpose, specify and designate, and such appeal shall vacate the judgment appealed from, and the case shall be tried *de novo* in the appellate court.   Appeals may be taken from both justices' and probate courts to the district court of their respective districts in cases where judgments have been heretofore rendered and remain unexecuted; but this provision shall not enlarge the time for taking an appeal beyond the periods now allowed by the existing laws of said Territory for taking appeals.   A writ of error from the Supreme Court of the United States to the supreme court of the Territory shall lie in criminal cases, where the accused shall have been sentenced to capital punishment or convicted of bigamy or polygamy.   Whenever the condition of the business in the district court of any district is such that the judge of the district is unable to do the same, he may request the judge of either of the other districts to assist him, and upon such request made, the judge so requested may hold the whole or part of any term, or any branch thereof, and his acts as judge shall be of equal force as if he were duly assigned to hold the courts in such district.

JURY LISTS—HOW DRAWN.

SEC. 4.   That within sixty days after the passage of this act, and in the month of January annually hereafter, the clerk of the district court in each judicial district, and the judge of probate of the county in which the district court is next to be held, shall prepare a jury-list from which grand and petit jurors shall be drawn, to serve in the district courts, of such district, until a new list shall be made as herein provided.   Said clerk and probate judge shall alternately select the name of a male citizen of the United States who has resided in the district for a period of six months next preceding, and who can read and write in the English language; and as selected, the name and residence of each shall be entered upon the list, until the same shall contain two hundred names, when the same shall be duly certified by such clerk and probate judge; and the same shall be filed in the office of the clerk of such district court, and a duplicate copy shall be made and certified by such officers, and filed in the office of said probate judge. Whenever a grand or petit jury is to be drawn to serve at any term of a district court, the judge of such district shall give public notice of the time and place of the drawing of such jury, which shall be at least twelve days before the commencement of such term; and on the day and at the place thus fixed, the judge of such district shall hold an open session of his court, and shall preside at the drawing of such jury; and the clerk of such court shall write the name of each person on the jury lists returned and filed in his office upon a separate slip of paper, as nearly as practicable of the same size and form, and all such slips shall, by the clerk in open court, be placed in a covered box, and thoroughly mixed and mingled, and thereupon the United States marshal, or his deputy, shall proceed to fairly draw by lot from said box such number of names as may have previously been directed by said judge; and if both a grand and petit jury are to be drawn, the grand jury shall be drawn first; and when the drawing shall have been concluded, the clerk of the district court shall issue a *venire* to the marshal or his deputy, directing him to summon the persons so drawn, and the same shall be duly served on each of the persons so drawn at least seven days before the commencement of the term at which they are to serve; and the jurors so drawn and summoned shall constitute the regular grand and petit juries for the term for all cases. And the names thus drawn from the box by the clerk, shall not be returned to or again placed in said box until a new jury list shall be made. If during any term of the district court any grand or petit jurors shall be necessary, the same shall be drawn from said box by the United States Marshal in open court; but if the attendance of those drawn cannot be obtained in a reasonable time, other names may be drawn in the same manner. Each party, whether in civil or criminal cases, shall be allowed three peremptory challenges except in capital cases, where the prosecution and the defense shal each be allowed fifteen challenges. In criminal cases, the court, and not the jury, shall pronounce the punishment under the limitation prescribed by law. The grand jury must inquire into the case of every person imprisoned within the district on a criminal charge and not indicted; into the condition and management of the public prisons within the district; and into the wilful, corrupt misconduct in office of public officers of every description within the district; and they are also entitled to free access, at all reasonable times, to the public prisons, and to the examination, without charge, of all public records within the district.

NOTARIES PUBLIC.

SEC. 5.   That there shall be appointed by the governor of said Territory one or more notaries public for each organized county, whose term of office shall be two years and until their successors shall be appointed and qualified. The act of the Legislative Assembly of the Territory of Utah entitled "An act concerning notaries public," approved January seventeenth, eighteen hundred and sixty-six, is hereby approved, except the first section thereof, which is hereby disapproved: *Provided*, That wherever, in said act, the words "probate judge," or "clerk of the probate court," are used, the words "secretary of the Territory" shall be substituted.

UNITED STATES COMMISSIONERS.

SEC. 6.   That the supreme court of said Territory is hereby authorized to appoint commissioners of said court, who shall have and exercise all the duties of commissioners of the circuit courts of the United States, and to take acknowledgments of bail; and, in addition, they shall have the same authority as examining and committing magistrates in all cases arising under the laws of said Territory as is now possessed by justices of the peace in said Territory.

FEES OF ATTORNEYS, MARSHALS AND CLERKS.

SEC. 7.   That the act of the Territorial Legislature

of the Territory of Utah entitled "An act in relation to marshals and attorneys," approved March third, eighteen hundred and fifty-two, and all laws of said Territory inconsistent with the provisions of this act are hereby disapproved. The act of the Congress of the United States entitled "An act to regulate the fees and costs to be allowed clerks, marshals and attorneys of the circuit and district courts of the United States, and for other purposes," approved February twenty-sixth, eighteen hundred and fifty-three, is extended over and shall apply to the fees of like officers in said Territory of Utah. But the district attorney shall not by fees and salary together receive more than thirty-five hundred dollars per year; and all fees or moneys received by him above said amount shall be paid into the Treasury of the United States.

APPROVED June 23rd, 1874.

AN ACT

To amend section fifty-three hundred and fifty-two of the Rivised Statutes of the United States, in reference to bigamy, and for other purposes.

(COMMONLY CALLED THE EDMUNDS LAW.)

Be it enacted by the Senate and House of Representatives of the United States of America in Congress assembled, That section fifty-three hundred and fifty-two of the Revised Statutes of the United States be, and the same is hereby amended so as to read as follows, namely:

POLYGAMY DEFINED, AND HOW PUNISHED.

"Every person who has a husband or wife living who, in a Territory or other place over which the United States have exclusive jurisdiction, hereafter marries another, whether married or single, and any man who hereafter simultaneously, or on the same day, marries more than one woman, in a Territory or other place over which the United States have exclusive jurisdiction, is guilty of polygamy, and shall be punished by a fine of not more than five hundred dollars and by imprisonment for a term of not more than five years; but this section shall not extend to any person by reason of any former marriage whose husband or wife by such marriage shall have been absent for five successive years, and is not known to such person to be living and is believed by such person to be dead, nor to any person by reason of any former marriage which shall have been dissolved by a valid decree of a competent court, nor to any person by reason of any former marriage which shall have been pronounced void by a valid decree of a competent court, on the ground of nullity of the marriage contract."

SEC. 2.   That the foregoing provisions shall not affect the prosecution or punishment of any offense already committed against the section amended by the first section of this act.

PROSECUTION FOR UNLAWFUL COHABITATION.

Sec. 3.   That if any male person, in a Territory or other place over which the United States have exclusive jurisdiction, hereafter cohabits with more than one woman, he shall be deemed guilty of a misdemeanor, and on conviction thereof shall be punished by a fine of not more than three hundred dollars, or by imprisonment for not more than six months, or by both of said punishments, in the discretion of the court.

Sec. 4.   That counts for any or all of these offenses named in sections one and three of this act may be joined in the same information or indictment.

PERSONS NOT COMPETENT TO SERVE AS JURORS IN CERTAIN CASES.

Sec. 5.   That in any prosecution for bigamy, polygamy, or unlawful cohabitation, under any statute of the United States, it shall be sufficient cause of challenge to

any person drawn or summoned as a juryman or talesman, first, that he is or has been living in the practice of
bigamy, polygamy or unlawful cohabitation with more
than one woman, or that he is or has been guilty of an
offense punishable by either of the foregoing sections, or
by section fifty-three hundred and fifty-two, of the Revised Statutes of the United States, or the act of July
first, eighteen hundred and sixty-two, entitled, "An act to
punish and prevent the practice of polygamy in the Territories of the United States and other places, and disapproving and annulling certain acts of the legislative
assembly of the Territory of Utah," or, second, that he
believes it right for a man to have more than one living
and undivorced wife at the same time, or to live in the
practice of cohabiting with more than one woman; and
any person appearing or offered as juror or talesman,
and challenged on either of the foregoing grounds, may
be questioned on his oath as to the existence of any such
cause of challenge, and other evidence may be introduced
bearing upon the question raised by such challenge; and
this question shall be tried by the court. But as to the first
ground of challenge, before mentioned, the person challenged shall not be bound to answer if he shall say upon
his oath that he declines on the ground that his answer
may tend to criminate himself; and if he shall answer as to
said first ground, his answer shall not be given in evidence
in any criminal prosecution against him for any offense
named in sections one or three of this act; but if he declines to answer on any ground, he shall be rejected as incompetent.

THE PRESIDENT MAY GRANT AMNESTY.

SEC. 6.   That the President is hereby authorized to
grant amnesty to such classes of offenders guilty of bigamy, polygamy, or unlawful cohabitation, before the passage of this act, on such conditions and under such limitations as he shall think proper; but no such amnesty

shall have effect unless the conditions thereof shall be complied with.

OFFSPRING OF POLYGAMOUS MARRIAGES LEGITIMATED.

SEC. 7.   That the issue of bigamous or polygamous marriages, known as Mormon marriages, in cases in which such marriages have been solemnized according to the ceremonies of the Mormon sect, in any Territory of the United States, and such issue shall have been born before the first day of January, Anno Domini eighteen hundred and eighty-three are hereby legitimated.

POLYGAMISTS DISQUALIFIED TO VOTE OR HOLD OFFICE.

SEC. 8.   That no polygamist, bigamist or any person cohabiting with more than one woman, and no woman cohabiting with any of the persons described as aforesaid in this section, in any Territory or other place over which the United States have exclusive jurisdiction, shall be entitled to vote at any election held in any such Territory or other place, or be eligible for election or appointment to or be entitled to hold any office or place of public trust, honor or emolument in, under or for any such Territory or place, or under the United States.

UTAH ELECTION COMMISSION CREATED.

SEC. 9.   That all the registration and election officers of every description in the Territory of Utah are hereby declared vacant, and each and every duty relating to the registration of voters, the conduct of elections, receiving or rejection of votes, and the canvassing and returning of the same, and the issuing of certificates or other evidence of election in said Territory, shall, until other provision be made by the legislative assembly of said Territory as is hereinafter by this section provided, be performed under the existing laws of the United States and of said Territory by proper persons, who shall be appointed to execute such offices and perform such duties by a board of five persons, to be appointed by the President, by and with the advice and consent of the Senate, not more than three of whom shall be members of one political party; and a majority of whom shall be a quorum.   The members of said board so appointed by the President shall each receive a salary at the rate of three thousand dollars per annum, and shall continue in office until the legislative assembly of said Territory shall make provision for filling said offices as herein authorized.   The secretary of the Territory shall be the secretary of said board, and keep a journal of its proceedings, and attest the action of said board under this section. The canvass and return of all the votes at elections in said Territory for members of the legislative assembly thereof shall also be returned to said board, which shall canvass all such returns and issue certificates of election to those persons who, being eligible for such election, shall appear to have been lawfully elected, which certificates shall be the only evidence of the right of such persons to sit in such assembly: *Provided*, That said board of five persons shall not exclude any person otherwise eligible to vote from the polls on account of any opinion such person may entertain on the subject of bigamy or polygamy, nor shall they refuse to count any such vote on account of the opinion of the person casting it on the subject of bigamy or polygamy; but each house of such assembly, after its organization, shall have power to decide upon the elections and qualifications of its members.   And at, or after the first meeting of said legislative assembly whose members shall have been elected and returned according to the provisions of this act, said legislative assembly may make such laws, conformable to the organic act of said Territory and not inconsistent with other laws of the United States, as it shall deem proper concerning the filling of the offices in said Territory declared vacant by this act.

Approved March 22, 1882.

AN ACT

To amend an act entitled "An act to amend section fifty-three hundred and fifty-two of the Revised Statutes of the United States, in reference to bigamy, and for other purposes," approved March twenty-second, eighteen hundred and eighty-two.

[DESIGNATED THE EDMUNDS-TUCKER LAW.]

Be it enacted by the Senate and House of Representatives of the United States of America in Congress assembled, That in any proceeding or examination before a grand jury, a judge, justice, or a United States commissioner, or a court, in any prosecution for bigamy, polygamy, or unlawful cohabitation, under any statute of the United States, the lawful husband or wife of the person accused shall be a competent witness, and may be called, but shall not be compelled to testify in such proceeding, examination, or prosecution without the consent of the husband or wife, as the case may be; and such witness shall not be permitted to testify as to any statement or communication made by either husband or wife, to each other, during the existence of the marriage relation deemed confidential at common law.

ATTACHMENT FOR WITNESSES.

SEC. 2.   That in any prosecution for bigamy, polygamy, or unlawful cohabitation, under any statute of the United States, whether before a United States commissioner, justice, judge, a grand jury, or any court, an attachment for any witness may be issued by the court, judge, or commissioner, without a previous subpœna, compelling the immediate attendance of such witness, when it shall appear by oath or affirmation, to the commissioner, justice, judge, or court, as the case may be, that there is reasonable ground to believe that such witness will unlawfully fail to obey a subpœna issued and served in the usual course in such cases; and in such case the usual witness fee shall be paid to such witness so attached: *Provided,* That the person so attached may at any time secure his or her discharge from custody by executing a recognizance, with sufficient surety, conditioned for the appearance of such person at the proper time as a witness in the cause or proceeding wherein the attachment may be issued.

ADULTERY.

Sec. 3.   That whoever commits adultery shall be punished by imprisonment in the penitentiary not exceeding three years; and when the act is committed between a married woman and a man who is unmarried, both parties to such act shall be deemed guilty of adultery: and when such act is committed between a married man and a woman who is unmarried, the man shall be deemed guilty of adultery.

INCEST.

Sec. 4.   That if any person related to another person within and not including the fourth degree of consanguinity computed according to the rules of the civil law, shall marry or cohabit with, or have sexual intercourse with such other so related person, knowing her or him to be within said degree of relationship, the person so offending shall be deemed guilty of incest, and, on conviction thereof shall be punished by imprisonment in the penitentiary not less than three years and not more than fifteen years.

FORNICATION.

Sec. 5.   That if an unmarried man or woman commit fornication, each of them shall be punished by imprisonment not exceeding six months, or by fine not exceeding one hundred dollars.

PROSECUTION FOR ADULTERY.

Sec. 6.   That all laws of the legislative assembly of the Territory of Utah which provide that prosecutions for adultery can only be commenced on the complaint of the husband or wife, are hereby disapproved and annulled; and all prosecutions for adultery may hereafter be instituted in the same way that prosecutions for other crimes are.

COMMISSIONERS MADE JUSTICES OF THE PEACE.

SEC. 7. That commissioners appointed by the supreme court and district courts in the Territory of Utah, shall possess and may exercise all the powers and jurisdiction that are or may be possessed or exercised by justices of the peace in said Territory under the laws thereof, and the same powers conferred by law on commissioners appointed by circuit courts of the United States.

MARSHALS MADE SHERIFFS AND CONSTABLES.

SEC. 8. That the marshal of said Territory of Utah and his deputies, shall possess and may exercise all the powers in executing the laws of the United States or of said Territory possessed and exercised by sheriffs, constables, and their deputies as peace officers: and each of them shall cause all offenders against the law in his view, to enter into recognizance to keep the peace and to appear at the next term of the court having jurisdiction of the case, and to commit to jail in case of failure to give such recognizance. They shall quell and suppress assault and batteries, riots, routs, affrays and insurrections.

MARRIAGE CEREMONIES AND CERTIFICATES THEREOF.

SEC. 9. That every ceremony of marriage, or in the nature of a marriage ceremony of any kind, in any of the Territories of the United States, whether either or both or more of the parties to such ceremony be lawfully competent to be the subjects of such marriage or ceremony or not, shall be certified by a certificate stating the fact and nature of such ceremony, the full names of each of the parties concerned, and the full name of every officer, priest and person, by whatever style or designation called or known, in any way taking part in the performance of such ceremony, which certificate shall be drawn up and signed by the parties to such ceremony and by every officer, priest and person taking part in the performance of such ceremony, and shall be by the officer, priest or other person solemnizing such marriage or ceremony filed in the office of the probate court, or, if there be none, in the office of the court having probate powers in the county or district in which such ceremony shall take place, for record, and shall be immediately recorded, and be at all times subject to inspection as other public records. Such certificate, or the record thereof, or a duly certified copy of such record, shall be *prima facia* evidence of the facts required by this act to be stated therein, in any proceeding, civil or criminal, in which the matter shall be drawn in question. Any person who shall wilfully violate any of the provisions of this section shall be deemed guilty of a misdemeanor, and shall, on conviction thereof, be punished by a fine of not more than $1,000, or by imprisonment not longer than two years or by both said punishments, in the discretion of the court.

PROOF NOT CHANGED.

Sec. 10. That nothing in this act shall be held to prevent the proof of marriages, whether lawful or unlawful, by any evidence now legally admissible for that purpose.

ILLEGITIMATE CHILDREN DISINHERITED.

Sec. 11. That the laws enacted by the Legislative Assembly of the Territory of Utah which provide for or recognize the capacity of illegitimate children to inherit or to be entitled to any distributive share in the estate of the father of any such illegitimate child are hereby disapproved and annulled; and no illegitimate child shall hereafter be entitled to inherit from his or her father or to receive any distributive share in the estate of his or her father: *Provided*, That this section shall not apply to any illegimate child born within twelve months after the passage of this act, nor to any child made legitimate by the seventh section of the act entitled "An act to amend section fifty-three hundred and fifty-two of the Revised Statutes of the United States, in reference to bigamy, and for other purposes," approved March twenty-second, 1882.

CURTAILING PROBATE JURISDICTION.

SEC. 12.   That the laws enacted by the Legislative Assembly of the Territory of Utah, conferring jurisdiction upon probate courts, or the judges thereof, or any of them, in said Territory, other than in respect of the estates of deceased persons, and in respect of the guardianship of the persons and property of infants, and in respect of the persons and property of persons not of sound mind, are hereby disapproved and annulled, and no probate court or judge of probate shall exercise any jurisdiction other than in respect of the matters aforesaid, except as a member of a county court ; and every such jurisdiction so by force of this act withdrawn from the said probate courts or judges shall be had and exercised by the district courts of said Territory respectively.

PROPERTY ESCHEATED.

SEC. 13.   That it shall be the duty of the Attorney-General of the United States to institute and prosecute proceedings to forfeit and escheat to the United States the property of corporations obtained or held in violation of section 3 of the act of Congress approved the 1st day of July, 1862, entitled "An act to punish and prevent the practice of polygamy in the Territories of the United States and other places, and disapproving and annulling certain acts of the Legislative Assembly of the Territory of Utah," or in violation of section eighteen hundred and ninety of the Revised Statutes of the United States, and all such property so forfeited and escheated to the United States shall be disposed of by the Secretary of the Interior, and the proceeds thereof applied to the use and benefit of the common schools in the Territory in which such property may be: *Provided*, That no building, or the grounds appurtenant thereto, which is held and occupied exclusively for purposes of the worship of God, or parsonage connected therewith, or burial ground, shall be forfeited.

PROCEEDINGS AGAINST CORPORATIONS.

SEC. 14.   That in any proceeding for the enforcement of the provisions of law against corporations or associations acquiring or holding property in any Territory of the United States in excess of the amount limited by law, the court before which such proceeding may be instituted shall have power in a summary way to compel the production of all books, records, papers, and documents of or belonging to any trustee or person holding or controlling or managing property in which such corporation may have any right, title, or interest whatever.

PERPETUAL EMIGRATION FUND COMPANY DISSOLVED.

SEC. 15.   That all laws of the Legislative Assembly of the Territory of Utah, or of the so-called government of the State of Deseret, creating, organizing, amending, or continuing the corporation or association called the Perpetual Emigrating Fund Company are hereby disapproved and annulled; and the said corporation, in so far as it may now have, or pretend to have, any legal existence, is hereby dissolved ; and it shall not be lawful for the Legislative Assembly of the Territory of Utah to create, organize, or in any manner recognize any such corporation or association, or to pass any law for the purpose of or operating to accomplish the bringing of persons into the said Territory for any purpose whatsoever.

PROPERTY OF THE P. E. FUND COMPANY ESCHEATED.

SEC. 16.   That it shall be the duty of the Attorney-General of the United States to cause such proceedings to be taken in the supreme court of the Territory of Utah as shall be proper to carry into effect the provisions of the preceding section, and pay the debts and to dispose of the property and assets of said corporation according to law. Said property and assets, in excess of the debts and the amount of any lawful claims established by the court against the same, shall escheat to the United States, and shall be taken, invested, and disposed of by the Secretary of the Interior, under the direction of the President of the United States, for the benefit of common schools in said Territory.

THE CHURCH DISINCORPORATED.

SEC. 17.   That the acts of the Legislative Assembly of the Territory of Utah incorporating, continuing, or providing for the corporation known as the Church of Jesus Christ of Latter-day Saints, and the ordinance of the so-called general assembly of the State of Deseret incorporating the Church of Jesus Christ of Latter-day Saints, so far as the same may now have legal force and validity, are hereby disapproved and annulled, and the said corporation, in so far as it may now have, or pretend to have, any legal existence, is hereby dissolved. That it shall be the duty of the Attorney-General of the United States to cause such proceedings to be taken in the supreme court of the Territory of Utah as shall be proper to execute the foregoing provisions of this section and to wind up the affairs of said corporation conformably to law; and in such proceedings the court shall have power, and it shall be its duty to make such decree or decrees as shall be proper to effectuate the transfer of the title to real property now held and used by said corporation for places of worship, and parsonages connected therewith, and burial grounds, and of the description mentioned in the proviso to section thirteen of said act, and in section twenty-six of this act, to the respective trustees mentioned in section twenty-six of this act; and for the purposes of this section said court shall have all the powers of a court of equity.

THE RIGHT OF DOWER.

SEC. 18.   (a) A widow shall be endowed of the third part of all the lands whereof her husband was seized of an estate of inheritance at any time during the marriage, unless she shall have lawfully released her right thereto.

(b) The widow of any alien who at the time of his death shall be entitled by law to hold any real estate, if she be an inhabitant of the Territory at the time of such death, shall be entitled to dower of such estate in the same manner as if such alien had been a native citizen.

(c) If a husband seized of an estate of inheritance in lands exchanges them for other lands, his widow shall not have dower of both, but shall make her election to be endowed of the lands given or of those taken in exchange; and if such election be not evinced by the commencement of proceedings to recover her dower of the lands given in exchange within one year after the death of her husband, she shall be deemed to have elected to take her dower of the lands received in exchange.

(d) When a person seized of an estate of inheritance in lands shall have executed a mortgage, or other conveyance in the nature of mortgage, of such estate, before marriage, his widow shall nevertheless be entitled to dower out of the lands mortgaged or so conveyed, as against every person except the mortgagee or grantee in such conveyance and those claiming under him.

(e) When a husband shall purchase lands during coverture, and shall at the same time execute a mortgage, or other conveyance in the nature of mortgage, of his estate in such lands to secure the payment of the purchase-money, his widow shall not be entitled to dower out of such lands, as against the mortgagee or grantee in such conveyance or those claiming under him, although she shall not have united in such mortgage: but she shall be entitled to her dower in such lands as against all other persons.

(f) Where in such case the mortgagee, or such grantee or those claiming under him, shall, after the death of the husband of such widow, cause the land mortgaged or so conveyed to be sold, either under a power of sale contained in the mortgage or such conveyance or by virtue of the decree of a court, if any surplus shall remain after payment of the moneys due on such mortgage or such conveyance, and the costs and charges of the sale, such widow shall nevertheless be entitled to the interest or income of the one-third part of such surplus for her life, as her dower.

(g)   A widow shall not be endowed of lands conveyed to her husband by way of mortgage unless he acquire an absolute estate therein during the marriage period.

(h)   In case of divorce dissolving the marriage contract for the misconduct of the wife, she shall not be endowed.

PROBATE JUDGES MADE APPOINTIVE BY THE PRESIDENT.

SEC. 19.   That hereafter the judge of probate in each county within the Territory of Utah, provided for by the existing laws thereof shall be appointed by the President of the United States, by and with the advice and consent of the Senate; and so much of the laws of said Territory as provide for the election of such judge by the Legislative Assembly are hereby disapproved and annulled.

FEMALE SUFFRAGE ABOLISHED.

Sec. 20.   That it shall not be lawful for any female to vote at any election hereafter held in the Territory of Utah for any public purpose whatever, and no such vote shall be received or counted or given effect in any manner whatever; and any and every act of the Legislative Assembly of the Territory of Utah providing or allowing the registration or voting by females is hereby annulled.

SECRET BALLOT.

SEC. 21.   That all laws of the Legislative Assembly of the Territory of Utah which provide for numbering or identifying the votes of the electors at any election in said Territory are hereby disapproved and annulled;

but the foregoing provisions shall not preclude the lawful registration of voters, or any other provisions for securing fair elections which do not involve the disclosure of the candidates for whom any particular elector shall have voted.

RE-DISTRICTING THE TERRITORY.

SEC. 22. That the existing election districts and apportionments of representation concerning the members of the Legislative Assembly of the Territory of Utah are hereby abolished; and it shall be the duty of the governor, Territorial secretary, and the Board of Commissioners mentioned in section 9 of the act of Congress approved March twenty-second, eighteen hundred and eighty-two, entitled "An act to amend section fifty-three hundred and fifty-two of the Revised Statutes of the United States, in reference to bigamy, and for other purposes," in said Territory, forthwith to re-district said Territory, and apportion representation in the same in such manner as to provide, as nearly as may be, for an equal representation of the people (excepting Indians not taxed), being citizens of the United States, according to numbers in said Legislative Assembly, and to the number of members of the council and house of representatives respectively, as now established by law; and a record of the establishment of such new districts and the apportionment of representation thereto shall be made in the office of the secretary of said Territory, and such establishment and representation shall continue until Congress shall otherwise provide; and no persons other than citizens of the United States otherwise qualified shall be entitled to vote at any election in said Territory.

ELECTION LAW REMAINS.

SEC. 23. That the provisions of section nine of said act approved March twenty-second, eighteen hundred and eighty-two in regard to registration and election officers, and the registration of voters, and the conduct of elections, and the powers and the duties of the Board therein mentioned, shall continue and remain operative until the provisions and laws therein referred to be made and enacted by the Legislative Assembly of said Territory of Utah shall have been made and enacted by said assembly and shall have been approved by Congress.

THE TEST OATH.

SEC. 24. That every male person twenty-one years of age resident in the Territory of Utah shall, as a condition precedent to his right to register or vote at any election in said Territory, take and subscribe an oath or affirmation, before the registration officer of his voting precinct, that he is over twenty-one years of age, and has resided in the Territory of Utah for six months then last passed and in the precinct for one month immediately preceding the date thereof, and that he is a native born (or naturalized, as the case may be) citizen of the United States, and further state in such oath or affirmation his full name, with his age, place of business, his status, whether single or married, the name of his lawful wife, and that he will support the Constitution of the United States and will faithfully obey the laws thereof, and espeeially obey the act of Congress approved March twenty-second, eighteen hundred and eighty-two, entitled "An act to amend section fifty-three hundred and fifty-two of the Revised Statutes of the United States, in reference to bigamy, and for other purposes," and will also obey this act in respect of the crimes in said act defined and forbidden, and that he will not, directly or indirectly, aid or abet, counsel or advise, any other person to commit any of said crimes. Such registration officer is authorized to administer said oath or affirmation; and all such oaths or affirmations shall be by him delivered to the clerk of the probate court of the proper county, and shall be deemed public records therein. But if any election shall occur in said Territory before the next revision of the registration lists as required by law, the said oath or affirmation shall be administered by the presiding judge of the election precinct on or before the day of election. As a condition precedent to the right to hold office in or under said Territory, the officer before entering on the duties of his office, shall take and subscribe an oath or affirmation declaring his full name, with his age, place of business, his status, whether married or single, and, if married, the name of his lawful wife, and that he will support the Constitution of the United States and will faithfully obey the laws thereof, and especially will obey the act of Congress approved March 22nd, 1882, entitled "An act to amend section fifty-three hundred and fifty-two of the Revised Statutes of the United States, in reference to bigamy, and for other purposes," and will also obey this act in respect of the crimes in said act defined and forbidden, and that he will not, directly or indirectly, aid or abet, counsel or advise, any other person to commit any of said crimes; which oath or affirmation shall be recorded in the proper office and endorsed on the commission or certificate of appointment. All grand and petit jurors in said Territory shall take the same oath or affirmation to be administered, in writing or orally, in the proper court. No person shall be entitled to vote in any election in said Territory, or be capable of jury service, or hold any office of trust or emolument in said Territory who shall not have taken the oath or affirmation aforesaid. No person who shall have been convicted of any crime under this act, or under the act of Congress aforesaid approved March 22, 1882, or who shall be a polygamist, or who shall associate or cohabit polygamously with persons of the other sex shall be entitled to vote in any election in said Territory, or be capable of jury service, or to hold any office of trust or emolument in said Territory.

OFFICE OF SCHOOL SUPERINTENDENT ABOLISHED.

SEC. 25. That the office of Territorial superintendent of district schools created by the laws of Utah is hereby abolished; and it shall be the duty of the supreme court of said Territory to appoint a commissioner of schools, who shall possess and exercise all the powers and duties heretofore imposed by the laws of said Territory upon the Territorial superintendent of district schools, and who shall receive the same salary and compensation, which shall be paid out of the treasury of said Territory; and the laws of the Territory of Utah providing for the method of election and appointment of such Territorial superintendent of district schools are hereby suspended until the further action of Congress shall be had in respect thereto. The said superintendent shall have power to prohibit the use in any district school of any book of sectarian character or otherwise unsuitable. Said superintendent shall collect and classify statistics and other information respecting the districts and other schools in said Territory, showing their progress, the whole number of children of school age, the number who attend school in each year in the respective counties, the average length of time of their attendance, the number of teachers and the compensation paid to the same, the number of teachers who are Mormons, the number who are so-called Gentiles, the number of children of Mormon parents and the number of children of so-called Gentile parents, and their respective average attendance at school; all of which statistics and information shall be annually reported to Congress, through the governor of said Territory, and the Department of the Interior.

CHURCHES MAY HOLD REAL PROPERTY.

SEC. 26. That all religious societies, sects, and congregations shall have the right to have and to hold, through trustees appointed by any court exercising probate powers in a Territory, only on the nomination of the authorities of such society, sect, or congregation, so much real property for the erection or use of houses of worship, and for such parsonages and burial grounds as shall be necessary for the convenience and use of the several congregations of such religious society, sect, or congregation.

THE MILITIA.

Sec. 27. That all laws passed by the so-called State of Deseret and by the Legislative Assembly of the Territory of Utah for the organization of the militia thereof or for the creation of the Nauvoo Legion are hereby annulled and declared of no effect; and the militia of Utah shall be organized and subjected in all respects to the laws of the United States regulating the militia in the Territories · *Provided, however*, That all general officers of the militia shall be appointed by the governor of the Territory, by and with the advice and consent of the council thereof. The Legislative Assembly of Utah shall have power to pass laws for organizing the militia thereof, subject to the approval of Congress.

March 3, 1887.

———

CIRCULAR FROM THE UTAH COMMISSION.

For the Information of Registration Officers.

Office of the Utah Commission,
Salt Lake City, March 19, 1887.

The Utah Commission being solicitous to secure a fair and impartial registration of the qualified electors of the Territory, in conformity with the acts of Congress, respectfully submit to the registration officers appointed for that purpose the following suggestions, in the hope that they will faithfully and impartially discharge their duties, according to law:

1. No polygamist, bigamist, or any person cohabiting with more than one woman, shall be entitled to register or vote at any election in this Territory; nor any person who has been convicted of the crime of incest, unlawful cohabitation, adultery, fornication, bigamy or polygamy; nor any person who associates or cohabits

polygamously with persons of the other sex; nor can any person register or vote who has not taken or subscribed the oath prescribed by the Twenty-fourth Section of the Act of Congress of March 3, 1887; nor can any woman register or vote.

The Commission is of the opinion that the above specifications include all the disabilities to which electors are subject under the laws of Congress, and that no opinions which they may entertain upon questions of religion or church polity should be the subject of inquiry or exclusion of any elector.

The first registration under the Act of Congress is to be an original and new and complete registration; and the County Registration Officer of each county should, by himself or deputies, register every legal voter in his county; and for this purpose should, if necessary, visit every dwelling-house therein.

The oath to be administered may be formulated as follows:

TERRITORY OF UTAH,   }
County of.......................... ...}

I, ...　　　.............　....... ..., being duly sworn [or affirmed], depose and say that I am over twenty-one years of age; that I have resided in the Territory of Utah for six months last past, and in this precinct for one month immediately preceding the date hereof; and that I am a native-born [or naturalized, as the case may be] citizen of the United States, that my full name is ....　....

.... ; that I am ......　.............　.... years of age; that my place of business is ..　　　　　　　　..........; that I am a [single or] married man; that the name of my lawful wife is ....　　　　.......　.　..　　.....; and that I will support the Constitution of the United States, and will faithfully obey the laws thereof, and especially will obey the Act of Congress approved March 22, 1882, entitled: "An Act to amend Section 5352, of the Revised Statutes of the

United States in reference to bigamy and for other purposes," and that I will also obey the Act of Congress, of March 3, 1887, entitled: "An Act to amend An Act entitled An Act to amend Section 5352 of the Revised Statutes of the United States in reference to bigamy and for other purposes, approved March 22, 1882," in respect of the crimes in said act defined and forbidden, and that I will not, directly or indirectly, aid or abet, counsel or advise any other person to commit any of said crimes defined by acts of Congress, as polygamy, bigamy, unlawful cohabitation, incest, adultery and fornication.

Subscribed and sworn to before me this   day of............., A. D. 188.....

Deputy Registration officer for ....   Precinct.

County.

Although the person applying to have his name registered as a voter may have made the foregoing oath, yet if the Registrar shall, for reasonable cr probable cause, believe that the applicant is then, in fact, a bigamist, polygamist or living in unlawful cohabitation, or associating or cohabiting polygamously with persons of the other sex, or has been convicted of bigamy, polygamy, unlawful cohabitation, incest, adultery or fornication —in our opinion the Registrar may require the applicant to make the following additional affidavit:

TERRITORY OF UTAH,   }
County of .... }

I,.... ...., further swear [or affirm] that I am not a bigamist, polygamist or living in unlawful cohabitation, or associating or cohabiting polygamously with persons of the other sex, and that I have not been convicted of the crime of bigamy, polygamy, unlawful cohabitation, incest, adultery or fornication.

Subscribed and sworn to before me this ... ...
day of ... ..., A. D. 188.....

Deputy Registration Officer for ....
Precinct,   County.

2. The Registration Officers and their deputies should carefully preserve the Registration Lists for each precinct, for use at the June Revision.

3. The first registration prior to June in .... precinct,   County, should be performed within .... days.

4. The County Registration Officers and their deputies will receive compensation as follows: For County Registration officers, four dollars per day; for each Deputy Registration Officer, three dollars per day; the compensation to be paid for the time during which said officers have been necessarily employed in the discharge of their duties.

5. The law requires each County Registration Officer, in person or by deputy, during the week commencing the first Monday in June, at his office, to enter on his Registry List, the name of any voter that may have been omitted, on such voter appearing and taking the oath aforesaid.

6. Upon the completion of the lists, each Registration Officer shall prepare triplicate lists in alphabetical order, for each precinct, containing the names of all registered voters, one of which lists should be filed in the office of the Clerk of the County Court on or before the first day of July next; one list to be posted up in each precinct, at least fifteen days before the day of election, at or near the place of election, and the other list transmitted by him to the Judges of Election of the several precincts for use at the poles: and the oaths of registered

voters, immediately after the day of election, delivered to the Clerk of the Probate Court of the proper County.

7. The law authorizes voters removing from one election precinct to another in the same County, to appear before the Registration Officer at any time previous to the filing of the lists in the office of the Clerk of the County Court, and have their names erased therefrom, and they may thereupon have their names registered in the precinct to which they may remove.

8. Prior to each election the Registration Officer of each County shall cause to be written or printed, a notice which shall designate the office or offices to be filled, and stating that the election will commence at................ (designating the place for holding polls,) one hour after sunrise, and continue until sunset on the................day of................188........ Dated at ....on this.... ....day of................ ....A. D. 188........

....

Registration Officer.

A copy of this should be posted up at least fifteen days before the day of election, in the three public places in the precinct best calculated to give notice to all the voters. It is the duty of the Registration Officer to give notice on the lists posted as aforesaid, that the Deputy Registration Officer of such precinct will hear objections of the right to vote of any person registered, until sunset on the fifth day preceding the day of election. Said objections shall be made by a qualified voter, in writing, and delivered to said Deputy Registration Officer, who shall issue a written notice to the person objected to, stating the place, day and hour when the objection shall be heard. The person making the objection shall serve, or cause to be served, said notice on the person objected to, and shall also make return of such service to the Deputy Registration Officer, before whom the objection is to be heard. In our opinion the objections should specify the grounds thereof, and should be made separately as to each person objected to; and actual personal service should be proved by the affidavit of the person making the same, unless served, and return thereof made, by an officer authorized by law to serve process, and at least three days' notice should be given. Upon the hearing of the case if said officer shall find that the person objected to is not a qualified voter, he shall, within three days prior to the election, transmit a certified list of all such disqualified persons to the Judge of Election appointed by this commission; and said Judges should strike such names from the Registry Lists before the opening of the polls.

9. The County Registration Officer should, as soon as may be after his appointment, recommend to this Commission, for deputy Registration Officers for the several precincts in his County, the names of reputable and discreet men, who are qualified and willing to take the official oath; and he should also recommend to the Commission, for their information, the names of four persons, two of whom should belong to the party being in the majority at the last general election, and two being of the party then in the minority, and who are eligible and proper persons to act as Judges of Election in each precinct of his County.

10. The Registration Officers and their deputies should each, before entering upon the discharge of their duties, take and subscribe an oath as required by the Act of Congress, the form whereof is endorsed on his commission and a duplicate thereof, signed and sworn to,

should be forthwith sent by mail to this Commission as evidence that the person accepts the appointment and has duly qualified.

By order of the Commission,

A. B. CARLTON,

Chairman.

APPENDIX.

With the exception of a few additions and corrections, the foregoing pages were written from time to time, from 1882 to 1889 inclusive. Since then important events have occurred in Utah strongly fortifying the position which the author took more than four years ago to the effect that the Mormon people had in good faith resolved upon a new departure. The following documents are self-explanatory, and they are therefore submitted to the reader without comment:

Salt Lake City.
December 12th, 1889.

To Whom It May Concern:

In consequence of gross misrepresentations of the doctrines, aims and practices of the Church of Jesus Christ of Latter-day Saints, commonly called the "Mormon" Church, which have been promulgated for years, and have recently been revived for political purposes and to prevent all aliens, otherwise qualified, who are members of the "Mormon" Church from acquiring citizenship, we deem it proper on behalf of said Church to publicly deny these calumnies and enter our protest against them.

We solemnly make the following declarations, viz:

That this Church views the shedding of human blood with the utmost abhorrence. That we regard the killing of a human being, except in conformity with the civil law, as a capital crime which should be punished by shedding the blood of the criminal, after a public trial before a legally constituted court of the land.

Notwithstanding all the stories told about the killing of apostates, no case of this kind has ever occurred, and of course has never been established against the Church we represent. Hundreds of seceders from the Church have continuously resided and now live in this Territory, many of whom have amassed considerable wealth, though bitterly hostile to the "Mormon" faith and people. Even those who have made it their business to fabricate the vilest falsehoods, and to render them plausible by culling isolated passages from old sermons without the explanatory context, and have suffered no opportunity to escape them of vilifying and blackening the characters of the people, have remained among those whom they have thus persistently calumniated until the present day, without receiving the slightest personal injury.

We denounce as entirely untrue the allegation which has been made, that our Church favors or believes in the killing of persons who leave the Church or apostatize from its doctrines. We would view a punishment of this character for such an act with the utmost horror, it is abhorrent to us and is in direct opposition to the fundamental principles of our creed.

The revelations of God to this Church make death the penalty for capital crime, and require that offenders against life and property shall be delivered up to and be tried by the laws of the land.

We declare that no Bishop's or other court in this Church claims or exercises the right to supercede, annul or modify a judgment of any civil court.

Such courts while established to regulate Christian conduct are purely ecclesiastical, and their punitive powers go no further than the suspension and excommunication of members from Church fellowship.

That this Church, while offering advice for the welfare of its members in all conditions of life, does not claim or exercise the right to interfere with citizens in the free exercise of social or political rights and privileges. The ballot in this Territory is absolutely untrammeled and secret. No man's business or other secular affairs are invaded by the Church or any of its officers.

Free agency and direct individual accountability to God, are among the essentials of our Church doctrine. All things in the Church must be done by common consent, and no officer is appointed without the vote of the body.

We declare that there is nothing in the ceremony of the Endowment, or in any doctrine, tenet, obligation or injunction of this Church, either private or public, which is hostile or intended to be hostile to the Government of the United States. On the contrary, its members are under divine commandment to revere the Constitution as a heaven-inspired instrument.

Utterances of prominent men in the Church at a time of great excitement, have been selected and grouped, to convey the impression that present members are seditious. Those expressions were made more than thirty years ago, when through the falsehoods of recreant officials, afterwards demonstrated to be baseless, troops were sent to this Territory and were viewed by the people, in their isolated condition, fifteen hundred miles from railroads, as an armed mob coming to renew the bloody persecutions of years before.

At that time excitement prevailed and strong language was used; but no words of disloyalty against the Government or its institutions were uttered; public speakers confined their remarks to denouncing traitorous officials who were prostituting the powers of their positions to accomplish nefarious ends. Criticism of the acts of United States officials was not considered then, neither is it now, as treason against the nation nor as hostility to the Government. In this connection we may say that the members of our Church have never offered or intended to offer any insult to the flag of our country; but have always honored it as the ensign of laws and liberty.

We also declare that this Church does not claim to be an independent temporal kingdom of God, or to be an *imperium in imperio*, aiming to overthrow the United States or any other civil government. It has been organized by divine revelation preparatory to the second advent of the Redeemer. It proclaims that "the kingdom of heaven is at hand." Its members are commanded of God to be subject unto the powers that be until Christ comes, whose right it is to reign.

Church government and civil government are distinct and separate in our theory and practice, and we regard it as part of our destiny to aid in the maintenance and perpetuity of the institutions of our country.

We claim no religious liberty that we are unwilling to accord to others.

We ask for no civil or political rights which are not granted and guaranteed to citizens in general.

We desire to be in harmony with the Government and people of the United States as an integral part of the nation.

We regard all attempts to exclude aliens from naturalization, and citizens from the exercise of the elective franchise, solely because they are members of the "Mormon" Church, as impolitic, unrepublican and dangerous encroachments upon civil and religious liberty.

Notwithstanding the wrongs we consider we have suffered through the improper execution of national laws, we regard those wrongs as the acts of men and not of the Government; and we intend by the help of Omnipotence, to remain firm in our fealty and steadfast in the maintenance of constitutional principles and the integrity of this Republic.

We earnestly appeal to the American press and people, not to condemn the Latter-day Saints unheard. Must we always be judged by the misrepresentations of our enemies, and never be accorded a fair opportunity of representing ourselves?

In the name of justice, reason and humanity, we ask for a suspension of national and popular judgment, until a full investigation can be had and all the facts connected with what is called the "Mormon" question can be known. And we appeal to the Eternal Judge of all men

and nations, to aid us in the vindication of our righteous
cause.

WILFORD WOODRUFF.
GEORGE Q. CANNON,
JOSEPH F. SMITH,

Presidency of the Church of Jesus Christ of Latter-
day Saints.

LORENZO SNOW,
FRANKLIN D. RICHARDS,
BRIGHAM YOUNG,
MOSES THATCHER,
FRANCIS M. LYMAN,
JOHN HENRY SMITH,
GEORGE TEASDALE,
HEBER J. GRANT,
JOHN W. TAYLOR,
M. W. MERRILL,
A. H. LUND,
ABRAHAM H. CANNON,

Members of the Council of the Apostles.

JOHN W. YOUNG,
DANIEL H. WELLS,
Counselors.

PRESIDENT WOODRUFF'S MANIFESTO.

PROCEEDINGS AT THE SEMI-ANNUAL GENERAL CONFERENCE
OF THE CHURCH OF JESUS CHRIST OF LATTER-DAY
SAINTS.

Monday Forenoon, October 6, 1890.

PRESIDENT WOODRUFF said: I will say, as the question is often asked, "What do the Latter-day Saints
believe in?" we feel disposed to read the Articles of
Faith of the Church of Jesus Christ of Latter-day
Saints, and should there be any strangers present, they
may understand our faith in this respect. The question

is often asked, " Do the Mormon people believe in the Bible?" so the principles that are read will show our faith and belief appertaining to the Gospel of Christ.

The articles were then read by Bishop Orson F. Whitney.   They are here introduced :

ARTICLES OF FAITH OF THE CHURCH OF JESUS CHRIST OF LATTER-DAY SAINTS.

I.   We believe in God, the Eternal Father, and in His Son, Jesus Christ, and in the Holy Ghost.

2.   We believe that men will be punished for their own sins, and not for Adam's transgression.

3.   We believe that through the atonement of Christ all mankind may be saved, by obedience to the laws and ordinances of the Gospel.

4.   We believe that these ordinances are: First, faith in the Lord Jesus Christ; second, repentance; third, baptism by immersion for the remission of sins; fourth, laying on of hands for the gift of the Holy Ghost.

5.   We believe that a man must be called of God by "prophecy, and by the laying on of hands," by those who are in authority to preach the Gospel and administer in the ordinances thereof.

6.   We believe in the same organization that existed in the primitive church, viz: apostles, prophets, pastors, teachers, evangelists, etc.

7.   We believe in the gift of tongues, prophecy, revelation, visions, healing, interpretation of tongues, etc.

8.   We believe the Bible to be the word of God, as far as it is translated correctly; we also believe the Book of Mormon to be the word of God.

9.   We believe all that God has revealed, all that He does now reveal, and we believe that He will yet reveal many great and important things pertaining to the Kingdom of God.

10.   We believe in the literal gathering of Israel and in the restoration of the Ten Tribes.   That Zion will be

built upon this continent. That Christ will reign personally upon the earth, and that the earth will be renewed and receive its paradisic glory.

11. We claim the privilege of worshiping Almighty God according to the dictates of our conscience, and allow all men the same privilege, let them worship how, where or what they may.

12. We believe in being subject to kings, presidents, rulers and magistrates, in obeying, honoring and sustaining the law.

13. We believe in being honest, true, chaste, benevolent, virtuous, and in doing good to *all men*; indeed we may say that we follow the admonition of Paul, "We believe all things, we hope all things," we have endured many things, and hope to be able to endure all things. If there is anything virtuous, lovely or of good report or praiseworthy, we seek after these things. JOSEPH SMITH.

APOSTLE FRANKLIN D. RICHARDS said: Beloved brethren and sisters, I move that we, as members of the Church of Jesus Christ of Latter-day Saints in General Conference assembled, do accept and adopt these Articles of Faith which Bishop Whitney has now read as the rule of our faith and of our conduct during our mortal lives.

It may be thought that it is superfluous to offer it; but it must be borne in mind that we have a rising generation since this was last presented to us, that are coming to years of judgment and understanding; and we wish to have all, old and young, rich and poor, bond and free, that have faith in the Lord Jesus Christ and in these articles, to have a chance to express it by their vote, i they wish.

The vote to sustain Brother Richards' motion was unanimous.

PRESIDENT GEORGE Q. CANNON said: President Woodruff, as doubtless the members of the Conference are aware, has felt himself called upon to issue a manifesto concerning certain things connected with our affairs in this Territory, and he is desirous to have this submitted to this Conference ; to have their views or their expressions concerning it, and Bishop Whitney will read this document now in your hearing.

Following is the manifesto as read :

OFFICIAL DECLARATION.

To Whom it May Concern :

Press dispatches having been sent for political purposes, from Salt Lake City, which have been widely published, to the effect that the Utah Commission, in their recent report to the Secretary of the Interior, allege that plural marriages are still being solemnized and that forty or more such marriages have been contracted in Utah since last June or during the past year ; also that in public discourses the leaders of the Church have taught, encouraged and urged the continuance of the practice of polygamy ;

I, therefore, as President of the Church of Jesus Christ of Latter-day Saints, do hereby, in the most solemn manner, declare that these charges are false. We are not teaching polygamy or plural marriage, nor permitting any person to enter into its practice, and I deny that either forty or any other number of plural marriages have during that period been solemnized in our temples or in any other place in the Territory.

One case has been reported, in which the parties alleged that the marriage was performed in the Endowment House, in Salt Lake City, in the spring of 1889, but I have not been able to learn who performed the ceremony ; whatever was done in this matter was without my knowledge.   In consequence of this alleged occurrence the Endowment House was, by my instructions, taken down without delay.

Inasmuch as laws have been enacted by Congress forbidding plural marriages, which laws have been pronounced constitutional by the court of last resort, ·I hereby declare my intention to submit to those laws, and to use my influence with the members of the Church over which I preside to have them do likewise.

There is nothing in my teachings to the Church or in those of my associates, during the time specified, which can be reasonably construed to inculcate or encourage polygamy, and when any Elder of the Church has used language which appeared to convey any such teaching he has been promptly reproved. And I now publicly declare that my advice to the Latter-day Saints is to refrain from contracting any marriage forbidden by the law of the land.

WILFORD WOODRUFF,
President of the Church of Jesus Christ of Latter-day Saints.

PRESIDENT LORENZO SNOW offered the following:

"I move that, recognizing Wilford Woodruff as the President of the Church of Jesus Christ of Latter-day Saints, and the only man on the earth at the present time who holds the keys of the sealing ordinances, we consider him fully authorized by virtue of his position to issue the manifesto which has been read in our hearing and which is dated September 24th, 1890, and that as a Church in General Conference assembled, we accept his declaration concerning plural marriages as authoritative and binding."

The vote to sustain the foregoing was unanimous:

PRESIDENT GEORGE Q. CANNON.

On the 19th of January, 1841, the Lord gave His servant Joseph Smith a revelation, the 49th paragraph of which I will read:

"Verily, verily, I say unto you, that when I give a commandment to any of the sons of men, to do a work unto my name, and those sons of men go with all their might, and with all they have, to perform that work, and cease not their diligence, and their enemies come upon them, and hinder them from performing that work; behold, it behoveth me to require that work no more at the hands of those sons of men, but to accept of their offerings."

The Lord says other things connected with this, which I do not think it necessary to read, but the whole revelation is profitable, and can be read by those who desire to do so.

It is on this basis that President Woodruff has felt himself justified in issuing this manifesto.

I suppose it would not be justice to this Conference not to say something upon this subject; and yet everyone knows how delicate a subject it is, and how difficult it is to approach it without saying something that may offend somebody. So far as I am concerned, I can say that of the men in this Church who have endeavored to maintain this principle of plural marriage, I am one. In public and in private I have avowed my belief in it. I have defended it everywhere and under all circumstances, and when it was necessary have said that I considered the command was binding and imperative upon me.

But a change has taken place. We have, in the first place, endeavored to show that the law which affected this feature of our religion was unconstitutional. We believed for years that the law of July 1st, 1862, was in direct conflict with the first amendment to the Constitution, which says that "Congress shall make no law respecting an establishment of religion, or prohibiting the free exercise thereof." We rested upon that, and for years continued the practice of plural marriage, believing the law against it to be an unconstitutional one, and that we had the right, under the Constitution, to carry out this principle practically in our lives. So confident was I in relation to this view that in conversations with President Grant, and with his Attorney-General, ex-Senator Williams, of Oregon, I said to them that if my case were not barred by the statute of limitations I

would be willing to have it made a test case, in order
that the law might be tested.   We were sustained in this
view not only by our own interpretation of the amendment to the Constitution, but also by some of the best
legal minds in the country, who took exactly the same
view that we did—that this law was an interference with
religious rights, and that so long as our practices did not
interfere with the happiness and peace of society, or of
others, we had the right to carry out this principle.   In
fact, it is within six or eight months that, in conversation with two United States Senators, each conversation
being separate from the other, both of them expressed
themselves, though not in the same language, to this
effect: "Mr. Cannon, if this feature that you practice
had not been associated with religion, it might have been
tolerated ; but you have associated it with religion and it
has aroused the religious sentiment of the. nation, and
that sentiment cannot be resisted.   So far as the
practice itself is concerned, if you had not made it a part
of your faith and an institution sanctioned by religion, it
might have gone along unnoticed."   I do not give the
exact language ; but these are the ideas that they conveyed to me.   Now, we were very confident that this law
was an unconstitutional one.   President Daniel H. Wells
will remember how he and I tried to get a case to test
the constitutionality of the law during the lifetime of
President Brigham Young.   We wanted to get Brother
Erastus Snow.   It was the last thing that we should have
thought of to put a man like he was in the gap if we
had not been firmly convinced that the law was unconstitutional and would be declared so by the United States
Supreme Court.   We telegraphed to Brother Erastus
in the south, thinking that his case would not be barred
by the statute of limitations.   He replied to us concerning it, and we found that it was barred.   Brother A. M.
Musser proposed himself, if I remember aright, to be a
test case; but there was a defect in his case.   We
wanted this case, whenever it was presented, to be presented fairly, that there should be no evasion about it,

but that it should be a case that could be tested fairly before the courts of the country.   Finally, Brother George Reynolds was selected.   I said to myself when I learned the result, "It is the last time that I will ever have anything to do with a test case again which will involve the liberty of anybody."   I was promised when he was sentenced, by one high in authority and who had the right to make the promise, that he should be released, when the circumstances were told to him; for they were laid fairly before him, and he was told that the evidence had been furnished by Brother Reynolds himself, and that everything had been done to make it a test case; the government had been aided in the securing of witnesses, and no difficulty thrown in the way.   Afterwards, on the second trial, I believe Brother Reynolds' lawyers got frightened, and there was something occurred then that gave it a different appearance.   But when the facts were related, as I stated, to one high in authority, he promised me that George Reynolds should be pardoned. There were those, however, in this city who were determined that he should not escape imprisonment, and the prosecuting attorney wrote a letter which changed the mind of this high official, as he afterwards told me, and he declined to carry out that which I had received as a promise.   But even then there were circumstances connected with this decision that made us reluctant to accept it.

Since that time the history of the proceedings is before you and before the world.   We have felt as though this command of God was of such importance to us, involving so many serious consequences, that we should do all in our power to have the world know the position that we occupied.   There may be men among us who believe they would be damned if they did not obey this, accepting it as a direct command from God.   Therefore, you can understand how tenaciously we have protested, and how vigorously we have endeavored, as far as we could, to make public our views upon this subject.

I suppose there are two classes here to-day in this

congregation—one class who feel to sorrow to the bottom of their hearts because of the necessity of this action that we have now taken; another class who will say: " Did I not tell you so? " " Did I not tell you it would come to this? "   " Did I not say to you that you ought to take advantage of and comply with this years ago, instead of enduring that which you have suffered since that time? "   There may be men here today who pride themselves on their foresight, and who take credit to themselves because they foresaw, as they allege, that which we have done to-day, and would lead others to believe that if their counsel had been adopted, if the views that they presented had been accepted by the people, it might have saved very serious consequences to us all and left us in a better position than that which we occupy to-day. But I, for one, differ entirely with this view. I believe that it was necessary that we should witness unto God, the Eternal Father, unto the heavens and unto the earth, that this was really a principle dear to us—dearer, it might be said, in some respects, than life itself. We could not have done this had we submitted at the time that those of whom I speak suggested submission. We could not have left our own nation without excuse. It might have said, "Had we known all that you tell us now concerning this, we should have had very different views about this feature of your religion than we did have. " But now, after the occurrences of the past six years have been witnessed by this entire nation and by the world, and by God the Eternal Father and the heavenly hosts, no one can plead as an excuse that they have been ignorant of our belief and the dearness of this principle to us. Upwards of thirteen hundred men have been incarcerated in prison, going there for various terms, from one or three months up to years. They have gone there willingly, as martyrs to this principle, making a protest that the heavens and the earth should bear record of, that they were conscientious in espousing this principle, and that it was not for sensual indulgence, because if sensual indulgence had been the object, we could have

21

obtained it without such sacrifices as were involved in obedience to this law—without going to prison, without sustaining wives and children, without the obloquy that has been heaped upon us because of this action of ours. If licentious motives had prompted us, we could have secured the results in a cheaper way and in a way more in consonance with universal custom throughout our own land and all Christendom. But the sacrifices that we have made in this respect, bear testimony to the heavens and to the earth that we have been sincere and conscientious in all we have done, and that we have not been prompted by a desire to use women for lustful purposes, but to save them, to make them honorable, and to leave no margin of women in our society to become a prey to lust, so that every woman in our land should have the opportunity of becoming a virtuous wife and an honored mother, loved and respected by her offspring and by all her associates.

If no other result has attended what may be termed our obstinacy, these results are, at least, upon record, and they never can be blotted out. The imprisonment of these men, the sufferings—the untold, unwritten yea, unmentionable, it may be said, sufferings—of wives and children, they are recorded in heaven and are known to men upon the earth, and they form a chapter that will never be blotted out.

Latter-day Saints, there has been nothing lost in the five years that have just passed. We have lost no credit. There has been no honor sacrificed. We can look God in the face—that is, if we are permitted to do so, so far as this is concerned, we can; we can look the holy angels in the face; we can look mankind in the face, without a blush, or without feeling that we have done anything unworthy of our manhood or of our professions and the faith that God has given unto us. This all of us can do; and if no other result has followed what may be called our obstinacy, than these which I now describe, they are grand enough to pay us for all that we have gone through.

But the time has come when, in the providence of God, it seemed necessary that something should be done to meet the requirements of the country, to meet the demands that have been made upon us, and to save the people.   President Woodruff and others of us have been appealed to hundreds of times, I might say;—I can say for myself, that I have been appealed to many scores of times to get out something and to announce something.   Some of our leading brethren have said: "Inasmuch as we have ceased to give permission for plural marriages to be solemnized, why cannot we have the benefit of that?   Why cannot we tell the world it, so as to have the benefit of it?   Our enemies are alleging constantly that we still practice this in secret, and that we are dishonest and guilty of evasion.   Now, if we have really put a stop to granting permissions to men to take more wives than one, why should not the world know it and we have the advantage of it?"   These remarks have been made to us repeatedly.   But at no time has the Spirit seemed to indicate that this should be done.   We have waited for the Lord to move in the matter; and on the 24th of September, President Woodruff made up his mind that he would write something, and he had the spirit of it.   He had prayed about it and had besought God repeatedly to show him what to do.   At that time the Spirit came upon him, and the document that has been read in your hearing was the result.   I know that it was right, much as it has gone against the grain with me in many respects, because many of you know the contest we have had upon this point. But when God speaks, and when God makes known His mind and will, I hope that I and all Latter-day Saints will bow in submission to it.   When that document was prepared it was submitted.   But, as is said in this motion that has been made, President Woodruff is the only man upon the earth who holds the keys of the sealing power.   These Apostles all around me have all the same authority that he has.   We are all ordained with the same ordination.   We all have had the same keys and the same powers bestowed upon us. But there is an order in the Church of God, and that order is, that there is only one man at a time on the earth who holds the keys of sealing, and that man is the President of the Church, now Wilford Woodruff. Therefore he signed that document himself. Some have wondered and said, "Why didn't his counselors sign? Why didn't others sign?" Well, I give you the reason—because he is the only man on the earth that has this right, and he exercised it, and he did this with the approval of all of us to whom the matter was submitted, after he had made up his mind, and we sustained it; for we had made it a subject of prayer also, that God would direct us.

There never was a time in the Church when I believe the leading men of this Church have endeavored to live nearer to God, because they have seen the path in which we walked environed with difficulties, beset with all manner of snares, and we have had the responsibility resting upon us of your salvation, to a certain extent. God has chosen us, not we ourselves, to be the shepherds of His flock. We have not sought this responsibility. You know Wilford Woodruff too well to believe that he would seek such an office as he now fills. I trust you know the rest of us sufficiently to believe the same concerning us. I have shrunk from the Apostleship. I have shrunk from being a member of the First Presidency. I felt that if I could get my salvation in any other way, I prayed God that He would give it to me, after he revealed to me that I would be an Apostle, when I was comparatively a child; and I have had that feeling ever since. These Apostles, all of them, feel the responsibility which rests upon them as leaders of the people, God having made us, in His providence, your shepherds. We feel that the flock is in our charge, and if any harm befall this flock through us, we will have to answer for it in the day of the Lord Jesus; we shall have to stand and render an account of that which has been entrusted to us; and if we are faithless, and careless, and do not live so as to have the word of God continually with us, and know His mind and will, then our condemnation will be sure and certain, and we cannot escape it. But you are our witnesses as to whether God is with us or not, as well as the Holy Ghost. You have received, and it is your privilege to receive, the testimony of Jesus Christ as to whether these men who stand at your head, are the servants of God, whom God has chosen, and through whom God gives instructions to His people. You know it, because the testimony of the Spirit is with you, and the Spirit of God burns in your bosoms when you hear the word of God declared by these servants, and there is a testimony living in your hearts concerning it.

Now, realizing the full responsibility of this, this action has been taken. Will it try many of the Saints? Perhaps it will; and perhaps it will try those who have not obeyed this law as much as any others in the Church. But all that we can say to you is that which we repeatedly say to you—go unto God yourselves, if you are tried over this and cannot see its purpose; go to your secret chambers and ask God and plead with Him, in the name of Jesus, to give you a testimony as He has given it to us, and I promise you that you will not come away empty, nor dissatisfied; you will have a testimony, and light will be poured out upon you, and you will see things that perhaps you cannot see and understand at the present time

I pray God to bless all of you, my brethren and sisters; to fill you with His Holy Spirit; to keep you in the path of exaltation which He has marked out for us; to be with us on the right hand and on the left in our future as He has been in the past.

Before I sit down I wish to call attention to one remarkable thing, and it may be an evidence to you that the devil is not pleased with what we have done. It is seldom I have seen so many lies, and such flagrant, outrageous lies told the about Latter-day Saints as I have quite recently. I have not time to read the papers, but I have happened to pick up two or three papers and glance at them, and the most infernal (pardon me for using that expression) lies ever framed are told. It seems as though the devil is mad every way. "Now," says he, "they are going to take advantage of this, and I am determined they shall have no benefit of it; I will fill the earth with lies concerning them, and neutralize this declaration of President Woodruff's." And you will see in all the papers everything that can be said to neutralize the effect of this. To me it is pretty good evidence that the devil is not pleased with what we are doing. When we kept silence concerning this, then we were a very mean and bad people; and now that we have broken the silence and made public our position, why, we are wicked in other directions, and no credence can be attached to anything that we say. You may know by this that his satanic majesty is not pleased with our action. I hope he never will be.

PRESIDENT WILFORD WOODRUFF.

I want to say to all Israel that the step which I have taken in issuing this manifesto has not been done without earnest prayer before the Lord. I am about to go into the spirit world, like other men of my age. I expect to meet the face of my Heavenly Father—the Father of my spirit; I expect to meet the face of Joseph Smith, of Brigham Young, of John Taylor, and of the Apostles, and for me to have taken a stand in anything which is not pleasing in the sight of God, or before the heavens, I would rather have gone out and been shot. My life is no better than other men's. I am not ignorant of the feelings that have been engendered through the course I have pursued. But I have done my duty, and the nation of which we form a part must be responsible for that which has been done in relation to this principle.

The Lord has required at our hands many things that we have not done, many things that we were prevented from doing. The Lord required us to build a Temple in Jackson County. We were prevented by violence from doing it. He required us to build a Temple

in Far West, which we have not been able to do. A great
many things have been required of us, and we have not
been able to do them, because of those that surrounded
us in the world. This people are in the hands of God.
This work is the hands of God, and He will take care of
it. Brother George Q. Cannon told us about the lies
that are abroad. It is a time when there have been more
lies told about Mormonism than almost any other subject
ever presented to the human family. I often think of what
Lorenzo Dow said with regard to the doctrine of election. Says he: "It is like this: You can, and you can't;
you will, and you won't; you shall, and you shan't; you'll
be damned if you do, and you'll be damned if you
don't." That is about the condition we as Latter-day
Saints are in. If we were to undertake to please the
world, and that was our object, we might as well give up
the ship, we might have given it up in the beginning.
But the Lord has called us to labor in the vineyard; and
when our nation passes laws, as they have done, in
regard to this principle which we have presented to the
Conference, it is not wisdom for us to make war upon
sixty-five millions of people. It is not wisdom for us to
go forth and carry out this principle against the laws of
the nation and receive the consequences. That is in the
hands of God, and He will govern and control it. The
Church of Christ is here; the Zion of God is here, in
fulfillment of these revelations of God that are contained
in these holy records in which the whole Christian world
profess to believe. The Bible could never have been
fulfilled had it not been for the raising up of a Prophet
in the last days. The revelations of St. John could
never have been fulfilled if the angel of God had not
flown through the midst of heaven, "having the everlasting gospel to preach to them that dwell on the earth,
and to every nation, and kindred, and tongue, and people, saying with a loud voice, Fear God, and give glory
to Him; for the hour of His judgment is come." Was
that angel going to visit New York, Philadelphia, Boston,
and the world, and call the people together and preach

to them? Not at all. But the Lord raised up a Prophet. The angel of God delivered that Gospel to that Prophet. That Prophet organized a Church; and all that he was promised in this code of revelations (the Book of Doctrine and Covenants) has been fulfilled as fast as time would admit. That which is not yet fulfilled will be.

Brethren and sisters, it is our duty to be true to God and to be faithful. Make your prayers known unto the Lord. The Lord has told us what He will do concerning many things. He will fulfill His word. Let us be careful and wise, and let us be satisfied with the dealings of God with us. If we do our duty to one another, to our country, and to the Church of Christ, we will be justified when we go into the spirit world. It is not the first time that the world has sought to hinder the fulfillment of revelation and prophecy. The Jewish nation and other nations rose up and slew the Son of God and every Apostle but one that bore the Priesthood in that day and generation. They could not establish the kingdom; the world was against them. When the Apostles asked Jesus whether He would at that time restore again the kingdom to Israel, He replied: "It is not for you to know the times or seasons, which the Father hath put in His own power." He did not say it would be established then; but He taught them to pray: "Our Father which art in heaven, hallowed be thy name. Thy kingdom come. Thy will be done on earth, as it is in heaven." It is a long time since that prayer was offered, and it has not been fulfilled until the present generation. The Lord is preparing a people to receive His kingdom and His Church, and to build up His work. That, brethren and sisters, is our labor.

I want the prayers of the Latter-day Saints. I thank God that I have seen with my eyes this day that this people have been ready to vote to sustain me in an action that I know, in one sense, has pained their hearts. Brother George Q. Cannon has laid before you our position. The Lord has given us commandments concerning many things, and we have carried them out as far as we could; but when we cannot do it, we are justified. The Lord does not require at our hands things that we cannot do.

This is all I want to say to the Latter-day Saints upon this subject. But go before the Lord and ask Him for light and truth, and to give us such blessings as we stand in need of. Let your prayers ascend into the ears of the God of Sabaoth, and they will be heard and answered upon your heads, and upon the heads of the world. Our nation is in the hands of God. He holds their destiny. He holds the destinies of all men. I will say to the Latter-day Saints, as an Elder in Israel and as an Apostle of the Lord Jesus Christ, we are approaching some of the most tremendous judgments God ever poured out upon the world. You watch the signs of the times, the signs of the coming of the Son of Man. They are beginning to be made manifest both in heaven and on earth. As has been told you by the Apostles, Christ will not come until these things come to pass. Jerusalem has got to be rebuilt. The Temple has got to be built. Judah has got to be gathered, and the House of Israel. And the Gentiles will go forth to battle against Judah and Jerusalem before the coming of the Son of Man. These things have been revealed by the prophets; they will have their fulfillment. We are approaching these things. All that the Latter-day Saints have to do is to be quiet, careful and wise before the Lord, watch the signs of the times, and be true and faithful; and when you get through you will understand many things that you do not today. This work has been raised up by the power of Almighty God. These Elders of Israel were called from the various occupations of life to preach as they were moved upon by the Holy Ghost. They were not learned men; they were the weak things of this world, whom God chose to confound the wise, "and things which are not, to bring to nought things that are." We are here on that principle. Others will be gathered on that principle. Zion will be redeemed, Zion will arise, and the glory of God will rest upon her, and all that Isaiah and the other prophets have spoken concerning her will come to pass. We are in the last dispensation and fullness of time. It is a great day, and the eyes of all the heavens are over us, and the eyes of God Himself and all our patriarchs and prophets. They are watching over you with feelings of deep interest, for your welfare; and the prophets who were slain and sealed their testimony with their blood, are mingling with the Gods, pleading for their brethren. Therefore, let us be faithful, and leave events in the hands of God, and He will take care of us if we do our duty.

I pray God that He will bless these Apostles, Prophets and Patriarchs, these Seventies, High Priests and Elders of Israel, and these Latter-day Saints, who have entered into covenant with our God. You have a great future before you. You have kept the commandments of God, so far as you have had the opportunity, and by receiving the Gospel of Christ and being faithful your reward is before you. Your history is written and is before you. I will say that this nation, and all nations, together with presidents, kings, emperors, judges, and all men, righteous and wicked have got to go into the spirit world and stand before the bar of God. They have got to give an account of the deeds done in the body. Therefore, we are safe as long as we do our duty. No matter what trials or tribulations we may be called to pass through, the hand of God will be with us and will sustain us. I ask my heavenly Father to pour out His Spirit upon me, as His servant, that in my advanced age, and during the few days I have to spend here in the flesh, I may be led by the inspiration of the Almighty. I say to Israel, the Lord will never permit me nor any other man who stands as the President of this Church, to lead you astray. It is not in the programme. It is not in the mind of God. If I were to attempt that, the Lord would remove me out of my place, and so He will any other man who attempts to lead the children of men astray from the oracles of God and from their duty. God bless you. Amen.

EXTRACTS FROM THE OFFICIAL MINUTES OF THE GENERAL
CONFERENCE OF THE CHURCH OF JESUS CHRIST OF
LATTER-DAY SAINTS, OCTOBER 6, 1891.

Misrepresentations of the Utah Commission denounced.

Elder John Clark said:

Reference has been made, my brethren and sisters, to the report of the Utah Commission. I am of the opinion, as the previous speaker, that the misrepresentations that have been placed upon us for a number of years, have been passed by too many times in silence. I think that some action should be taken, and that some resolutions, before this Conference adjourns, should be placed before the Conference for their action. I have read the report of the Utah Commission, and from my knowledge of the affairs in this Territory, I am satisfied, as has been stated, that statements made in that report are incorrect and maliciously untrue, and have been gotten up for the purpose of injuring the Latter-day Saints. I therefore move, if it be in order, that a committee of five be appointed by this Conference to formulate such resolutions as will refute, and deny these statements, and set in proper order our views in regard to these matters.

The motion instantly received a large number of seconds. It was put to the audience by President Cannon and carried unanimously.

President Woodruff then named the following as the committee on resolutions:

John Clark, chairman, William H. Rowe, Charles W. Penrose, John T. Caine and Franklin S. Richards.

The motion to accept of the committee thus constituted was unanimous.

COMMITTEE REPORT.

President Wilford Woodruff and members of the

Church of Jesus Christ of Latter-day Saints, in General Conference assembled:

Brethren and Sisters.—Your committee appointed to formulate an expression of the Conference relative to certain statements made by the majority of the Utah Commission in their report to the Secretary of the Interior for the year 1891, beg leave to report the accompanying Preamble and Resolutions, and recommend their adoption by the Conference.

Very respectfully,

JOHN CLARK,
W. H. ROWE,
CHAS. W. PENROSE,
JOHN T. CAINE,
FRANKLIN S. RICHARDS.

SALT LAKE CITY, Oct. 6th, 1891.

PREAMBLE AND RESOLUTIONS.

Whereas, the Utah Commission, with one exception, in their report to the Secretary of the Interior for 1891, have made many untruthful statements concerning the Church of Jesus Christ of Latter-day Saints and the attitude of its members in relation to political affairs; and,

Whereas, said report is an official document and is likely to greatly prejudice the people of the nation against our Church and its members, and it is therefore unwise to allow its erroneous statements to pass unnoticed;

Now, therefore, be it resolved by the Church of Jesus Christ of Latter-day Saints in General Conference assembled, that we deny most emphatically the assertion of the Commission that the Church dominates its members in political matters and that Church and State are united. Whatever appeerence there may have been in past times of a union of Church and State, because men holding ecclesiastical authority were elected to civil office by popular vote, there is now no foundation or excuse for the statement that Church and State are united in

Utah, or that the leaders of the Church dictate the members in political matters; that no coercion or any influence whatever of an ecclesiastical nature has been exercised over us by our Church leaders in reference to which political party we shall join, and that we have been and are perfectly free to unite with any or no political party as we may individually elect; that the People's Party has been entirely and finally dissolved and that our fealty henceforth will be to such national political party as seems to us best suited to the purposes of republican government.

Also, be it resolved that we do not believe there have been any polygamous marriages solemnized among the Latter-day Saints during the period named by the Utah Commission; and we denounce the statements which convey the idea that such marriages have been contracted as false and misleading, and that we protest against the perversions of fact and principle and intent, contained in the report of the Commission, and declare that the manifesto of President Woodruff forbidding future plural marriages was adopted at the last October Conference in all sincerity and good faith, and that we have every reason to believe that it has been carried out in letter and in spirit; and all statements to the contrary are entirely destitute of truth.

And be it further resolved, That we appeal to the press and people of this country to accept our united declaration and protest, to give it publicity, and to aid in disseminating the truth, that falsehood may be refuted and justice be done to a people continually maligned and almost universally misunderstood. And may God defend the right.

DECLARATION BY THE FIRST PRESIDENCY OF THE CHURCH.

Concerning the official report of the Utah Commission made to the Secretary of the Interior, in which they allege "During the past year, notwithstanding the manifesto, reports have been received by the Commission of eighteen male persons who with an equal number of females, are believed to have entered into polygamous marriages, during the year," we have to say, it is utterly without foundation in truth. We repeat in the most solemn manner the declaration made by President Wilford Woodruff at our General Conference held last October, that there have been no plural marriages solemnized during the period named.

Polygamy or plural marriage has not been taught, neither has there been given permission to any person to enter into its practice, but on the contrary, it has been strictly forbidden.

WILFORD WOODRUFF,
GEORGE Q. CANNON,
JOSEPH F. SMITH,

First Presidency of the Church of Jesus Christ of Latter-day Saints.

Apostle Moses Thatcher moved that we receive, endorse and adopt as true, the statement of the Presidency. Unanimously adopted.

VIEWS OF CHIEF JUSTICE ZANE.

In the *Forum* for November, 1891, there is an able and eloquent contribution from the pen of Hon. Charles S. Zane, Chief Justice of Utah, first appointed by President Arthur and re-appointed by President Harrison. Judge Zane has had a larger experience in dealing with the vexed questions pertaining to Utah, than any other man; and it is gratifying to the author of this volume to find his oft-expressed views confirmed and corroborated by the learned Chief Justice. From the article in the *Forum* we select a few passages. Speaking of the manifesto of President Woodruff and the resolutions of the Conference, he says: "By this action I am convinced that the Mormon Church abandoned polygamy and that it will never adopt it again in the United States." Continuing, he says:—There are probably a hundred and fifty thousand Mormons in this Territory, but of that number many are only nominally so. Amid the contentions between them and the Gentiles, many have sided with the church in which are their parents, relatives and friends, without embracing its faith. It is idle now to think of disfranchising the Latter-day Saints. They are an industrious, temperate people, as a rule; and my observation has led me to believe that they are law-abiding since the church took its stand under the law against plural marriage. I am aware that now and then individuals will report violations of that law since the manifesto; but upon investigation such charges are seldom sustained. It would be strange if there were no breaches of it; there are some such cases among non-Mormons. I do not believe that such marriages have been authorized or sanctioned by the officers of the Mormon Church since the manifesto.

Gentiles have said to the Mormons, "When your Church abandons polygamy, and you take a stand in favor of obedience to the law and disband your party, we will welcome you in with us politically." But when the Church declared against polygamy and in favor of obedience to the law and the "Church Party" as it was termed, disbanded, and its members proposed to unite with the national parties, the Mormons were charged with hypocrisy in so doing and were told that they could not be believe, and that their object was political ascendancy for the Church through statehood. They were asked to do what was patriotic and right; and when they did as asked—without an opportunity to show by their conduct that they were in earnest, and without any evidence since then that they were not—they were charged with sinister designs upon the rights of those not of their religion; in fact, with a purpose to gain political power that they might deprive the Gentiles of their political and civil rights; and heap wrongs and indignities upon them.   In view of the multitude of counsel, of the disapproval and denunciation that the Latter-day Saints were receiving, the venerable man at their head remarked to his brethren, that he often thought of what Lorenzo Dow once said of the doctrine of election. "Said he, 'It is like this: you can and you can't, you will and you won't, you shall and you shan't, you'll be damned if you do and you'll be damned if you don't.' "That," he continued, "is about the condition we as Latter-day Saints are in."

From the realities of the past, among conditions differing widely from those of today, many Gentiles fear that the Mormons will return to the old practices and ways of Brigham Young and others of his time.   To these people I say that the face of Utah is toward the sun.   The darkness is at her back.   She is not on the retreat.   We are climbing the hills of progress: higher planes and brighter lights are ahead, and I trust we shal all get clearer and better views of human duty.

The Mormon is with us.   The same nature is common to us all.   The Power higher than ourselves has so ordered.   So far as he and we obey the law, we are all equal before it.   The forces of nature are changing the most durable objects in the finite world.   Our natures and our beliefs are changed by the influences around us. So of that organization of which we are units—society. A better feeling is growing; prejudice and hate are losing their grip, slowly it must be conceded.   But I have no doubt that confidence, good-will and harmony will be

restored sooner or later, and that ere long these valleys and mountains will be the home of a patriotic, har-
monious, progressive and great people.

Charles S. Zane.

THE ANTI-MORMON CRUSADE.

CAPTAIN CODMAN SAYS ITS EFFECTS HAVE BEEN EVIL.—AN
INTERESTING LETTER FROM AN ABLE WRITER.

Soda Springs, Idaho, Sept. 9, 1890.

Sir:—I have carefully read the communication of
Judge Carlton to the *Democrat* of August 30, and fully
endorse every word of it. If proof is needed of the vera-
city of his statements it is furnished by the Salt Lake
Tribune, which, without undertaking to disprove them,
attacks their author in the most venomous personal abuse
which forms the staple argument of that newspaper when
it has to deal with an opponent.

I have been intimately acquainted with the Mormon
people for seventeen years, have traveled through the
length and breadth of their land before the railroads came
there, and have had business relations with them in which
I always found them trustworthy. Barring their practice
of polygamy, now fallen into "innocuous desuetude," there
is not such a law-abiding people within the limits of these
United States. And yet these are the men who in Idaho,
where I have resided for many summers and know them
to be the most honest, conscientious, industrious and
sober among the inhabitants of this new State—these are
the men who are disfranchised, excluded from the jury
box and denied every political right excepting that of being taxed.

Judge Carlton says: "Of the whole Mormon popula-

22

tion in Utah, only a very small per cent. are in polygamy. Out of the adult males, from 85 to 95 per cent. are not living in a polygamous relation."

In Idaho the proportion of polygamists is much less.

Of the 5,000 disfranchised voters, there are not 200 who are amenable to punishment for transgressing the law. It is not pretended that there are more, but their crime is that they "belong to an organization that teaches polygamy," and it is made a condition of their voting in future that they shall produce satisfactory evidence that they have left the Mormon Church two years before asking for registration. It is in vain that they urge that the Mormon Church no longer teaches polygamy and that they produce the authoritative declaration of its president to the Associated Press that he has given *positive orders that no more plural marriages shall be solemnized."* They are asked: "Do you believe that Joseph Smith was a prophet? Do you believe that he had a revelation instituting polygamy?"

It might as well be asked of the Presbyterian: "Do you believe that Jehovah was God, and that he "gave wives" to David; that he sent down fire from heaven to destroy the prophets of Baal, and let loose the armies of Israel to murder the Canaanites and the Philistines?". Of course the true Presbyterian believes all that, or at least he says that he does; but as he is not a polygamist or a murderer himself, he is allowed to vote. Why, then, should the Presbyterian be ruled in and the Mormon ruled out in Idaho? The answer is ready. Presbyterians belong to both political parties. The Mormons are mostly Democrats, and they are Democrats not because they know or care much about the tariff, but because the infamous legislation against them has been enacted by a Republican Congress that has sent corrupt governors and judges to oppress their co-religionists in Utah; that has taken advantage of an obsolete territorial law to rob them of their church property, and has made a law of its own unparalleled in the meanness of such sneak thievery, which confiscated the hard-earned savings contributed to the "emigration fund" for the purpose of bringing their converts away from their poverty in Europe to the enjoyments and the blessings of this free (?) and happy land.

The Mormons are accused of disloyalty. What wonder would it be if the charge were true? And yet, in spite of every device to bring them into rebellion, they remain quiet under the indignities heaped upon them, still adhering to the belief that the Declaration of Independence and the Constitution of the United States were inspired by the Almighty, who, in his own good time, will see that they obtain justice at the hands of their country.

The Mormons are by no means the ignorant people that those who are themselves as ignorant of them, of their habits and their religion, as Judge Carlton has amply proved that they are, suppose them to be. It is true they are not "up" in the classics or in the higher branches of literature, but common school education is as generally diffused as in the most favored States of the Union. Comparatively uneducated men are annually sent to foreign lands as missionaries, but they are close observers of what they see abroad, and on their return, in the long winter evenings they disseminate among their neighbors the intelligence they have acquired, so that the Mormons know vastly more about what is going on in the outside world than the world knows about them. Even in educated Boston it is common to hear that polygamy is the corner stone of Mormonism, when it is only a stone that has now fallen from its superstructure, and to be told that the "Mormon Bible" has superseded the sacred scriptures which are more firmly believed in by Mormons than by any Christian sect. The article of Judge Carlton is unanswerable. How comes it then that the other members of the "Utah commission" to which he tells your readers that he was attached for seven years, differ so materially from him.

In the first place this Utah commission never had any *raison d' etre*. It has never accomplished any work that could not have been done by the secretary of the Territory single-handed. It was the child of prejudice and congressional ignorance.

Judge Carlton is the only one of its members who has the candor to admit that it was a piece of useless legislation, and he values that more than his salary of $5,000 a year. Those who have signed the majority reports valued their salaries more than the truth. That is the whole of it. Hence their labored efforts to prove that their semi-annual visits to Utah were necessary for the suppression of polygamy and disloyalty. They are upheld in this pretense by the newspaper already referred to, but there is not a Mormon or a Gentile in the common walks of life who does not look upon them as actors in a ridiculous farce. The effect of the anti-Mormon crusade for all these years has been for evil, and that continually.

It has got the community of Salt Lake City by the ears. It has demoralized society by introducing obscenity into the press and into daily conversation even among ladies of culture. By giving the impression that life and capital were not safe in the Territory, it has retarded the influx of a good and varied population, and has prevented the investment of money there. All that was needed was to have made polygamy punishable like any other crime, according to its degree. Criminals of all sorts frequently escape conviction everywhere, but in Utah, where the whole power of the courts is in Federal courts, who construe the laws of evidence to suit themselves, conviction of polygamy is almost always sure, though other crimes may be unpunished.

The fear of the law may have had a restraining influence upon polygamy, but the contact with outside civilization which absurd prejudice and the malignant lies of those whose main object has been political control, could not repel, would alone have accomplished its overthrow.

This is fully proven in the admirable paper under review.

Now that all we have a right to ask of the Mormons has been yielded, it would be the part of a generous government to restore to them the property it has stolen; but if it is unwilling to do this, it might at least for the future abstain from the enactment of needless and unjust laws against a people whom no tyrannical legislation has driven or can drive from their allegiance to the Constitution of the United States. JOHN CODMAN.

FAIR PLAY FOR THE MORMONS.

SOME MISREPRESENTATIONS CORRECTED—THEY ARE NOT DISLOYAL TO THE GOVERNMENT—POLYGAMY TO BE DISCONTINUED.

BY A. B. CARLTON.

It is sixty years since the organization of "the Church of Jesus Christ of Latter-day Saints," commonly called the Mormon Church. During the whole of that time the public mind has been more or less interested and perturbed in regard to this strange people, who have been more talked about, and written about, in books, pamphlets, magazines, brochures and newspapers than any other religious sect that has arisen in this century.

Many, perhaps most of the books of Gentile or anti-Mormon authors, are utterly unreliable. Some are characterized by the acrimony of apostate rancor, and some by the *odium theologicum* of rival sectarianism; while others are filled with sensational stories more or less apocryphal or fabulous, and illustrated with monstrous pictures. A few deplorable facts in Mormon history, are eked out with imaginary padding invented by the author, or copied from some preceding and equally unreliable writer; the object being merely to make a book that will sell, by pandering to the popular taste for the marvelous.

Thus it has come to pass that there are many prevalent popular errors in regard to the Mormons and their real character: and I propose in this paper to point out and correct some of these errors. Concerning my opportunities for a knowledge of the subject, it will not be improper for me to state that for nearly seven years I was a member of the Utah Commission, appointed by President Arthur in 1882, under the anti-polygamy act of Congress of that year; and that I was the chairman of the commission during the latter half of that period.

The task I undertake is a difficult aud ungracious one, because there are many persons who would rather believe a lie in regard to a hated religious sect than to be enlightened with the truth; and it is easy, as well as agreeable, for some people to indulge in hyperbole and fiction against any whom it is the fashion to despise.

But it is my deliberate judgment that the Mormon people have been more misrepresented and misunderstood than any other community in modern times. I therefore deem it to be a duty, as well as a pleasure to give the truth as I understand it.

Error No. 1. It is a common belief, propagated by sensational writers, and designing and interested persons, that the Mormons are a gang of incorrigible rogues and criminals; when, in fact, according to the testimony of every unprejudiced man who is acquainted with them, that for honesty, industry, sobriety, neighborly kindness and peace and good order, the Mormons are at least equal, if not superior to any other community on this continent. Over 95 per cent. of the saloon keepers and gamblers of Utah are anti-Mormons, and while the Mormons are over 75 per cent. of the population, yet six or seven eighths of the heinous and felonious offenses, as murder, manslaughter, burglary, robbery, rape and the like, are committed by the Gentile or non-Mormon minority.

Error No. 2. That the Mormons are a sort of pagans, and do not even profess to believe in the Christian religion.

On the contrary, they believe in the Old and New Testament—in the Father, Son and Holy Ghost—in all the cardinal doctrines of the Christian religion, as baptism, repentance, the resurrection, etc. They believe in the Bible absolutely and literally with an undoubting faith. Whatever they find recorded in the New Testament concerning the creed and practice of the first Saints in the days of Jesus and his apostles and the early disciples they adopt as the creed and practice of the "Latter-day Saints;" for example, the gifts of the Holy Ghost, such as healing by the laying on of hands, speaking in tongues and the intrepretation of tongues, prophesying, etc. They say that these gifts, in different degrees, inhere " to all them that believe " in all ages and countries; and they will not allow that a plain passage of scripture should be done away with, as typical, figurative, or as having gone by lapse of time, into "innocuous desuetude."

That the Mormons as a rule, are intensely devotional and honest and sincere in their religious profession has been confirmed by the unanimous opinion of the five members of the commission in their official reports.

Error No. 3.   That the Mormons are disloyal to the government.

This is a charge, that, in process of time, has been made against more than one religious denomination, and has a certain degree of plausibility from the oft repeated declaration of ecclesiastics and religious enthusiasts, that the law of God is superior to the laws of the land; and that the laws of God are to be obeyed rather than the laws of men.   Add to this the idea of the "Kingdom of God on earth," which all good Christians pray for; and that in former times some enthusiasts among the Mormons believed (and some, perhaps, still believe) that the Kingdom has already come, and the reign of the Saints has already begun in Zion; fulfilling the prophetic oracles of the Book of Daniel and the Revelations of St. John; and it will be seen upon what theory the Mormons are charged with disloyalty to the civil authority, especially as it is claimed that they are bound to obey the head of their church, just as it has been maintained that the Catholics are bound to obey the Pope of Rome.

Accordingly, at an early day in Missouri, about the time Governor Boggs issued his Herod-like proclamation that all the Mormons should be exterminated, when one of the "Saints" was on trial before a Dogberry justice of the peace on a charge of "treason," the prisoner was asked the question, "do you believe in the Book of

Daniel?" The prisoner answered in the affirmative. "Put that down," said the justice to his clerk, "that is evidence of *treason*." However, the leading Mormons of this day, hold with other denominations that the "Kingdom" is yet to "come."

Again; there were troublous times in Utah between thirty and forty years ago, growing out of a conflict in the jurisdiction of the courts. An army was sent out by President Buchanan in 1857. In this "Mormon war," I believe nobody was hurt—and Brigham Young sent out his hosts to meet the invaders with the extraordinary order that "no blood should be shed." Under the excitement many intemperate speeches and threats were made by Brigham and others.

The Mormons vow their fealty to the government under the Constitution, which they say is of divine origin; and during my seven years sojourn in Utah there was no attempt and there did not appear to be the slightest disposition to raise an insurrection or oppose the execution of the laws by force.

But it is true that from time to time they criticised the judges of the courts and other Federal officers, charging them with violating the law, and cruelty and injustice in its administration. For example:

The Federal judges in Utah a few years ago made an extraordinary decision in the application of what was called "Segregation." The third section of the so-called Edmunds act of 1882 makes it an indictable offense for any male person to cohabit with more than one woman, and fixes the maximum punishment at a fine of $300 and imprisonment for six months. But the judges invented a new doctrine and called it "Segregation," the gist of which is that, if a man had been living with two or more wives for three years, the period of the statute of limitations, the grand jury might "segregate;" that is, divide up the three years into periods of a year, a month, a week or a day each, and bring in a separate indictment for each one of these "segregated" periods; so that the three years being "segregated" into periods of one day each the offender, for three years' continuous cohabitation, might be indicted 1,095 times, with cumulative fines and imprisonments, amounting to $328,590 fines and 547 years and six months' imprisonment.

This doctrine was applied in many cases. The Mormons criticised it as contrary to law, and against the whole course of judicial decisions, in similar cases, both in England and America, and that by a sort of judicial legislation the judges sought to punish a man an indefinite number of times for one offense in violation of the Constitution. But the judges gave no heed to these "disloyal" complaints and went on "segregating" until the Supreme Court of the United States reversed the cases and decided that the Mormons were right, and the Utah judges were wrong. In re Snow, 120, U. S. S. C. Rep. page 274.

Another case of Mormon "disloyalty" occurred in the autumn of 1882. A majority of the Utah commission decided that a man was not entitled to be registered as a voter who had married a plural wife subsequent to July 1, 1862, (the date of the passage of the first act concerning polygamy) although all his wives, or all but one, had died from ten to twenty years before.

The Mormons were so disloyal that they criticised this ruling as absurd, unreasonable and contrary to law. "How," they asked, "can a man be a polygamist who has no wife at all?"

This doctrine, however, continued to be enforced by the commission for over two years, and many of the leading citizens were denied the right to vote or hold office, (among them Wm. Jennings, the mayor,) although they had had no more than one wife for many years. Finally, after the customary "law's delay" the Supreme Court of the United States decided that this ruling of the commission was erroneous. Murphy vs. Ramsey et al, 115, Supreme Court Rep. page 15.

Another rare specimen, a new variety of the *scarabæus segregationis* of Utah was examined, dissected and immolated by the United States Supreme Court in the case of Hans Neilsen, 131 United States Supreme Court Rep. page 176.

Error No. 4. There is a general misapprehension in the public mind in regard to the extent to which polygamy is practiced, and also as to its present status.

Of the whole Mormon population in Utah only a very small per cent. are in polygamy; and of the adult males, from 85 to 95 per cent. are not living in a polygamous relation.

But, before proceeding further in relation to the present condition in regard to polygamy, I will give my solution of the very natural and reasonable query: "How did it come to pass that a people so intensely devotional and religious and possessed of so many good qualities should have accepted the creed and practices of polygamy, so repugnant to European and American civilization?"

For a right understanding of this question, it is necessary to consider the Mormon doctrine of "continuous revelation."

They believe, as before stated, in the revelations of Moses and the prophets, as recorded in the Old Testament, and also in the "gift of prophesy." as promised in the New Testament, "to them who believe."

They say that from the days of the Patriarchs of Israel down to the revelations of John on the Isle of Patmos, after the death of Christ, there was a long line of prophets, seers and revelators, who appeared at different ages and through many centuries, such as Daniel, Isaiah, Jeremiah, Habakkuk, Nahum, and so on. They declare that it is not consistent with the divine wisdom, after centuries of communication from the celestial kingdom through the prophetic oracles, mankind should have been suddenly cut off; and enclosed as with a canopy of brass from all further light from above.

Accordingly when Joseph Smith appeared and was accepted as a "prophet, seer and revelator" in "these latter days," and proclaimed the "dispensation of the fullness of times," the revelations claimed to have been received by him were accepted by his followers as emanations from his divine will. These "revelations" are printed in a book entitled the "Book of Doctrine and Covenants;" and among them is one sanctioning a plurality of wives. This is the real origin of polygamy among the Mormons; although the example of Abraham, Isaac and Jacob, David and Solomon and other noted personages among the chosen people made it easier for the Mormons to accept the modern "revelation;" and yet when the doctrine was first publicly promulgated in Salt Lake City in 1852, it was received by many of the "Saints" with reluctance or aversion. However, the power and influence of Brigham Young were so potential; and the confidence of the people in him, as a wise lawgiver and a prophet, was so great, that polygamy was accepted as a part of the creed.

But sagacious men among the Mormons have long foreseen that the practice of polygamy must eventually be abandoned; and since the death of Brigham Young in 1877 there has been a constantly increasing disposition among the people to unload this incubus from their shoulders. The difficulties in the way of an immediate change in this respect can be readily imagined.

Three years ago, however, important steps in this direction were taken by a great majority of the Mormon people. An act of Congress, which took effect on March 3d, 1887, required of every voter, as a condition precedent to registration, that he should make an affidavit, declaring among other things, that he would not enter the polygamous relation nor commit fornication or adultery, and that he would not aid or abet, counsel or advise others to commit any of such offenses.

A few Mormon voters and a good many Gentiles declined to be registered on such conditions; but the great mass of the voters among the Mormons took the oath and voted. The next important step in the direction of reform, was the holding of a constitutional convention on June 30, 1887, with delegates from all the counties in the Territory. The Gentiles having declined to participate, the convention was composed entirely of Mormons. The constitution thus formulated contained a provision prohibiting polygamy and making it a crime, with a severe penalty, and at the August election following 95 per cent. of all the Mormon voters in the Terriory voted for the ratification of this constitution.

Following up the reform movement thus inaugurated, the legislative assembly composed of 31 Mormons and 5 Gentiles, which met in Salt Lake City in January 1888, enacted a very well considered marriage law, declaring among other things, all plural marriages to be illegal and void, and making it a crime with a heavy penalty for any clerk of a probate court to issue a license for a plural marriage; and also providing for the punishment of any minister, preacher of the gospel, or any officer or other person who solemnizes any such marriage.

The same legislative assembly passed a concurrent resolution in favor of the enforcement of the laws against polygamy and unlawful cohabitation as well as fornication and adultery, "to the end that all such offenses may be prohibited."

From the facts, as well as official information and personal observation, there can be no reasonable doubt that the Mormons have wisely resolved on the discontinuance of polygamy, and that during the last three years new polygamous marriages in Utah have been very rare, probably not more numerous in proportion to the population than bigamous marriages in any of the States.

It is true that some non-Mormons say they have no confidence in the good faith of the Saints, and claim to believe that their movements for reform are all a sham; that, "nothing good can come out of Nazareth," and that they are obstinate, stiff-necked and fanatical, that they are incorrigible and their reformation utterly hopeless. But it should be borne in mind that churches and creeds are subject to the laws of evolution, of which many illustrations can be given from ecclesiastical history, and of which notable instances were furnished by a very respectable religious organization in New York and Chicago early in February of this year, favoring radical changes in their confession of faith.

Utah is not now and never can be again what it was in the days of Brigham Young, who, with all his faults, was as brave, wise and able a leader of men as ever led his hosts into the "startled solitudes of an unpeopled land."

As a born leader of men, and esteemed by his followers, a prophet, seer and revelator, he dominated with almost absolute authority over his people, isolated for many years, from all the world in the secluded valleys of the Rocky Mountains. But all this is changed. The railroad, the telegraph, free speech, a free press, schools, colleges, churches of many denominations, and last, but not least, the real estate boomers are there now. Polygamy cannot stand up before modern civilization. The Mormons are wise enough to see this and to act upon it.

The practice of polygamy, which has so long been the reproach of the Mormon people, and has been the cause of so much suffering and distress, should be abandoned in good faith and forever. This being accomplished no just ground will remain for pursuing them with further hostile legislation. Any further discrimination against them should then be indignantly resented by all American citizens who are imbued with the true principles of civil and religious liberty. In Utah there are persons of multifarious religious creeds, and some with no religious belief at all. There we find perfect religious freedom for the Catholic, the Jew, the Episcopalian, the Presbyterian, the Methodist, the Baptist, the Campbellite and the Congregationalist, all of whom have churches, or houses of worship there. Besides there are many infidels, skeptics and spiritualists. Shall we allow to all these freedom of religious opinion and worship and deny it to the Mormons, those who, for the rights of conscience, sought a home in the wilderness, which they have made to "blossom as the rose?"

Shall we, now, in the most enlightened age of all the centuries, invoke legal coercion over the consciences of men in the matters of religion; and resort to the thumbscrew and the rack, political proscription and disfranchisement, as modes of religious instruction and persuasion?

HISTORY REPEATING ITSELF.

MORMONS AND CATHOLICS.

The advocacy of religious freedom is no new thing with the author of this volume. More than a third of a century ago, he defended the Catholic against the Know-Nothing crusade. He was not a Catholic and is a native of America as were his ancestors for many generations; but a sense of justice and devotion to the Constitution, together with a natural disposition to take the side of the under dog in the fight, impelled him to take an active part in opposition to bigotry, intolerance and persecution. It is curious to observe that the same war cries and catch-words were invoked in the crusade against the Catholics as are now employed against the Mormons for example, "allegiance to a foreign power;" "abject obedience to the commands of the head of the Church;"—danger of the government being overthrown;" "Americans must rule," etc.

In those days, too, similar means were employed to inflame the public mind. Books purporting to be written by apostate priests and escaped nuns embellished with monstrous pictures, were circulated all over the country. This craze prevailed for one or two years, and finally met with an ignominious defeat in Virginia. In August, 1855, the spirit of persecution culminated in the murder of a large number of Catholics and foreigners, and the burning of churches and dwellings in Louisville, Ky. This tragic event and the spirit of the times which led up to it were commemorated at that time by the author of this book in some stanzas, written in imitation of the "Battle of Blenheim."

It should be explained that "Sam" was a name assumed facetiously by the Know-Nothing party, "Cheyennes" and "Hindoo" were epithets bestowed upon them by their opponents.

[From the Bloomington (Ind.) *News-Letter*, of Aug. 11, 1855.]

THE BATTLE OF LOUISVILLE.

BY A. B. CARLTON.

It was on an August evening;—
The bloody work was done,
And "Samuel" at his cottage door
Was sitting in the sun;
And by him sitting on a stool
His little grand-child, William Poole.*

They saw the dead with ghastly wounds
And limbs burnt off, borne by;—
And then old Sam, he shook his head,
And with a holy sigh,
"*They're only Dutch and Irish,*" said he,
"*Who fell in the great victory!*"

"Now tell me what 'twas all about,"
Young William Poole he cries,
While looking in his grand-dad's face
With wonder-waiting eyes;—
"Now tell me all about the war,
And what they killed the Irish for."

*NOTE—Named after the great prize-fighting bully, who was canonized in New York, and followed to his grave by eighty thousand men.

"They were Know-Nothings," Samuel cried,
"Who put them all to rout;
But what they shot and burnt them for,
I could not well make out.
But Mayor Barber said," quoth he,
"*That 'twas a glorious victory!*"

The Dutch and Irish lived in peace
Yon silvery stream hard by;
The Hindoos burnt their dwellings down,
And they were forced to fly;
So with their wives and children fled,
Nor had they where to rest their head."

"With fire and guns the city round
Was wasted far and wide;
And many an Irish mother then,
And new-born baby died;
But things like that you know *must be
At a Know-Nothing victory.*"

"They say it was a shocking sight,
After the day was won;—
For twenty bloody corpses there
Lay rotting in the sun;
But things like that you know *must be
After a Know-Nothing victory.*"

"Great glory George D. Prentice won,
And also Captain Stone;"—
"Why 'twas a very wicked thing,"—
Quoth Samuel's little son:—
"Nay, nay, my little boy," said he,
"It was a famous victory!"

And *Cheyennes* said: "Americans
America shall rule;"—
"But what good came of it at last?"
Quoth little William Poole;—
"Why, that I can not tell," said he,
"But 'twas a glorious victory!"

EPILOGUE.

To all them which dwell in the Valleys of the Mountains, called to be Saints, I send greeting. To all Christians, Jews and Gentiles in Zion, I send my benediction. To all Apostates, Infidels and Sadducees which say there is no resurrection, I send my best wishes for their conversion. If I have any enemies in Utah, I will freely forgive them, if they will repent. Some of them are great sinners; but I hope they may finally be saved, albeit this carries the doctrine of universal salvation to its utmost limit, and strains the quality of Mercy. I bear them no malice. I would not break a butterfly on the wheel nor put an ephemora to the rack. I will conclude with Uncle Toby, in Tristrem Shandy: "Go, poor little fly:—the world is wide enough fo' thee and me."

ERRATA.

THIS volume is, in general, so correctly printed that it is with reluctance that the author points out a few typographical errors, which no doubt are mainly attributable to the fault of the manuscript rather than that of the printer or proof-reader.

On page 57, line 3, for "State" read "slate."

On page 84, line 19, for "attributes" read "attributed."

On page 117, line 9, for "except" read "accept."

On page 118, line 27, for "law" read "saw."

On page 145, line 10, for "fair minds" read "far winds."

On page 161, line 16, for "state" read "stale."